SCRIBE

The Story of the Only Female Pope

A Novel

Hugo N. Gerstl

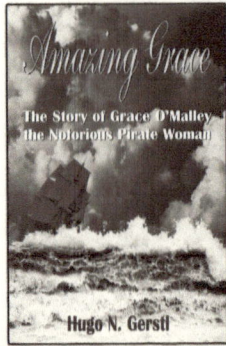

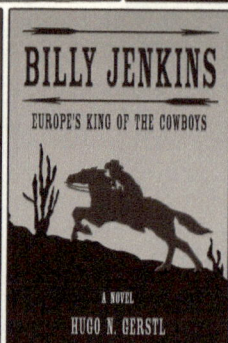

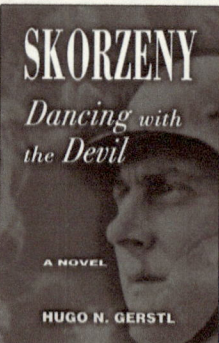

SCRIBE

The Story of the Only Female Pope

A Novel

HUGO N. GERSTL

PANGÆA
PUBLISHING GROUP

SCRIBE: THE STORY OF THE ONLY FEMALE POPE

ISBN 978-1-950134-16-8
Pangæa Publishing Group
www.PangaeaPublishing.com

Cover design and typesetting by
DesignPeaks@gmail.com

For information contact:

PANGÆA PUBLISHING GROUP
25579 Carmel Knolls Drive
Carmel, CA 93923
Telephone: 831-624-3508/831-649-0668
Fax: 831-649-8007
Email: info@pangaeapublishing.com

To my late parents, Alfred and Trudy Gerstl

AND MOST OF ALL,
FOR MY ETERNAL LOVE,
LORRAINE

Translator's Note

Outside, the static sound of rain kept up its onslaught. Despite my precautions, water had seeped down the legs of my pants and onto my shoes. I shivered in the cold of the stone basement.

Signor Bertelli, the curator of the museum here in Viona, trembled with an excitement I couldn't share. His red face smiled uncontrollably, and his agitated hands kept waving me to follow.

"Here!" he exclaimed. "See, Professor!" He plopped down a metal box on a shaky wooden table, then pulled up a chair for me. In a split-second swirl, he'd snapped on the hanging light bulb, thrown me a pair of latex gloves, and had the lid off the box.

"The most amazing thing you ever saw!" Bertelli insisted. In my wet condition, I didn't even try to feign enthusiasm.

Before me sat a dusty pile of crumbling old parchments. "Read it!" Bertelli insisted.

Holding my hands in front of my nose to keep out the dust, I looked over the first few pages. Bertelli's eyes remained fixed on me. I huddled in my overcoat, trying to keep warm.

"Interesting," I finally said. "Interesting."

Bertelli beamed. I added, "A forgery, of course."

Bertelli's beam lost its wattage.

"But interesting nonetheless. Quite a find."

Bertelli smiled again.

"Of course, you know it's not authentic. If it were authentic, it'd be long fallen to dust. Parchment doesn't last a thousand years"

He gave a noncommittal shrug.

"From the condition of the parchment and the style of lettering, I'd place it around the 16th century," I said.

Bertelli rose. From somewhere in that grimy collection of statues, stoneware, and sarcophagi, he produced a bottle of port and two glasses. Before I could decline, he'd filled the two glasses and set one in front of me. I took a generous swig and immediately felt warmer. After a second sip, I started to apologize for not being more enthusiastic.

Bertelli pointed to the old parchment and said, "It's from Siani."

I looked from him to the manuscript.

"Siani," I repeated.

Bertelli nodded.

"The monastery?"

Again he nodded.

"My God," I said.

The monastery at Siani was famous throughout the academic world for its library. The monks of medieval days routinely obtained ancient, crumbling manuscripts and recopied them. Scholars had found a treasure trove of books and pamphlets a thousand or more years old that had been recopied in the practiced hand of the Sianian monks several centuries after their original writing.

"But how can that be?" I said. "I've studied the contents of the library at Siani extensively. Nothing like this ever came up."

Bertelli nodded and grinned. At once, the answer seemed so obvious, I couldn't believe I'd even asked the question. A monk producing this sort of blasphemy in the 16th century would have burned at the stake, along with his book.

"Where was it found?" I asked. Now I found my own voice starting to shake with excitement.

"Hidden in a wall in the cellar. Even then, we had to smuggle it out."

I nodded.

"You know, even today, the church has no desire for these kinds of things to get out," he added.

I looked over the first page again.

~ ∫ ~

I started reading it with great difficulty, for several words were faded or obliterated altogether. It took me just over a year to translate and edit the document so that it made any sense. Yet, as difficult as the task was – more than a year of slow, exceedingly painstaking effort, working every day for three or four hours – I was tantalized, consumed by its contents. Now, at last, I am satisfied that my translation is as accurate as I can make it.

In order that you may read it more easily, there are numerous places where I've substituted language in common use today for the often almost untranslatable style, words, and phrases in which it was handed to me. There are geographical places where I've juxtaposed the present-day names with names that were used at the time the document was written.

I am still profoundly perplexed. Is the document a fraud, or is it the truth? I don't know. I suppose I never will.

Oberlin, Ohio, January, 2019. – HNG

ANNO DOMINI XX AUGUSTUS DCCCLVII
THE FIFTEENTH DAY OF THE SIXTH MONTH
OF MY IMPRISONMENT
IN HADRIAN'S TOWER

By the Grace of one whose name I dare not mention, who has provided me with materials and implements with which to write, and who has arranged to preserve what I write for safekeeping,

I, MARTIN PASCHAL, FORMERLY AND BY THE GRACE OF GOD STILL A CARDINAL IN THE ROMAN CHURCH AND SCRIBE TO THE LATE POPE,

DEPOSE AND STATE AS FOLLOWS:

Hearken well to what I say, you who are now alive! For all I know, these pages may even have been preserved until your lifetime. For all I know, by the time you find these pages, they may have been gathering dust for so long that the days in which I lived, and the people who were so important in my time are no more remembered than clouds scudding across the sky.

This is the true story of a time that was. Every minstrel and seer and sayer meddles with the history which he sings or writes or tells, trimming it or elaborating upon it to beguile those who hear or read it, or to flatter his patron, his ruler, his god – or to malign the enemies of his patron, his ruler, or his god – until the truth is obscured by veils of falsehood, sanctimonious pretension, or invented myth.

So that the truth of the events of my time might be truly known, I set them down here, without embellishment, without partiality, and, because of the low station to which I have sunk and the uncertain future which I face, of which I do not care, without fear of reprisal.

IN THE NAME OF THE FATHER AND THE SON AND THE HOLY GHOST, AMEN. I swear upon my immortal soul that what I say herein is the truth and is known to God Almighty to be so, regardless of what is now being said.

According to the official Catalogue of Popes, after the Holy Father Leo IV died in the Year of Our Lord, Eight hundred fifty-five, he was succeeded by Pope Benedict III.

I, Martin Paschal, swear upon my eternal soul that the Catalogue lies. Leo died on the twentieth day of June, EIGHT HUNDRED FIFTY-FOUR, and to him succeeded John, who was a woman, who sat on the Papal Throne for two years, five months, and four days ...

BOOK 1.
WESSEX

Chapter 1

It is impossible to begin my tale without telling of the time and place in which I lived. After the demise of Rome-in-the-West, more than three hundred years ago, Britannia escaped the ravages of Visigoths and Ostrogoths, of Vandals and Danes, simply because it was too far away, too cold, and too wet to be of much use to anyone. Britannia was nothing more than a series of small landholdings, with each manor lord the kinglet of his own small demesne, until the accession of the Great Charles, who had been invested Holy Roman Emperor shortly before my birth.

By the time I was born in the Year Of Our Lord Eight Hundred Nine, three kingdoms, Wessex, Mercia, and Northumberland, dominated the large island of Britain. Of these, Wessex, which is situated in the southeastern portion of the island, and where my father served as Shire Rief, was the most powerful.

Scarcely ten years before my birth, the Danes and the Northmen had begun to make war on our coasts. At first, they plundered our land, but returned to their ships. As years went by, I heard from others that these Scandinavians had come ashore and made mockery of the kingdoms of my homeland.

But that was to come later. I recall the years of my youth as a time of adventure. One born fairly high on society's scale usually survived to adulthood, unless cut down by the axe of plagues which regularly ravaged Wessex.

I was born on a manor one score miles from the fortified town of Winchester. My father, who'd been awarded the position of Shire Rief and a freehold of ten prime acres, as a result of having served honorably as an officer in Lord Ramsey's army, had built a house of stone and hewed timber sixty feet up the hill from the twenty thatched peasant huts which formed the nearest village. For its time, it was a mansion. There were four rooms. Stretched goatskin windows, through which we had an opaque view of the morning light, gave a feeling of openness to the place. At night, or when it was cold, we were kept warm by a covered, wood-burning fireplace, with a dampered chimney.

By contrast, the village huts had no windows at all. They belched greasy smoke from unvented roofs at all hours of the day or night. We lived far enough removed from these hovels to escape the eye-smarting smoke, and we avoided the stench that emanated from the accumulated urine and feces that wound through the village to the bottom of the hill.

Although my father could have made his home in Winchester itself, he chose to live farther north, where, he often said, a man could walk in the nearby forest without hearing the sounds of his neighbor's sheep.

My mother, a large, rawboned woman, nearly as tall as my father, had stringy, black hair and rough, red hands. She awoke before my father each morning to milk the cow, put our few scruffy sheep out to pasture, and slop the pigs. She, and the baby who would have been my sister, died in childbirth when I was five years old. My father and I buried them both a few days later, and I was left as the only child. I have no other memory of my mother.

Within a month, my father hired a young village peasant to look after our livestock. More important — at least to me — my father devised a clever contraption that allowed me to ride in front of him on his horse, so we could patrol his quarter of the shire together.

My father's territory extended from Andover on the west, to the Mercian frontier, halfway to London. I remember, even now, the Hampshire hills, lush and green, dotted with oak, alder, and thick brush. My father warned me to use caution on any segment of the London Road, for highwaymen invariably hid in the crevasses of the hills and preyed upon those bound for the city.

Twice a year, he and I went down to Portsmouth to conduct business and trade stories with such law enforcement officers as there were in those times. They came from Sussex and Dorset. These were grand times, for Portsmouth was a large, exciting metropolis, or so I thought then.

The city, positioned fortuitously at the confluence of river and sea, was the major port in southern England. The center of the city was its waterfront, with its gambling and drinking establishments, cheap hotels, and the like. Inland, the trading area was arranged about a large, rectangular plaza. Stalls of all shapes and sizes filled its central market. Jewelers peddled their wares in one part of the marketplace, fishmongers in another, cloth merchants in a third. There were egg sellers and butcher shops. Everywhere I looked, boys ran through the market delivering mugs of warm beer. A large, stone bakery stood near the plaza, steam rising from its roof. The City Hall and several inns ringed the central square.

Portsmouth's alleyways were narrow and there were the strong, commingled odors of frying food, tallow and urine. The dirt streets were free of dung, for most horses and mules had burlap or canvas bags fitted over their rear ends. "They save everything here," my father told me. "They sell the manure to farmers in surrounding villages."

Here and there throughout the city were wider roads, which had occasional strips of very old, cracked paving in dismal disrepair. "Those were built by the Romans hundreds of years ago," my father said. "No one knows how they managed to do it, but it was a waste of money, as you can see. That type of waste brought down the Roman Empire."

There were hundreds of stone buildings. I saw a few of the wealthiest citizens carried about in closed conveyances, but most people in the city walked where they needed to go. At night, torches standing on posts on the each side of the main streets lit the city. There was a noisy, often frayed, but definite sense of order, a hum of vibrancy marking the comings and goings of Portsmouth's inhabitants.

I enjoyed better meals in Portsmouth than any others I can remember until I was grown and had left Angle-land. Meals would start with wonderful soups of mixed vegetables and lamb, seasoned with salt from the mines of Germany and pepper from the far, Far East, even beyond Constantinople. There was always fresh, hot bread. My father and I ate heaping trenchers of well-browned roast lamb, greasy with fat and seasoned with rosemary, crackling and crisp on the outside, tender and pink inside. The meat was served with rice, a rarity in the England of that day. We always finished the meal with sweet apples and bread pudding followed by warm beer.

I loved my father beyond any other being. As much of a man's man as he was, he never neglected me or bade me sleep at night without a tender, encouraging word. He taught me to fell a deer with a single arrow at twenty yards and to bring down a bird on the wing.

By the time I was sixteen, I had grown to pretty much the height I stand today, five feet ten inches by the English measure, taller than most. I am told I was passably handsome, with sand-colored hair and light blue eyes, but I have never been one to use vanity as an artifice. It was more important to me that I could comport myself honorably with short sword by that time.

During my childhood, my father had told me over and over that London was, with the exception of Constantinople, the largest city in the entire world. He had so piqued my interest that when, shortly after my sixteenth birthday, my father told me that since he now considered me a man grown, he would take me to London within a fortnight, I could hardly sleep at night for the excitement he'd generated within me. Unfortunately, the following week, while we were hunting in the woods northwest of Winchester, my father was bitten by a rabid wolf. I cringe even now as I recall the excruciatingly painful and horrid death he suffered within less than a month.

After my father died, I did not care to languish on his estate. His position was neither inherited nor inheritable, nor did I think myself appropriate for that position. Thus, I sold my father's ten acres and the home in which I had grown up, back to the lord's estate. His retainers were most generous and agreed to invest the proceeds on my behalf.

Early one evening, just before I was to leave the property, I went to the southeastern corner of the plot. Taking care to make certain that no one was about, I unearthed the treasure my father had told me existed, but which he had never described. I was overwhelmed when I found out how vast it truly was. I could easily have retired a rich man, even then: solidi, gold and silver beyond counting.

But to whom could I entrust this treasure? I'd acquired no close friends. To disclose this treasure to no one was to subject me to a lifetime of furtively hiding the fortune, which would tie me to wherever it was buried or hidden. To give it for safekeeping to the Jews of Portsmouth and hope to earn interest on it? Perhaps, for they were said to be scrupulously meticulous in their record-keeping.

In the end, I deposited virtually all of my fortune for investment with a well-reputed Jewish agent, a man of forty in Portsmouth, whose name was Isaac HaCohen. My father had told me that despite the disdain in which the general populace held this race, Jews as individuals were intelligent, possessed of a wonderful sense of humor, and honest in their dealings. Over the years, I found that the HaCohens lived up to this reputation and my money grew at an incredible rate each year. I kept with me only as much as I could safely afford to lose, and even then it was an unheard-of amount of money.

When I completed my initial transaction with him, the Jew handed me several small pieces of parchment, about the size of my hand, which were stitched together with thin, strong leather sinews. Looking at the miniature codex, I saw a series of indecipherable writings and figures carefully written on the document. HaCohen explained that this was a form written in Hebrew and accepted by any Jewish moneylender anywhere in the civilized world. It stated that I had such-and-such an amount on deposit with him, and I could draw on that sum anywhere I found a Jew who could direct me to such a moneylender. That moneylender would, in turn, enter the amount I had drawn, subtract that from the amount written by my money manager, and enter the new balance. This was an elegantly simple means of functioning anywhere within the area I could reasonably be expected to travel.

HaCohen told me that each year, as close as possible to the anniversary of the date of my original deposit with him, he would balance the books of my accretions and withdrawals, and would issue a new – and newly dated – codex, certifying what was then available in my account, and as soon as possible after each anniversary, I should write to him, telling him where I would be for the next few months, and he would arrange to have a trusted messenger – a Jew, of course – deliver the new codex to me.

It took me the better part of six months to settle everything concerned with my father's bequest to me, and by then I was more eager than ever to see the great city of London.

I longed for adventure, as I suppose every young man does, and every young woman, too, for all I know. I was, I thought, better prepared than most to deal with life. Few in Angle-land possessed the wherewithal to make good on their dreams of travel.

Isaac HaCohen, my agent, suggested it might be safer and less daunting for me to travel to London for the first time, if his son Micah, who was two or three years my senior, accompanied me to London, since he was well familiar with the road. I readily agreed, for over the time it took to put my affairs in order, I had found Micah, a tall, robust, red-headed young man, to be the closest thing to a friend I'd yet encountered.

Thus it was that in July of the Year of Our Lord 826, when all matters pertaining to my father's estate had been settled and the homestead had been sold, Micah and I found ourselves on the road to London. The weather was clement. More important, it was a rare time of peace. Egbert had subdued the Mercians at Ellandum and it appeared the whole of Angle-land would be unified at last. All about me, there were signs of construction and active labor. As my father had predicted, England was pushing back the beasts and the wilderness, taming the land with mattock and plow, planting fruit trees, herding flocks, tending vines, the hard life tempered with love and prayer, flowers, music and ale.

The highway to London, which had been tamped dirt and gravel less than a year before, was covered and lined with wood planks from Boroughneck, fifty miles outside the city, all the way into London itself. I had inherited my father's sturdy horse, an eight-year-old gelding named Arca, and him I kept, as he would prove not only a staunch companion, but also a mount whose habits were familiar to me.

~ ∫ ~

For all its wild antics, Portsmouth was an orderly place that had definite boundaries. It described an arc around its bay, but no sooner it came to the first of the low hills behind it, it ceased. London, on the other hand, seemed to straggle on for endless miles.

"This is not really London," Micah HaCohen said. "What they call the City itself is quite small, less than a mile square and surrounded by sturdy walls."

"Why, then, does it feel so much like a city?"

"That's a good question," he responded equably. "The City of London is the seat of government, but it is not the residential city." He chuckled as our horses stopped to nibble at a few errant blades of grass by the side of the graveled road. "I'm told London is really one hundred towns in search of a city. We're in Westholme now. Within a few miles we'll be in some other townlet that claims independence from the City.

We'll pass through several more hamlets until we arrive at Kensington, where we'll spend the night."

My horse whuffled and glanced up at me as though placing a period at the end of Micah's sentence.

"Not London?" I asked.

"No, there are no inns in London proper," he said.

He kicked his horse and we were on our way once again. It was high summer, and the sky, gray for a good part of the year, was surprisingly blue, with only a few fleecy clouds and a light breeze to temper the warmth of the sun. The horses must have felt frisky, since they broke into a light trot, then a canter.

Soon the buildings of London's outskirts, some an astounding three full stories high, hove into view. In my haste to grasp all the rich, new sights and smells, my eyes swept the area to the left of my mount and I momentarily lost sight of where I was headed until I heard a small shriek. Startled, Arca veered to the right and my head instantly snapped forward, just in time to see a young girl of about twelve years trip and fall right in front of my horse.

I reined Arca in so tightly that he reared and would have come down right on top of the girl, but for the fact that I pulled his checkrein hard right. When he came down, he missed the girl, because she'd deftly rolled to the left. Even had Arca landed where he was planning, she would not have been underfoot.

As I was thinking whether to scold the young girl for running into the path of the horse or to congratulate her for her cool grace in such a dangerous situation, she quietly gazed at me, and through me, taking my measure as if to say, "Is that all there is to you?" Stunned, I simply sat astride my mount, looking sheepishly back at her, struck dumb for a few seconds.

"I …" Suddenly she and I were in verbal collision.

"Should have been looking where I was going …"

"Should not have run into the road …"

It was an awkward moment for both of us. She was by no means unattractive. Her blonde hair was cut short in the fashion favored by both sexes at that time. Her eyes were deep green, flecked with sparks of yellow. Her skin was flawless and quite pale. I dismounted my horse and led it to the side of the road. From ground level, the girl was not so small as she had appeared from above, but she was still not full grown.

"Are you all right?" These were my first words to a creature four years my junior, who one day would become the center of my universe. I smiled to cover my embarrassment.

"And if I weren't, kind sir?" she chided. "Would you then summon a barber to bleed me?"

It took me a moment to see she was teasing me. When I answered, it was defensive. "Surely I could …"

"And where, pray, would you find one? Your accent is that of the southwest. I daresay it sounds as though you've never been within a week's journey of London town. At least by your clothes, I would assess you are more than a peasant."

"And you?" I asked. Micah chuckled softly. The age-old battle of the sexes begins even in the very young, and I think he knew, even at that moment, that I was using words to surround myself with a verbal fence, lest she gently tear down my resistance.

"I," she said regally, "am Joan, and one day I shall be famous throughout the world."

At that, I laughed, and roundly, for the very seriousness of her demeanor was itself a delightful mocking of self-important adults who'd always made me impatient. I bowed low and said, with the same mock seriousness, "I am at your service, my lady. And what would you have me be? Your servant? Your slave? Your minister?"

Still with a straight face, but with eyes now alight with the humor of the game, she remarked, "Perhaps you shall be of some service to me when I attain my calling."

"Well said, young lady," Micah remarked. "Would you, perhaps, know of a decent inn where my friend and I might spend the night, Miss Joan?"

"Indeed, Sir," she said, straightening up and becoming serious. Both my parents died of the plague two years ago. I live with my uncle and aunt, who operate the cleanest inn in these parts, and at a reasonable price as well. Come, it's but a few blocks away and I shall lead you there myself."

The girl was accurate in respect of the cleanliness of her relatives' inn. There was ample fodder for our horses and the rooms were comfortable, if quite simple. There was a bed for Micah and me, a stool at the foot of each where we could unhitch our boots, and a metal pan with which we might perform our ablutions. The outhouse was not far from the main building and, surprisingly, its stench did not permeate the inn itself.

Dinner that evening was as spare as the room — a scrawny chicken that looked as though it had been roasted for the minimum time necessary to draw the blood out, then scalded with hot water, a few turnips and some unidentifiable greens that might have been chard or spinach.

Joan's aunt and uncle were drab and elderly, probably forty-five years or even more, which, even today, is significantly older than the age most people attain before they die. They were pleasant enough, but so innocuous they almost faded into the wall. I was surprised that these quite ordinary people were related to Joan, who, even at twelve years, exhibited a store of knowledge greater than mine.

"They say Egbert will unite all of Angle-land within the next five years," she said at dinner.

"Who are they?"

"Traveling Normans who've stopped at the inn, a professor from the newly formed university in Athens, even a Reverend Father who came all the way from the seat of Rome-in-the-East and spent time here yesterday fortnight."

"Say you so. You listen to these people then?"

"Yes," she said. "God gave us two ears and one mouth, so perhaps 'tis best we listen twice as much as speak."

"Well said."

I watched Joan closely as she continued to speak. In the gentle torchlight, her white skin had taken on a red-gold tint, reflecting the flickering light. Her eyes were large and luminous as she spoke, but what I noticed most were her expressive hands — hands that didn't seem to stop moving, as if she were using them to illustrate her every point.

"Soon you'll see how London is bursting outside its walls and growing in every direction. It'll be a proper city before you know it. Like Rome and Byzantium and Ravenna and ..."

"How come you to know such things?"

"What I don't hear from travelers, I read about," she said.

"You read?" I asked in awe.

"Of course," she said. She walked over to the sideboard and poured a large tankard of ale for me and one for herself and brought them over. As she hoisted her arms, I saw the faint beginnings of budding curves beneath her wool tunic.

"Where did you learn to read?" I asked.

"My parents were my first teachers. Both of them could read and write. My father practiced law in London's court system. Three years before he died, he was called upon to resolve disputes and dispense justice in the city's open-air markets. He grew wealthy and, as far as I could tell, we lived very well. My mother acted as his secretary. My dad treated everyone as an equal, including my mother and me. He never saw me as a mere child, and a girl at that. My parents hired a private tutor for me when I was five."

"How long did the tutor teach you?"

"Until my parents died. But that wasn't the only place I learned. There was an abbey with a small library near our home. Ever since I can remember, I loved to go into that library to smell the old parchment scrolls and watch scribes recording so much knowledge. By the time I was eight, a few of them had grown used to me and they taught me to write some.

"When I moved here, I discovered a stone kirk less than a mile from here. The head priest is a doddering old fellow, but there is a young man, a postulant named Nicola, who grew up in northern Italia and recently came here from Avignon, to serve an internship in Angle-land. He's not much older than you," she said, glancing at me. "Nicola doesn't seem to care that I am a girl, and half Saxon at that. Perhaps we'll meet him while you're here."

"Perhaps," I murmured. By this time, my eyelids were getting heavy, because of the excitement of the long day, the heat of the roaring fire, the ale coursing through my body, or perhaps all of them. I pleaded exhaustion, and Micah and I retired to our room.

CHAPTER 2

Next day, Micah and I went into London proper. I imagine I must have looked like a true rustic, gaping in wide-eyed wonder at everything I saw. There were huge stone buildings, streets paved with cobblestones, horses pulling wheeled carriages – carrucas they'd called them in the old Roman days, and even raised sidewalks. To be sure, there had been such buildings and carriages and streets in Portsmouth, but never so many in such close proximity to one another.

By afternoon, Micah and I said our fare-thee-well's to one another. He told me he was going to remain in the city overnight with family friends. I don't think he was unhappy that I declined his invitation to stay with him. He told me he'd be leaving London next morning and riding straight through to Portsmouth, in order to be home for the Jewish Sabbath. Micah had been a boon companion, albeit for a brief time, and we vowed to stay in touch with one another, and often.

When I returned to the inn, I told Joan's uncle and aunt I would like to stay with them for a month, while I decided where I might find more permanent lodgings. They quoted me a quite reasonable price, and I'm sure they were gratified when

I paid them for a month in advance and added one-fourth again over what they had quoted me. Joan's uncle and aunt were noticeably friendlier to me that evening, and for every evening I stayed with them thereafter, even though the food was only marginally better than it had been the first night.

The news of my pending long stay spread quickly, and Joan squealed with delight when she heard I was going to be there more than a couple of days. At dinner that night, Joan and I exchanged more intimate conversation. "My early life was wonderful," she said. "My parents guided me, they didn't force anything on me, and they allowed me the independence to make my own mistakes. They were gone much too soon." She sighed.

"I'm sorry," I said, not knowing what else to say.

"For the first several months I couldn't believe it. They were so young, not much more than thirty-three. Of course, no one could have predicted it. One out of every four people in our area died. I was luckier than most. My father's older brother – my uncle – inherited the family fortune, which, I learned, was quite a bit smaller than I had thought."

"So you work for your keep?"

"Not really," she said. Then, more quietly, "As you must have noticed, they are not young people, and never having had children of their own, they find it easier to let me do what I will, just as long as I don't upset their peaceful existence. Between you and me, I don't think they see me as particularly relevant to their lives."

"But you do chores?"

"When I'm needed. They've run the inn for so many years by themselves – actually, they have a hired girl who helps out. Aside from being friendly enough and easy to live with, they don't pay me much mind and I try not to disturb them."

"Do they know you meet with this Nicola you mentioned last night?"

"If they do, we really don't discuss it. I suppose they've heard me talking about him, but they're about as curious as two mushrooms. I'm sure that if I suddenly disappeared, they'd fret for a couple of days, and then just go about their lives the same as before I came here two years ago. I'll be thirteen in November, and I suppose I should start thinking about what I want to do with my life. What about you, Martin?"

"My dad died eight months ago. I find it hard to believe, but I guess I had to learn to function on my own pretty quickly. I haven't given much thought what to do with my life, either. My Da left me with enough money that I'll never have to worry."

"Are you sure you want to tell me these things?"

"Why not? I don't carry much on my person. Most of it is in Portsmouth with a Jewish broker."

"You trust him?"

"Why do you ask?"

She scratched her chin. "No reason, really. People talk – "

"Your parents?"

"Ne, they saw no differences in people of one group or another. To them, a person was a good person or a bad person. I just wondered what experience you'd had with them. The young man who came with you last evening, was he Jewish?"

"Aye."

"I thought as much. He wore the skullcap they all wear and he had locks of hair over his ears. What was your father like?"

"A good, good man. Strong, gentle. I suppose every boy thinks of his father that way."

Joan fetched us two tankards of ale – smaller than last night's draughts, and returned to the table. "Not every child feels that way, at least not in London." She switched the subject deftly. "I've let slip that I'm almost thirteen. How old are you, Martin?"

"Seventeen. Well, almost seventeen. September fifth, a month from now."

"You said you'd learned to function on your own?"

"To the extent I learned to ride and hunt. I've been to a city…"

"Portsmouth?"

"Aye." I felt momentarily uncertain as I saw her grinning. "Well, somewhat of a city, then."

"Have you a trade?"

"Ne."

"So you'd be a hunter and rider, then?" She giggled impishly.

"Hardly."

"Well, my new friend. Since we two seem to be cast adrift from our elders a bit earlier than we would have liked, perhaps we'll have to learn to help one another determine what we want to do in our lives." As she said this, I began to realize that although she was much smaller than me, she was worldly-wise as well as book-wise, and we might very well help one another into a more mature adulthood. The day had been long. I'd seen an enormous city, ridden to and from it, independently arranged for a month's lodging for myself, and engaged in a wonderful conversation with an intelligent and attractive young person. I found myself eager to start my new life on the morrow, and early went to my room for a good night's rest.

~ ∫ ~

The dining room was gray in the morning light. It smelled sweet from the burnt embers of the fireplace and sour from dried old ale, which felt sticky as I walked across the floor. The sideboard was loaded with an array of heavy, dark breads, sweet jam and butter. A pitcher of warm ale and five goblets had been placed next to the food. As I tore off a chunk from one of the loaves, I sensed the approach of a small figure, heralded by a clean, youthful fragrance. "Good morning, dear lady," I said, turning and bowing.

"And you, kind Sir," she said, granting me a serious-faced mock curtsy. "Are we to be one another's companions today?

"I don't know, Joan," I replied. "I thought to go into London town and explore those parts I've not yet seen."

"Oh, you can see London anytime. Today, I'd like you to meet Nicola, the man I told you about. He stays not far from here, at the small stone kirk in Kensington."

So we finished our breakfast and not long after, I helped Joan up on my horse. I was about to mount behind her when she said, "We needn't overburden your steed. It's not far from here to the Stone kirk and it might be best to save his strength for the longer ride to London."

"Very well, M'lady," said I, bowing in what I felt was my most gallant manner.

The church was, as she had said, less than a mile away and it took us only a short time to get there. I had seen places of Christian worship in the villages near where I grew up. I'd been to Portsmouth, of course, but the church I'd seen there was a rude affair compared to what Joan had called a small kirk. The church was built of stone, with a nave and apse taller than any of the buildings I'd seen in Portsmouth. When I entered, I marveled at the soft glow of hundreds of candles and a buzzing in my head from the cloying, oily sweet smell of burning tallow. The light from the flickering tapers cast ever-changing bright spots and shadows on the stone walls. Because of the height and shape of the building, my voice echoed when I spoke.

At the front of the church stood a raised platform. Beyond the platform, a carved figure depicting an agonized Christ suspended from a large wooden cross hung from the wall. I heard the chanting of prayers, enhanced by the echoes the sounds made as they bounced from floor to ceiling.

Joan went to a small door beyond the nave and knocked softly. The door opened and I saw a pleasant-looking young man about my height and build and, I guessed, not more than a few years my senior, with dark hair cut very short. His complexion was darker than hers and sallow, rather than ruddy. Looking up, he saw me standing to the right and slightly behind Joan. He signaled us to enter the door from which he'd come. The door led down a small hallway, at the end of which was a room about the same size as my bedroom at the inn. There was a rough wooden table and three chairs. The young man bade us sit.

"Nicola," Joan burst out, in an impatient, impetuous way I later came to know so well, "this is my new friend Martin. He reads, too," she added, as though this joined the three of us in some sort of secret cabal.

"I'm delighted to meet you," the young man said, smiling. I immediately took a liking to him. "Of course, you've noticed Joan makes friends quite easily."

"No, I haven't had that opportunity," I said. "You must be Nicola of whom she spoke so highly."

"I am," he said, grasping my hand in the Christian fashion and tugging it firmly. "Born in Italia, late of Avignon, and learning what I can about your land. You're not from London?"

"No, from the west."

Before long, we were learning not so much about Angle-land as about one another. Nicola was lonely for male companionship near his own age. He told me that each of the postulants who had been with him at Avignon had been sent to churches in different Bishoprics to broaden their worldview. "I was in the middle of my class. The best of the assignments, Ostia Antica, Brigantium and Athens, went to the top three students. I got the next choice, and I preferred Angle-land over the land of the Franks. Winters are said to be brutal there, and the recently converted heathens are little more than Goths with the thinnest veneer of Christianity."

But, he told me, Angle-land, too, was of recent conversion. Those who labored in the arms of Mother Church were elderly, and their ideas were as conservative and crystallized as, in Nicola's words, "a bunch of dry bones from which all the sap has been bled." That was why he'd found Joan so refreshing. "An eager young mind, even a female one, is preferable to what I see each day."

"Are there no young male students?" I asked.

"There are, but they seem dull and insipid. They'd clearly rather be out in the fields than here," he replied. "It seems a new habit has sprung up among the Angle-landers. The first-born son inherits everything, so fathers eager to avoid resentment between brothers, developed the idea of sending every second son to us, where he becomes the child of Mother Church. Of course," he looked around to make sure no one was within earshot of his small room, "Mother Church exacts her price from these fathers. Our Church is not a free dumping ground, regardless of what Saint Paul might have said in an earlier day. Nowadays, each son who comes to us brings a plot of land as well, to insure that Mother Church may support that son in the manner the father expects."

"A bit of heresy," Joan chided him, winking. "Nicola has some very advanced ideas. The elders would not be thrilled to hear them."

Nicola grinned. "I would be long gone if the Holy Fathers heard some of the things I say — or, for that matter, if the fathers who send such sons, or even the doltish sons themselves knew what I thought."

I soon fathomed why Joan's and Nicola's relationship was an easy one. He viewed her as someone who was not a threat, since she was a "mere girl," someone who would listen as he tested ideas that would clearly have been heretical, if not outright blasphemous, to the Church fathers. She was young, eager to hear new ideas, apparently quite capable of keeping his confidence, and properly worshipful of him. Joan, on the other hand, used Nicola to broaden her own knowledge. Since she did not know how she would fare had her uncle and aunt suspected how much she truly knew, Nicola was charged with keeping their secret. It was a fair exchange. I felt honored that they were making me a part of their unspoken pact.

What was to have been the briefest introductory visit consumed several hours. Early on, Nicola told me I might simply call him "Nico," if I felt more comfortable doing so. Using the guise of showing us the Church and proudly explaining everything that was within, he took us deeper and deeper into his confidence. I learned that Joan was fluent not only Latin, but also Greek. She had learned these tongues in the sanctuary of Nicola's "office," under the pretense of studying verbal conjugations, lingual syntax, and Pater Nosters. She was familiar with Lucretius' *De rerum natura* and she had read the works of Boethius, who had written a life of the Goth Theodoreikhs, the Barbarian conqueror of Western Rome.

At the time, none of this meant anything to me. I realize now I was a primitive. I'd learned prayers and minimal precepts of Church dogma, but I had been reared as a child of the great outdoors. What mattered it to me what angels did to, for, or with one another? Better a hare stewing in a pot, or a broiling haunch of venison from a deer I'd slain, than a dispute over differing dogmas within the Church.

Joan and Nicola vehemently but amicably argued over positions the Church had taken on one issue or another. Joan tested the limits of Church writ, pushing, prodding, knocking over those tenets she found to be hypocritical.

It was not long before the two of them enticed me to study with them. I engaged my room for another month, then another, and then for a far longer period, much to the apparent joy of Joan's aunt and uncle.

For the next several months, as friendship grew between the three of us, Nicola and Joan, together and separately, imparted much of their knowledge to me. Several afternoons, by the light of the sun, and several evenings by the light of large candles, which I had purchased on my own, so as not to cut into the small profit my hosts derived from me, I worked hard to learn Latin and Greek, how to read, and even how to write. This was difficult at first, for I was a bit old to be a primary student, but with Nicola's and with Joan's help, by the time a year had gone by, I was adept at my studies. Indeed, I had taken a particular liking to writing and had started keeping a journal – a lifelong habit, as it was to turn out.

Within that year, Joan had grown. By the time she was fourteen, she was not a beauty in the delicate, slope-shouldered fashion of the day, but she was by no means unattractive. She was shorter than me, but womanly built. What attracted me to her was her pale skin, white-blonde hair, and amazing deep green eyes.

Her uncle and aunt appeared to have withered and shrunk in the year I'd been staying with them. They reminded me of exhausted plants in a garden, which, left without care too long, had gone to seed.

By this time, Joan's knowledge exceeded even Nico's. I have found that young children can be particularly vexing when they reduce everything with which they do not agree to the ultimate question, "Why?" Joan might also ask, "Why?" but unlike a stubborn child, she would invariably search deeper to find the answer to that question. While Nicola and I were content to absorb what we saw, to discuss it, and to move on to other matters quickly, Joan would pursue the deeper meaning of almost everything. She would seek out an abbot, find an out-of-the way library of rare and arcane books, accost a student, a barber, a dentist, or anyone else who possessed expertise in her current interest.

Increasingly, however, she complained to us that she found doors barred to her, first, because she was no longer a child and, more important, because she was female. At first, she shrugged off these rejections, but as time went on, she expressed her increasing frustration to Nico and me. "It's so bloody unfair!" she roared one day in a fit of pique and a spate of language I'd have never expected from a girl. I noticed, not for the first time, how rich and full her voice could be when she wanted to project force, nearly as deep as that of young man. Nico and I tried to humor her, but without success. As she stomped angrily away, I winked at Nico and together we blessed the fate that had made us men.

CHAPTER 3

Joan did not appear for two days thereafter. When I asked her uncle and aunt where she was, they shrugged their shoulders. On the third morning, they received a short note stating that Joan was staying with a friend in London. As Joan had said, they were about as curious as mushrooms, and they questioned the issue no further.

That afternoon was particularly lovely, a rare day of dry sunshine in southeastern Angle-land. Nico and I had decided to read in the garden at the rear of the Stone kirk. We'd been at it about an hour when a young man we had not met before joined us. He wore the cowl and tunic of a newly ordained brother, and we bowed respectfully.

"It's such a pleasant afternoon, do you mind if I join you?" the young friar asked.

"Not at all, Brother … umm … Brother …?"

"Joannes," the young man answered Nicola. "Come from the monastery at Ghent, across the Channel."

"Ah, then you must know my friend Benedict," Nicola said excitedly. "He and I were postulants together at Avignon."

"And you are still a postulant?" Joannes asked, widening his eyes. There was something very familiar about those eyes. I couldn't place it at that moment, but I began to wonder where I had seen this Brother Joannes before.

"Yes," Nicola replied, looking toward the ground. "The fathers seem to believe I need a bit more seasoning in the conventional wisdom. I fear I am a bit liberal for their thoughts. But tell me, Brother," he said, recovering quickly, "did you perchance see my friend, Benedict?"

"Ah, Brother Benedict ..."

"Yes, yes," Nicola said, his voice rising in barely masked excitement.

"A young man of twenty years or so, about your height, lighter hair color than yours ..."

"That's him, that's certainly him! You've seen him, then?"

"Well, no," said Brother Joannes. "But I've heard you speak of him often."

"How could that be?" Nicola asked sharply. "We've never met before." He now became suspicious. "Have you, perchance, been spying on me for the perfidious Fathers?"

"Ne ... I mean Nein, nicht war," Brother Joannes said, quickly slipping into a language I did not know.

"Wait a minute," Nico said. "I know you. We've met before, but where? Avignon? Tours?"

At that, Brother Joannes could control himself no longer. He burst out in most un-Brotherly laughter, so much so that his face started to color a high pink. Nicola and I stood helplessly by until he'd recovered. "No, you ninnies," he finally said. "Right here. You are Nicola and you Martin, are you not? Your powers of observation are as sharp as a pair of donkeys, and that is exactly what you are!"

With that, Brother Joannes insouciantly flipped back his cowl to reveal ...

"JOAN!" we gasped in unison.

"Well, now, my wondrous lads, your powers of observation have increased somewhat."

It was Joan, all right, no question of that. But her hair was cut short and there was a small, bald tonsure in the middle of her pate. No one could make out her womanly curves because of the loose-fitting wool tunic. She told us that even were the tunic to be tighter, it would make no difference, for she'd flattened what curves she had with a binding cloth and her voice was deep enough that she could pass for a soft-spoken man. There were many women taller than she was. Conversely, I had met many men shorter. Our Joan had truly metamorphosed into Brother Joannes.

"Why?" I asked. I was genuinely confused.

"Because this is the only way I'm going to unlock the doors that have been closed to me."

"You would give up your, your... you know?" I stammered.

"My what, Martin? My chance to help my aunt and uncle run a country inn? My chance to marry a man who'd most likely beat me and keep me pregnant with numerous babes 'til the day I was worn out, when he'd run away with some young bawd? My grand opportunity to be a curious oddity, an object of derision among men, who would view me as a lesser creature simply because I'm a female? To gossip with womenfolk, with whom I have nothing in common?" Her voice was rising with indignation.

"But ...?"

"Yes?" she asked, softening her voice, her green eyes alertly awaiting my response.

There was nothing I could say. Her reasoning was unassailable. I looked for help to my friend Nicola. He simply grinned.

"Where did you get the priestly garb and the new hairstyle?" he asked.

"London is a huge city. You can find tailors who'll make anything you want. Had I been so possessed, I could even have ordered papal robes," she said. "Barbers do more than bleed people. No one ever thought to ask if I was male or female," she added. "Because I was green-eyed and light-haired, the darker people from Italia took me for a Saxon. Because I was beardless, the northmen who occupy many of the city's streets took me for a Latin."

We were standing in bright sunlight. If Joan could pass for a man in such conditions, how much easier it would be for her be mistaken for a brother in the darkened corridors of an abbey. What Joan was suggesting was a monstrous fraud on no less than Mother Church herself. It was unheard-of, it was blasphemous. And, given her shrewd intelligence it might just work. And thus was our plan hatched.

I had money enough to sustain the three of us. Nicola, who had traveled in Gallia, Italia and even Frankland, admitted he was on a trail to nowhere and had tired of his time in Angle-land. Joan was independent, and, at almost fourteen, most women in Angle-land were already married and starting families.

Our plan could take no longer than three months, for after the autumnal equinox the weather grows bitter and crossing the Channel would be hazardous. Joan would leave first. Indeed, she would not return to her uncle's and aunt's abode at all. Nicola was certain the Holy Fathers at the stone kirk would greet his news with relief rather than concern. And

I, completely on my own, with no ties to anyone and nothing to hold me anywhere, was free to go when and where I desired.

~ ∫ ~

Joan's aunt and uncle were sanguine when they received a polite note from her. Their sole concern was that they were now older and had anticipated that Joan would be doing more to help them at the inn. I expressed my sympathy on their loss and promised I would go to London and find them ample replacement for Joan's services. To further ease their loss, such as it was, I insisted on paying the first six months' wages to the new serving wench.

From that day forward, until the day I announced my own departure, I was treated with even greater deference than before. There were other benefits as well. The new serving maid I retained for them, Hilda, was twenty years old, buxom and possessed of a generous nature. It was not long before she realized I was responsible for the best job she could ever hope to receive and that, in addition to having paid a substantial portion of her wages, I made certain to leave ample extra money to enable her to have something to spend on her days off. One evening in August, after she'd assured herself that the master and mistress were soundly sleeping, she came quietly to my room. As I have said, Hilda was of a generous and giving nature, and I was a bright, eagerly receptive student of what she had to teach. Thereafter, I seldom slept alone during my time at the inn. I think of Hilda now and again, even to this day.

During those three months, Nico and I saw Joan only when we visited London. Our visits were brief and circumspect. She was masquerading as "Brother Joannes," and had taken up residence as a visiting monk in a nearby monastery.

Nicola and I were frankly curious, and asked our friend questions which, but for our friendship, would have been mortally sinful, or at least venally so. Joan answered cheerfully. "The monks look upon the body as a sinful vessel, which must be concealed to the maximum degree possible. Saint Benedict clearly dictated that brothers must sleep in their robes and reveal no more than their hands or feet. Only the sick are allowed to bathe." Here she stopped and giggled. "I manage to go to the public baths whenever possible and I find it very easy to keep my distance from the brothers, since they generally smell quite horrid."

"What about the latrines?" I asked.

"There are concealing partitions between each of the stone seats."

"Yes, but Joan, you are a woman, and …"

"I manage to control my monthly bleeding with absorbent leaves. I either bury them at night in the abbey's garden, or simply drop the soiled leaves down the deep holes of the necessaria. They smell no worse than what's down there already."

"No one suspects?" Nicola asked.

"Not in the least. Once one's gender is established, no one gives it a second thought."

~ ∫ ~

"You're certain you want to go through with this?" Nicola asked.

"Absolutely," Joan replied with resolve, after a particularly difficult day of training to erase everything she had done by instinct as a girl.

Nicola and I worked with her to lower the register of her voice, but, as it turned out, we needn't have done so, for Joan, who never ceased to surprise me, had studied folk medicine and had found a particular root or plant that deepened her voice and made it sound appropriately throaty or scratchy.

Joan also solved our knottiest problem. As with many things in the world, it was resolved with a rather large bribe. In retrospect, it was certainly one of the best investments I ever made. One morning in September, just after my eighteenth birthday, Nicola and I forayed into London, where we met Joan. "We've a busy morning ahead of us," she said, "and one which will prove most valuable to our futures as well. We need proof of our bona fides as Benedictine Brothers. Something that will allow us to cross borders and stay where we need to stay."

"I've got sufficient money to enable us to stay wherever we want," I said. "If it's a quality hostel you need — "

"Ne," Joan replied equably. "What I need is a passegiata into the abbeys, the libraries, the places where I need to be to learn more and more. It cannot hurt either of you to have such proof as well. Nicola, how long have you been a struggling postulant?"

"Five years."

"And you've still no hint of when you might become a Brother?"

"None," he said, looking down at the earth.

"Martin, how much money have you on your person?"

"Twenty solidi," I replied. "Why?"

"You'll need that and perhaps more."

"More than twenty solidi? Why a rich man lives on that for three months."

"Trust me, my friend," she said.

Without more, she led us out of town. Soon we came to a rolling, green meadow, abutted by a small wood. At the point where the field met the trees, there was a well-constructed one-story building of wood and pitch. Joan knocked on the door and after a few words to a florid-faced, paunchy man of indeterminate middle age, introduced us.

"This is Andros," she said, simply. "Andros, these are my friends, Brother Nicholas and Brother Martin." We were shocked at our sudden elevation, but said nothing.

"Ah, yes, Brother Joannes," Andros said smoothly, after giving us a mild nod. "Umm – you brought the money?"

Joan nudged me. I nodded. "How much do you require?" I asked, not knowing what we were asking for, but knowing Joan expected me to bargain.

"Fifty solidi," he said, without blanching.

"Five," I responded.

"Impossible!" Andros said angrily. "Do you have any idea of the expenses involved? Joannes, you said your friend would pay an honest price."

"Ah, yes," Joan said quietly. "An honest price for honest work." She suppressed a smile only by covering her mouth with the back of her hand. "There are those who would eagerly do this for five…"

"Yes, of course," Andros replied oilily. "And you would get precisely what you paid for. It might get you as far as Tours, but not through the door of that abbey."

"Nonsense," Joan retorted. "Most of the Brothers there can hardly read the prayers."

"But the Abbott would know, and surely the librarian and the copyists would know, and where would you be then, young man?" Nico and I winked knowingly at one another. If she could fool this fellow into believing she was a man — they stood at a distance of less than three feet from one another, and she was wearing only a tunic and no cowl — then how much easier would it be to pass as a Brother in the abbey, where one's word went unchallenged?

"You are Greek?" Nico asked.

"But of course," the older man said. "From Athens."

"Ne, ne," Nicola said knowingly. "You speak with the accent of the Peloponnesus." Nico launched into a spate of rapidly spoken Greek. At Nicola's mention of the name Michaelis Amorianus, Andros' face suddenly broke into a broad grin.

"You never told me your friend was a Greek," he said to Joan, clapping Nico on the back. "Of course, this makes all the difference in the world. For him, I will charge twenty solidi, less than half of my normal price."

"D —," Joan started to say, but I interrupted her rudely.

"Eight."

There was more animated jabbering between Andros and Nicola. Finally, the man, Andros shrugged and said "Dhodhekah."

"Ohkee, ahkreevo. Enia."

"Endhekah!"

Joan translated for me. "Andros has gone down to twelve. Nico offered nine and Andros came back with eleven."

"Tell him ten and be done with," I whispered.

"Kirios," Joan said, switching to Greek. "Dhekah solidi and finished."

At that, Andros looked from Nico to Joan. "What's this? You both speak Greek? You are ganging up on a poor old man? You would see me starve?"

"By the looks of you, Kirios Andros, you've not missed one meal in your life," Joan said, manly punching him softly in his large gut.

"Very well, ten, then," he said, resignedly.

"As I told you last week, we are in a hurry. Are they finished?" Joan asked. "We'll pay you immediately they're delivered to us."

At that, the fat man rubbed the fingernails of his right hand against the palm of his left. "Of course," he said. "I defy the Pope himself to prove they are anything but genuine. But first, the money."

I reached into my purse to gather the payment demanded, happy that my friends had saved me half of what I had been told I would have to pay. As I withdrew my hand, Nicola pushed it aside. "First, the parchment," he said.

"Yes, of course." Andros went into another room and emerged with three beautifully illuminated writings. At the top of each, in bright red letters, was the name "Schola Alcuinicus, Angliorum" and the date of its founding, "Anno Domini DCCLXXV," seven years before Charlemagne had summoned the renowned scholar, Alcuin, to teach at the palace school in Aachen." There was a great deal of exquisite handwriting on the parchments, but none of them were signed nor bore any seal.

Joan nodded to me and I handed Andros the money. He disappeared into another room and emerged a few moments later with a man whom he introduced as Deacon Paulus Magnus. The Deacon had the crepecious skin of the very old, almost the same color as the parchment. His voice was as brittle as the crackle of browned and dying leaves which have fallen off an oak in late fall. And, as sometimes is apparent in those whose age has deprived them of the grosser aspects of sexual identity, there was no odor about the man other than what one would have found in that same pile of dried leaves.

"Tell these young people about yourself, Your Worship," Andros said, with effusive deference to the old fellow.

The man accepted a drink of hot cider from our host and told us he had, indeed, studied under the great Alcuin himself, when that renowned scholar had served at York. He'd accompanied Alcuin when the great man went to teach at Charlemagne's palace school at Aachen, some forty-four years before. When Alcuin left the school to assume the role of Abbot, eight years later, Paulus had followed his master to the huge abbey at Tours, where he remained as an assistant to Alcuin until the revered Abbot's death in 804. Over the next hour, almost without stop, the old man filled us in with so many details of his life, so many apparently accurate snippets about the life of Alcuin, that we would be hard-pressed to doubt his veracity. I noticed that Joan, unlike Nico and me, hung on every word, mentally putting the old man's words away for further use.

Paulus sadly concluded that the politics of the Church were no different than the politics of politics anywhere. After Alcuin's death, he found himself relegated to ever lesser positions at Tours. "I was eighty-one last month," he concluded. "My friend Andros says you are seeking admission to the old school at York, where I myself studied and he asks that I sign a letter of recommendation on your behalf."

At that, I looked from Joan to Nicola, momentarily ashamed of the duplicitous trick we were playing on an innocent old man.

"You'll forgive me if my eyesight is not what it once was. I've come to rely on Andros to draft letters on my behalf. But you seem a pleasant enough group of youngsters," he said. "You are familiar with your prayers? Your knowledge of Latin?"

"We are, Father," Joan said, and she rattled off dialogues between Founding Fathers of the Church with an eloquence that startled the old gentleman.

"Young man, you remind me of the day I met the Master himself," he said. "You will undoubtedly be admitted into the Schola with no difficulty." Paulus turned to his friend and said, "Andros, hand me the quill and the seal."

With that, Deacon Paulus Magnus, a well-known, if somewhat faded star in Mother Church's firmament, launched into a detailed lecture about his years at Tours, which happened to be our first intended destination. At the end of an hour, he set his signature on all three of the documents, then watched with approval as Andros heated and dripped purple wax onto the bottom of the first piece of parchment. With a strength we would not have believed he had, the old man lifted and applied a heavy bronze seal to the hot wax on those and the other two certificats.

"You must now excuse my illustrious friend," Andros said. "He is exhausted by his labors and should rest."

He took the old man out of the room in which we were standing. As they left the room, Andros handed the Deacon two solidi.

When he returned, Andros sat at a table and, in a firm and flowery hand, made three perfect copies of a signature above and to the left of the deacon's spidery handwriting. "Finished," he said, after scattering drying talc on the parchments. He handed one to Joan, one to Nico, and one to me. Not only was the handwriting exquisite, but the verbiage was elegant and laudatory. It went on for most of the page, describing in detail how Fra. Martinus Paschal, Fra Nicholas Baptista Generola, and Fra. Joannes Angliorum had excelled in all fields at Alcuin's Schola at York with the highest honors, and how each had been certified as a Brother in Christ in Holy Mother Church. The certificat was countersigned by the Archbishop of Reims himself, and, as I looked at the original and reputedly true signature, I succumbed to Andros" representation that even the Archbishop himself would never be able to swear that this was not his signature.

The certificat requested that as designated emissaries of His Holiness the Archbishop of Reims, we were to be afforded the utmost courtesies as Scholars in Residence acting under his aegis wherever in Church lands we might find ourselves. And with these in hand, we were now truly ready to embark on our journey.

~ ∫ ~

After the autumnal equinox, the days started to grow noticeably shorter and colder. The world in which we were about to venture was very nearly as uncertain about its identity and destiny as we were about our own. For a brief period, Charlemagne had united the whole of at least what had been the Western Roman Empire, but since his death, even that was falling into disarray. Charlemagne's son, Louis the Pious, had held the Empire together for barely three years after his father's death until, in 817, he had divided France among his sons. Lothar, the eldest, had become co-regent; the second son, Ludwig, had received Bajuwaria; and Pepin, the youngest, ruled Aquitania.

In Rome, Paschal had been Pope from 817 through 824, three years before the onset of our journey. However, in 824, when Paschal died, a state of near anarchy erupted until the Franks, by show of sheer force, imposed the Constitutio Romana on the Holy See, giving the Frankish emperor the right to approve any newly-elected Pope. Eugenius now wore the Shoes of the Fisherman.

Farther east, Michael the Amorian, had become Byzantine emperor in 820, ending the Syrian dynasty, and the Saracens, heathens from Araby, had advanced as far as Crete and the islands of Greece, and were said to be preparing to attack Sicily and Sardinia, two islands right off the coast of Italia.

And we — Nicola, Joan, now confirmed in her identity as Brother Joannes, and I — were about to descend into the center of a world in turmoil.

BOOK 11.
AQUITANIA

CHAPTER 4

Two days later, we departed London. The land was gentle, the weather kind as we negotiated the terrain south toward Tunbridge Wells. The first evening, we made camp in a clearing two hours' ride south of Woodbridge Down. We could have spent the night at an inn, but we'd been cosseted in a city for several months, and we knew that with winter coming upon us no more than two months hence, a night under the stars, breathing the fresh air of an open space, would be a welcome change.

My father's training enabled me to shoot a couple of fat marmots and a large hare, certainly enough for a magnificent feast. Meanwhile, Nicola had started a small fire and had erected a spit of crossed-carved branches. Joan found wild onions and edible greens in a nearby copse. From out her horse pack, she produced a small iron pot with an arched handle over the top. This she laid directly on the fire, just below where the spitted marmots were roasting. When the bottom of her pot was lined with melted marmot fat, she used a small tree branch to move the pot away from the marmots, but still over the fire, placed the wild onions and greens in the pot, and started stirring the combined vegetables in the sizzling fat.

Before long, the roasting carcasses were browning. I watched the drippings of fat sizzle as they dropped onto the fire and inhaled the sweet, pungent aroma of the onions and greens. My stomach groaned with hunger. After a sufficient time, the three of us enjoyed a delicious and filling repast.

I heard the dull thud of two church bells as the sun set. Village lights flickered in the distance. Soon, night was upon the land. There is something lonely, awesome, and beautiful about being close to a forest, away from the noises and smells of a town or city. The stars seem somehow more numerous and brighter, the sky larger. Distant sounds seem muted and less intrusive.

Nicola brought out a small stringed instrument and the three of us sat around the fire, listening as he strummed simple chords. Joan's eyes widened as she recognized a ballad about a young girl who was in love with a young Celtic boy. The boy had gone off to war and she lamented she'd never see him again. He'd returned, but he'd been horribly injured and deformed, and now her sad song turned to thoughts of a life she could have had. Dare she give up her life for a suddenly cynical cripple, or free herself from the bondage of young love destroyed? There was no answer to the question. After Nicola finished, we all sat quiet, humbled by the words, lost in our own thoughts.

After a while, Joan said, "Thank God I've vowed never to let myself come to such a state."

"How would you know?" Nicola rejoined. "Have you locked yourself in a cage at fourteen years, never to come out? And you, the most brilliant g–," he stopped himself. "The brightest youth I've ever met?"

"If I am to achieve my goal, I cannot let such a thing as wasted emotion stand in my way."

"And is love such a waste of emotion?" I asked mildly.

"Yes, it is," Joan responded with what I thought more heat than the question demanded. "What does 'love' produce except loss of your senses to momentary pleasure" — she blushed — "at least I've been told it's pleasure — and a sackful of babies. You wipe their spittle and their filthy skeit, and, before you even know it, you confront old age, pain and death. No, my friends, that is not something for me. I want more for myself."

"Such as?" Nicola spoke.

"I want to find out what is truly right, and help teach people to know what is right."

"Ah, yes," Nicola said gently. "Isn't that something we all want?" We were all silent for a few moments. "I came upon a very old farmer outside the monastery at Avignon," he continued. "I had seen him from a distance before and knew he was not attached to the monastery and that he had been long a widower. He was leading a shambling ox, who limped in pain, toward a small balsam forest some distance away. He rubbed the ox's back and talked to it softly, and I thought he must be a bit crazed to be talking to a dumb animal. Having nothing better to do that day, I followed the man until he entered the forest.

"He stopped and removed a mallet which had been in a sack tied to the ox's back. Still talking to the ox in the same low, soothing voice, he reared back and struck the animal between its eyes with the mallet. The blow was so sudden and so hard that without so much as a whimper, the ox fell over and lay still. The old man pulled a knife from the same sack and cleanly slit the ox's throat. The ox barely twitched before a pool of its blood ran in small rivulets at the farmer's feet.

"I was outraged at the farmer's cruelty and ran into the woods to tell him so. When I reached the old fellow, he was sitting on a stump, mumbling words I could not comprehend. When he saw me, he seemed quite composed and at peace.

"'Old man,' I shouted. 'How could you have done such a thing? Surely you know right from wrong?'

"The farmer pondered the question for several moments, before he looked at me, not unkindly. His hair, which was a mottled gray, was wispy and stood out from his head. 'Young man,' he said, 'this may be hard for you to understand. I only ask that you think back to what I say when you're twenty or thirty years older. When I was young, I was no different from you. I certainly knew right from wrong and thought I was chosen by the Merciful God to bring right to the world. I didn't. In the real world, you do what you must to survive as best you can. Along the way, you start to ask different questions, the kind it never occurred to you to ask when you were young. Such as, is it more important to stand for what you believe is right at the cost of another creature's pain? You saw me kill the old ox, did you not?'

"'Of course.'

"'And you believe I was unkind because I struck the beast beforehand with a hammer?'

"'Yes. How could you bring such pain to the animal not once but twice? And for what purpose?'

"'Trust me when I say that what I did was a kindness to the animal.'

"'That is like asking me to believe that what my eyes show me is wrong is not. That if enough people tell me that black is white I will start to believe it.'

"'On the contrary, young man, if you hear me out, you may come to understand right and wrong more deeply and perhaps understand your own shortcomings the better. You say it looked cruel to you when I knocked the ox between its eyes?'

"'Yes.'

"'Consider this, then,' the old man continued. 'The ox was very old, blind, stiffened, and very much in pain. He might have died in agony in another month or even another year, and his suffering would have been greatly lengthened. The last memory the old fellow had was that he was walking with me — I, who have been his friend and raised him from a calf newly born. The day was sunny and the load he was carrying unusually light for him. He was always used to the sound of my voice and he felt my hand gently, lovingly upon his back.

"'When I struck him with a blunt instrument, it took but an instant for him to fall into a swoon and he truly did not feel a moment's pain. He simply, quite suddenly, was sleeping deeply. He died, not even knowing he had died. And he is no longer in pain.'"

Joan wasn't chastened by Nicola's words, but she was wise enough, even at fourteen years, to weigh and evaluate something that was said, rather than assume it was wrong simply because it did not meet with her own expressed beliefs.

The crescent moon in the sky sank beneath the treetops. We opened our mats, wrapped ourselves in cloaks, and before long the world softened and started to become a blur. My last conscious thought was that if the old farmer's ox had died in this manner, maybe it was not wrong after all.

~ ∫ ~

I don't know how long I had been sleeping. It was not yet light and the fire had not yet turned to coal and ash. I felt the need to void myself of liquid and walked deeper into the woods — not so far that I could not see our distant fire, but far enough so as not to disturb Joan and Nicola.

I had just finished my business and was lowering my tunic when I saw a flickering light in the midst of trees. Startled, I thought to run back and wake the others. The light might be caused by a highwayman, or by a group of them, and we'd best not be caught unawares. I clutched at the short knife sheathed at my side.

I crept as quietly as I could toward the light. Soon I came near enough to see that the light came from a smoky torch of bundled pitch wood. I closed to within three man-lengths and hid behind a thick tree. From there, I had a clear view of a man in a short, dark tunic and trousers, leading a horse tethered to a rope. Man and horse stopped every few steps, as if thinking what to do next. Because of the wavering light, I could see that the horse carried a burden, a shapeless thickness across its back like a large, lumpy sack filled with clothing.

As I watched, the man set his torch in the soft earth, then sat on a small rock nearby and drew his knees up so his head rested on them. He sat silently for a few moments, then started a keening kind of moan. "Oh, God, God," he started to wail. "Why? Why? I have lusted and it has come to this." He rose abruptly and started to bang his head rhythmically but not, I noticed, with great force, against the nearest tree.

"God, I am damned. What to do? What, oh what to do? I am only twenty-three years old and I long for your service, Oh God. Help me return to your fold as clean as a newborn lamb, so that I may lay cleansed in the fold with Your Shepherd."

The religious babble surprised me. It seemed so out of place and filled with an emotion that seemed to be heartfelt. The man sat on the rock again, his head down, and rocked from side to side.

I wondered how best to handle this situation and thought, *This man is no highwayman and he is so consumed by his own unhappiness that he means no harm to us.* I had just taken the first steps back toward our encampment when the man stood and went over to the horse. He walked to the horse's far side and began trying to lift the bundle off the animal's back. The horse shifted nervously and pulled back its ears, whuffling in an agitated manner. Could it have sensed my presence? I saw the whites of the horse's eyes and it whipped its head rapidly up and down.

"Steady, fellow," the man said, ignorant of whatever it was that had bothered the horse. After some more groaning and pulling, and a great exhalation of breath, the man finally got the bundle off the horse and over his shoulder. When he emerged, staggering, from behind the horse, I barely stifled a gasp as I realized that he was lugging a woman. Her long, black hair cascaded toward the ground and one of her arms was swinging unrhythmically. The woman was not conscious, but her body seemed pliable rather than stiff.

The man lowered her to the ground, sat on his rock once again, and began sobbing. He pulled a knife from somewhere about his person and sat staring at it in the firelight, turning it first one way, then another. He looked toward the prostrate figure lying in front of him, rose from the rock, and rolled her over onto her back.

In the blaze of the torch's smoky light, I could see that whoever the woman was, her stomach protruded and showed she was with child. The man took hold of a huge cross, which hung on a thin rope around his neck, took it off and laid it between the curves rising from the woman's chest. He grabbed the knife in both hands and raised it up above her inert body.

"In the name of the Father and the Son and the Holy Ghost," he intoned in Latin.

What occurred next seemed to happen much more slowly that it probably did. The man started to bring the knife down in a slow arc. I burst from my hiding place, shouted, "No!" and knocked the man's arm away so that the knife came down in the dirt and skittered away.

The woman, still unconscious, did not move. I unsheathed my knife and glared down at the would-be murderer.

He looked up at me with a resigned stare.

"Step away from her," I ordered. I found I was breathing heavily and my voice was husky. "Get over here where I can see you." As he came closer to me, I could see he was half a head taller than me, but of slighter build. "Stop right there," I ordered.

"The Lord has answered my prayer," the man said humbly. "You are a messenger from God, telling me not to do what I would have done."

He took another step toward me. As I raised my own knife and glared at him menacingly, he dropped to his knees, fell forward and hugged my legs. I shoved him away. He turned his face up to me and, in the light of the torch, I could see that it was shiny with tears. I struck the man rather a mild blow with the flat of my hand, and he toppled helplessly back onto the ground.

"I deserve that and I thank you for it," he said.

"You deserve to be killed," I said. I looked over to where the woman lay, still unmoving. "I might still do it," I added.

"Don't kill me, I'm a man of God."

"Aren't we all?" I responded.

"A priest is what I mean," he said. "I'm an ordained priest."

I looked at him uncomfortably. "Is she dead?"

"No."

"What's wrong with her?"

"As you can tell, she is with child. I gave her some, ummm, medicine."

"So I see. From a barber or an old witch?"

"From a peddler. He said it would put her to sleep hard until morning."

"You're the father?"

"What concern is that of yours?" Those words answered my question.

"You're not married to her?"

"I said I'm a priest."

"Obviously not a very observant one."

"No." He stood up unsteadily. "You must understand, certainly. You and I are of an age. The devil tempts even a holy man."

"But surely you know what's right and what's not?" I faltered slightly in my stern tone, remembering the story Nicola had told earlier in the evening.

I knelt down close to the body — it was a girl no more than fifteen — put a hand to her dark head and lifted it. She was breathing softly, shallowly, with a kind of faint snore. Her face was slack and the shadows from the torchlight did nothing to flatter her. Still, she was a pretty thing and I could see where a man, even a priest, might find restraint a burden. I lowered her head back to the ground.

"Put her back on the horse," I ordered. I stepped away, keeping my knife unsheathed, knowing that the bulk of my body in the firelight and the firmness of my voice was enough to control the man. He knelt and struggled to lever the girl off the ground. He rose and half dragged, half stumbled to the horse, the girl an obvious burden to his slight frame.

"Can you help me?" he asked.

"You managed to get her here yourself."

"Yes, that's true," he said. "Our Lord Jesus bore a cross as well, you know."

"That's so."

I heard the noise of footsteps tramping toward us. The man was far enough away that he could do me no harm, but now I felt trapped between a known would-be assailant and an unknown force. Without turning, I said, "Hold right there!" in a voice I hoped was more controlled than I felt.

"It's all right, Martin. It's only us," I heard Nicola say.

"Nicola, Jo—"

"Joannes, too," she finished, her voice man-husky. "What have we here?"

Relieved, I explained quickly what I had come upon, and how I had happened to come upon it. The man stood there by the horse, saying nothing. By this time, the woman was once again draped over the horse's back.

"What now?" the man asked, when I was finished.

"Do you have a name?" Joan asked in the same tone a man would have asked, "Who dropped this turd in the middle of my kitchen?"

"Anastasius," he said. His speech was accented.

"Not from near here, obviously," Joan continued in the same tone.

"From the Holy See."

"A priest from Rome itself," she said. "Are these the morals they teach you there?"

"What do you know you of such things?" the man said sharply, pushed almost over the brink by Joan's scalding tone. Then, abashed, Anastasius continued, in a half-pleading, half-confiding manner which I found disgusting. "Surely you, yourself, have felt the need for a woman, felt your fascinum tingling at the curve of a woman's breast?"

"What of it?" Joan answered coldly. "I'm a man of God just like you purport to be. Only I have learned to control my manly urges and kept what's inside my tunic *inside* my tunic."

Despite the intensity of the moment, I suddenly developed a huge spasm of coughing in an effort to stop myself from an outbreak of uncontrollable laughter. *My God, she's convincing enough that I believe her!*

"Enough," Joan barked, now taking full control of the situation. "Where are you from?"

"Rysley, a small village near Tunbridge Wells."

"Walk ahead of us and show us the way there."

"But I cannot return there. I've been summoned back to Rome and I've already made my farewells. Who knows what they'll do when they see —?"

"Whatever they'll do, it's nothing more than you deserve. Move!" she commanded, pointing in the direction of our camp.

By the time we got to where we'd made camp, the darkness had given way to a misty dawn. Each of us grabbed a handful of cold marmot, took a sip of water from our skins, and packed and mounted our own horses. Anastasius watched in silence while we ate.

We started toward Tunbridge Wells, Anastasius leading his horse by its rope, the young woman still in a state of senselessness. The road soon climbed and crossed a small ridge. It wound through low, rolling hills. We left the forest behind and now the land lay open in great patches, where much of the woodland had been burned away, whether by nature or by the hand of man. It was a country of black stumps and dark brown soil, stretching away to a far horizon.

Anastasius was sweating, despite the cold, and every now and again the girl draped over his horse shivered. After some hours, the weather finally warmed and we could see the small town of Tunbridge Wells in the distance.

"What do you intend to do with me? Anastasius asked.

I was the first to respond. "I'm thinking about it. How came you to such a state, Priest? "

"She promised me she'd become a nun. She lives with an old grandfather so weak-eyed he can hardly see, so deaf he can hardly hear. It was easy for us to slip away into a haymow behind her grandpa's place or even go into the woods. I'm ashamed to say we spent a good part of the summer doing just that."

"Crafty as a fox. Is that what I'm hearing?"

"Well, yes, you might say that."

"But not crafty enough to avoid what happened? How did it all start?"

"In the usual way. A certain look of the eye at church. A brush of the hands after services. A touch during a visit to her grandpa's place for dinner."

"There's a far way from that to naked in a haymow."

"Yes."

"An even longer way to you drugging her and getting ready to end two lives with one blade in a forest twenty miles away in the middle of the night."

"It's more complicated than you make it out to be. You know how strict the Church is."

"But you could have left the Church, gotten married, and done the honorable thing," Joan said. "People do that. God understands."

"Maybe you didn't hear me, young sir," Anastasius turned toward her. "She was about to become a Sister in the Church, a Bride of Christ. They'd have found out —"

"Say you so," Joan replied.

"Yes. And I've anguished over it through many a night."

"I'm certain you did," Joan said. "On rainy nights when the haymows were too damp."

"Could you not both have left the Church and simply taken up life in a new place?" Nicola asked.

"You don't seem to understand," the priest said. "I am not some country fellow with no future. I was sent here from Rome for a first posting and now I've been asked to return to the Holy See. My uncle is a Prince of the Church at Rome. They say there are plans for me," he finished miserably.

"So you would rather marry her if you could?" Joan asked.

"I did not say that," he said. "She is nothing more than a country commoner."

"I'm sure you didn't tell her that when you were preparing to upend her," Joan said caustically. "Or when you needed a vase in which to stick the flower of your manhood."

The sarcasm went right over Anastasius' head. The fool actually took Joan's words to be an indication of complicity. "Ah, you've been there," he said, winking. "So you must know what I mean, then."

Joan abruptly changed the subject. "The girl seems to be coming out of her stupor. Let us feed her a very small bit of mandragoras root. If the grandfather's as blind and deaf as our priest says, we should be able to put her back in her bed like this never happened. Have either of you a bit of cloth?" she asked, turning to us.

"I do," I said.

Joan quickly dismounted and commanded Anastasius to lie down on the ground.

"What do you intend to do?" He seemed humiliated but defiant nonetheless.

In reply, Joan unsheathed a large knife and nodded her head, silently commanding him once again to lie on the ground. "Martin, take the rope off and hold the horse for a moment." I did, and at her signal, tossed it to her. Joan trussed the struggling Anastasius with the rope, then, despite the priest wagging his head from side to side, she managed to stuff the wad of cloth into his mouth. She signaled Anastasius to rise.

"Why did you do that?" I asked her.

"Had we all paraded into town, he'd have called to the nearest passing man or woman. He's known in these parts and would undoubtedly have blamed us for everything. Since he's the village priest, people would certainly take his word over ours. Now, let's go around the outside perimeter of the town."

When we were on the outskirts of Tunbridge Wells, some barking dogs approached us. When they recognized the priest's familiar smell, they trotted away, satisfied.

"Which way to her house, Priest?" Joan asked.

Anastasius nodded toward a grove of poplars to beyond the edge of town. Soon we came to a tiny cottage in a clearing, just one room, covered over with bare boards. Anastasius looked toward it and pointed.

Just before they reached the house, Joan indicated a lone oak at the edge of the clearing.

"Back up to that oak," Joan said, her mood calm but unyielding. When he had done so, she took the long length of rope that was left after binding him by his wrists and, wrapping part of it around Anastasius' neck, bound the priest to the tree. Nicola brought another length of rope from the bag on his horse, and with that we were able to secure his legs to the tree as well.

At a nod from Joan, I lifted the girl from the horse. I put one arm under her waist, the other under the backs of her thighs. Her dark head rested on my shoulder. Despite all she had been through, there was a pleasant scent about her. She moaned softly and my heart went out to her. She was tiny and helpless, even more so because she knew nothing of what was going on. Anger rose in me as I thought of this girl, barely out of childhood herself, now with child. I ought to kill that priest, I thought.

I carried the girl to the house as gently as I could. The door was not closed. I heard the sound of hard snoring from within. The grandfather slept on a pallet by a slow burning fire. The room was dark and smoky, even in the full light of day. When I tried to raise the man by clapping my hands, he simply snored on. I decided it was safe to go in. I saw another, smaller pallet a few feet from where the old man was sleeping. I took the girl to the pallet, pulled off her rough shoes, and covered her as far up as her bosom. I left as quietly as I could.

When I came to where the priest was tied to the tree, I hawked up what phlegm I could, and spat full in his face. I suppose that was a needlessly cruel thing to do, for Anastasius was helpless and had no possible way either of fighting back or even wiping the spittle from his person. But, somehow, I thought the girl deserved that small bit of retribution to her dignity. Joan and Nicola looked at me and said not a word.

I reached in my horse's pack for a piece of parchment and a quill. As simply as I could, I printed what had happened in plain letters. When I was finished, I punched the parchment onto a tree branch above Anastasius' head. The priest, who had read what I was writing, thrashed about and made angry gargling noises. He tried to chew through the wad of cloth in his mouth.

I had no stomach for this man. I yanked the cloth out of his mouth. "What is it you want to say?" I demanded. "And I warn you that if you speak one word above a whisper, I will carve a deep cross in your despicable body."

"You're ruining my life," he said hotly.

"So say you," I said, surprised at the bitterness of my tone. "You think about ruining lives while you're tied here. If I didn't do what I'm doing, you would probably take the girl back out in the forest tonight and finish what you tried to do last night."

"Why not just kill me then?"

"Don't think I haven't thought about it."

"God damn you to hell!" This time he surprised me by spitting toward my face, though he was still bound. I moved fast enough to avoid it for the most part, and by that time, my anger had abated, so I simply wiped the residue away.

With not another word, Joan picked up the cloth, stuffed it back in Anastasius' mouth, and took a narrower piece of rope by which she insured that the gag would not come out before we were far away.

We let Anastasius' horse run free, readied our own steeds, and within a few moments we were riding south, trying to put as much distance as possible between us and what we had left behind.

CHAPTER 5

Gull's Landing, from whence we intended to debark, was a filthy seaport town of six hundred souls. It was the most likely point from which we could make passage to St. Valery. Its buildings were grimy with the accumulated grease of countless years. Gull's Landing was aptly named. Those birds had indeed landed and shat on every wharf in the area. The town's two jetties were slippery with fish slime. The odor of the place was of salty air, soured by bird droppings, rotting entrails of sea creatures, and the stench of strong ale and ale-ripened vomit.

Nico found us a large, rough-wood hewn inn, where we enjoyed a delicious fish stew. We took lodging in the place, stabled our horses, and enjoyed a good night's sleep, accompanied by the comforting sound of a rainstorm pelting the roof over our beds.

By next morning, when we left the inn to seek passage to St. Valery, the storm had passed, and the fresh breeze had dried mud-girdled streets, so that it was easy to walk at the high ridge in the center of the way. Not long afterward, we came to the harbor.

As we were discussing where best to go to find someone to take us across the Channel, a voice boomed out behind us. "Did I hear you were looking for passage to St. Valery?" When we turned, we found ourselves facing a man of thirty-five, considerably shorter than any of us, who had a luxuriant, bushy moustache and clear, brown eyes. He wore a nondescript coat and fisherman's hat. "My name is West. I can get you there safely."

"I'm Joannes Angliorum," Joan said, nodding her head. "My brothers-in-God, Martin Paschal, Nicholas Baptista Generola."

"Priests?" He crossed himself, hawked up a wad of phlegm, and spat it toward the sea. "Sorry, it's this blasted wet wind."

"Not priests," Joan continued. "Brothers traveling to our first posting in Aquitania."

West – we didn't know if this was his first or his last name – looked us over cautiously. "You're not dressed as holy men."

"We've but one cassock apiece and no need to betray who or what we are on the road," Joan said. As West's face fell, Joan continued smoothly. "Never you mind our appearance, good captain. We're able to afford reasonable passage to Europa. We have three steeds as well. I trust your boat can make the voyage with all of us?"

He looked toward the quay uncertainly, shrugged his shoulders and grinned unabashedly back at us, displaying a mouth half filled with brown, mottled teeth. "Of course."

West quoted us a price that was outrageous, although affordable. Nico, who'd taken this sea voyage before, offered barely a third of what the ship's captain had asked. West laughed derisively and said, "Find passage with anyone else you choose, then. You'll not find many a captain in Gull's

Landing or, for that matter, anywhere on the southern coast, who'll take you through Dane-filled, monster-infested waters for twice the price I've asked."

"Fine, then," Joan said equably. "That's a chance we'll gladly take. Come, fellows," she addressed us. "Tonight we'll indulge ourselves. We're in no hurry, there's no need for us to bother ourselves with a robber. Good day, sir, and good luck." She clapped us on our shoulders and herded us toward the nearest bar.

"But you said you were brothers-in-God," West wailed.

"Mayhap," said Joan. "Friars we are, and newly graduated. We've years of celibacy ahead of us, but those years don't start tonight. Come fellows! Now!"

We'd gone no more than a dozen paces before West followed us, wheedling and importuning. "You don't understand. You expect me to carry three grown men *and* three horses. Mine is not a Norse war vessel and it is not equipped to carry stupid, skittish land animals. They would have to be lashed down. The wind would have to be just right. You said you need to travel there tonight?"

"Not necessarily," Nico said. "We've got several weeks before we need even think of landing there, and there's enough activity around here to sustain us 'til then."

"Would you be willing to man the oars, if need be?" he asked slyly.

"Of course, man."

"Well, why didn't you say so?" he said. "In two days' time, I can find an additional passenger, which will allow me to cut my own expenses."

Within a few moments, a deal was struck. Without seeing West's vessel, we agreed to pay him two-thirds of his original asking price, half due when we set sail, the other portion on our safe arrival at St. Valery. We would make the voyage by day, three days hence, and he would honor the agreement, whether or not he'd secured other voyagers.

"Fine, and done," said Joan, shaking West's hand. "Now that that's finished, we'll meet you where you've indicated at sunrise in three days. For now, we've things to do. Why not join us?"

"It would be my pleasure," West replied.

After we'd walked several hundred yards, Joan said, "Why don't we traverse Front Street and find the least disreputable looking place?"

"But I thought you wanted ...?"

"Well, I've changed my mind. Mayhap you're right. I should start thinking as a man of God."

I glanced over at Nico, who'd raised his own eyebrows in response to the blank, innocent look I shot his way.

As we walked, I asked West, "Is Gull's Landing your home port?"

"For now," he said, and shrugged.

"From whence come you originally?"

"The North – but not from the land of the North*men*, you understand. Germania and the Low Countries. One day, when I've saved enough and can sell my vessel, I shall return to Fulda."

"I'm told there's a great *schola* there," Joan said.

"True, but not for the likes of me. Gull's Landing is one of the few Angle-ish ports not under blockade between the Islands and Europa. Would you like to see the vessel now?"

"Ne, we'll meet you two days hence and examine your vessel then."

~ ∫ ~

As I had surmised, it was a plain barque of the kind that plied the coastal waters in those days, more a barge than a boat, really, with a wide deck and a shallow draft. The vessel had two masts with square-rigged sails of the old Roman style, and a small below-deck area that could accommodate two oarsmen on each side. West told us the journey, which approximated eighty Roman miles, would take two full days, the weather gods willing. When Joan enquired why it would take so long, West said that although it was too early for the raging winter storms, which were known to savage the Channel, he intended to stay as close to the coastline as possible. We would sail east from Gull's Landing, thence north to the chalk cliffs of Dover, where we'd lay off the coast 'til nightfall. From there, under cover of night – a period when the Northmen were known not to haunt the seas – we would set a course across the Strait of Dover until we came to the Neustrian coast. Thence, we would resume our journey down the Coast until we came to the mouth of the Seine, where West would deposit us at Cape Havrus, near St. Valery.

"Have you found the fourth passenger you talked about when we booked passage?" I asked.

"Indeed," West responded, rubbing his hands together in a brisk motion to assuage the cold morning. "A man-of-God like yourselves, who told me he would debark at the mouth of the Seine as well. Like you, he did not wear the priest's cassock. Quite a tale he told, and I must say even as hard a heart as mine was softened by the harsh treatment he'd received."

As I listened to West's review of what he'd been told, I felt an icy chill.

"Ah, yes, the poor young man, lately come from Tunbridge Wells. Just outside that town, he was waylaid by three highwaymen, who robbed him and left him tied to a tree."

"A shame," Joan said. She turned to us and said, in Latin, "This does not bode well."

"Should we abandon the voyage on this barque then?" Nico replied in the same language.

"After we've already paid half our passage? Ne," said I. "There are three of us, and if we are indeed 'highwaymen', that 'priest' would do well to fear us."

"It's not the journey that bothers me," said Joan. "It's the part about being sent from the Holy See and debarking with us. Remember, he said his uncle was a prince of the Church? He could have connections at Tours."

"What then?"

"In his Christian heart he must feel the need to repay our 'favor'," she said. "Perhaps we might think of another abbey? Rouen or even Fulda?"

"I think it best just to keep an eye on him," I said. "What can he do or say that we cannot refute?"

~ ∫ ~

It was indeed Anastasius, and if he recognized us, he gave no indication of it. We thought it best to keep up the pretense, and listened sympathetically as he repeated to us the tale he'd told the ship's master.

Next morning, West seemed unaccustomedly dour and suggested we might want to wait a day or two before setting forth. "Why?" I asked. "There's a glorious sun rising in the east. Surely it bodes a fair day and easy sailing."

"Ne," said West, glowering. "Look toward the opposite horizon."

I did, and saw a few red-tinged clouds reflecting the sun's rays. "Beautiful," I said.

"Ne, ne. Damnable. Have ye not heard the saying, 'Red sky in morning, sailor take warning?" I fear we've a dangerous journey ahead should we proceed this day."

But we managed to convince West that he himself had told us the barque would stay close to shore and that, at the very worst, it was no farther than thirty-five Roman miles across the Strait of Dover. So it was that we cast off, and although the day got progressively grayer and more sultry, by the time we made landfall at Dover in late afternoon, the wind had dropped altogether and the water was calm.

During the day, Anastasius kept to himself, but well within earshot, reciting prayers.

"'Tis the new style from Rome," Nico told us. "They say, it's named after the late Pope Gregory, of blessed memory and it became obligatory once Charles accepted the orb as Holy Roman Emperor."

"'New?'" Joan remarked archly. "Blessed Gregory died more than eleven score years ago. Rather ancient, I would say."

"Well, let's just say new to *us*, then. It would not harm us to listen and learn. If, as he says, his uncle is well placed at the Holy See, we would do well to learn the current manner of the court."

By nightfall, the waves approaching Dover were choppy. There was still no sign of a storm. What little wind there'd been, had abated. West looked about nervously. "T'would be dangerous to cross now."

"Nonsense," said Joan. "If four of us take turns rowing, it will take a few hours at most to make the crossing."

"'Tis on your head, then, not mine," said West. "I've weathered many a storm and if there's one a'sea, I'll weather that one, too. But I warn you two" – here, he pointed to Joan and me – "you've not been on the water before. Can either of you swim?"

"Ne," Joan answered. I responded likewise.

"If fools ye be, then decide among yourselves who'll row first. I'll remain topside to steer the vessel."

For the first watch, all went well. The weather remained calm. When I could barely make out the Neustrian Coast in the distance, the gale hit with a suddenness that overwhelmed all of us. Before we knew it, the small craft was rocking from side to side, out of control amid waves twice as high as a man. Several waves washed completely over our vessel, and when other waves hit us broadside, the horses pawed the deck and screamed shrilly in terror, even though they were secured with stout ropes.

Within moments after the storm struck, I was heaving my innards out over the side of the boat, and while the icy water shocked me into consciousness, I was trembling all over with fear. Then the waves turned the boat, first hard left, then hard right. From my vantage point, bleak and terrifying as it was, I saw Joan approach Anastasius from the rear. *My, God*, I thought, *she's going to push him overboard and we'll be done with that devil.*

Anastasius had no inkling of Joan's plan. He turned sharply to avoid falling over the side of the boat, just as Joan lunged forward to push him. I tried to move as quickly as I could to grab Joan, but it was too late.

"Man overboard!" shouted the captain.

I gasped, helpless, as I saw her topple over the deck, into the roiling waves. "Joan!" I shouted, forgetting in my panic the masquerade. Joan bobbed up and down near the boat. Although I could barely see her in the dark, she was nearly hysterical with fear. What happened next seemed more dream than reality.

Anastasius shucked off his protective garment, quickly tied a length of rope about his chest, and jumped into the savage waters, paddling his arms and kicking his legs as he raced toward Joan. He reached her quickly and shouted something to her. She stiffened and lay prone on her back. Anastasius grabbed her around her armpits. It was then that I saw a sudden, almost imperceptible spark of shock in his eyes. It was gone in an instant and he kicked violently toward the boat, dragging Joan and shouting to anyone who could hear to pull the rope in.

God, he knows. But I said nothing.

Joan's tunic had come off in the water. I had the presence of mind to have a large blanket ready when Nico and I pulled her back onto the boat. Joan was shivering, covered with those tiny red welts called "duck bumps," as I quickly spirited her belowdecks.

None of us spoke for the rest of the sea journey. The storm abated as suddenly as it had come upon us. By daylight, we came upon the Neustrian coast. We sailed south under a gray, but benevolent sky. By midday, we debarked just south of where the River Seine meets the sea. As soon as we had the mind to do so, we all three glared at Anastasius with a mixture of thanks and venom.

"I swear I never suspected —" he said, shakily.

"And *I* swear if you so much as utter it to a soul, you will be a dead man the moment I learn of it," I said.

"I as well," said Nico in a quiet, seemingly mild voice, which carried far more menace than mine. "But we thank you nonetheless."

"The debt is repaid, to God and to man. You know this means that none of us must ever disclose any of our secrets," Anastasius said. "We are all young. We have many years ahead of us. Mayhap our paths will not even cross again."

"I have difficulty believing that," Joan said. "No one would have believed the impossible coincidence of your escaping so quickly from Tunbridge Wells, coming to Gull's Landing, and booking passage in the one space remaining on the same boat as us. Is your destination Tours?" I noticed there was high color in her cheeks.

"*Ne*, my uncle has summoned me to Rome. There has been another shakeup there."

"What say you?" I asked.

"Eugenius died mysteriously two months ago. My uncle said that Valentinius, who succeeded him, stood in the shoes of the Fisherman for a mere forty days. Now, Gregory the Fourth has ascended Peter's throne, and God only knows how long he'll last."

"Well," I said. "As long as we're traveling to Tours, I suppose there's no harm if we travel together. That is, if we can find a way to trust one another."

"I need hardly think you'd fear me after what happened back in Angle-land," Anastasius said, with what passed for a smile, but seemed to me more of a smirk. "Besides, you've got three horses and I've but one pair of legs."

"True," Nico said. "I suggest for the time being, we ride two on one of the horses to the nearest town and get our bearings before we start south toward Tours."

We found shelter at Cape Havrus, near St. Valery, that night, no better nor memorable than where we'd lodged in Gull's landing. Next day, under a still gray sky, we traversed the Seine until we came to the large town of Rouen, which had its own abbey. That structure was, by far, the largest series of buildings in that place and dominated the countryside.

We were welcomed warmly when the three of us presented our documents, and especially when Anastasius made known his intimate connection with Rome. This was the first time I'd seen an abbey of some size, and, bumpkin that I realize I must have been back then, I was momentarily stupefied. The main building was larger than any structure I'd ever seen. It was made of hewn stone, was of a grayish brown color, and as high as ten men. It was cruciform in shape – that is to say in the shape of a cross – with four towers, one at each end. These towers were square and gave the place a sense of great strength and solidity. It was built in a style that I learned, much later, was called Romanesque, after some of the early buildings still standing in Rome.

The sleeping quarters consisted of forty cubicles, each a very small, windowless room that held one narrow cot and a rough, small table, on which sat a single large candle. These cells were lined up on both sides of one wing of the abbey's cross-arms. Each cell was equipped with a metal basin, set below the table, which was used for washing one's hands. There were six rere-dorters – *necessarias* – outside the wing, and a communal washroom nearby. While the lodgings were cramped, stark and drab, they were relatively clean and safe, and they were free.

Our horses were stabled in a separate building some distance away. There seemed to be more animals than men at the abbey that night.

During supper, which consisted of a thick broth and heavy, broad-grained bread, a young monk of my own age, Eridius, engaged me in conversation. He told me that on Sabbath, townfolk came to the abbey for a prayer service that lasted from sunrise to mid-afternoon. Two days a week, Rouen's populace set up a trade fair on the meadow between the abbey and the town proper. The monks participated in the fair, trading some of the wine, cheese and sausage they made at the abbey for seeds, blankets, baskets and such.

"Even asses, kine and horses when we need them," he said.

"When our abbot finds need to travel any distance, or to exchange important Church documents and such, they serve him and his retinue well."

"How frequently does your abbot travel?"

"Not much, anymore," Eridius replied. "He is old and seized of the gout, which makes riding uncomfortable. Lately it seems we have more animals than we need."

Nico moved from the wooden bench where he sat and joined us. "Think you the abbot could spare a mount?" he asked.

"I don't know," Eridius answered. "Best ask Brother stableman."

After supper, Nico and I found that fellow, short, stocky, barrel-chested and smelling of farm animals, at his evening chores, cleaning the stables of dung and piling the manure outside to be used as fertilizer at a later date. He was a merry sort, and offered us some red wine, which, I daresay, we welcomed after our harrowing time a'sea. After we'd told him of our need, he asked, "Where are you going next?"

"Tours," I responded. He brightened visibly.

"Father Abbot's scriveners have just completed a manuscript in the new Carolingian minuscule script. He wants the Bishop at Tours to review the last segments of the work before it is placed in its cover. We've not been able to find anyone to travel to Tours for the past fortnight and, as you might have heard, our Abbot is an old man and he becomes more impatient as he senses his end approaching."

"Surely with so many monks and priests at Rouen you can send one or two of them?"

"*Ne*," the stableman replied. "Of forty-three permanent residents of the abbey, we've four kinds: those who are too old and feeble to travel, those who fear attack from highwaymen, those who are too rash and young to have judgment and who might be enticed by the … sports along the way; and those who, like me, are said to be indispensable to the day-to-day activities of the abbey."

"Surely your monks could obtain an escort?

"Ne. Every spare man can usually be found fighting a war for some lord, a petty king, even for Louis himself," the stableman replied. "Every spare man, that is, except the serfs, the clergy, the highwaymen, and those too besotted with wine or whoring to care."

"Why would you trust us to carry the manuscript safely to Tours?" Nico asked.

"It's not for me to trust or distrust you," said the stableman. "I simply asked because people who need a horse and who are not townspeople are generally journeyers passing through Rouen. Trust is something dispensed by the Father Abbot and his underlings, who are appointed for such things. I simply stable horses. But should you meet with the Abbot's favor, you may be in luck."

"What mean you?" I asked.

"Horses are valuable to the townfolk, but they have precious little value here. They're neither as strong nor as stolid as oxen, they are more skittish than asses, and their skeit is far less productive than that of a cow, a pig, or even a chicken. The manuscript, on the other hand, may one day be of inestimable value. Father Abbot may well elect to entrust you with the manuscript, and should he do so, he'll no doubt provide you with the means of transporting it to Tours."

Nico and I said nothing, but I could hardly believe our good fortune.

Next day, we met with the Abbot, who, indeed, was old and enfeebled. It seemed he could hardly believe his good fortune when he learned that we were not only traveling to Tours, but were – at least Nico, Joan and I – going to Tours, to attend the *schola* there. The elderly Abbot waxed eloquent about that great school.

Just before we'd left Angle-land, I had taken to writing accounts of our journey. No sooner were we beyond the Abbot's presence, I wrote down all I could remember of what he had said. I asked Joan to read over what I had written. She was remarkably perceptive. By the time she had finished reciting small, what seemed to me insignificant details, my writing had more than doubled.

Father Abbot provided us with a horse, not the best of the abbey's lot, but a serviceable chestnut mare.

The following morning, each astride our own mount, we left Rouen for Tours.

Chapter 6

I packed the abbot's manuscript in a flat leather pouch, and hid it between Arca's saddle and the larger saddlebag, which carried my single change of clothing and winter cloak.

It was some three hundred Roman miles from Rouen to Tours. Since we'd be traveling part of the way on water, I envisaged a twenty day voyage to our destination. We'd follow the Seine until it joined the Iura River, some distance west of the new city of Paris. From there, we would catch a ferry-barge to take us south to the small abbey at Chartres. After another three days, we would come to the lesser Loire River. From there, it would take less than a fortnight for us to get to Tours. It was now the middle of October. Hopefully, the weather would remain clement until we arrived at the great abbey. Father Abbot admonished us to avoid the Collinius mountains, which, he told us, contained treacherous weather, treacherous highwaymen, and a surly populace that was decidedly unfriendly toward Mother Church.

The autumn of that year – in Aquitania it's called the "old women's summer" – was particularly lovely. The first evening after we'd left Rouen was warm enough to spend the night under the stars. Still, I had a disquieting feeling. Less than a fortnight ago, we'd surprised Anastasius in an unnatural act and left him to be dealt with by an outraged village. Tonight, we were under the stars of Neustria together. Anastasius had repaid our "kindness" by saving Joan's life, and in the process had discovered her secret. I still did not trust him. The world moves in odd directions.

Joan and I took the first watch. In order to stay awake, we talked quietly about our past days in Angle-land. It struck me, not for the first time, that despite her close-cropped hair and shapeless tunic, Joan had become a very attractive *woman*. I confess that at that moment I felt a tingling, distinctly *un*brotherly feeling toward her and found myself mute in her presence.

Next morning, we traversed the valley of the Seine. The hills exploded in a wild array of fall colors – red, yellow, orange, green, ochre – in several shades and gradients. I'd never seen such beauty in Angle-land. If you allow a horse the freedom to do so, it will stop at every bush or blade of grass. Arca, fine and loyal steed that he was, was no different from his brethren, and since I was enjoying the warmth and beauty of the place, I had no desire to urge him forward, so I lagged behind the others.

Nicola led our small group. Joan and Anastasius rode side by side. Often, when I looked up, I saw them in converse. Since I was several yards away, I could not hear what they were saying, but I noticed Joan's face displayed a high color. I kicked Arca's flanks to catch up with them and asked if anything were wrong.

"*Ne*," Joan said. "Anastasius was telling me about his childhood in Rome. I would love to see it some day. Did you know it's over a thousand years old, Martin?"

"Who can even imagine a place of such an age?" I said, but I wasn't thinking of Rome. I was thinking of last night, and of Joan, and I felt a tingling once again. Anastasius, who'd certainly had a history with at least one woman, must have sensed Joan's budding sensuality, but he continued talking, without surcease, about the once-great city on the River Tiber.

"South of the Vatican, the imperial city still exists, but in a badly deteriorated state. There are still entertainments in the Colosseum, chariot races from time to time, but no longer the way it was. I'm told that five hundred years ago, there was a man-made lake *inside* the Colosseum, and small naval vessels actually staged battles there."

Nico, who'd slowed down for us to catch up, added, "Early Christians were given the choice of fighting a lion bare-handed or fighting one another to the death."

"Yes," Anastasius said. "That was before Rome became a part of Christendom and reached its greatest glory."

"If it reached such a high state, why is the City in decline today?" Joan asked.

"That is a long and complicated story, Brother Joannes," Anastasius replied easily. I glanced at him sharply, wondering if the "Brother Joannes" was for Nico's and my benefit. "The Emperor Constantine moved the imperial capital far to the East and created the city that bears his name. When that happened, much of Rome's wealth, the civil servants, and the army followed him. Not long after, the Empire became divided. The old city of Romulus and Remus continued to claim *its* right to be capital of the Empire. Constantinople and Rome spent so much time debating their respective rights, not only as *the* Imperial City but the seat of *true* Christendom, that Rome ignored the threat from without, while Constantinople ignored the danger approaching from the shores of Africa and

Araby. Before anyone knew it, the last of the *Roman* emperors, Romulus Augustulus – the so-called 'Little Augustus,' was toppled from the Imperial throne. Then came Audawahkirs and anarchy, followed by Theodoricus, and the final flowering of true order. By the time he died, the Western Empire was finished and the Holy Fathers assumed control of their very small remnant of the City."

"*Sic semper gloria*," I added mildly.

Our journey on the Iura was so gentle that ferrymen did not find the journey upstream to Chartres to be difficult. We arranged for transport for ourselves and our four horses at a quarter of what we'd paid to cross the Channel. The next few days were peaceful and pleasant. The barge-ferry was much wider than the seagoing vessel on which we'd come to Neustria, but with a shallower draft. The horses were tied, one at each corner of the barge, to maintain balance. They did not seem ill at ease, even though they were off their natural turf. They ate and shat at will. When the latter happened, one of the bargemen simply swept their droppings into the river with a stiff broom. The three bargemen took turns propelling and steering the boat. Two of them, one on each side, moved the barge upstream by means of long wooden poles, while the third steered the vessel by means of a flat, moveable wooden board attached to its rear.

The Collinius Mountains to the west were purple in the morning light. Trees lined both banks of the river and beyond – balsam and poplar, oak, elm and willow – all dressed in their garishly beautiful autumn colors. We spoke about everything and nothing, and when we tired of that, we sang songs of our childhood, and when we tired of that, too, we set lines in the water. We caught numerous fish that day, trout, fat grayling and bass. That night, the bargemen grilled those fish on a charcoal brazier. After some more quiet singing – the bargemen taught us some ribald songs they'd learned in their youth – they secured the vessel to two large oak trees. We spread out bedclothes and sleeping gear on deck and slept the deep sleep of peace.

~ ∫ ~

The foothills of the Collinius were filled with trees in those days, but the forests were even then giving way to a number of manors along the highways. When we stopped outside a village some distance from Chartres, I approached what I took to be an elderly man with stooped back, who seemed to be laboring mightily under a large load of wood, and asked for directions to Bonneval, where we intended to spend the night. I was shocked to learn that the fellow was only thirty years old, no more than twelve years my senior.

Since the fellow was loquacious, I soon found out why he appeared so ancient. "Life's been hard and it don't get easier. The lord lives in his manor house and owns all the best land. Us who work the land, we get the rotted gullies, the hills, the thinnest soil. The lord lets us use old, half-broken tools for nothing and he lets us farm our own plots, but for that privilege we work in *his* great fields first, and our womenfolk cook, weave and care for the lord's livestock from dawn to nearly sundown, six days out of each week. On Sundays, we attend chapel on the manor proper. That leaves us precious little time to work our own plots. If the lord's fields don't need work that day, there's hay to cut and haul from the meadows, and wood from the forest to carry to the lord's manor house. Oh, yes, we is the ones what work on the bridges, the roads and the walls. We is the ones what has to pay the taxes and fees and tolls to the lord, so he can afford to buy the tools he allows us to use.

We can't even leave the manor without the lord's permission. My daddy lived that way and his daddy before him and there aisn't no other way to live."

The man pointed toward a small group of windowless cottages. "That's where we're born and that's where we'll die. Most of our lives, we survive on black bread and ale, limp vegetables, or handouts from the lord. Once a year, on Christmas, he gives a haunch of meat for each family. That's not bad when the family's small, but me and my goodwife, we've raised eight kids. She's my second wife, by the way, the first died in childbirth five years ago. I've only sired two by this'un and another on the way."

I gathered our small group together, outside the man's hearing, and said, "We're men of God. How can we not help this poor man in some way?"

"I agree," Nico said, "but he was proud enough to refuse our offer to help him carry wood. He'd never accept what he saw as charity, and if we gave him something outright, it would crush his spirit even more."

"I say we move on," said Anastasius. "He is one peasant out of thousands in Europa. If we gave him something, every beggar between here and Rome would know of it, and we'd be besieged. Let him be, leave him to his land and his lord. It's his lord's responsibility, not ours."

Anastasius was not stilled by my hostile glare. He continued, "He was born to his fate. That's God's doing, not ours. That we're privileged to be smarter, better educated ..."

"Better connected," Nico intoned, his tone flat.

"Yes, that too," Anastasius said. "But that is his problem, not ours."

At that, I lost my composure. Perhaps it was because of the circumstances under which we'd met Anastasius – or was it perhaps because I sensed, through nothing I could explain, that he could become my rival for Joan's attention? "I daresay *you* certainly had no hesitation in dealing intimately with a certain peasant back in Tunbridge Wells."

"That is not your concern!" he snapped back. "I thought we'd agreed that certain debts were paid. If you're so concerned about how one should treat a peasant, why didn't you do something *for* her instead of *to* me? Why should you be interested in this shabby old wretch?"

I would have struck him with my fist, when Joan intervened. "Easy, fellows," she said. "We've got a long ride ahead of us and nothing to be gained by bickering." I was irked at her placating tone, annoyed that she should sense anything of value in what Anastasius said.

"Martin's right," she continued. "He who saves one human being, it is as if he saves the entire world. There's no harm in helping this poor fellow out, but how?"

"Which is your house, sir?" Nico asked the peasant, smoothly.

"Yonder," said he, pointing to a thatched cottage set back one from the road, but otherwise indistinguishable from the others. "Why d'ye ask?"

"We are monks at the abbey of Tours some days' journey from here. The Reverend Bishop has sent us out to learn about the lives of Christ's lambs, so we might better their lot. Would it be possible for Brothers Joannes and me to visit with you for a short while? Brother Martin will ensure there will be no punishment if we can but speak with your goodwife and yourself for some moments. I would like to see your home. Then, mayhap, you can show me your plot and the lord's best meadows. We've been told to learn about conditions in yonder village, your lord's village I presume?"

"Aye," the man replied, looking warily at Nico, with peasant cunning. "But since there's two of ye and one of me, ye'd not mind if my wife's two brothers be with us?"

"Of course not," said Nico.

As the man shambled toward the cottage, his back still bent under the wood, Nico said, "Martin, ride quickly back to the large village we passed a mile or so ago. Find what provisions you can – warm blankets for winter, seed for wheat if you come upon it, wine, but the good stuff – I'll wager this fellow has never had anything other than sour wine in his life – and a large ham. Anything more you can think of that will make his life a little easier. Make whatever excuses you can – we're on a long journey, we don't know when we'll have time to stop, that sort of thing. Purchase also a pair of long-handled metal hoes and a scythe."

"I understand the rest, but the man said his lord provides him with tools," said I.

"Trust me, do as I say. When you return, proceed straight to his cottage."

"You said he'd never accept charity."

"And he won't. The door will be unlocked. I'll make sure that anyone who's been there, the man, his goodwife, whatever children there are, have come with me to show me the lord's fields."

"I see," I said, grinning. "While they are showing you the lord's fields, the Lord will provide."

"What of you, Anastasius?" Joan asked. "You've no desire to be part of this plot?"

"Indeed not," said the priest huffily. "I'll busy myself finding provender for *us*. Charity begins in one's own home."

"Very well," said I. "I am certainly willing to contribute to our victuals and the lord's gift." "Contribute" was an odd term, since I'd paid for everything but Anastasius' passage thus far. I handed Anastasius more than enough to provision us for the journey to Tours. Nico obligingly lightened Arca's load and off we went.

For the first time in months, I gave Arca free rein. That splendid beast raced through field and meadow with the abandon of a colt. Soon, we arrived at the lord's larger village. Eight children, the man had said, plus his wife and himself. I packed in ten blankets, two smoked hams, a peck of turnips, another of dried beans, a burlap bag filled with winter wheat seeds, two large jugs of good wine, plus another for ourselves, two sturdy long-handled hoes, and a large scythe. Arca was a strong horse, who'd carried me from London to Gull's Landing, and from the Neustrian coast to Rouen without protest, but this load was equal to the weight of two fully grown adults. I walked him back toward the peasant's village.

It was not a long walk, but I felt cold, unseen eyes on me, from back in the hills adjacent to and above the roadway. Arca whickered uncomfortably from time to time, but nothing came of my uncomfortable feeling and soon we were back on the lord's manor. I saw Joan and Nico with a large group of people, surveying a field far above the group of hovels.

A horse loaded with more provisions than a peasant will ordinarily see in five years is something that will gather attention very quickly, but it was my good fortune that this was a workday, and only one or two of the oldest inhabitants of the village — I wondered how old they really were — saw a man and a heavily-laden horse approach the peasant's quarters. It took me half a dozen trips to unload the provender and deposit it in the rude, single-roomed hut.

I let Arca graze in an unfarmed field of grass nearby, while I kept a keen eye on our peasant friend's cottage, lest anyone had seen me and thought to help himself to what lay therein. No one bothered the hut, and when I saw Joan and Nico descending from the hills, I called out, "Hail, Brothers, goodmen!" We must be on our way before sundown."

"Ah, yes, Brother Martin," Nico responded. "I fear we've seen so much to report to the Reverend Holy Father that we took far more time than we thought. Did you attend to that other errand we spoke about?"

"Yes, Brother Nico. Let us rouse Brother Anastasius and be on our way."

Anastasius had spent wisely and provisioned us well. Since money was a scarce commodity in those parts, a little of it went a long way. Anastasius had packed in dark bread, cheese, ale, celery root, beetroot, sausage and ale sufficient for three days' journey. We were civil to one another, but no more than that.

We'd scarcely entered the hills between the village and Bonneval when I felt the same chill at the back of my neck I'd felt on the way back to the peasant's hut. Unseen eyes, *unfriendly* unseen eyes, seemed to pierce the back of my head. It was late afternoon and we still had, by my reckoning, ten Roman miles to traverse before we came to that town. The village we'd left was the same distance behind us.

"Ride close," Nico said, as though reading my thoughts. "You got the hoes? The scythe, Martin?"

"Aye."

"Good. Anastasius, you and Martin each take a hoe." He took them from my saddle pack. "I'll take the scythe."

"So you feel it, too?"

"Aye. Six of them, but ragged and scrofulous. Look up the hill, slowly. Don't give any sign that you see them."

There were indeed six, although only three rode small ponies and the others were on foot. They were positioned well above us, on a trail which gave them a view up and down the highway. They paralleled our ride for the next mile, neither gaining on us nor lagging behind. Almost unconsciously, we made sure Joan was protected in the center of our group.

Just after we'd done that, the three mounted highwaymen accelerated and rode forward, while their cohorts formed a sort of rear guard. "Let me do the talking," Nico whispered. We nodded, frightened because we were outnumbered, but Nico's certainty gave us confidence. The three mounted brigands sat astride their steeds, blocking the highway as we came round a bend.

"Good afternoon, young sirs," the one nearest us called, raising his hat. He was very lean and very dirty, with a poxed face and a greasy beard. "You're new to these parts, are ye not?"

On Nico's instruction, we said nothing, but sat quietly. Neither us, nor the three mounted outlaws moved. The highwaymen seemed to enjoy the superior knowledge that while only three of them faced four of us, they knew, and we did not, that three more of their number were stealthily approaching us from the back.

Nico smiled at the highwaymen. "We mean you no harm. We are brothers in Christ and we give you blessing. Perhaps you might tell us the way to Bonneval."

"Perhaps we might tell you the way to Bonneval," the leader mimicked Nico. "Perhaps you might tell us the way to your possessions, young sir," he said, bowing with mock gentility from the waist.

"I think not," Nico said, his easy smile remaining in place. Joan, Anastasius and I were astonished by his calm in the face of the onslaught. "There are but three of you and four of us."

"Aye," said the leader, with an evil grin. "Mayhap the odds are different."

At that, Arca whuffled. I heard a very slight roll of pebbles behind us.

Still smiling, Nico said, "Ye'll not get to heaven by such vile threats, man. Not unless I help you."

"You help us?" the ringleader guffawed. "How? By your prayers, priest? By the castrated balls of your martyred Saint Damien?"

"Ne, ne," said Nico. "Watch and you shall see the miracle." Nico lifted his eyes heavenward and intoned some kind of Pater Deum I'd not heard before. What happened next astounded all of us. Nico wheeled his horse around, unsheathed his scythe and, faster than anyone could react, rode straight at the three men who'd crept up behind us. As Joan, Anastasius and I, and the mounted brigands watched, Nico hacked and slashed, using his sickle with deadly accuracy. Fountains of blood gushed from the ruptured necks of two of the footmen, who screamed in their death throes. The third had been about to brandish his short sword, but Nico, reacting faster than that villain, pulled sharply back on his steed's rein, causing the horse to rear up, turn in his tracks, and come crashing down on that wretch. We heard the snap of the man's neck followed by another slash from Nico's scythe, and that man breathed no more.

I was the first to recover from the shock. "The hoe, Anastasius!" I shouted as I spurred Arca at the three mounted highwaymen. Using the farm implement as a truncheon, I unseated the leader. Bereft of his horse and whatever weapon he had when he rode up, he was at my mercy, and I showed none. Over and over again, I hacked at his back, his neck, and his head with the hoe, until he neither moved nor breathed. The two remaining outlaws, seeing the trouncing inflicted on their fellows, took off at a dead run in the direction from whence they'd come. Anastasius pursued them for some moments, then turned back to rejoin us.

"I guess I helped them get to heaven, all right," Nico said. "Not in the way they anticipated, I am sure, but effective just the same." We were all trembling.

"I think we might wish to calm ourselves with some of this," I said, handing around the flask of wine I'd purchased earlier that day.

"What do we do with these ... these ...?" said Joan, shuddering as she pointed at the four dead bodies around us.

"From dust we come and to dust return," chanted Nico. "They will be food for the worm and the carrion raptor, which is as much as one could have expected from them."

After a brief draught of wine, we were on our way once again. The remainder of our journey to Tours passed without serious incident.

Chapter 7

The huge, ancient towers of the cathedral more than dominated the city, they ruled the landscape for ten Roman miles on every side.

"God be praised," Joan breathed in awe. "This place has been teaching every subject known to man for more than eighteen generations – four hundred fifty-six years. Why, there are Saints who graduated its *schola*."

"Indeed, it was founded by the sainted Martin himself," Anastasius said.

At that moment, I didn't need a history lesson from someone I viewed as … as what? Inherently evil? But he had risked his life to save Joan. A coward? Because he tried to drug and butcher a helpless girl-child whom he'd impregnated? That wasn't the right word. No, he was an opportunist in every sense of the word. He would do whatever was necessary to propel him to the height of his ambition. But what was that ambition? According to him, he was already well-connected at Rome. No, my distaste for him came from a far deeper source. I somehow sensed that Joan was intrigued by Anastasius, someone I viewed as an immoral rogue disguised in priestly garb. In order to dispel my anger, I rode closer to the great abbey, whose very stones breathed an aura of ancient glory and stolidness. In some places, the stones were covered with moss. They were wet to the touch, slippery, and cold, despite the warmth of the sun. Many of these stones were charred and blackened, survivors of centuries of burning, razing, the abuse of conquerors, then rebuilt by nameless hundreds of laborers. It never ceases to amaze me, even to this day, and mayhap it will always be so, that mankind celebrates "courageous" warriors who commit splendid crimes and is quick to forget those who bear the weaknesses of virtue. As I have learned during my life, no good deed goes unpunished.

Tours was the seat of the Most Reverend, His Excellency Numenior, Bishop of Aquitania. His See was housed immediately adjacent to the cathedral. The abbey itself was situated some four Roman miles away from Tours. It was a much larger version of the one at Rouen and it was built in the Roman style. Its print upon the ground resembled that of a great cross. While Rouen permanently housed somewhat more than forty monks, the abbey at Marmoutier, which had been surrounded, then digested by Tours, was home to three hundred monks and students. And those students were not just limited to men, as I was to learn. Many sisters from the abbey of Saint Amoria three miles distant, attended classes, too. They did not study with the male students, for that would cause unbearable temptation. Rather, they learned to teach small children, to serve as nurses to the sick and mendicants to the poor.

There were cells sufficient for the more than one hundred students that presented themselves to the *schola*, from whence went forward a veritable army dedicated to Christ and to higher learning. How large was the abbey? I cannot say for certain, but I counted the length of one wall at two thousand, seven hundred paces.

When we presented our credentials to the Brother Hosteler, he showed us to our cells. The bed in my tiny room was the usual narrow cot with a straw mattress, but there was a smaller mound of straw encased in burlap that served as a pillow and, at the foot of the bed, a thick, woolen blanket. Each cell had a window with waxed covering that faced onto the inner courtyard and provided light during daylight hours. There were two candles, a small, fat one that sat atop a desk, and a larger one, housed in a stand that came to my shoulders and which, I was to learn, shed a great deal of light after sunset in the small space where I was to sleep and study.

We shared a most generous lunch in the common hall, which consisted of a huge tureen of thick soup containing all manner of vegetables – beans, onions, garlic, and various roots – as well as real chunks of fatty beef. One scooped up the soup with trenchers of rich, fragrant bread, still warm from the oven, and drank from large tankards of ale and new wine laced with honey. Neither the scholars, the teachers, the monks, nor those officials who toiled in the Bishop's see in the town, had taken vows of poverty. The abbey's fields were as rich as those of any lord's estate in the Loire valley. Everyone, from student to monk to visiting priest, was expected to do his fair share of physical labor for the benefit of that vast institution.

Anastasius was to remain at Tours for a fortnight before he departed for Rome. Nicola, Joan, and I were tested to determine at what level we'd be placed in the *schola*. Not surprisingly, Joan was placed in the highest *stratum* of classes. I was assigned to the larger *median* classes. At least I was not relegated to the very lowest, beginning classes where more than forty students attended at a sitting. Nico was designated a proctor and was given upper level seminars in lieu of large classes.

Nevertheless, because of our bond, both of country and of friendship, we studied together and often discussed what we were learning. Joan's disputatious nature was welcomed in her philosophy and rhetoric classes. She read Plato and Aristotle, Vergilius, Horatius, Pythagoras and Ovidius.

"If we are to be the strongest warriors in the army of Christ, we must be armed with the greatest knowledge of every age," she said.

"A saying of Joannes Angliorum?" I asked.

"*Ne*," Nico said, laughing. "An admonition from Pater Euphronius, Philosophy Secundum. I remember that quote from some years ago."

Our daily routine was unflagging. We awoke at dawn, performed our ablutions in silence and, after early prayers and breakfast of porridge and ale, worked in the fields until the sun was midway between the horizon and its zenith. Thence, after a short prayer service, we engaged in classes in *schola* until the noontime meal. When we'd eaten that large meal, we spent a brief time at rest before it was time to return to afternoon classes. These lasted until sundown, when we held a longer evening prayer service, ate a light meal, and retired to our cells to study until, exhausted, we fell into a deep sleep. Occasionally, Joan or I would knock on one another's door to ask or answer a question posed by the other, but from not long after sunset until dawn our time was our own.

We would see Anastasius at the evening meal, but otherwise hardly at all. I have no idea how he spent his days. Occasionally I saw him conversing with Joan or with Nico, but he and I avoided each other. The rift between us had not healed.

I was heartened when it was time for Anastasius to leave. I knew I would feel at greater ease once he had ceased breathing the same air as me. Most urgent to me, he would be gone from Joan's presence. From time to time during that week, she would mention some bit of gossip she'd heard from Anastasius, some story about Saint Martin, the founder of the abbey, which he'd told her, a bit of knowledge about the Eternal City of Rome. I feigned interest, but seethed inwardly.

The evening before Anastasius was to leave, Joan presented him with a small gift at the post-sundown meal and we all spent time reminiscing about the strange twist of fate that had brought us together. Even I was more civil to him than I'd been at any time since he'd boarded West's vessel back at Gull's Landing. After dinner, I retired to my room and started writing notes about the day. It had become my practice, just before I started my evening studies, to write everything I could recall about the events of the day. I detailed such matters as the strangely attractive wood-stench of vinegar made from Balsam sap, the fibrous feel of shredded beef as it mingled with the crunch of cut green beans, the enduring aroma of falling leaves as they wafted over the Loire valley.

I had begun my instruction in astronomy earlier that day, and I wanted to share that knowledge with Joan, since I knew she would not be taking that class until the following January. Her cell was two away from mine. I knocked on her door in the code we'd agreed upon, two short, one long, two short. She did not answer immediately, nor did she answer on my second or third series of knocks. "Joannes?" I called softly, then louder.

When there was still no answer, I shook the door, which, as an abbey rule, was never barred or locked. There was still no response. I opened the door. "Joannes?" I called. The room was empty. Perhaps she'd gone for an evening walk. The area around the abbey was perfectly safe after dark. There was a wide meadow on one side and a small, thin forest on the other. After I'd concluded that she was not in one of the outhouses, I went out into the fields.

The night was warm and balmy. There were a few dim lights in the city of Tours below, and, of course, I could easily see the cathedral. I heard the sounds of the night – shouting, singing, the mooing of cattle as they were led to their stalls. On one of my ventures outside the abbey, I'd discovered a particularly lovely, sheltered area, up the hill from the abbey, hidden from general view. It commanded a fine view of the entire valley and it was a place of great peace. I'd found this knoll a wonderful place from which to view heaven and earth, to contemplate my life, and to simply enjoy the beauty that was the world.

As I came nearer the knoll, I heard a whimpering noise, like an animal in distress, and harsh, labored breathing. The noise rose and fell in a distinct rhythm. I'd heard such whimpering before, but I couldn't place where. I approached the crest of the hill slowly and cautiously to avoid detection. The whimpering became louder and the sound was muffled. There was another sound, that of a larger, deeper-voiced animal, also breathing harshly.

As I came around a rise and into the small clearing which was the knoll, I heard a sudden sharp gasp and a shrill scream, followed almost instantly by a bellow like that of an enraged bull. As I looked at the source of the noise, my heart felt as though it had jumped into my throat and stopped.

Joan was nude. Her breasts were high and silky. Her nipples were hard, taut, pink in the half-moon light. Her legs were splayed, her wondrous body covered with perspiration. She was moaning incomprehensible nothings. Atop her lay a naked, obviously spent Anastasius, moaning in a paroxysm of harmony with her. They were oblivious to anyone and anything in the rapture of their passion. They did not see me and they did not move.

Somehow, I found my way back to my cell, but I did not sleep at all that night, nor the next. I did not attend classes. I ate sparingly, if at all. I took long walks in the evening and cursed God and life. I avoided contact with anyone. It was my first lesson in learning that life can be unbearably painful, and it was a lesson I would not soon forget. When I finally roused myself to go back to class, Anastasius had left for Rome.

~ ∫ ~

As I wrote about what was going on inside of me, the poison seeped out of my soul, slowly at first, then in great measure, and by the time the moon was new once again, memory of what I had witnessed was softening. Not that I didn't awaken each night during that first month with a stabbing pain in my stomach and not so that I slept a night through without cursing her – without cursing them.

It is just that, as is well and truly said, young hearts crack but they do not break. I had just passed my nineteenth birthday, and I was by no means ready to drown myself in the nearby Loire. Within a month and a fortnight, I'd decided that Joan was by no means "the only fish in the river." Not every scholar at the abbey's *schola* was destined to become a cleric, so long as the knowledge gained there would be of use to the Army of Christ. That army was not limited to foot soldiers – monks, priests, and the like, nor was it limited to its high ranking leadership – the bishop at Tours, the cardinals, or even the Pope himself. Like any army that has ever existed in this world, Christ's Army needed provisioners, architects and builders, warriors and librarians, scriveners and emissaries to the heathen and to the emperors.

The Abbott turned a nearsighted, if not blind, eye to the extracurricular activities of those enrolled in the *schola*, provided their studies did not suffer. I was a young man, filled with the sap of young manhood, and it did not take me long to bury my memories of Joan in the arms of more than one willing young woman in Tours. By that, I don't mean only those *noctulucas* who plied their trade at night. There were ample lasses about who were not Sisters-in-Christ, unmarried daughters of the townfolk, who had a wonderfully refreshing attitude toward amorous dalliances, and who knew that scholars at the abbey might be tempted by a good time to become husbands and fathers of great means.

Chapter 8

The schola was set up in several small rooms. We students sat on hard-backed wooden benches, usually five, sometimes as many as eight in a row. Since learning was paramount and hygiene was not, and since the rooms were windowless and light was provided by candles or torches, the odor in these rooms was rank. They emanated not only from my fellow scholars, but from the accumulated stink of more than four centuries. During their initial period, which lasted a year, all first-time students were exposed to reading, writing, mathematics, and Church history. This was designed to give each of us an opportunity to select areas of study in which we became most interested.

Classes were conducted by a *magister* who, for the most part, dictated the lessons. We responded *ad rotum* every few moments. There was neither room nor desk upon which to write down what the teacher had said. We were supposed to do that each evening. We were given small rolls of old parchment or bound *codexes* to take back to our cubicles at night. Not all of the documents contained the same writings. We would return them to class the next day, and each of us would read two or three pages out loud to the entire class. Only the *magister*, of course, knew what we were reading, and if we read our passages correctly or not – unless one or more of us had already read that parchment roll or *codex* before.

It did not take long for us to figure out that we could escape the humiliation of a public reprimand if some of us banded together at night and *each* studied the rolls or booklets we'd been given, together. In this way, we achieved the benefit of a collective intellect and were well able to move the class forward much faster. It took me the better part of ten years to find out that what we had believed was a morally dishonest sin of cheating was precisely what the *magisteria* of the *schola* hoped we would do, for that made their job much easier.

Not every student studied all day, every day. We were expected to teach children and, occasionally, preach homilies and such to the inhabitants of Tours and surrounding towns and villages.

In those days, and even now, good and evil were living companions to people in Aquitania – indeed, to all Christian people in Europe and in Angle-land, and even in far-off Ireland. When someone was said to have the Devil in him, people took it quite literally. Jack Frost was a kinsman to the Devil, nipping noses and fingers, and making the ground too hard to work. There was a legion of little people, elves and trolls and fairies, who were very real to the village folk.

But the Church had its own army of spirits, the saints, who had lived their lives – and often lost their lives – for the glory of Christ's teaching. There was at least one, usually many more than one, saint for each day of the year, and we students were expected to teach the common folk about a saint, or a number of saints, on that saint's – or those saints' – special day.

Kings and emperors were depicted as symbolic and idealized figures on their coins. But when it came to saints, these were real people, albeit sometimes a bit strange. I recall with amusement teaching about two saints in particular. The first, and most curious, was Saint Simeon Stylites, who lived four hundred years ago. That odd fellow spent much of his life living naked on top of increasingly high pillars, and I was told by authorities, who said this with utter seriousness, that when he let loose his *skeit* from atop these pillars, merchants in the area gathered this holy manure and sold these droppings to pilgrims.

Then there was Saint Mary of Egypt, the patron saint of fallen women. Mary left her home at the age of twelve and went to live in Alexandria, where she became a prostitute for seventeen years. She was curious to make a pilgrimage to Jerusalem, and paid for her passage by offering herself to the sailors. But when she arrived at the holy city with her fellow pilgrims, she felt herself held back from entering the church by an invisible force. When she lifted her eyes to an image of the Virgin Mary, she heard a voice telling her to cross the River Jordan, where she would find rest. Mary of Egypt supposedly bought three loaves of bread and spent the rest of her life living in the desert on dates and berries. When her clothes wore out, her hair grew long enough to cover her modesty, and she dedicated the remainder of her days to prayer and contemplation. We students often joked irreverently that the *real* reason for her "redemption" may well have been that she'd been used so often that she could no longer make a living plying her trade.

Saints Simeon and Mary of Egypt were colorful, but their stories were actually quite typical of what we taught, for the common folk were eager to hear about these persons – eager because these saints lived lives that were so much larger than their own. After we had told our flock these often wondrous tales, we prayed to that day's holy figures. Prayer was a way of asking a saint to pay attention to the parishioners' own particular worries. Singing was a beautiful way of saying, "Please listen." There was no question but that God intervened actively in daily life. Thus, one function of worship was for the common folk to secure divine intervention in their own behalves. And, of course, that is still the way the Church operates today – or at least it was when I was cast down into my present station.

~ ∫ ~

I have here a confession to make. It was not a particularly egregious sin, and at this time in my life, it is of no moment, but I make it anyway. The means by which we came to Tours was fueled by the Abbot's desire to have the Bishop sanction certain writings that had been produced at Rouen. Neither Nicola, nor Joan, nor the accursed Anastasius, seemed to have remembered that sealed pouch I was supposed to have presented to the Bishop on our arrival. I secreted it in my cell, and, in January, I did the unthinkable. I slit the pouch at the bottom, where it was not sealed, and extracted a few sheets of the precious parchment.

Each student was expected to wear one of two *schola* tunics issued to him for the duration of his stay at Tours. Tunics wore out and each of us was expected to know how to mend his clothing. We were permitted to borrow needles and binding thread from the *commissarius* to accomplish this. It did not take me long to learn that some of the binding threads used on our clothes were of the same kind and size as those used to bind the individual sheets in parchment rolls or codexes. I had also noticed that individual sheets which made up the rolls or codexes were not of uniform color or quality.

I selected one single sheet of parchment from the Rouen codex, slit the binding threads on each side of that page, removed the page from the codex, then painstakingly reattached the two adjacent pages together. So careful was my surgery that not even I could make out that a page had been removed unless I had been an *investigator scrupulorum*. I hid the purloined sheet of parchment along with the unbound sheet from the Rouen codex among my clothing.

One of the earliest lessons I had learned was that in the abbey gifts were exchanged for gifts. The *commissarius* was the abbey's purveyor of its finest quills, inkwells and ink, as well as the sparkling colors with which Tours' finest writings were illuminated and even spare pieces of parchment. He was also a man who each night imbibed heavily of every sort of alcoholic beverage available. In short order I convinced the *commissarius* that a substantial amount of quills, inkwells, ink and colorants, and a single page of used parchment, about the same size, color, and texture as the one from the Rouen codex, which I'd secreted, were a wonderful trade for an entire month's supply of the finest Aquitanian wines.

By means of a *strygil*, I carefully rubbed off everything that had been on parchment given to me by the *commissarius*, until that sheet was *tabula rasa*. I then sliced the tell-tale part of the parchment containing the binding holes. Now, the most difficult part of my deceit was to begin.

During February and March, I set aside time each evening for my task. If the deception were to work, the workmanship must be perfect. Letter by laborious letter, I copied the single page from the Rouen codex. I make haste to say that I was not forging a document. Rather, I was copying it in my own best hand. It was a matter of some pride that each scrivener at Rouen had set his initials at the bottom of each page he had written. When I finally came to the end of my page of writing, I carefully inscribed my own initials, MP. I looked at the two pages purporting to be parts of the Rouen codex, one real, one counterfeit. If pride truly be a sin, I suffered that sin, for I felt my work was better than the original. I dusted my work with colorant and let it dry for three days. At the end of that time, I placed my writing in order among the other sheets of the Rouen codex, slipped the entire manuscript back into its pouch, and sewed up the bottom.

Shortly afterward, I begged an audience with no less an Excellency than the Bishop himself. I told his secretary that I bore an important codex from the Abbot of Rouen. After a fortnight, I was granted an audience at midmorning at the See, and was ushered into the Bishop's chambers.

Bishop Numenior"s chambers were more luxurious than any I'd ever seen. The hardwood floors were graced by tightly woven carpets, said to come from the looms of Constantinople. The walls were adorned with glorious paintings, and the Bishop's monumental desk was of incised oak. The Bishop himself was taller than I by half a head, and had a ruddy complexion. He was clearly a man who had lived well, and his ample girth displayed someone who had not missed many meals. Even from our first meeting, he surprised and amazed me.

"Martin Paschal – our Angle-ish brother. Greetings, young Sir and welcome. It took you long enough to get here."

"W—what do you mean, Your Excellency?" I stuttered.

"According to my informants, you left the abbey at Rouen last October. I've made the journey from Saint Valery, where you landed, to Tours myself, and were you to have walked the entire distance, it would not have taken you five months to get here."

"I was … I was so filled with awe at becoming a scholar — " I mumbled. My face felt like it was on fire and I stared determinedly at the floor.

"Nonsense," the great man said. As I glanced up, I saw a merry twinkle in his eye. "Your teachers report you have an astounding recall, that your language skills are exemplary, and that you write with the finest hand they have seen in years. It seems that you and the young men you came with, Nicolas, whom I knew from before, and especially the young Joannes Angliorum have dominated this year's entering class. I would hardly call that 'filled with awe.'"

"True," I said, "but even Your Excellency must know how difficult is the first year of *schola*."

"But not that difficult that you haven't tasted the sweet, earthly delights of the city below the abbey," he said. I blushed yet deeper. "Never you mind, Martin. I was young once, myself. What is your business here?"

"I … I have a manuscript from Father Abbot at Rouen. He asked that Your Excellency grant an imprimatur and sanction."

"Ah, yes, Ronolf would want the approval of the Bishop – and not necessarily the approval of *this* Bishop – reactionary conservative that he is. Never had an original thought in his head. How is that old man, anyway?"

"As of last October, I was told he was failing."

"That old scoundrel has been failing or plagued by the gout for the last thirty years. Ronolf was born a stingy old man.

I'll wager he gave you a scrawny old beast and some sour wine and sent you on your way thinking he'd brought the entire abbey to ruin."

As we talked on and on, far longer than the few minutes' time I'd been allotted, I found I genuinely liked this man. He was a Bishop, yet he seemed so ordinary, so human. I found myself thinking, "If I could but labor in the service of such a man, I would be happy." Too soon, Bishop Numenior dismissed me, wishing me well in my studies, saying, earnestly I believed, that he hoped we would meet again soon.

~ ∫ ~

"Soon" was less than a fortnight later, when I was asked to stay back after writing class adjourned. "Martin, the Bishop commands an audience with you, within the hour."

The Bishop was sitting at his desk when I was escorted into his sanctum. To his right, there was a stack of parchment sheets. I had a suspicion what they were. I made the sign of the cross, knelt, and awaited word from Numenior. The Bishop dismissed the escort. "Sit down, sit down, Martin Paschal," Bishop Numenior said. "You've seen these parchment sheets before?"

I didn't know what to say. If they were the Rouen Codex and I said I hadn't seen them, I'd be lying. I knew from my earlier conversation with Numenior how perceptive he was.

"Are they the pages of the Rouen Codex?" I asked.

"They are. I thought the Abbot Ronolf had told you they were a manuscript. How would you surmise they were a codex unless you had read them?"

"Does that not answer your question, Excellency?"

"Well spoken, Martin, answering my question with the one question that would answer the question. Would you like some wine? Don't look so shocked, young Martin. There is nothing sinful in that which the Lord hath brought forth." At that, he brought forth two cups and a flagon of sweet wine from a counter behind his desk. He filled the cups, passed one to me and took a long draught from his own.

"So you disobeyed old Ronolf and read the *Codex*. I cannot determine how you were able to replace the seal so perfectly. Even my *scrupulores* could not find a break in it."

"I didn't break the seal, Excellency. I slit the bottom of the pouch, then resewed it."

"I see. Did you find the work 'illuminating?'"

"May I be truthful, Your Grace?"

"By all means."

"I found it almost incomprehensibly dull."

"Including the page you copied and slipped in as if it were an original?"

Both of us were silent for what seemed the longest moment of my life. The greatest deception I'd ever planned, one to which I had devoted as much care as any King planning an entire campaign, and it had come unraveled in less than two weeks.

"I will leave the abbey in disgrace tomorrow, Your Excellency," I finally managed. "But may I be permitted to ask one final question before I go?"

"You may, but I think I know what it is, and I can answer it for you before you ask." He extracted the page I had written from among the stack of parchment sheets. I could tell from the "MP" in the lower left hand corner, which I'd so foolishly cast on the parchment, that it was my writing.

"This page is very slightly smaller than the others. The parchment on which it has been written is older, as anyone can see from the yellowish margins on the unwritten side. The lighter color on the written side convinced my *scrupulores* that this page had been freshly cleaned and prepared. But even that would not have been enough to convince me of the deception."

"What then, Your Excellency?"

"It is the handwriting itself." He extracted two other sheets from the *Codex* and shoved the three pages at me. "Can you not tell the difference?"

I examined all three sheets. Mine was somehow different, but I still could not understand what he meant. I shrugged, speechless.

"Look carefully, Martin. Do you want to look at more sheets?" He shoved the entire manuscript to my side of the desk. "Let me tell you, then. These sheets – the manuscript that Ronolf sent to me. Pedantic, dull, dry, brittle as bones. Dutifully and obviously written by scriveners who were being dutiful. Now look at the page done in your hand. Clear, bright, *alive*. Can you not see that, Martin? Are you truly that dense?"

I hardly dared look at the Bishop, for my shame weighed heavy upon me, but ultimately I had to look at him. Not only were his eyes smiling, but his entire face as well. "It would have taken an ignoramus not to have noticed the difference in the writing, Martin. While I have been accused of being many things, an ignoramus is not one of them. Now, I will make you a proposition, and I ask that you consider it carefully.

"I sense in you an intelligence, but, more than that, a boldness of thought and deed, which I find might be useful to me. You may leave the abbey in disgrace this very day, or you can agree to serve as a very junior member of something I call my "Council of Friends," with payment of a slight stipend, by the way, starting tomorrow morning. You might wonder why a Bishop would associate with a young student. The answer is very simple. I have always learned that to keep abreast of current developments, new thoughts, and new insights, it pays to have at least one or two younger men in my inner council. The young and the not-so-young profit equally from their association with each other.

"Your lessons at the abbey will continue but will be at, shall we say, a much *higher* level. You will learn anything you want to learn – the history of the world, languages, an even better hand, and, most important, the art of diplomacy. You will work harder than you have ever worked in your life, and there will be times when you curse the day you ever crossed my path, but in the end you will be a better man for it."

I could not believe what I was hearing. "How … how much time do I have to decide, Excellency?"

"I expect your answer before you leave this room."

CHAPTER 9

There were five of us in Numenior"s "Council of Friends." Filomen, who, at seventy-nine, had served the bishop before Numenior and the bishop before *him*, was a man tremendously wise in years and experience, but often forgetful in his dotage. Numenior told me he kept the old man on because, given his high station and seniority, there was simply no place else to send him. I did not mind listening to Filomen's tales, for I learned more about the history of the Bishopric and of the abbey at Tours than most historians might have forgotten.

Filomen, despite his subordinate position to our Bishop, never referred to our leader as "His Excellency," or "His Grace," or even "the bishop." It was always "Numenior," more often "young Numenior."

Magister Hudsonius, the head of the *schola*, was a huge man of fifty-five, who added a wonderful balance to the council. He was old enough to have the wisdom of years of experience, yet he was constantly exposed to the new ideas gleaned in conversations with the brightest youths to pass through the *schola*. It was his philosophy that the finest teachers are not those who demand *ad rotum* learning by repetition, but rather those who create that rarified aura – an *atmos-sphere* to use the ancient Greek – in which one wants to learn.

Gurgis, older than Hudsonius, but younger than Filomen, was Numenior"s treasurer. He was a bitter, stingy man, the only one on the Council to whom I took a dislike. I suppose he did not particularly care for me because of my youth and my obvious, often vocal, support for any argument opposed to his own. Gurgis was testy about every *nummus* that went out of the abbey's treasury. He proposed, among other things, that the abbey pay for itself by admitting to its *schola* only those sons whose fathers were willing to endow the abbey with substantial assets – land, gold, coin of the realm, or property in kind. Although I was abashed and dismayed at what seemed to be the very opposite of what the founder of the abbey, Saint Martin, stood for, I held my tongue.

Not so the youngest, brashest of Bishop Numenior"s counselors, John Scotus Erigena – John the Irishman, who, I was to learn, had been born in Paris. John was one year my junior. I met him at the first meeting I attended. I was as attracted to Scotus as I was repelled by Gurgis. We councillors sat around a large, oak table at these meetings, so that no one claimed to be at its head, nor was anyone's position viewed as superior to that of anyone else. Bishop Numenior sat at a different table, slightly removed, elevated above us.

Gurgis had just tried to make what I felt was a rather coldhearted point about placing gates at each of the four entries to the abbey and charging a *nummus* or half-penny for the privilege of attending Mass at the abbey on Sundays.

John Scotus placed his hairless chin in a cup formed by his thumb and forefinger and scratched gently with the forefinger. "I suppose, Your Excellency," he said mildly, "that Saint Peter might want to place such a toll gate at the entrance to heaven, in order to keep out those who had proved to be such poor money managers that they could not afford to enter."

Gurgis bridled at the temerity of this young upstart, but continued to argue his point. I watched with glee as Erigena adroitly demolished each of Gurgis' arguments. Bishop Numenior hid his chuckle behind a cough, but when I looked over at him, he rolled his eyes. I was later to learn that Gurgis had been foisted on the bishop by Rome, but there was nothing he could do about it, the politics of Holy Mother Church being what they were.

Ultimately, Gurgis, in utter frustration, hurled at Erigena, "What separates a fool from an Irishman?" — a direct play on John Scotus's name. There was a shocked intake of breath among all of us at the viciousness of this personal insult.

Without batting an eye, John Scotus smiled and blandly responded, "This table."

Even the Bishop choked, so hard was he laughing. Gurgis' face turned white with rage. Without another word, he rose and stomped out of the room. It was decided to delay indefinitely a decision on his proposal.

~ ∫ ~

As Bishop of Tours, which meant Bishop of the entire northern half of Aquitania, Numenior was responsible to officers in the Army of Christ, both up and down. There were priests, Monsignors, lesser Bishops and greater Bishops. Nicocepherus, the Cardinal of Aquitania and Neustria, was a frequent guest at Tours, just as Numenior periodically traveled to Rome, to the Western March, which was only now starting to be called Spain, and elsewhere within Christ's realm.

Nor was Numenior's circle of influence limited to the Church. He often engaged in audiences with Louis Pius,

Charlemagne's tall, handsome, aging son, who had been Holy Roman emperor since his father's death fifteen years before. On one occasion, Bishop Numenior commanded John Scotus Erigena and me to accompany him.

This was a time of great trembling upon the land. Louis was a decent, gentle, and gracious man, who was unfortunately too lenient and forgiving for his own good. Early in his reign, he had divided his empire into three kingdoms, each ruled by one of his sons, Pepin, Lothar and Ludwig. On the death of his wife, Louis had married again. I first met the emperor at the Imperial Residence in Aix la Chapelle, on the frontier between Neustria and Austrasia, in May 829. Louis' throne room was grandiloquent in size, but plainer than Numenior"s offices.

Our bishop was ushered into the throne room by six pages. John Scotus and I followed in his wake. A number of lesser nobles followed us. All but our coterie of three bowed humbly before the emperor. Numenior nodded his head respectfully, but not deferentially. We did the same. I looked up to see a striking, olive-complexioned young woman, nearly as tall as the emperor.

"The Empress Judith," Erigena whispered to me. "The little fellow sitting on her lap is the cause of all of the emperor's problems."

The "little fellow" to whom Erigena referred was a tot whom I took to be about three years old. On seeing Erigena, whom he must have known from before, he issued a most un-royal whoop and bounded from his mother's lap into John Scotus' arms. "Thcotuth, Thcotuth, Thcotuth!" he repeated happily.

"Hey, Charliebald, you little troublemaker!" John said, making no attempt to hide his affection for the child.

"Twubble makuh?"

"Never mind, puppy! How's your beautiful mommy?"

"Mommy!" chirped the child, and toddled back to the Empress" side.

I have said before that John Scotus Erigena was brash and bold. Even then, he assumed he was no one's inferior, not even the emperor's. Neither the emperor nor his empress seemed perturbed by this outburst. Louis' eyes followed the child with adoration. Anyone who gave the son of his old age pleasure was a person to be treasured.

Some time later, Numenior, John Scotus and I were ushered into the emperor's private chambers. There were only two other persons, guards, present.

"The war?" Numenior began, without preamble.

"It is sad," Louis said. I noticed his right arm shook with a palsy. "Can you imagine, Excellency, three sons rebelling against their father?

"It is sad indeed, Your Imperial Majesty," Numenior rejoined. "Charles is not their full brother. They say you've displaced them and gone back on your word."

"You've spoken with them, then?" the emperor asked.

"Through their intermediaries."

"Lothar's still the most adamant?"

"He feels the most threatened. Pepin and Ludwig feel more secure on their thrones."

"It's been three years. I cannot abandon Charles. He's as much the son of my loins as they are. I made a promise to Judith when he was conceived."

"True Your Majesty, but twelve years ago you made what they felt was a fair division. They feel your annulment of that division betrayed them."

The emperor sighed heavily, walked over to a corner of the chambers and rested his hand on a large, beautifully illustrated map. "My father fought so hard to unite his dominions as a single empire. Is it all to fall apart in one generation?"

"If you don't mind my asking Majesty, why did you divide the empire so early in your reign?"

"Administrative reasons, Numenior. Father held it together by constant campaigns and by the force of his personal magnetism, something with which I was never endowed. I believed if I had three trusted lieutenants ruling on my behalf – and who could a father trust more than his own sons? – they would somehow consolidate what my father had won. Ah, well, you've done what you could. How does the clergy view the rebellion?"

"Honestly, Sire, I would say two out of every three favor your rebellious sons. They feel it politically expedient because they live in your sons" domains."

"So the news is all bad, then?"

"*Ne*, Majesty. In their hearts they'd all like to see a truce. John Scotus, what say you?" the bishop said, turning to Erigena.

"While the loyalist or rebellious lords play games using live soldiers to fight for one side or the other, the great mass of your subjects could not care less who prevails, for it only augurs poorly in their own lives. Soldiers trampling here and there over the manor means less food for the serfs, harder work to produce more, and the death of their sons who are sent off to the wars. Majesty, your worry need not be with the vicars in the army of Christ, which is nothing but a shadow army, even though it has great influence. You would do better to consolidate your influence with the common man."

"Out of the mouths of the young often come great truths," the emperor said. "My Charlie adores you, Erigena. Would you consider staying at court to help shape the little fellow?"

"So, husband," Judith said, walking over to Louis, putting her arm about his waist and most unregally, sensually pressing her bosom into his arm, "we battle to the end – and beyond that, for whoever 'wins' this paltry war, the other side will be lying in wait for the next series of battles. What difference does it make? My Charles will survive them all, so everyone will have wasted countless lives and scraped the bottom of four treasuries without accomplishing anything." She did not so much sound bitter, as determined.

"Still, it would be nice to have some peace, darling," Louis said.

"Well, Your Imperial Majesty, talking about peace won't bring it. Let us live for the fine times we can enjoy while we're alive," said Bishop Numenior. "No one can take back yesterday by feeling badly about it, and who knows if we will even be alive tomorrow? So let us enjoy every day as if it were our last. I've brought several flagons of the finest aged Aquitanian sweet wine. I hope your Imperial Majesties have laid in viands worthy of a high ranking cleric like me."

We remained at Louis' court three days and three nights, and we were well and convivially fed, wined, and entertained.

~ ∫ ~

"Your Excellency, how did your council of friends originate?" I asked.

"When I became bishop, fifteen years ago, I determined I would not lose touch with the real world. As bishop, I have all the advice and counsel one needs from officials, those of the Church and those of the lords. I wanted something more honest, more private, a balance of young and old, established ideas and heresies, men who were not so overwhelmed by my bishop's miter that they would tell me what I wanted to hear and cloak the truth. Filomen and Gurgis are approaching the end of their ecclesiastical careers, so they don't care what they say. Hudsonius is at the peak of his somewhat less-than-illustrious career. He knows he's not going higher in the Church, he has reached his level of comfort and security, and he knows he will be around for as long as I. As for each of you, well, you will be what you will be, and that's something over which I have no control. Only, perhaps, some slight influence. Your gift to me is that spirit which enables me to maintain my touch with the future. Mind, I am your Bishop and confidant, not your jailer. Thus, you need be a member of my Council only so long as you desire."

We rode awhile in amicable silence. The bishop continued. "Filomen is harmless, but remarkably wise, even in his dotterel. Although he repeats himself interminably, you'd do well to listen to what he has to tell. Say what you will about mean-spirited Gurgis, he is scrupulously honest and diligent. Under his stewardship Tours is one of the wealthiest Bishoprics in Western Christendom. Besides, how would you expect me to understand the reactionary element in our Bishopric unless I had some hint of what motivates them? Gurgis is emblematic of the lot."

At that, Erigena smiled. It was the lusty month of May, late in spring. All about us, flowers had blossomed in profusion. As Austrasia gave way to Neustria, and Neustria, in turn, gave way to the soft hills of Aquitania, we experienced the abundant, fresh growth of nature. The valleys were redolent with the sweet, heavy fragrance of roses, carnations and jasmine. In the villages, we heard the sound of laughter, particularly after dark, even more particularly among the young. The sap had risen, not only in the trees and flowers. I wondered whether

Gurgis, that cold, stiff old man had ever given his emotions to the warmth of May sunshine or shared the hidden delights of a first love. Had he ever been with a woman? Or was he born an old, barren soul? At that moment, I truly felt pity for Gurgis, hidebound as he was in his fundamentalist views and his devotion to coins, numbers and old, worn traditions.

~ ∫ ~

"Your Excellency, Your Excellency!" Hudsonius had actually ridden out to meet us some ten miles from the abbey. Now the magister magistorum was not a man given to excitement, nor, since he must have weighed nearly twice as much as the Bishop, was he a man given to much of anything that resembled physical exertion. But here he was on a warm day, sweating as profusely as an animal, very red of countenance, almost in tears. "You must come immediately. There's been a dreadful crime. A murder most foul. It's … it's Gurgis. And the treasury has been looted!"

CHAPTER 10

"When was this discovered?"

"Last evening, half to midnight, Excellency."

"How much is missing."

"One thousand gold *solidi*, Excellency."

"Hmmm. Six months' worth of donations. Very well, there's not much to be done on the road. Let us proceed to the abbey and find out what we can."

When we arrived at Tours, nothing seemed out of the ordinary. The *schola* was in its regular session. There seemed to be no uproar. On Numenior's direction, Hudsonius, Erigena and I met in his chambers. We agreed not to disturb old Filomen.

"Where is the body?" the Bishop asked Hudsonius.

"I dragged it into a nearby closet in the counting house, close to where I'd found it. I did not think it would decompose before you arrived."

"Has anyone else seen the body?"

"No, Your Excellency."

"Murder, you say?"

"I can think of no other answer. Else why would the treasury door be open and funds missing?"

"Let us look."

One by one, we slipped unnoticed into the counting house. Since Gurgis had not been known for his congeniality, it was not a place of common assemblage, so there were few monks in the vicinity when we gathered there. Hudsonius opened the closet. Gurgis' body was rigid. There was an odor of burned nuts about him. Erigena and I carried what had been Gurgis to a better lit area while Hudsonius barred the door.

We cut away his robes to inspect his body. Unclothed, Gurgis looked smaller, spindlier than in life. There were no signs of a struggle, save for a single bruised lump of no great size high on his forehead. "That bump would hardly have killed him. There's no sign of blood," I said.

"That old stick probably had no blood," Erigena mumbled in an undertone. He was silenced by Bishop Numenior's glare.

"None of us is in a position to speculate," Hudsonius said. "But there are two investigators, teachers in the *schola*, with great expertise in the science of the human body. While they are not as knowledgeable, perhaps, as *detectores*, I understand they have had some experience in criminal matters. Perhaps I should call upon them?"

"Certainly, once they're consulted, Gurgis' death will no longer be secret," I said. "But sooner or later the news will be found out in any event. I say we ask them in."

"I agree," said Erigena.

"Then it is unanimous," the Bishop announced. So it was that I met Brothers Willibald and Bernd, the first from London, the other from the mountainous land of Helvetia. Through these *professores biologias*, we learned much about the body.

"There is no question that a single, sharp blow to the head could cause death," said Willibald. "But I have performed autopsies in the past and I do not detect that here. The bump on this man's forehead would have rendered him momentarily unconscious, but would not have killed him. Brother Martin, you said earlier that you had smelt something unusual when you picked the body up?"

"Burnt almonds," I replied.

At that, Bernd opened the corpse's mouth and sniffed its odors. His fingers rummaged around in Gurgis' mouth, until he found a few remaining drops of the old treasurer's spittle. He rolled that moisture between thumb and forefinger, then wafted it under his nostrils. Looking at Willibald, he said, "Poison."

"I suspected as much," Willibald said. "Bar the doors to this counting house, Your Excellency. Let us spend some time searching for clues to this man's death. This man may have been killed, but it was by poison, not by force."

It was Erigena who found the note an hour later, buried between the leaves of one of Gurgis' old books of account, on an upper shelf of his counting room. The note contained a stark confession, "I can no longer live with my sin. My reputation is gone and so am I."

"A suicide?" Hudsonius remarked.

"A rather suspicious suicide," Brother Bernd responded.

"Why do you say that?" asked Bishop Numenior. "What could be clearer than a handwritten note?"

"In every case of suicide where I have been called upon to assist, we found a writing very near to the suicide himself. The suicide is driven by a desire to explain *why*. Here, I have heard nothing of any great crime or, for that matter, any great sin committed by this man that would destroy his reputation. I believe you said that money was missing from the treasury?"

"Aye," remarked Hudsonius.

"How much?"

"A thousand gold *solidi*."

"When was it discovered?" asked Brother Willibald.

"When I found the body," said Hudsonius.

"How did you discover the funds to be missing?"

"The outer vault where we keep the current treasure was open and it was empty. I recall Gurgis reporting to Bishop Numenior the day before His Excellency left for Aix la Chapelle that we kept one thousand gold *solidi* in the outer vault at all times."

"Could anyone have overheard that conversation?" Willibald asked.

"Hardly. It was spoken in His Excellency's private chambers."

"So …" Bishop Numenior fingered the beard beneath his chin. "We have the strange, sudden disappearance of a large sum of money, a bump on a man's head designed to make us feel he was killed by the blow, the discovery of poison, and a note that tends to incriminate him."

"Not necessarily Gurgis, Your Excellency," said Erigena. "Does the note bear his name?"

"No," said Brother Bernd, "but that's not unusual. Many notes are not signed. One simply assumes they were written by the suicide."

"Your Excellency," I said. "Do you have anything in Gurgis' proven hand?"

"I have one or two writings. Not many, for Gurgis was no more loquacious in his writing than he was in his speech. I shall fetch them and return shortly."

Not long after, the Bishop returned with two single pages of papyrus. "At one time, this was much less costly than parchment," Numenior said. "Now, since we no longer enjoy trade with Egypt, it has become very dear. These were part of an accounting report he wrote to the Bishop at Avignon, for transmittal to Rome twenty years ago. Even then, Gurgis had a reputation for punctiliousness."

I compared the sheets he had brought with Gurgis' alleged suicide note. Although the handwriting looked similar, after half an hour, even allowing for the twenty year hiatus, I concluded they had not been written in the same hand. When I pointed out the most obvious differences to my audience, they seemed convinced as well that something was odd about this situation.

An enormous series of questions now confronted us. If we truly had a murder on our hands, was it from within the abbey? If so, why? Were we of the Bishop's inner council safe? For that matter, was the Bishop safe? What of the missing money? Exchange was not easy to come by in those days, and a thousand gold *solidi* meant six months of collections not merely from the abbey, but from the entire Bishopric, and that included contributions from the lords of several manors. Gone without a trace. A vault that did not look as though it had been forced or pried open. It was a problem of alarming proportions. I could tell from his demeanor that the Bishop himself was most concerned.

~ ∫ ~

Early that evening, after supper, I wanted time alone to ponder the problem. The well-traversed road from the abbey to the city was a public thoroughfare, used by large numbers of the local populace, pilgrims, penitents and clergy each day, but this evening the road seemed mine alone. Or so I thought, until I surmised a presence behind me and to my right. As I walked faster, the presence increased its pace. As I slowed, it slowed, like a shadow. But it was not a shadow.

"Are we never to be friends?" she asked.

"I think not."

"You found out." It was a statement, not a question. I refused to answer. I walked resolutely on. She remained my shadow, neither speeding up nor slowing.

"How could you *dare*?" I finally said. My voice was venomous. "And with that ... that *skeit* Anastasius."

"Would you have been so sanctimonious had it been you?" she shot back.

I did not want to speak with her, wanted nothing to do with her, wanted at that moment to kill her, wanted to slowly cut out her nether parts with a rusty knife. Perversely, I wanted to embrace her, cry until my heart had torn itself from inside me, have her cry, kiss her tear-stained face 'til the hurting stopped and we were whole again. I had buried Joan so deep in my past. I had tried to purge the memory of her completely from my heart. I was high in the Council of the Bishop and she was still a lowly student plodding her way through the *schola*. I had shown her, that betraying, conniving, heartless, soulless wanton.

With only a few words, she slashed my heart and nullified everything I'd been and done in the past ten months.

"Whatever else you might think of me, I was with you in the hardest times —"

"I don't want to hear it. Leave me be, for God's sake."

"What do you think I felt when I knew you were with Hilda?"

"I said leave me be. You are not my friend."

"You loved me once."

Four more words. Four more heart slashes.

I walked on, a lump bigger than that on Gurgis' head in my throat, saying nothing, lest I choke on the words. *Think of something. Think of anything. Gurgis' murder.* The silence mounted.

Finally, I broke it. "You knew what he was, you saw what he did. You damned him with your own mouth."

"And you knew me only as a boy, as a man. You were unattainable, untouchable. You were a man and I was a child. I had needs, too."

"So you chose the worst possible slime and you allowed him to impale you on his pole like a bitch in heat." I was blazing with anger, with righteous indignation, with the most desperate pain I'd ever felt in my life, more than even when I had seen her with him.

I turned off the road and into a copse, less than half a mile from town, and sat on a large rock outcropping. She approached me, planted herself directly in front of me, where I'd have to face her. I turned aside, my face in my hands.

"Look at me, Martin. Are you trying to pretend we've been nothing to one another? I dare you to tell me that."

What seemed like an eternity went by. When I looked up, it was hard to see clearly, so copious were my tears. "I d..." I barely whispered.

"What?" she asked.

"I ... I ... Why, Joan? Why?" It was the first time I'd even spoken her name in months.

"Because I did have needs," she said, softly. "Because I'd never been with a man. Because it was no longer enough to ... do it to myself. Because no one perceived me as a woman. Because of his supposed connections which might help me later in life. Because, because, because ... does it really matter why?"

"Was it … was it the only time?"

"No." She looked at me calmly, levelly.

"When?" My voice was a raspy, choked whisper.

"It started a week before we arrived at the Abbey."

"How? I was there, Nicola was there every night."

"There are always ways, there are always times. Do we really have to talk about it? How important can it be? We are here and this is now." She was now very much the Joan I had known before, rational, collected, matter of fact, the Joannes persona. The little girl who'd stood calmly by when my horse had almost come down on her head. Was she acting this way for my benefit? Who was she? What was she?

I started to say, "It's different, I'm a man," but that would have led the conversation nowhere except to continued anger. So I said nothing.

"I'm not asking you to love me, nor even to like me, Martin," she said, more gently. "I'm not asking your forgiveness. What I did is what I did and I cannot take that back. I need not apologize to you or to anyone else for who I am and what I am. I would have liked to be your friend. That was all I came to ask. And you've given me your answer."

She turned, her head held high, her shoulders squared, and, with not a backward glance, walked up the road, toward the Abbey.

If you let her go, if you abandon what she is to you, you will damn yourself 'til the day you die.

Don't counsel me. She is faithless, an opportunist who will do whatever she needs to do to make the best of any situation.

Do you truly believe that? She's a fifteen-year-old-child.

Who fornicated with a man much older. Who debauched herself, who… who fucked herself into oblivion for her own pleasure.

Who was with you when this all began.

Who risked everything to betray her own relatives for your benefit.

Whom you love from the very depths of your soul.

Whom you love from the very depths of your soul. Whatever she is, whatever she will be, whom you love from the very depths of your soul. Lose her now, lose her forever, lose your life, lose your own soul.

"Joan ... wait ... please."

She was several yards ahead of me. She marched resolutely on.

"Joan ..."

She stopped, turned ever so slowly. She smiled – an enigmatic smile.

"Joan ... I felt so betrayed."

"Why?" she asked. "Did I ever mislead you? What did I ever do that you yourself haven't done with a woman? Or do you think I didn't know about the young serving wench Hilda, or a handful of women in Tours city?"

"But that's different."

Now it was Joan's turn to be angry. "How is that different?"

We were some distance from the abbey and the dim lights from the town beyond the abbey softened the countryside. We continued walking up a small hill, each of us now consumed in suspended, uncomfortable anger.

I was momentarily speechless, amazed. *As wise as Joan was, how could she not innately know how different a man was from a woman?*

"Well?" she continued hotly. "Explain to me how a man is different from a woman? Is one better, smarter, more understanding than the other? Must a woman always be subordinate to a man? Suppose it had been Nicola and you'd come upon him rutting with another woman who meant nothing to you?"

"But you — ?"

"I what? Do you honestly feel you have the right to consider yourself morally – sexually – superior to me? Or must I remind you that, to everyone in the world except you, Nicola, and Anastasius, who learned quite by accident that I was female, I am a man?"

My anger of the last months withered under her devastating anger. Yet, who was she to be angry with me? Had I betrayed her? Of course not! Hilda had been a long time ago. But other women had not.

During the next hour or more, sometimes shouting, and then, when the hot flames of our anger had consumed themselves and become ashes, with deeper understanding, I started to realize that every human being suffers from the same disease – that of humanity, with all its strengths and weaknesses, failures and faults, and yet, if we come to our highest selves, perhaps we each possess a spark of the divine.

And when we walked back down the hill and returned to the abbey, I also realized that Joan and I would be the closest of lifelong friends, since we need never have a secret from one another again.

Chapter 11

The investigation into Gurgis' death consumed the next sixty days. There were few times during that period when Bishop Numenior called a meeting of his Friends.

Joan and I, on the other hand, conversed every day about anything and everything, and, in that summer of the year of Our Lord eight hundred thirty, there was much to talk about. Our home, Angle-land, fell under siege from the Danes. Spain was in constant battle with the Moors of Africa. Saracens ransacked the shores of the Eastern Roman Empire and the sands of the Italian peninsula with equal disdain and equally ineffective resistance. More than once, Joan suggested that our time at Tours might be approaching its end.

"Martin, I've heard it told that all the great minds are turning toward Fulda."

"Do you know how far Fulda is from here? How inhospitable the climate?"

"Aye, but I'd be indoors studying most of the time. Besides," she laughed, "It might be time for me to search out my Saxon roots."

One evening, in mid-September, we were walking toward our special spot, when, with no advance warning, Joan told me, "I heard from Anastasius today."

I must have turned white. I felt, dizziness, revulsion and, of course, jealousy. I held myself in control as best I could and said nothing. While Joan could not see my expression, she knew me as well as I knew myself. "You needn't be concerned, Martin. He is a part of my past, and an unimportant part at that. He means nothing to me. You should have known that by now."

"You may think you are finished with him, but he obviously does not feel that way toward you."

"Then that's his problem, not mine. I did not say I'd seen him. I heard from him through an emissary."

"An emissary?" I repeated.

"Yes, and what he had to say pertains more to you than to me."

"How say you?"

"You are special friends with the Bishop, are you not?"

"Aye."

"I was told I should distance myself from Numenior as rapidly as possible."

"Why?"

"There are those at Avignon, powerful men, who believe Numenior was responsible for Gurgis' death and for the supposed theft of the thousand gold *solidi* from the abbey's treasury."

"That's nonsense. I was with him when Hudsonius led us to the body. I saw that the forward vault door was open."

"Did you see any sign that it had been forced open?"

"*Ne.*"

"Nor was there a sign of violence that would have killed Gurgis."

I thought for a moment. How could she know this? Superb at divination she might be, an intelligent, articulate scholar she most certainly was. But no one had been there except Hudsonius, John Scotus, the Bishop and the two investigators, and we'd been sworn to absolutely secrecy.

"The emissary told you this?"

"Aye, and more. He said Gurgis had been poisoned and a note had been written and placed where it would be conveniently found. He said he could prove the Bishop was not only involved, but he knew where the Bishop had hidden the supposedly missing money."

"I don't believe it."

"Neither did I, but he said if I wished – he said he was doing this because his friend Anastasius owed me a great favor – Hah!" she laughed bitterly. "Now I know exactly what he thought me worth – a *favor*. He told me exactly where I could discover the missing money, down to the very last *nummus*. *And* he told me the Bishop had hidden several vials of poison for some time in future when he planned to take care of other enemies. Martin, I worry for you."

"Why?" I asked, feeling faint again.

"The emissary told me the Bishop's so-called Council of Friends would be the first to be poisoned, to allay any suspicion from Numenior. After his Friends were killed, it would appear as though he would be the next to die. There would be no possible suspicion of the Bishop and he could consolidate his power through his untrammeled use of the entire treasury for his own purposes. If one or more of his enemies – he told me the Bishop has many enemies – were conveniently to disappear or suffer sudden, unexpected deaths, then so be it. No one would dare accuse him."

"How would this ... this emissary know to seek you out?" I stammered.

"A scoundrel Anastasius may be, and the devil incarnate in your eyes, but at least he was honorable enough to keep my female identity a secret. The fellow came this morning as an ordinary messenger from Avignon with a sack full of messages, and asked to present one to Brother Joannes Angliorum. I'm sure he believed I was a man, even to the moment he departed back to Avignon."

"Did he offer you any further proofs?"

"Only that if the Bishop seemed more out of sorts than usual, it was because he knew he was under investigation by Cardinal Alcinorius, who was never a friend of our Bishop."

"I've heard that before."

"What if the emissary's tale is true?"

I had not even considered the possibility that it could be true. I knew Numenior to be a good and worldly man, knew him to be beyond such a nefarious plot. Or did I? Joan said she'd been given proof. Perhaps it was time that I learned not to be so trusting of those who befriended me. And who better than Anastasius had taught me that lesson?

~ ∫ ~

The Bishop was obliged to travel throughout his dominion no less than four times each year. Not counting the journey to Aix la Chappelle, it had been nearly three months since he'd done so. Less than a week later, he convened his Council of Friends and advised us he would be leaving within the fortnight. I asked whether there was anything I could do to assist him in his absence.

"Yes, find the man who killed Gurgis," he said.

When the rest had left, I asked, "Excellency, what was Gurgis' primary job?"

"He kept all the books of account of the Abbey."

"Was he the only one with access to those books?"

"Yes, until two years ago. Gurgis was foisted upon me by Rome. My great and good friend Cardinal Alcinorius," he snorted with derision, "sent an auditor from Avignon to assist Gurgis with accounting for the Abbey's business. That auditor stayed on for more than a year and a half, and then returned to Avignon."

"What was this auditor's name?"

"Marius."

"Have you heard from him since?"

"Ne," the bishop responded. "As far as I know, he has not come back for three months."

"Who has been keeping the books of account for the Abbey since Gurgis' death?"

"Why, no one, Martin. Why do you ask?"

"I have an idea, Excellency. I am by no means an investigator, but I have watched and learned from two of the best young minds I've met, John Scotus Erigena, and Joannes Angliorum, my close friend. I would like to beg a privilege, Your Eminence. While you are gone, would it be possible for Scotus, Joannes, and me to examine the Abbey's ledgers in private?"

The bishop smiled. "I know of Joannes Angliorum. He's reputed to be a brilliant scholar, but why do you require his help?"

"Excellency," I said. "I may be an astute recorder of others' ideas, but Joannes has an amazing grasp of numbers –

not only the numbers, but the meaning behind those numbers. If there are any irregularities, he would find them more quickly than I."

The bishop signaled me to come into his private chambers. Once we were there, he locked the outer door. "Do you truly think there could be a relationship between accounting records, the missing money, and Gurgis' death?"

"My intuition tells me there is."

"Very well, then. I trust John Scotus implicitly. If you vouch for Brother Joannes, so be it. During my absence, you will be responsible for the accounting cubicle and bearer of the key. You will see that the office is opened on time and closed when the work is done. All ledgers are your responsibility, and you will lock them up each night."

~ ∫ ~

When I returned to the Abbey, John Scotus accosted me and said, "All right, Martin, you obviously know something you've not mentioned about the murder."

"*Ne*, that is not true."

"You may swear it's not true, but I saw how you stayed behind and asked to speak with the bishop when you asked what we could do to help and he responded "Find Gurgis' murderer." You both entered his chambers for a private conversation. That crime is now several months old. Even though it hangs heavy on our necks, we, of all people in the abbey, know it is destined to remain unsolved." John Scotus Erigena had become my friend. I'd mentioned him to Numenior and I felt I could place my faith in him. But unless Joan felt likewise, she'd feel I'd betrayed her. "Truly, I know nothing, Erigena, but there is someone who might have information – a student in the *schola*. Would you give me a day to ask if he would consider my telling you?"

"Would you want your friend to test me?" Erigena said.

"Why do you say that?"

"Placed in possession of such information, I would hesitate to disclose it to anyone I did not trust. I gather you share such a relationship?"

"Aye," I replied. "He and I traveled from Angle-land to Aquitania with Nicola and another. I've known Joannes half my life."

"So you've traveled together, grown up together, wenched together — ? Never mind, you need not blush, your answer is clear enough. His information, is it dependable?"

"I cannot say. It came from Avignon, by way of a priest with whom we traveled."

"I won't ask you to disclose your friend's identity, Martin. Tell your friend you have someone you'd like him to meet. In that way, he and I might test one another and see how we get on. Let me know tomorrow after vespers."

Next morning, I met Joan at breakfast and disclosed I had a friend who was interested in meeting her, a member of the Council of Friends itself.

"Let me see," she remarked, scratching some of the blonde down on her cheek. "It could not be Hudsonius. I've met him several times. Nor could it be the Bishop. That leaves you and two others, one an old man who wouldn't stretch his brain to even remember me. There is only one other in the group, a very young man."

"John Scotus Erigena."

Joan's hand flew involuntarily to her mouth and she gasped. I was surprised by the unusual force of her response. "That young man – he is John Scotus Erigena?"

"You know him?"

"I know *of* him. Who in this abbey does not? Even now there is talk in the *schola* of his one day becoming the Pope himself. More than one *lectorus* has told our class that Erigena is the greatest mind they've ever reckoned with, perhaps the greatest mind in the past century. There are all kinds of stories about how he learned an entire six month period of lessons in three days, how the teachers refused to engage him in debate for fear of being humiliated in front of their class, how, in secret, they asked him to help them gain a greater understanding. He wants to meet me?" Joan asked.

"Aye."

"Why?"

I told Joan the details about my meeting with the Bishop the day before, of John Scotus' suspicion that I knew something I was not telling, of his desire to become involved, but not until he could gain her trust.

"He doesn't know — ?"

"Of course not. I promised you years ago I would not betray that to anyone and I have kept that promise. He knows of you only as a Brother who accompanied me from Angle-land with two others. I told him someone had disclosed information about Gurgis' murder to you."

"I have no difficulty in meeting him, once I get over my awe, given his reputation. Might Nicola go with us?"

"I see no reason why not. I only hesitate because right now the secret is between you and me. By speaking with Nicola and perhaps with Erigena, we double the number of people who know. We multiply the risk of news spreading throughout the abbey."

"You trust me?"

"Of course."

"You trust Erigena?"

"Yes."

"Then why mistrust our oldest, dearest friend?"

"Very well, I'll introduce you to Erigena tomorrow after Vespers. While you are talking with him, I will absent myself for an hour, fetch Nicola and return."

So it was and so it became. That evening, we met as planned, outside the abbey.

"John Scotus Erigena, this is my friend, Joannes — "

"*This* is the friend of whom you spoke? Brother Joannes Angliorum?"

"None other. Why do you seem so surprised?"

It was the first time in nearly a year of my acquaintanceship with Erigena that he seemed at a loss for words. Joan, however, was not at a loss.

"John Scotus Erigena," she said, her voice low pitched, masculine. "I am humbled to meet you. Your reputation has preceded you, and not merely with Martin."

"My reputation," he repeated. "Fra Joannes, I must beg your indulgence, but your reputation has well preceded you. You are aware, of course, that I have close friendships among the *lectores*."

"Naturally. I'm certain you are aware of your reputation."

He smiled and seemed to relax. "From the way you greeted me, Fra Joannes, I am equally certain you are not aware of your own reputation." Now it was Joan's turn to blush. Within a very few moments, they appeared at ease with one another.

I left to seek out Nicola. When I told him the story, Nicola chuckled with gentle irony, "The two titans have met? Yet the walls of the abbey still stand?"

"Aye, my friend."

"She told me about the messenger from Avignon." I was not greatly surprised. I wondered, for an instant, whether she'd told him more. But he said nothing else.

When we approached Erigena and Joan, I saw Joan was almost out of control, so hard was she laughing. As I came closer, I could hear them. "That old miser was more shocked that I *wasn't* shocked than when I said, 'This table' Ah, Martin returns with another man. This must be Father Nicholas – the one you call Nicola?"

"It is." Introductions were made all around. Joan returned to the matter at hand. "Very well, I've told you Nicola knows. Martin told me you suspect there's something I know. I have satisfied myself of your *bona fides*. Let us talk together about this."

For the next hour, Joan outlined in detail what she'd learned from Anastasius' courier. Although Nicola and I each stopped her several times with what I thought were piercing questions, Erigena said nothing until she'd come to the end of her discourse.

"How well do you know this messenger?"

"It was the first time I'd ever met him."

"How well do you know the man who sent the messenger? More than that, do you trust him? You three were with him for several weeks, ate with him, slept alongside him" – I winced inside, as though slapped hard in the face – "rode along new roads together."

Joan replied with no trace of emotion, "I know more about you than I do about Anastasius."

"Martin, you know the man."

"Not well."

"Nicola?"

"The circumstances under which we met this – Priest – were not such as would engender trust." Nicola told Erigena how we'd met Anastasius. "It surprised us all when he appeared at Gull's Landing, more so when he risked his own life to save Joannes at sea. He was a pleasant enough companion on the way to Tours, although I never saw him part with a *nummus* to help defray our expenses. Between Martin, Joannes and I, there was a history, a friendship going back some years, so we knew and trusted one another. Do I trust Anastasius?" Nicola thought for a long moment. "No, Erigena, I do not trust the man."

"Why?" I asked.

"Because Joannes told me Anastasius had sent the emissary because he felt he owed Joannes a favor. Not only could I not surmise any favor that Anastasius would owe Brother Joannes – after all it was he who had saved Joannes' life, not the other way around – but in all my time with him, I found Anastasius was not the kind who would do anything for anyone unless it could promote his own ends. He always told me there were 'plans' for him, that he was related to a Prince of the Church – I assumed a Cardinal. And Cardinals, though they may detest one another in private, are part of a Sacred College. They are members of their own Brotherhood, each one washing the hands and feet of the other. Furthermore, I suspect that the motive in warning you to leave to avoid suspicion is really so that it would look like rats leaving a sinking ship – an interesting comment on his character and proof that he has underestimated ours."

"So," Erigena continued, "Anastasius' friend, supposedly sent by the Cardinal, or someone close to the Cardinal, told Joannes that Gurgis was poisoned, that he knew exactly where a thousand *solidi* were hidden, and where numerous vials of poison could be found. All this from someone who had never before met Joannes. The emissary knew that Joannes and Martin were close comrades. He seemed to possess information only available to insiders, which means that either Numenior is guilty as he says, or that someone was working inside without our knowledge. Joannes, did you, by any chance, learn the name of this emissary?"

"He only told me his first name, which was very common. Marius."

"Bishop Numenior told me the auditor forced upon him was named Marius," I said. "Joannes, you said the emissary's name was Marius. You're correct that Marius is a common name. There are at least twenty scholars named Marius at Tours Abbey. But I have a suspicion that may be worth testing. Is there somewhere we might adjourn to in private? Somewhere we cannot be heard?"

"Why not the council chambers?" Erigena asked. "You and I each have a set of keys and the Bishop has gone traveling— "

~ ∫ ~

"Did any of us see the money go missing?" I asked.

"Ne," said John Scouts. "It had something to do with the account books being out of balance. There was a physical count while we were gone to Aix la Chappelle, and that's when they determined that a thousand gold *solidi* were missing."

"I thought as much," I told my three friends. "On a hunch, I asked the Bishop if I could have access to the ledgers in his absence. Numenior not only granted my wish, but also gave me full charge of the records while he was gone."

"What do you suggest," Joan asked.

"The four of us should work in teams of two. Joannes, you have a great grasp of numbers. I would like you to help me audit the Abbey's books for the most recent five years. It will take us the better part of a week. Scotus, see if the Abbey has changed its way of doing business during that time.

"And I?" Nicola asked.

"You, Nicola, are *everyman* – the common denominator in any group, and the one with whom the average inhabitant of this Abbey would feel most comfortable speaking. Listen to the talk of the humble. Draw out conversations if you have to. Learn what you can. Time grows short. We will meet after Compline, one week hence. When we have learned more, we will better know how to proceed."

CHAPTER 12

When we met, the information we'd gleaned started to paint a vivid picture of something very much amiss.

Joan was the first to report her findings and mine. "The ledgers show that while the See relies on donations, more than half of the Church's income is derived from the sale of the Abbey's wine. Martin and I looked carefully at the ledgers for more than the last five years. We went back this far to establish the normal flow of money and goods. It became evident that when Gurgis took over the accounting, the amount of money generated by the Church increased significantly.

"Gurgis did this by using the excess labor to make brooms and other inexpensive items instead of buying them. The stipends to the Pope increased substantially. He also changed the system so that only he could draw money from the vaults. His second in charge would submit a list of materials required by the Church, most of which consisted of fresh fruit and vegetables which the Church did not produce. He would also estimate the cost and increase it by one-fifth measure to allow those monks in charge of purchasing to take advantage of much lower prices for increased quantity and other variables including price fluctuations, depending on availability."

"How did this work?" Nicola asked.

"Fairly easily, Nico. If the estimated cost of purchases was sixteen *solidi*, Gurgis would advance twenty *solidi*. After the goods were purchased, his aide would provide the list of purchases and the prices and the balance of the money. The cost of the goods purchased plus the returned money was to equal the money advanced to balance the ledgers. The returned *solidi* were entered into the journal by the newest monk accountant. Nothing seemed amiss, and everything was in Gurgis' very exacting hand."

"An elegant system," John Scotus remarked dryly. "I do hope it gets more exciting than this, though."

"Oh, but it does," I said. "Bishop Numenior told me that two years ago, an accountant named Marius was sent from the Cardinal in Avignon to audit Gurgis' books. Marius was placed in charge of the purchase ledgers. Apparently, they worked on the same set of books, for beginning about that time some of the entries were in Gurgis' hand and some were in a different hand. Joannes and I decided to check these more carefully. We found that the first of the irregularities started about eighteen months ago."

Joan continued. "Starting at that point, the cost of goods gradually increased, so that within six months they were eleven percent higher than they'd been. When I enquired about this rise, our purveyors told me that the market price has been stable for the past six years or more. When I pointed this out to Martin, he examined the ledgers and found nothing out of the ordinary. The books balanced. It was when we examined the invoices that supported those costs that we found something out of the ordinary. It was quite subtle, really. If a lamb shank cost five *solidi*, that cost on the invoice changed to a six, simply by adding another digit – VI. The change was easy to make, since the monks who handled the purchasing were not adept at writing. Nothing was altered except that the spacing was slightly different. If there were five purchases for twelve *solidi*, marked up by one *solidi* for each unit, the invoice showed seventeen *solidi*, and this was duly recorded in the cost of goods ledger."

"I see," Scotus said, perking up. "The actual expenditure was twelve *solidi*, but the books showed seventeen *solidi*. There would be five unaccounted-for *solidi* floating around."

"Aye," Joan continued. "Whoever knew about the discrepancy could easily pocket or distribute the five *solidi* that the purveyors returned. Marius was clever and never took more than ten percent for himself."

"Martin," Scotus said, "you asked me to see if the Abbey had changed its way of doing business. It did, and, so far as I can tell, it all happened within a month after this Marius fellow was assigned to the Tours."

Nicola raised his eyebrows. "I think we should all have some wine while we're discussing this," he said. He rose and poured each of us a draught.

"Nicola, your sense of timing is almost poetic," Scotus said. "What I found has to do precisely with wine."

"What do you mean?" I asked. I felt a warm buzz of anticipation.

"It has always been the Abbey's practice to auction its wine to the highest bidder. Because the monks in charge are always casking and barreling and aging wines, the Abbey is able to conduct such an auction every two or three months.

"Yes, go on," I said.

"About a month after Marius' arrival, the Abbey conducted its usual auction. There was a stranger who attended this auction. He bid twice the highest bid and made a bold proposal to the brothers who conducted the auction. He said he would buy the entire year's production of wine, and what's more, he would guarantee to pay the same price per cask for the entire vintage.

"The other bidders stormed out of the Abbey, so bitter were they, both with this rebuke to business-as-usual, and at the stranger's guarantee, which was more than they could afford, even if they had formed a cooperative group and purchased wine together.

"Marius, who was in the cellar at the time the man made his proposal, was very enthusiastic, according to the brother vintners with whom I spoke. He heartily endorsed this fellow, said he had known him for years, and said that he had purchased wine all over Aquitania and had a reputation for prompt payment and no haggling. Thus, in one instant, Marius convinced his brethren that they should accept the man's offer, and they did."

"And Marius was the keeper of the books," Joan said. "The books were out of balance by exactly one thousand gold *solidi* when a physical count of the money was made against the report in the books. But even if Marius was working in concert with this wine merchant, and even if Marius were somehow altering the ledgers, we have no proof that either was responsible for the missing money. If we assume that the wine merchant paid in coin, then a purchase this large would have to have been recorded in the accounting ledgers."

"Unless," Nicola said, smiling enigmatically, "some of the money coming in was going out of the Abbey just as fast, or even faster."

"You're speaking in riddles," I said. "What have you found, Nicola?"

In order to understand how Nicola was able to gather his knowledge, one must understand the cycle of life at the Abbey of Tours – or, for that matter, at virtually any abbey or monastery in those days. The Church obviously included parish clergy, who served as shepherds to the lay folk. But there was an even larger group of holy people, men and women, who did nothing but pray and study, contemplate and copy manuscripts. These folk had dedicated their entire lives to God. While the Abbey at Tours employed local laborers to work the hardest jobs in the fields, the monks, scholars, and attendant priests carried out most of the rest of the required tasks, including agricultural ones, themselves.

The singing of the Divine Office was the heartbeat of religious devotions for the monks, just as study was at the core of the *scholars'* existence. The life of a monk, while not always rigorous, was certainly not conducive to complete rest. A day in such a life began at midnight, even in the cold and dark of winter, when the monks would descend from their dormitory into the chapel for *Matins* and *Lauds*. Afterward, the community went back to bed and slept again until rising at first cockcrow to sing *Prime*.

There were five other prayer services during the day – *Terce* three hours after *Prime, Sext* three hours after that, when the Sun was at its highest, *None* three hours later, *Vespers* at sunset, and *Compline* three hours after sunset. After *Compline*, everyone went to bed.

While Saint Benedict of Blessed Memory, who had founded the Order, decreed that monks should be silent for as much of the day and night as possible, he must have known that social intercourse was as natural among monks as among other human beings, so he authorized monks to communicate with signs. The sign language they developed became quite complex and almost any idea the monks needed to convey could be transmitted.

If one wanted wine, for example, he would signal with two fingers as though he were undoing the tap of a cask. To ask a Brother to pass the butter, a monk would stroke the inside of his hand with three fingers. For pepper, he knocked with one index finger on the other, and for salt he shook his hand with three fingers together, as if he were salting something. Occasionally, I would dine with the monks, and I found it amusing to watch the vigorous beckoning, squeezing of ear lobes, rubbing fingers up and down the sides of their noses and smoothing their hands over their stomachs.

The abbot was described by putting two fingers to one's head and taking hold of a hank of hair, as if tugging a forelock. The bursar was indicated by a single index finger raised over the head, the sign of the ox, because he provided such things. One described the cellarer by a circular turning of the hand and wrist, as if unlocking a door with a key. The magister of the elementary school was described by putting two fingers to one's eyes and holding up the little finger.

Nicola's mastery of the signs enabled him to accomplish a major breakthrough in our private search for evidence. For man is by nature garrulous – a natural gossip – and many a snippet of gossip contains monumental truths.

"When Marius and the other fellow watered the wine in the casks, they slipped the coins right back into the cask."

"The small amounts that Marius had put by over the preceding several months! How did you ever find that out?" Joan asked, almost gasping with excitement.

"From one of the youngest and lowest monks, who'd been assigned to mop the floors in the wine cellar. He and three others were also assigned to haul the wooden wine casks up the stairs and into the merchant's cart. Monks aren't supposed to curse, but this one did, and not in sign language either."

We laughed. Nicola went on to tell of how, for the past three days, he'd disguised himself as a monk from another Abbey. Nicola told the young fellow that there had been complaints about how monks were treated at certain Abbeys in the district, that he had been sent from the See to investigate these complaints, and that anything the young monk told him would be held in strictest confidence.

"The monk didn't need a second invitation. He immediately started complaining about anything and everything: he never should have entered the monastic life, he had left a girl back home in the mountains to the east, that the food was abominable, but mostly that the men of privilege, particularly the wine merchant and that son of a fitchet bitch accounting fellow, were outrageous in their arrogance.

"He told me that the accounting fellow in particular – and his description fit your description of Marius, Joannes – was so self-important that he thought his *skeit* didn't stink. Those are the monk's words, not mine, by the way. He also told me he recognized the man who came to pick up the wine as the same one who had shocked everyone by making such a high bid on the wine.

"He said that the wine merchant always came at times when the bishop was away from the See. On those occasions, he'd worn robes of rich Tyrrhian purple, stayed in the Privileged Visiting Quarters, and told our young friend that he was an old friend of Bishop Numenior. He even produced a key to the Bishop's chambers and the monk had seen him go in and out of those chambers in Numenior"'s absence. He enlisted – nay, ordered – the monk to assist him in, as he put it, cleaning out the Bishop's unnecessary detritus, so that, when the Bishop returned from his journey, he would have offices appropriate to welcome a Cardinal, for whom he, the wine merchant, supposedly worked.

"So badly was the monk treated, he was more than annoyed when the wine merchant left without even having the decency to thank him for his efforts – or to give him recompense of any sort. He vowed he'd have retribution.

"The wine merchant was to make three trips a year. Each time, he would cart away one-third of the year's purchase. The last time was about four months ago."

"Just before Marius returned to Avignon," I said. "He must be due back any day now."

"Our monk was by no means as stupid as Marius and the wine merchant thought he was. He felt there was something very odd about the wine merchant – an outsider, not even a priest – staying in the bishop's privileged quarters, and being so obviously friendly with the Abbey's accountant. On the last night of this particular visit, he saw Marius and the wine merchant descend the steps into the cellar after the sun had set. This seemed even more odd to him, and he followed, quiet and unobserved, at some distance. He said he was so shocked that he was frightened to tell anyone what he saw."

"Which was?" Joan prompted.

"The wine merchant untapped each cask set to be shipped on the morrow. 'Is it well watered?' he asked the accountant Marius. 'Aye,' said Marius. 'And I should be well watered as well.' With that, he handed the wine merchant a large bag of coins. The merchant dipped into the bag, brought forth a handful, and passed them over to Marius. 'A portion of water for you, a portion of water for His Eminence, and a portion of water for Anastasius.'"

"Anastasius?" I gasped.

"That's what the monk said the merchant had said. He told me the wine merchant poured about a third of the coins into one cask, a third into another, and the remainder into yet another cask. In all, there were eight casks to be loaded that day. Apparently the merchant and the accountant had agreed that the three casks containing the coins would be carried up first, and loaded into the front of the cart, farthest from where anyone might be tempted to look. That was the last time our monk saw the wine merchant or Marius. Oh, and he told me one more thing of interest."

"What was that?" Joan asked.

"The wine merchant bought a year's worth of product. Yet, he only took possession of nine months' worth of wine. He is supposed to come in the next week to pick up the remainder of his purchase."

"That, my friends, may be the answer to our mystery," I said. "It is likely that Gurgis, who knew the books better than anyone, either discovered the accounting error, or, what is even more likely, Marius believed that Gurgis might uncover the discrepancies in the books and point the finger of suspicion at Marius. I believe that Marius was responsible for Gurgis' death in one way or another. But there remains the question of proving Marius' involvement and that of the villainous wine merchant."

"How could we do that?" Scotus asked.

"I have an idea," Joan said. "I'll wager our friend Marius will suddenly appear in the next few days. It's a week before the bishop is scheduled to return, and he'll undoubtedly have one last piece of business to settle – and a little bit more 'water' for his needs."

~ ∫ ~

As Joan suspected, Marius came to Tours two days later. He approached Hudsonius, who'd been briefed on what to expect, and who was in charge of the abbey in the bishop's absence. Hudsonius told me he'd told Marius that the accounts of the abbey were in dreadful shape since Gurgis' unfortunate death, that the bishop had asked me to try to sort out the books, but that I was having the devil's own time trying to balance them.

Not unexpectedly, Marius volunteered to help, and I met him the following morning.

"Ah, young Martin," the man said, introducing himself. "Magister Hudsonius told me you were having a dreadful time trying to learn bookkeeping in a very brief time." The man was shorter than I, very dapper for a man of the Church, with soft, scrubbed hands and neatly pared fingernails.

"I'm afraid so," I sighed. "If only Mother Church could find me a helping hand. It's certain that I'll never be an accountant."

"It so happens I am an accountant," he said. "Why, I'll wager if you give me two days, I can have these books in fine shape."

"Oh, wonderful!" I said, feigning exuberance. "I'd be so happy to have you working beside me, supervising me, pointing out where I've made my mistakes."

"And well you shall," he said convivially. "But I'll need the first day to work here on my own, sorting through some months of records – invoices, donations, wine sales, and such. Indeed, I believe any day now the source of our great wealth, the wine merchant, will show up to take delivery of the last eight casks of wine. You're fortunate that I'll be able to deal with him."

"You've no idea how much I appreciate your help. I'll see you at midday tomorrow?"

"Fine," the accountant said.

Just before vespers, I "remembered" that I'd promised Bishop Numenior I'd lock the door to the accounting cubicle and carry the keys with me. I had barely entered the cubicle when I saw Marius held in the iron grip of the two investigators. I say held, but actually he was shackled.

"What is this?" I asked, sounding convincingly surprised.

"None of your business," barked one of the investigators, Willibald. "We'll deal with this."

Marius was pale and perspiring. "This is all a mistake. Tell him who I am, Martin."

"This man is Marius. He told me he was familiar with the accounting office in the abbey … that he'd worked here for nearly two years. He was helping me to clear up the books. I thought — that is, the bishop will be annoyed."

"I said this is none of your business. Now begone, and quickly unless you want to share a cell with him in the lower depths of the dungeon."

I scurried away quickly, winking at Willibald as I left.

Shortly after sunset, the wine merchant arrived at the abbey. Nicola had identified the young monk to me, and he and I had dressed alike, in rough wool garb, our heads hooded, with vapid expressions on our faces. We watched as Nicola went to the merchant's cart to greet him.

"Where's Marius?" the merchant asked suspiciously.

"He was delayed enroute from Avignon. Something about Anastasius being recalled to Rome, or such."

"Aye, I'd heard that," the man said, still not letting down his guard. "But why would that cause an accountant to remain at Avignon?"

"I've no idea," Nicola said smoothly. Then, more quietly, "But he left word with me that the wine was to be well watered, and there'd be something for me to drink as well."

At that, from some yards away, I could see the wine merchant's expression relax. "Oh, ho!" he said. "This is the last shipment of the year, and the largest."

"I'm aware of that," Nicola said. "I saw you brought a much larger cart than usual. And four oxen."

"True. Did he tell you about our, umm, arrangement?"

"Of course," Nicola replied. "I've already made sure the accounting ledgers were properly balanced. I suggest we drink the water in five draughts this time. One never knows who might want some wine while you're on the road."

"And the measure?"

"As always. A fourth part wine, the rest water. Since you're so late, I've already drained off the top. We can go now and be done with in time for you to be gone by morning. The bishop's chamber?"

"He really did train you well," the merchant said, grinning.

"Let's not tarry, then."

They didn't. The young monk and I followed at a respectful distance, and made as though we were cleaning out the floor on the far side of the cellar. We both heard and saw the exchange, and it was exactly as the monk had told us. At one point, the merchant became nervous and said, "What about those fellows yonder? The ones scrubbing the floor."

"You needn't worry," Nicola said easily. "They're both deaf and dumb. They couldn't hear anything if they wanted to, and even if they could, who would they tell?"

"Aye, you're right," the merchant replied.

They were finished with their business within the hour, and the following morning that monk and three others dutifully lifted the twelve casks into the merchant's cart. The five casks containing the coins were placed in rows of three and two at the bottom front of the cart. The other casks were stacked atop of and behind them.

The merchant departed and was less than a Roman mile away when four inspectors came riding up and asked for a word with him.

Although it was ultimately of great benefit to me – as well as to Joan, John Scotus, and even Nicola – it is not necessary to this tale that I relate in detail what ultimately happened when we disclosed the results of our actions direct to the Bishop upon his return. Aye, at this time in my life, I can scarcely remember the way in which Numenior dealt with the problem.

Shortly thereafter, Cardinal Alcinorius was recalled to Rome for consultations with the Holy Father, Pope Gregory IV, and since Cardinals served at the pleasure of the Pope, the Holy See announced that Alcinorius had received a substantial promotion. I was mystified, and not a little annoyed that Alcinorius had benefited so greatly from his own foul doing, until Numenior told me, with a wink, "Ah, yes, Martin, my Brother in Christ has been afforded a rare promotion and a splendid opportunity indeed. He has just been designated the Archbishop of no less a See than Sarmatia."

"Sarmatia, Excellency?"

"Indeed, Martin. A most … 'provocative' assignment. He will be a pioneer for Christ, defending, let us say, 'Christendom's ultimate borders.' I've never been there, but I've heard stories about it." He walked over to a small table adjoining his bed and came back with a large map-scroll, which he rolled out onto a much larger table. Pointing out to me that Alcinorius' new see

was four times larger than that of Avignon, he said, "Ah, yes
… from the flat lands of Lviv in the south to the amber coast
of Pomore on the Wendic Gulf, and from the Viswa River in
the west to the River Volga, my Brother in Christ will be the
head and voice of Rome in all of it. Nine months of the fiercest
cold you could imagine, nearly three months filled with the
most pestilential vermin on the face of the Earth, and ten days
a year of gloriously sunny skies. If I may use language that
may scandalize you, Young Brother Martin, among our more
elevated Brethren, I believe it is called 'God's *skeit* hole.'"

CHAPTER 13

At the beginning of June, 831, Nicola told us he was moving on to be a priest in Ravenna. We were happy for him. John Scotus announced the following month that he'd been offered a position of great prominence and promise in Angleland and had decided to take it.

Although Bishop Numenior and I were almost like an uncle and his favored nephew, I noticed that he and Joan were engaged increasingly in lengthy conversations during August, converse from which I was not excluded, but in which I was not really interested, since my days were busily spent as Numenior"s Vicar General *pro tempore*. Besides, I missed none of the substance of their talks, since Joan and I spoke with one another each evening before *Compline*.

"Our bishop feels I have acquired all the knowledge I can acquire here," she said, "and he has asked about my future. He seems to share the same opinion of me as did John Scotus. Remember last year, when I remarked on Fulda?"

"I do," I said, although, for myself, I had no great desire to spend God knows how many more years in dreary study in a cold, inhospitable land. Still, Joan had become so much a part of my life that I dreaded any lengthy separation from her.

"Well, now I am not so sure," she said, to my immense relief. "Fulda is too close to Alcinorius' See, and I'm told our old friend, Anastasius, has cast his lot with Avignon's erstwhile cardinal. I believe the world is wider than northern Europe."

"Are these your words, Joan?"

"Not mine alone. Our bishop has told me of other places. Constantinople, Rome, the Holy Land — "

As we sat on "our" hillock in the pleasant evening twilight, I felt my own heart racing. I agreed with Joan that Tours had been a wonderful learning place, but that there must be more to life than the great abbey. Without Nicola or John Scotus or Joan, the abbey would be a lonely and forlorn place. I said as much to Joan.

"Come with me, then," she said.

"Whither would we journey?"

"Athens would be as good a place as any."

"Athens? Isn't that rather a tired backwater."

"*Ne.* I've heard tell that Rome has certainly declined from the city it was during the reign of the Caesars, and we know that Constantinople is in the ascendant, though Rome would never admit to that. Athens was the parent to both Rome and Byzantium. It's located between both of those cities, and thus is enemy to neither."

I knew that more than a millennium ago Athens had been a center of the world's most profound ideas. While Constantinople and Rome – and even Avignon, Aix La Chapelle, and Fulda – quietly but viciously competed with one another for prominence and dominance of the Christian world, Athens had no desire to do other than what it had done in the past several hundred years. It was a marketplace of the world's ideas. If that made it a backwater, so be it, for that great city somehow seemed to believe it would outlast them all.

That evening, and for several nights thereafter, Joan and I warmed to the idea of the new adventure. Joan felt that in Athens she would be far away from the scheming and posturing and intrigues of the Western Church's leadership, and that she could pursue her own ideas in a relatively safe and sunny place. In the fifteen years since Saint Leo had passed away, there had been four popes before the current prelate, Gregory, stood in the shoes of the Fisherman.

"Of course, we could go to the Holy See before we went to Athens," I said, becoming increasingly eager and excited as we planned out the next stage of our lives. "We could go overland to Rome, spend as much time as we like there, then cross the Hadriatic Sea from Brindisium — "

Joan smiled enigmatically and listened to what I had to say.

"Martin," she finally replied. "How old are you?"

"Twenty-two," I said.

"I'll be eighteen next month. Hardly what one would call old people. It is for the elderly to make a trip such as you propose. I have another idea."

I looked at her uncomprehendingly.

"Our bishop has been kind enough to loan me a recently completed codex of maps. Could you arrange to meet us tomorrow after *Terce*?"

I could and I did. When I arrived, Numenior had already poured draughts of wine for himself and for Joan. They appeared to have been chatting convivially before I arrived. "Welcome, Brother Martin," the bishop said congenially, offering me a goblet of wine. "I understand from talking to Brother Joannes that I am about to lose my vicar general and my most brilliant remaining student. Not that I blame you," he said. "Even our great abbey can become stifling after awhile. My only regret is that, after hearing Joannes' tale of where you and he propose to go, I am too old, too fat, and too high risen in Mother Church to accompany you. Also, as you undoubtedly know, I am too accustomed to my comforts to desert them now."

"Surely, Excellency, a journey to Athens would not tax you?"

"An ordinary journey, no. But what Brother Joannes and I have been lately discussing is a bit longer and a great deal more strenuous." The bishop bade Joan and I sit down at the large oak council table. He refilled his own goblet with a large draught of the hearty burgundy red wine he so favored. I had not taken the first sip of my wine, and Joan declined politely. He motioned toward the scrolls in Joan's arms, and she placed them on the table.

"Brother Joannes and I have given some thought to this matter," Numenior continued. "Like Erigena, Joannes Angliorum is an extraordinarily brilliant scholar. In some quarters, this makes for a most favorable impression. In other quarters, this can be a great danger. It is not the rank and file clerics that worry the Papal intriguers. *Ne*, it is the young who show the greatest promise that threaten their security – and their own futures."

"Is that why Brother Joannnes elected to go to Athens?" I asked, leaning back in the soft council chair and taking a first sip of the strong, heady red wine.

"Let's say it was a decision we arrived at together. Joannes told me you said Athens was not of great importance to the Church. While that may presently be so, it is also a much safer place than Rome or Fulda.

"Pope Gregory and our beloved Archbishop of Sarmatia are no closer than Alcinorius and me. I have little doubt that Alcinorius will be keeping an eye on you, Joannes, for you could represent either a threat or an opportunity to him. While Gregory is a good man, the average tenure of the last five Popes has been less than three years each – not what one would call a sinecure. Despite Alcinorius' 'promotion' last year, he has powerful friends at Rome."

Joan touched my arm. "Remember when I spoke of Fulda last year? His Excellency related to me that Alcinorius relishes my going to Fulda, which is close enough for him to keep an eye on me."

"I think," Bishop Numenior said, "it would look best, and it would certainly be politically astute, if Brother Joannes were to announce, with great panoply, that he has decided to attend the great abbey at Fulda, and that you will remain here as my vicar."

"What will really happen, Excellency?"

The bishop rolled rather heavily to his feet, took the scrolls from Joan, and unrolled the largest of them. The scroll contained a large map that portrayed the entire area from Angle-land to Constantinople. I noticed that while Charlemagne's Empire, the Peninsula of Italia, the Eastern March, and the entire area south of the Danuvius River all the way to Constantinople was rendered in exquisite detail, the area entitled "Sarmatia – Terra Incognita" was a large, undetailed space on the map.

"Joannes will leave within the next fortnight on the road to Fulda. It is a well-used road that passes through Aix-la-Chapelle, or Aachen as our Germanic friends call it, then turns northeast toward Fulda. The journey should take a month or two at most, and Alcinorius' people will be watching as Joannes crosses the border into northern Germany.

"Brother Joannes, alas, will not arrive timely in Fulda, and a rumor will go out that he has succumbed to a remnant of barbarian Goths. I will direct my vicar to leave for the area where Brother Joannes was last seen, to investigate this unfortunate situation."

"You have another route in mind, Excellency?"

"Indeed," he answered. "Brother Joannes will travel north and east toward Aix-la-Chappelle. He will take lodging at Vesontio – the Franks have recently renamed it Besançon, where, the next morning, an old friend of mine will meet him in Vesontio, and spirit him to Basilea, which is where you, Martin, will meet him a month later. You can winter safely there, then travel east when spring arrives."

"How will I manage to find him?"

"My friend is very resourceful."

"How will I recognize your friend?"

"Of that you need not fear."

"Wouldn't it be simpler to travel south of the Alps and east through the Piedmont?"

"Simpler, yes, but for your purposes, not wise. Churchmen much prefer the route of least resistance. Alcinorius' spies would learn quickly of the deception should you somehow appear on that road which remains free of snow during the winter. It is best you tarry in Basilea or St. Gallen, where you will be far less conspicuous."

"Still," Bishop Numenior resumed, "you should not arrive in Athens too soon, for word might get out about your ultimate destination. I suggest a period of at least a year, perhaps two –"

"So long a time," Joan murmured under her breath.

"Joannes, when you're young, as you and Martin are, time is very much on your side. In two years, the ardor of those who seek you will have cooled. Alcinorius will forget that you ever walked the earth. And in that time, if you make this truly a voyage of discovery, you will learn more about life than you would had you spent five years in the learning centers of Athens. I can advise you of a reasonable route to take. But, if you are wise, you will deviate from that route, and you will see places and experience things that will last you for a full lifetime."

The morrow of the day following a fortnight, Joan bid a well-heralded farewell to Tours and, with several others in train, mounted her horse and started north toward Aix-la-Chappelle.

BOOK III.
ORESTES

CHAPTER 14

The world – the universe, for all I know – is reduced to a single being, and that being is you or I, or, for that matter a king or a pope, a lion or the smallest insect that creeps upon the earth.

Every being is the center of his own universe. And while we are so busy being the center of the universe, we seldom, if ever, realize that so is everyone else.

That does not mean to say that everyone is the master of anything. A man may worship or be bound to God, family elders, a pope, or an emperor. Indeed, I have often felt, particularly in later days, that I loved Joan more than myself, and sunk to my low station, as I presently am, I do not feel important at all. But then again, very few people ever really have any legitimate reason for feeling important.

Nevertheless, I have come to believe that to any man's sight and hearing and understanding, every other thing in the universe revolves about him. How could it seem otherwise? From inside his head, he regards everything else as outside, existing only to the extent that it affects himself. What he believes is, to him, the only necessary truth. What he does not know is not worth knowing. What things he does not love or hate are of no concern whatever. His own wants and complaints deserve the most immediate attention. If he awakes with an aching head or a sore shoulder, it is of more moment to him than another's dying or losing a limb. His own impending death means the veritable end of the world.

Even in my low state, I challenge you: Can you conceive of the grass growing when you can no longer feel it springing under your feet? When you can no longer smell its sweet aroma after rain? When you can no longer walk your horse and watch him graze upon it? When the grass has no other reason for its existence but to cover your grave – and you not able even to look upon and admire it?

So, in my present suffering, in my fear, and even in my blasphemy, I believe that regardless whether someone is a bishop, a prostitute, even like myself a high-risen clergyman now brought low, the grass grows, the world exists only because this person lives. His or her concerns are the most pressing that have existed from the beginning of the world. And then, I must remember that whatever this center of the universe does, or thinks, or says, will, in some way, affect other centers of the universe. But I digress from my story. Suffice it to say that whatever was going on in Constantinople or in Angle-land, in Rome or in Alcinorius' territories in the far away, vast, and reportedly inhospitable lands of Sarmatia, neither concerned nor affected me as I began my journey north and eastward.

~ ∫ ~

I left Tours on the fifth day of November 831, two months beyond my twenty-second birthday. A quite friendly priest in a church in Vesontio told me, "You'll be going into the Hrau

Albos, the foothills of the high Alps. When you have traveled a day with the Alps on your right, turn left the next morning and keep going in that direction. Eventually the land will descend and you will come to Basilea."

I had pared my belongings down to the bare minimum necessary to travel – two changes of clothing, a heavy, fur-lined coat and hat, high boots, a metal canteen to drink out of and a small fry pan in which to cook my food, a broadsword, a small, sharp knife, a hunting sling, and, of course, a type of fleece-lined bag, which covered me from head to foot, and in which I could sleep on the ground at night.

I carried sufficient money for my needs in a wallet that fit on a band inside my breeches. The pockets of this device were fulsome and the whole thing fit across my waist and extended up to my chest. I also carried several small flint stones and puffball tinder in my waist wallet, and these I guarded with the same zeal as my money.

All of my supplies except my bursary and my fire-lighting apparatus were wrapped in a canvas sack and hung on the left side of my horse. A similar sack hung from its right side. This sack contained supplies for my worthy steed, a winter blanket to keep out the bitter cold, and fleece stockings, which fit all the way to the horse's knees, and which could be bound by one set of leather thongs suspended from the saddle, and another set of thongs that I could tie closer to the horse's hooves. There were also special treats, carrots and turnips, and a refillable feedbag for my mount.

During my first two days, the journey was easy and remarkably pleasant. Between the western and eastern arms of the Dubis, there were many vineyards, and of course they bore no grapes in wintertime, but I found them quite useful nonetheless. I stole several bits of twine with which the vines were tied to their stakes, and those I tied together to make a fishing line. I improvised fishhooks by cutting the spiny hawthorn twigs that grew in the foothills. As I rode along a narrow dirt rut, I would, from time to time, notice tiny pieces of rodents on which raptors had gorged themselves, then left behind. I did my fishing at night. I made a torch of dead brush, which could be found everywhere, then set it afire. The light would attract the fish to the bank. Since my fishhooks were not stout enough to land larger fish, I was limited to grayling, trout, and loach. But these were plentiful, easy to catch, and delicious. My horse was able to forage happily in the area, because the snows had not yet come.

On the third morning east of Vesontio, I found myself in the deep woods, the trackless wilderness. Except for the comparatively few places on this continent where men have long been settled as farmers, herders, vine growers, miners, merchants, and timber cutters, almost all of Europe, from Angle-land to the Black Sea, has been densely forested since the beginning of time, and still was when I wandered over it, and still is, for all I know. However extensive may be the cleared and cultivated patches, and however numerous may be their human inhabitants, and however imposing may be their towns and cities, those clearings are but islands in the great primeval sea of trees.

Up to this point in my journey, the winter weather had been tolerably mild. But now I was in the high forelands of the immensely higher peaks of the Alps. The *Hrau Albos* are nowadays called the Jura Mountains, but I prefer the more descriptive Old Gothic name for them, the *Hrau Albos* – the *Raw* Alps – because of their savage winters. Unfortunately, I soon found that this winter was already savage, and it became even more so as I pressed eastward. Even at midday, the woods were dark and bleak and cold, and soon snow fell on snow, and I was forever confronted with an ice-flecked wind that might have flayed an ox. Both the horse and I were grateful for the protective winter clothing.

Even though snow covered most of the ground, I was capable of finding deadwood with which to build a fire, and I knew enough never to make a fire under a tree or a rock shelf burdened with snow, since the snow would loosen in the heat and fall and kill the fire. I had become proficient enough with my sling to drop an occasional tree squirrel or snow hare, even though squirrels were few and the white hares were difficult to see. The mountain brooks were too small to contain anything but minnows, but they were plentiful and nourishing. Thankfully, my horse had the sense to poke its head beneath the layers of snow covering the ground and find food. He also cropped everything from dry grass that poked up from snowbanks to edible bushes that grew above the snow.

Early in my journey, I believed eating snow would allay my thirst but, curiously, it did not. Soon, I learned how truly little water there is in snow. Thereafter, I tried to camp as often as possible beside a brook that was of a size to have some water flowing beneath its coating of ice.

It was my horse who taught me how to find food more easily. I noticed that he always seemed to investigate clefts in the rocks, wherein he'd find grass and other edibles protected from the ever-present snow. By following my horse's lead, I was often able to find a small cave in the rocks or a cranny in the ground that turned out to be the den of a hibernating hedgehog or dormouse or tortoise. I was delighted to find that marmots inhabit this area, for marmot meat is both very tasty and loaded with fat. Also, a marmot's den is always full of nuts, roots, seeds, and dried berries, and those make a delicious side dish with the marmot meat.

I was prudent enough not to investigate any large caves that I came across, for I'd learned years ago that they might be the winter quarters of hibernating bears. I also took care to avoid animals bigger than myself that were still awake and active in winter. Several times, I was able to see, and fortunately to keep my distance from, a massively-antlered elk or a high-humped bison.

~ ∫ ~

On the sixth night out of Vesontio, I crested the crown of a small hill and found myself looking down a good hundred paces below, into a dale that was nearly barren of trees and lit by a number of campfires. I saw a few crude huts encircled by a number of mean, patchwork hide tents. At the farther side of the dale I beheld a line of tethered horses, much smaller than mine and very shaggy. I had heard about these scruffy animals. They had been ridden into Europa by the legendary Huns, those same people who had rampaged and pillaged and destroyed the earth and its peaceable peoples everywhere they came, some four hundred years ago.

As I stared down toward the dale, I saw people moving around. These people rather resembled their horses. They were smaller than average. Both the men and the women were exceedingly ugly, of a dirty yellowish-brown complexion with long, stringy, greasy black hair, eyes that were only slitted pouches. The men had no beards, but some of them had straggly wisps of moustache. There were some twoscore persons moving about the camp. I could not tell from their ragged and shabby dress which were men and which were women, and I did not care to make their acquaintance.

Still, I was fascinated to sit quietly and observe them. They all seemed to walk bowlegged. I could hear several of them grumble to one another when they met, something that sounded to my ear like, "*Aruv zerko kara*," then spit on the ground. Drawn in by the magnet of what I was seeing, I neither listened, nor heard, nor saw anything out of the ordinary, high above the encampment as I was, until suddenly, with no warning at all, I felt a sharp, agonizing pain as a dagger was thrust into my shoulder blade and I felt a warm rush of blood, and smelt the most awful odor I have ever experienced.

My horse whinnied in terror and bolted into the woods. I heard a man's voice, harsh, guttural, speaking no language I knew. Quite quickly, my wrists were bound behind my back with a rough rope, and I was rudely pushed down a path toward the encampment. Halfway down the path, we stopped only long enough for my captor, whoever he or it was, to club me on the head with a blunt rock, after which everything went black.

I awoke to find myself bound to a stake, my hands tied behind my body. Five of the largest persons in the camp, all smaller than I, were shouting what I took to be questions of me in a language I did not understand. All I could do was shake my head. Each time I did not answer one of their questions, they seemed to exhibit a special glee by poking me – hard – with sharp sticks, the ends of which had just been removed from a nearby fire.

My misery appeared to work them up into a frenzy of blood lust. One of the men started to rip my shirt off my body. "NO!" I shouted at them, with what I hoped would be a terrifying roar, but seemed to emerge as nothing more than a bleat. As I twisted and turned every which way I could, as tightly bound as I was, to avoid them finding my body wallet, which, mercifully, they had not yet discovered, a man smacked me across the face with a broad wooden trowel. Tears came to my eyes, so great was the pain, and I felt my knees buckling once again.

I heard higher-pitched, shrill, screaming voices – some of their womenfolk I supposed. They had abandoned their effort to tear off my shirt because they had found a more amusing target. I felt my breeches quickly slit by a knife and pulled down around my legs, leaving me to my ultimate embarrassment. I am certain what they were looking at, and the women were pointing to, and laughing derisively at, was, to them, so pale, puny, shriveled, and paltry, that they reckoned I was probably not a man at all, but a eunuch. Truth to tell, I felt as violated as if I had been raped.

Just as I had descended into the lowest depth of my being, which is why, even now, even having fallen to my present low estate, I can look back and say perhaps there were worse times than the present, the camp suddenly went deadly silent in shock.

Then I heard another sound – the distant thrum of a bowstring and the whir of a flying arrow as it hurtled into the camp. I was astonished to hear a rapidly repeated thrum-thrum-thrum and whir-whir-whir. It must have been an entire army sent to save me. It seemed to take only a few seconds, but in those seconds ten men – fully one of every four in the encampment – lay dead or dying or desperately mutilated.

I gazed up toward the hill from which I'd been dragged down. Those around me had abandoned me altogether and were racing to their mean huts. Not quickly enough. I saw a single man at the top of the rise, who, with the speed and agility of a young athlete, was whipping other arrows from his quiver and nocking them to his bow and shooting them so fast that his right arm was almost a blur, while his left, holding the bow grip, stayed as steady as a statue. Within a few more moments, there were five more bodies writhing or still on the ground, and a tremendous wail went up from the huts.

The voice from the hill barked at my captors, obviously in their own language, which I did not understand, for they quailed and slowly moved out from the huts, into that corner of the camp farthest away from their horses.

My body was a massive lump of pain, my spirit had nearly been destroyed, and not long before I had found myself praying for a swift end to my suffering. I did not know what to think or what to believe or even what to hope for. Had Mother Church or Father God truly sent an avenging angel or was the body coming down the hill, who was grasping the reins of two horses, one of them mine, simply another, larger captor, coming to seize the prey earlier taken by the scrofulous bunch who'd initially bound me to a stake?

I had not long to wait. Whoever it was shouted at the cowering people in the corner, and almost immediately thereafter, I felt myself bathed, almost gently, by warm water and covered with a warm, if odoriferous and greasy, over-wrap.

As I opened my eyes, I beheld a man wearing an outfit of rough buckskin. His face was so tanned and wrinkled it looked like a continuance of his leather coat. While he may have been as old as sixty, he appeared to be in strong and robust old age, not the weakness and decay and thin flabbiness that presages the onset of one's final days. He had all of his teeth, and they were white.

"Good evening," he said in perfect, unaccented Latin. "Bishop Numenior sent word you might be difficult to find. But I didn't surmise you'd be this difficult to find. My name is Orestes, by the way, and I've been asked to take you to Brother Joannes Angliorum, who, even now, is waiting for us in Basilea."

CHAPTER 15

"Huns? Did you say *Huns*, Master?" I didn't know how to address him. He could have been a high clergyman, since he instantly referred to our bishop by his first name. I did not know exactly what he was, save that he had saved my life in the most explosively amazing display of marksmanship I'd ever experienced.

"Aye, young Martin."

"But they came and went hundreds of years ago."

"Well, let's say they came and destroyed everything in their way. After the death of their leader, Attila, most of them returned from whence they'd come, but small groups of them remained in the West and did not go back."

We were riding along a ridgeline, but I had no idea where we were. My horse was content to follow Orestes' large chestnut, and beset with sores and wracked with pain as I was, I was in no position to question his route. A gibbous moon had risen halfway in the sky, and however inclement the weather had been that day, the night was clear and crisp and there was no wind.

"Why would they stay in the West, Master?"

"Comfort, I suppose," he said.

"Comfort? These hills are frigid day and night."

"Ach, yes," Orestes replied. "But the lands to the far east, from whence they came, are far harsher, rocky steppes where, I'm told, the wind never stops blowing, there are almost no trees, and the land is covered by sheets of ice for the greater part of the year."

"Then why wouldn't all of them have stayed here?"

"Many reasons, Martin. The two that come to mind most immediately are that when they invaded the last time, the Romans and their allies, in a last show of their declining strength, somehow managed to push the Huns back after Attila had died in 453."

"And the other reason, Master?"

"You know," Orestes said, "you really aren't my slave and "Master" seems a bit obsequious — "

"What do I call you, then?"

Orestes scratched his bearded chin thoughtfully. "Let me think on that awhile."

"Perhaps if I addressed you by title? What is it you do – or, if you may forgive me for being so callous, for you don't seem a young man – what is it you did?"

"Nothing of significance," he replied. "Not many do."

We had reached the end of the ridgeline, and now a small, but well-defined trail led down into the forest. Orestes noticed my discomfort. "We'll be at our campsite soon," he said. "The second reason is that every man feels more comfortable, more secure in his own place. I've seen hundreds of men moved against their will to an infinitely more clement place than where they'd lived before. The vast majority pined for their old homeland. I'm told the Jews still endure only until the day they can return to Judea or Samaria. What a pestilential hellhole that is."

"You've been there?

"I have, on two occasions, for six months each time, and I couldn't wait to leave. The Huns may have had a *skeity* homeland, but it was *their* homeland, and when they made their bed under the stars, they had no need to worry that their every step would be marked and followed, and that they would be hated. They say the sky is somehow larger on those great steppes and that there are very few *Rus* people to interfere with them."

Orestes found a flat place at the bottom of the trail, which was circled by a protective group of trees. Although I could hardly dismount my horse – and he helped me to do that – I felt I had to somehow be of some use to him.

"Don't bother," he said. "You're going to be very sore for the next couple of days, and there's truly not a damned thing I can do about that. Your job is to heal. Eventually you may be of some little use to me."

"Master!" I let the word slip out hotly. "I can well take care of myself. I can certainly be of help to you, even in my … my present condition. I can hunt, and …"

"You may think you are a great hunter," Orestes remarked, ignoring my use of the honorific. "But I can tell you that when it comes to being a woodsman, you are a bit of a bumbler. I've been following you for the past three days."

"I never knew."

"Of course not. How would you have known? All kinds of forest animals have come galloping past me, fleeing from the noise and commotion you made. You are obviously new to the woods. I have occasionally halted just to get a look at you and marvel at how clumsily you move along, and how unskillfully you wield your sling, and how you often fail to see good, meaty animals that stand still while you pass."

As Orestes spoke, he was working swiftly to start a campfire. Old he might have been, but he was as strong as any man I've ever seen before or since. He carried at least two logs on each trip from the edge of the woods. "Are you hungry?" he asked, of a moment.

"More thirsty, and very sore," I mumbled.

"There's a brook trickling just behind those bushes yonder, if you still have the strength to crack the ice on it."

He kept on talking while I went and gratefully took a long drink. On my return to the fire, I noticed Orestes had erected a spit-and-brace over the flames and had installed a small pot filled with water over the fire. The water had become little warmer than tepid when he said to me, "I think this would be a good time for you to let me see how badly you've been injured. Off with your clothes, then."

I disrobed, and Orestes looked me over appraisingly, as one would examine a horse. "Doesn't look like any bones were broken. A lot of bruises and bumps, but in a week they'll be gone. Your face will take a bit longer to heal."

He dipped a soft piece of *chamois* in the warm water, and applied it to the affected parts. "Can't help you until I clean the dirt off," he remarked. After he was done with this cleansing, he applied a poultice of some sort to the painful areas of my face and body. It stung sharply at first, but momentarily it took the edge off my pain.

Now that my immediate needs had been attended to, I felt ravenously hungry. Orestes went over to the small brook where I'd been, pot in hand. As I lay on the flat ground, he walked to the edge of the encircling trees. "Just looking for some of my treasure," he called back. Shortly, he returned with a large, dried chunk of some kind of meat. "Dried venison," he said. "It's old, but it'll do."

With that, he dumped the hard block into the pot. He foraged around the field in which we found ourselves and came back not long after with two handfuls of vegetables or greens or herbs of some kind. He scrubbed them with the *chamois* he'd used on me, and then dumped them unceremoniously into the pot.

Soon, a rich, piquant aroma penetrated the air. My stomach growled with eager anticipation, but before eating, I checked the horses to ensure they'd been fed and watered. They had been – I might have known that Orestes would have thought of everything – and they were contentedly munching away. Orestes had also put blankets on our two steeds.

I was grateful to find that the two packs on either side of my horse not only had *not* been taken by the Huns, but that everything seemed to be in order within them. I extracted my bedding and returned to the campfire. Orestes ladled a bowl of stew for me before he ladled his own. It was warm, rich, and very filling. After I'd finished, I completed laying my bedding out by the fire. While I was still very uncomfortable, it was not long before I fell into a deep sleep.

Next morning, I still felt stiff and sore, but unquestionably better than I had the evening before. Whatever unguent Orestes had given me had worked in the night. I touched my face and felt two large lumps, but they did not concern me, since I was looking *out* from myself and there were few, if any, in this vicinity who would see my face.

As we gathered our belongings in preparation for the day's ride, I said, "I heard you shouting at the Huns in their own language last night. How many languages do you speak?"

"I stopped counting after six," he said. "I really know only a few words of the abominable Hun language."

"I only learned one phrase while I was held captive, and that only because it seems that's the *only* phrase they spoke while I was with them."

"*Aruv zerko hara,*" Orestes said mildly.

"Yes!" I replied, amazed that he knew even that phrase. "What does it mean?"

At that, the old man burst into almost raucous laughter. "What a skeity foul night!"

"But it's daytime, fr –."

"Or "What a skeity foul day!" depending on when it's said. It's one of their standard greetings to one another."

"But last evening was quite pleasant."

"Doesn't matter. To the Huns, all things are foul."

As Orestes began rolling his own belongings into the fur that had been his bed and blanket, I saw two objects on which he had protectively lain all night: a bow and a quiver of numerous arrows, the same as had delivered me from my doom the night before. Orestes saw me looking. His voice softened as he picked up the bow and fondled it. "Ja, this is my beauty, my treasure, my ever-reliable."

"My father had a bow," I said. "But his was much longer, and shaped in a single arc, like the Latin letter C. I have never seen one like yours before. It looks more like a crooked snake, winding upon itself."

"That's so. Each arm curves one way, then the other. Notice, where an ordinary bow is made of wood and has only the recoil strength of wood bent and tensed, this war bow starts with wood and adds to it." He gently stroked the outer curves. "See, the back of it here – "

"It looks like the front to me."

"*Ne.* Here the bow's wood is backed with dried animal sinews, because they resist being stretched. And it is bellied with horn, because that substance resists being compressed. So to the recoil of the bent wood's trying to straighten is added the horn's strong urge to stretch and the sinews' strong urge to shrink. With all that power together, this bow would make an arrow pierce clear through a young tree, at fifty paces. Even at two hundred paces, the arrow, should it hit a man, will usually hit hard enough to kill him."

He continued to talk as he belted the bow and the quiver of arrows to his fur coat. "It may take a bowyer five years or more to fashion a single bow like this one. Finding the wood, the bone, and the horn, then aging them and cutting them to shape. Then intervals of drying and seasoning them, reshaping and reshaping them again, making minute adjustments many times during its first months of use. Aye, Martin, the Goths may make the world's best swords and knives, but the Huns make the world's best war bows."

"A Hun gave you that bow?" I asked, amazed. "I'd have thought you were certainly no friend to any Hun."

Orestes laughed caustically, almost a snort. "*Ne*, young Martin, he did not *give* it to me. I *took* it from him."

"You *took* a bow from a Hun?"

"Well," Orestes said dryly, "not until I was sure he had no further use for it."

I considered what he had just said, and then, cautiously, so as not to insult or arouse Orestes' anger, I said, "I suppose you were, uh, quite a bit younger in those days?"

"Ja," he said, sounding not at all insulted. "That was three years ago. Before then, I had to rely on an ordinary hunting bow, such as you've seen. But enough. Now we are wasting time. I would like to make Basilea three or four days hence, and I wish to make tonight's destination before dark."

Before he swung into the saddle, Orestes went over to last night's campfire and started stirring it about.

"How come you're stoking the fire?" I asked. "I thought we were about to leave."

"We are leaving, and I am not stoking the fire," he replied, although he had laid two fresh branches on the few remaining embers and was blowing on them to set the branches" tines aflame. Shortly afterward, he handed me one of the branches. "When I travel on a day as cold as this, I always carry a firebrand and hold its flame near my mouth and inhale the warm air. Very comfortable, it is."

As we started riding – and once again I relied fully on Orestes to know the way to Basilea, he asked how I had intended to get to Basilea without him. "What do you mean, Sire?" I thought I would try the simplest honorific I knew. "I followed the directions given me by a kindly Dom in the abbey at Vesontio. He told me that as soon as I saw the high Alps on my right, I was to continue riding in the same direction until day's end, then turn left the next morning, and when the land descended, I would find my way to Basilea."

"I see," Orestes said. "And did he tell you how far left to turn?"

"Only until my back was to the high Alps. When I left Vesontio, I headed due east and three days later, I did indeed see the high Alps to my right. But then the storms started. During most of the day, the heavy clouds hid both the sun and the Alps from my sight, and at night I was so tired that I did not bother to look up for the north star."

"And has the land descended during your journey?"

"*Ne.* But the Dom did not tell me how many days it would be before the land started to descend." The horses were walking into deeper snow and I could feel my mount struggling a bit as it slogged through the powdery mass.

"I've been watching you for the past three days. Dom Clement is a good man, but he's never been beyond Aquitania and the Burgund lands. By any chance, have you felt the wind?"

"Ja," I responded. "How could I not? Since I entered the *Hrau Albos*, the damnable wind has been blowing almost all day, every day. Thank God, the wind has been at my back."

"At your back," Orestes intoned mildly. "And did Dom Clement ever tell you the direction of the wind in these forelands?"

"*Ne.*"

"I thought not," Orestes said. "The prevailing winds in the *Hrau Albos* are what the Romans called the *Aquilo* – the eagle's wind – from the Northeast. You may have come to Basilea eventually, had you gone entirely around the world – unlike most modern thinking today I believe in the theory of the ancients, that the world is a globe, not flat – but you would have approached it from the north. You have been heading south and west. In a few days, you would have been entirely lost, and most likely frozen to death in the Alps themselves."

"You've been following me for three days, and didn't even try to warn me?"

"Oh, I'd not have let you get too far into the Alps. I promised Numenior I would get you to Basilea."

"*Iésus Christos*," I muttered, using the Lord's name profanely as I had never done until then, but have done many a time since. "How does one find direction, then, when you can't see either the sun or the north star?"

"It is rather simpler than you might think," Orestes replied. "One uses a sun-stone." With that, he took something from inside his voluminous fur coat and held it out to me. It was only a piece of that common stone called *mica* in Latin, an opaline and blurrily transparent stone made up of many overlaid flaky leaves.

"It will not show you the north star," he said, "for it works only in daylight. But no matter how dark and cloudy the day, hold that to your eye and scan the heavens. If you look through the stone, most of the sky will look pink, but in the place where the sun stands unseen, the stone makes the sky look pale blue. Thus, you easily determine your direction." Indeed, many times during that bitter gray day, I asked Orestes to allow me to look through his sun-stone, and in every instance I found he'd been correct.

As the sun reached its zenith, I felt hungry and Orestes concurred that it would by pleasant to have a midday snack. I brought forth from my saddlebag a hunk of dried sausage which I'd purchased in Vesontio. Since I had not yet gone hungry, and since Orestes had indicated his intent to proceed as rapidly as possible, each of us cut small chunks from the sausage and ate it while we continued riding. The horses caught the smell of the meat, and, while they were not interested in such stuff, they, too, started combing the trees and those bushes sticking out from the snow, for something with which their own hunger might be assuaged.

Late in the afternoon, Orestes signaled me to halt. Before I could even ask why, he had swiftly brought up his bow, snatched an arrow from the quiver behind him, nocked it, bent the bow, and let fly. By the time I looked back at him questioningly, Orestes' prey had already fallen, some forty paces distant.

It was something like a goat, except that it had horns much more impressive than any goat's: thick, long, and backward-curving. I had never before seen such an animal. "An ibex," said Orestes. "They usually stay high on the peaks of the upper Alps. They only come this far down in deep winter. They're as curious as cats, which is our good fortune. Their meat is lean, since they don't fatten up to hibernate, and very tasty. We're only a short distance from the clearing where we'll stop for the night." He dismounted, asked me to help him strap the ibex onto his horse's back, and led the horse downhill to a clearing less than half a Roman mile away.

I noticed it was much warmer than it had been last night and, indeed, during this entire day. "Ach, ja," said Orestes. "We have been descending for most of the day. By midday tomorrow, we should come to the environs of Basilea."

This time, I was able to help set up the camp. I tethered the horses, and was pleasantly surprised to find long shoots of *green* grasses on the plain. I found plenty of wood and kindling nearby and stacked the wood, not as I had been used to doing, but as I had seen Orestes do the night before. I then started a fire. Not far away, under a thin sheeting of ice, I found a rill of cold, sweet water.

Meanwhile, Orestes had started skinning the ibex. I went to fetch the pot he'd used last night, but Orestes stopped me. "Not necessary," he said. "I'm removing the skin so I can cook the meat in it."

"Couldn't you sell the ibex's skin in town?" I asked.

"In summer I would. But its coarse winter coat has no real value. I can, however, get a good price for the horns."

With that, Orestes hefted the ibex's skin. I noticed he had left the hoofs and a pocket of skin at the four corners of the hide. He stuck four sticks into the ground around the fire, and used the hide's corner pockets to hang it over the blaze, fur side down. Once the fur was singed away, he filled the sagging hide with water. While that came to a boil, he brittled the carcass into wieldy chunks – brisket, ribs, plate, flank, and so on – and put those into the water. He tossed the remaining scraps into a far corner of the clearing. Shortly afterward, a number of birds and small animals descended on the scraps. "Nothing need go to waste in nature," Orestes said.

Once again, my mouth watered as the delectable aroma wafted from the skin pot, and the bubbling water darkened, and the bobbing chunks of meat turned from red to brown. At last, Orestes prodded a piece of meat with his knife and pronounced it done. It was, indeed, done, and done to perfection. It was so tender we did not have to gnaw at all and hardly had to chew. We had only to lip it off the bones. We gorged ourselves on it, but we could not finish all there was. Orestes set some by for the morning, and hung other bits over the fire to smoke and cure for carrying with us. Then, well and fully fed, we rolled into our furs for the night.

~ ∫ ~

That same night, totally unknown to me of course, Joan had been wandering through the streets of Basilea and had noticed three men talking at a corner of one of the side streets. Two of them were much older, but the third, who did little more than nod at what they said, was about her own age, blond, tall, and, to her eyes, very handsome. She found herself trembling, and strange, most unmanly thoughts assailed her as she walked slowly back to her lodging.

CHAPTER 16

Eventually, we came to the River Birse. It was nothing more than a small stream at the point where we reached it, and it was frozen all the way across, just like any of the other mountain brooks and rills. We followed the Birse downstream, and where it joined that great river, the Rhenus, we came in sight of Basilea. My first view of the city was the ruin of a garrison, built on a terrace that towered high above the rivers' junction.

Orestes explained to me that here the westward-flowing, narrow and rapid Rhenus makes an abrupt bend to flow northward, and also widens into a broad and easy-running river. So here was the upstream limit of navigation on that much traveled river that stretched all the way north across Europe to the Germanic Ocean.

"Five hundred years ago, Basilea was only a small and minor Roman garrison town," Orestes said. "These Roman fortress towns were all alike in the way they grew and developed over time. The walled camp occupied the most prominent and easily defensible place. It was encircled by ramparts, sentry towers, ditches, moats, thorny hedges, and other such barriers. Immediately outside those barricades, villages, then towns, then even cities grew up, divided by streets into blocks, market squares, and other elements of a real town. No doubt, these towns started out as merely the shanty booths of camp followers who peddled commodities that the Roman army did not always provide for its troops – rich foods, good wine, cheap women, and lusty entertainments, but as time went on these *cabanae* became the cornerstones of the civic community."

"Sire," I said, and with sincerity, "I mean no offense, but I am flabbergasted by your knowledge of … well … everything about *everything*, from a woodsman to an expert on military matters, to languages, to — "

"*Ne*, young Martin, I am none of the above. But when you have resided on earth for sixty-eight summers, as I have, you simply absorb things by keeping your eyes, your ears, and mostly your mind active and inquisitive. Although, I must say I fancy myself fairly well-read in Roman military history."

In that offhand way, I learned how old Orestes truly was. My mind reeled back to things he had told me during the journey. I had no reason to doubt anything he had said, but that meant he must have been well into his middle sixties when he had taken his war bow from a Hun. I could certainly testify to his speed and skill and stamina when he had rescued me from the Huns a scant few days ago. My God! What must he have been like when he was my age?

There were two broad, well-kept roads leading into Basilea from the south and from the southeast. "The center of the city has, of course, expanded northward these last several hundred years, but before we come to the center, I'd like to show you parts of the old garrison town that have somehow survived."

We turned onto a street far narrower than those we'd recently traversed. Although it was cracked and in disrepair in most places, there was still evidence of the military road that had, at one time, been a pride of the Roman Empire. The street led uphill. As we approached the half-ruined fortress atop the terrace, we rode a zigzag path that led through thorn thickets bridging the ditches, and trapfalls – a path easy enough for a pedestrian to negotiate, but capable of stopping any headlong charge of either foot or horse soldiers.

Finally, Orestes and I stood at the base of a high wall. Just one side of it was some four hundred paces from corner to corner. The wall, though constructed of stone or brick, was faced on the outside with a heavy layer of peat turf. "To soften the shock of even a battering ram," Orestes said. "This fortress was built in the days of Valentinian, the long-ago emperor under whose reign the fort had been established. It was headquarters to the Legio XI Claudia.

"Calculate how old this fortress is, young Martin," Orestes said. "It is now the middle of December 831. This garrison was established in the third year of the reign of the emperor Valentinian, just before he served as co-emperor with Gratianus – that would have been in 367."

I mentally calculated in my head. Four hundred sixty-five years. Twenty-one times my lifetime. Nearly seven times *Orestes'* lifetime. Once upon a time, young men my own age ate, drank, fought, impregnated other human beings who gave birth, and died. Men and women with the same wants, desires, needs, pleasures, and pain as every other man or woman who has, to this day, lived and died, and who, for all I know, will continue to do so until time out of mind. I was silent, unable to answer Orestes, overcome by the moment. Orestes, wise as he was, must have known this, and allowed me my time and my silence.

We rode back down the hill without a word.

~ ∫ ~

"Is this a night for carousing or a quiet one for catching up on the news between you young men?" Orestes asked.

"I think the latter, General," Joan spoke. "But don't let us stop you from doing what you planned to do, whatever that may be."

"*General*?" I gasped, astonished. "Is that the name you've given him? I've been calling him 'Master' or simply 'Sire.'"

"No, Martin, he truly is a general – more than that, actually."

As the story unfolded, I could barely contain myself, consumed as I was with admiration, astonishment, and, most of all, awe. Orestes seemed almost embarrassed by the attention, but it was plain to see that Joan had spoken truthfully, for everywhere we went – in the fine *deversorium* where we stayed, in every *caupona* or tavern, even when we walked in the street, well-dressed burghers, churchmen, and mostly military men of every petty king or nation respectfully doffed their hats, bowed, or simply gave the humble sign of the cross.

"General Gallianus has been retired for eighteen years," Joan began.

"My employer passed away, and after thirty-two years, I didn't feel the need to stay on with the new management," Orestes said quietly.

"Orestes is a shade too modest," Joan continued. "His former employer was a tall gentleman by the name of *Karl der*

Grosse – in English Charles the Great, in French *Charlemagne*. An emperor usually needs an army to ensure that he becomes an emperor – and that he stays an emperor – and an army needs a single Field Marshal – a general of generals."

"And General Gallianus – Orestes – was that Marshal?" I stammered.

"For the last half decade of Charlemagne's reign," Joan replied. "Before that, he'd been a mere General for a dozen years."

"I never knew," I said, looking directly at Orestes, then looking down at the floor. "I am humbled, Your … Highness? Excellency?"

"Orestes, if you will. Joannes, has had little trouble calling me what he wills."

We had moved into the *taberna*. A waiter silently brought us a fine Burgund wine. Orestes sipped thoughtfully. "There's only one thing wrong with retirement, and growing old," he said. "The Army of Charlemagne ceased to exist the day after I retired. The greatest armed force of our age, dashed in an instant, and me left with nothing more than memories, prestige that is dying as slowly and steadily as my former comrades-in-arms. The Romans said, '*Sic semper Gloria*,' and they were right.

"Year by year by year, there are changes," he continued, sad, but not maudlin. "The road to glory comes to a sudden end. The hurrahs of your troops, the sound and sight of an army on the march, the human stink of the campground or the barracks, filled with unwashed bodies, nervousness, young vigor unassuaged, excitement, life. All gone in the blink of an eye, and you're suddenly left with nothing but a chest full of medals and awards, children grown and gone – children you didn't take the time to know because you were on the battlefield, or in a faraway land. Then, slowly, slowly, it all starts to die a little more. Eight years ago, my Karenna – we'd been married forty-five years and, I say it proudly, I never strayed from our marriage bed."

"But surely you've kept active," I interjected. "Physically you look like a young man."

"One can put on an act for awhile – four, even five days, if the need arises. I exercise and I eat sparingly and try to maintain my condition as best I can. But when I rise up each morning, the aches in my body – in my shoulders and elbows, my knees and my neck – remind me that I am fighting harder each and every day just to try stay where I was the day before."

"You must be known to everyone." Joan said. "You don't seem poverty-stricken."

"My late ruler ensured I would never want for anything. He put by a retirement for me with the Helvetii bankers, who seem immune to every war and rebellion and revolution. And," he chuckled gently, "I am known to your bishop Numenior, who, if he is not quite my age, is at least of my generation."

As the evening wore on, we talked – or rather Orestes talked, while Joan and I listened in rapt attention – until some hours after the sun had gone down.

"All right, young fellows," the general finally said. "It's been a long day for you, and an even longer ten days for me. I was able to find separate rooms for each of us, which I hope you'll find to your liking. I trust we'll all sleep in late tomorrow, but let us meet at midday to discuss where – and how – the two of you will travel from here.

~ ʃ ~

Joan and I spent half the night talking with one another. Her passage to Basilea had been unobserved, and she was far more interested to hear of my rather wayward journey to the same place. She speculated on what might have happened had the Huns discovered her true sex.

"Ah, but didn't you tell me men and women are the same?" I remarked.

"Oaf!" she said, but laughing. "Did you have to take me entirely at my word? I said we shared the trait of being human. From the way you speak, the Huns may have seemed a bit less than human."

"Aye," I said.

"But both of us had the good fortune to meet Orestes," she said. "I'd certainly give what money I have to hear some of his life adventures. Of course, he's not hesitated to share many of them with me already. Have you ever noticed how old people are like that?"

"I have. He's never been at a loss for words since I met him. Still, I've learned a lot from him since he rescued me."

"It seems that older men – and older women, too, so far as I know – want to somehow shield us from discovering on our own what life is all about," she said.

"That's true. But sometimes the things they say make sense. It might be worth listening to what Orestes says, since some things may indeed make it easier to deal with our future. Speaking of which, have you changed your mind about going all the way to Athens?"

"*Ne*," Joan said. "Other than your harrowing experience, we've not encountered anything out of sorts. It should be quite easy from here."

How wrong Joan was. There were to be many events along the way, and had I know what was to befall us... But then, what human being ever knows what life holds?

CHAPTER 17

We decided to spend the winter in and around St. Gallen, the largest city on Lake Brigantinus – the Germans call it the *Bodensee* and the French and Saxons call it *Lake Constance* – a short and pleasant ride down the Rhenus. Four small kingdoms come together there, and each maintains its capital on the shores of the lake. St. Gallen is situated at the southwest corner of the lake.

Orestes, was in no hurry to depart, he having found two pairs of young ears who hung on his every word. He, in turn, was a master guide to the area. At one point, the three of us stopped beside the falls of the Rhenus, a grand, high, and tumultuous cataract that spanned the entire breadth of the river in three successive tiers. They were quite dramatic – rainbowed in daylight and moonbowed at night. What gives pleasure to one does not necessarily give pleasure to another. Watermen, in their shallow skiffs, found the falls a great nuisance. They plied up and down the stream. Coming from either direction, the boatmen had to unload their goods and portage them up or down the riverside around the falls, and then wait for another skiff to arrive from the other direction, when the two crews would exchange vessels to keep going. There were permanent skiff houses built above and below the falls, to shelter men and freight if they had to wait for long.

"*Ja*, it is a splendid sight," Orestes said. "But yonder, on the other side of the river, is the Black Forest, where you'll travel in about a month. It is no blacker than any other dense forest, but that has been its name since time out of mind. And in there, some minor streams unite to become the beginning of a far mightier river than this Rhenus. That river is called the Danuvius, and it flows all the way from the Black Forest to the Black Sea. Winter or summer, you can always find boats large enough to easily accommodate you and your steeds as far as Singidunum, for the river flows ever downstream."

As he was talking, my mind's eye pictured the codex maps that Bishop Numenior had shown us, and my mind boggled at the thought of the legendary, places we'd see: Passau and Juvavum, Lentia and Vindobona, Aquincum and, yes, Singidunum – maybe even the fabled Iron Gate itself. As much as I enjoyed Orestes, and as much as I treasured everything he taught me, I was eager to be enroute to what I believed would be my destiny, beyond the abbey, beyond the security of the *Schola*, to places where I would be responsible to and for only Joan and myself.

~ ∫ ~

Orestes helped keep us busy all through that winter. Sometimes he accompanied us, other times he suggested we strike out on our own. Much as I relished Joan's company, there were times when I wanted to be by myself.

I missed the flirtations, the chase, and those feminine wiles that, despite what Joan said, underline the basic differences between a man and a woman. As feminine as Joan might be once she shed her identity as Brother Joannes Angliorum, I cannot deny it was more exciting for me to gaze upon a half-revealed pair of creamy breasts rising from the low-cut bodice of a serving wench, or to the flush on the face of a woman alighting from a *carruca* when she saw me gazing in rapture at the turn of a half-hidden ankle or thigh, than it was to walk side-by-side with someone dressed in the shapeless habit of a monk or Church scholar.

Several nights during the time we were in Basilea or its environs, I did not return to the *hospitia* where we were ensconced, but rather spent these nights in the arms of more than one fragrant and truly feminine woman, of differing ages and states of matrimony. Each one of these females was, in her own way, exciting, noisy, and appreciative.

I do not know how Joan occupied herself during those times. But, as both of us would find out much sooner than I thought, Joan would become involved in a relationship – one that would ultimately lead to great tragedy, and one in which we proved our loving friendship for one another. It happened some time later during our next month in St. Gallen.

Chapter 18

St. Gallen was one of the wealthiest cities I had yet come across. I am told it has been that way for hundreds of years, since the days of the Roman Empire. Small wonder, for it is not only situated on Lake Constance – where the Rhenus is navigable in both directions, but it is also located at the confluence of several ancient Roman roads, which have been kept in remarkably good repair, and several recent roads, which, it seemed, had not been kept in such good repair. There were even roads that still traversed the passes through the High Alps and went all the way to Rome.

The lake itself, though large enough to be called the Swabian Sea, is not my favorite body of water. Since it has no nearby mountains to shelter it, the least wind makes it turbulent and storms are frequent and scarifying. Even on a calm and sunny day, the lake seems to be sullen and brooding. But the land surrounding the lake is pleasant, even cheerful. I found well-tended vineyards and trim orchards, and colorful fragrant gardens starting to bloom, even in late January.

St. Gallen itself does not stand on a hill, and its only view is of the melancholy lake. The inhabitants of the city are descended from the Helvetii, once a wandering and warlike people, who long ago settled down when they learned that instead of making war, they would do far better to make a profit from those who made war. Indeed, by making neutrality a vocation, they profit far more from wars than any victors do.

Of course, because it flourished by trade with many nations – indeed, such trade was often called "gray trade," because even if nations may, from time to time, have been at war with one another, one still needed what the other produced – there were times when the residents seemed vastly outnumbered by transient visitors, who hailed from every empire, kingdom, even fiefdom for that matter, in Europe and Asia and Africa. So staid and smug and fat were these people that they were on the receiving end of foreigners' snide ridicule, never spoken to the Helvetii, who were known to have precious little sense of humor.

Although Orestes ranged between Basilea and St. Gallen during the latter part of the winter of 831-832, we saw him less and less. In retrospect, I believe he was gently weaning us from himself, the better to enable us to prepare for the long journey that lay a few weeks hence.

I have always enjoyed exploring a new city on foot, for it is only when you are not rushing about and when you are close to the ground that you can see and hear, and, mostly, allow the feel of a place to surround you, and you can really learn about the people's habits, their mores, their jokes, and what is going on at the moment in the environs. I learned during my later days in the service of Mother Church that the best informed person is the one who is least noticed, one who can blend in with his surroundings, and who listens much more than he talks.

So it was that I found myself wandering about St. Gallen, getting to know that city. I soon discovered, from what I overheard in public places, that St. Gallen's citizens were in a state of some commotion. The permanent residents of the city were excited – or at least as excited as I'd ever seen the stolid Helvetii be – over the matter of choosing a new priest for the city's Basilica of St. Beatus. Its old priest had recently died, supposedly of a surfeit of beer. The matter of deciding on a new priest was on almost everyone's lips, and I, as always, was inquisitive. So, whenever I heard anyone discussing the subject in a language I could comprehend, I would loiter in the vicinity and listen.

"I shall nominate Schweitzermann," said one of a group of middle-aged men, all of whom looked exceedingly prosperous and well fed, and all of whom were speaking Latin. "He has long wanted to be something more than a successful and tightfisted merchant."

"An excellent choice," said another man. "Schweitzermann owns more business establishments and warehouses – he employs more commoners and purchases more slaves – than any other proprietor in St. Gallen."

"There are rumors from the other end of the lake," said a third man, "that Lindau and Brigantium may also soon be needing a new priest. Suppose those people should think of Schweitzermann? *Per Christo*," he continued, "Schweitzermann has wanted a priesthood – any priesthood – so long and so badly that he would move all his holdings to any dog-skeit excuse for a town if he were offered a priesthood."

"We must keep him here at all costs," the first man, who seemed to be the most senior of the group, concluded. "We must offer him the *stola!*"

And so it was that some days later, when it was announced throughout the town that Schweitzermann had been offered – and had accepted – the noble appointment, my curiosity took

me to the Basilica of St. Beatus – not a very noble edifice, if
I may be blunt – to watch the investment of the new priest.
Schweitzermann was, like the men I had heard talking about
him, of middle age, of amply well-fed girth, and nearly bald. He
would not have to shave his head to display a tonsure. He was
also beardless, and when I came close to him, I could discern
that he powdered his face to dull what would have been an
oily sheen about his head.

Without stammering, modest bobbing of his head, or
awkward shuffling of his feet, Schweitzermann announced his
acceptance of the priesthood in a strong voice that emphasized
that the great honor was nothing more than his due, and,
indeed, overdue at that. He had not condescended to dress
humbly in a robe and cowl. No, the new priest was dressed
as what he was and what he would always be – a peddler of
the products of others' labor – a very successful, rich, vain,
and preening peddler. It would have been offensive, even to
his merchant friends and colleagues and sycophants – and
especially to his competitors – to see the pure and simple white
stola draped across both his shoulders, over his expensive and
gaudy clothes.

He concluded the opening remarks of his priesthood
thus: "In reverence to that long-ago saint, I am adopting the
cognomen *Petrus* as my priestly name. I shall henceforth
be your stern but adoring father, *Tata Petrus*. However, as
required by tradition, I ask if there is any single person among
this congregation who challenges my fitness for this priestly
service."

The church was packed chockablock, as they say,
but no one in the congregation raised his voice. That was
understandable, since the entire congregation consisted of
eminently practical Helvetii, all engaged in commerce, and the

man standing before and above them could, with no more than a glance of rebuke, have withered any parishioner's business prospects forever.

To my surprise, *ne* to my astonishment, I heard a strong voice raised from the far corner of the church. As I glanced quickly around, I saw it was, of all people, Orestes, to whom I'd thought we'd bidden farewell not more than two nights ago, and I gaped as he called loudly up to the altar: "Dear father, dear *Tata* Petrus, how do you reconcile your Christian principles with the fact that this city owes so much of its prosperity to the perpetual waging of war between various factions of the empire? Will you preach against that?"

"I will not!" *Tata* Petrus snapped. He cast a withering glare in Orestes' direction, clearly intending to intimidate and humiliate my friend. "Christianity does not forbid the making of war, so long as it is a *just* war. Since every war has its end in peace, and since peace is a divine blessing, then every war can be called just."

Petrus solicited no further challenges. Orestes smiled – as smug a smile as I had seen on the faces of the merchants. Tata Petrus continued. "Before I pronounce the Dismissal of this service, my sons and daughters, I beg leave to read to you a section from the Epistles of Paul."

Schweitzermann had cunningly culled from the saint's letters to please his fellow tradesman and, in case some visiting noble was present, to flatter him appropriately.

"St. Paul spaketh thus: 'Let every man abide in the same calling in which he was called. Whosoever are servants under the yoke, let them count their masters worthy of all honor, lest the name of the Lord and His doctrine be blasphemed. Let every soul be subject to higher powers, for those that are, are ordained by God. Render therefore to all men their dues.

Tribute to whom tribute is due; custom to whom custom; fear to whom fear; honor to whom honor.' So says the sainted Paul."

By now, I was edging my way through the captivated crowd, to be early out the door, and perhaps to share a last farewell with my friend. I concluded that St. Gallen had acquired not only the priest it wanted, but one that it fully deserved. He was coming to the end of his address: "Let St. Augustine speak the only homily on that text: 'It is you, Mother Church, who makes wives subject to their husbands and sets husbands over their wives. You teach slaves to be loyal to their masters. You teach kings to rule for the benefit of their people, and it is you who warn the peoples to be subservient to their kings.'"

In my haste to be first out the door, I was saddened to see that Orestes had departed long before me and was nowhere to be found. But as I reached the door, I collided with a young man who was also evidently eager to escape. We backed apart, murmured apologies, and motioned to one another to go first, stepped forward together, collided again, laughed, and then carefully departed side by side. And that was how I came to meet Torvald.

~ ʃ ~

During the next week, Torvald and I walked through St. Gallen for hours at a time. We always made it a point to meet at the Basilica, usually shortly after midday. We talked comfortably about everything. Indeed, I cannot recall making such a close friend so quickly, save perhaps Nicola. Torvald was as congenial a young fellow as ever I'd met. He was a year younger and half a hand taller than me. He was well built, handsome, intelligent, and of almost unfailingly cheerful demeanor. It seemed strange to me that he never seemed to have any friends. I could not make out whether he shunned every other person of his own age or whether they shunned him. All I know is that not once did he greet anyone in the streets of St. Gallen, and not once did anyone greet him in return.

Torvald made no secret that he was, by any standard, on the lowest rung of St. Gallen's societal ladder. He was a day laborer. Each morning at cockcrow, he would line up with other hopefuls to secure such employment as might be needed – spreading manure in the fields; standing neck-deep in a pit filled with rancid urine and other smelly ingredients in a tannery; carrying splintery boards or heavy pipes to construction sites. He worked until noon, then washed himself clean of whatever odors hung about him, then met me in front of the church.

I could not, for the life of me, understand why someone as obviously bright and attractive as Torvald should ever have accepted these dismal occupations, or why his superiors had never promoted him to some more estimable position, or why he toiled uncomplainingly in these menial tasks, or why he seemed reconciled to working in this fashion for the rest of his life.

Every merchant in St. Gallen should have been fighting to hire him as a welcomer of customers, to put them at their ease before the merchant himself would slither out to handle the hard haggling. Torvald would have made a superb welcomer. But since he did not volunteer any information and he was my new friend, I thought it best not to enquire.

There was only one aspect of Torvald that not only bewildered me, but troubled me. Now and again – and we might be joking about a small thing, or munching on a sweet roll, or even mock wrestling – Torvald would suddenly stop still, look solemn, or even worried, and ask me something like, "Martin, did you see that orange bird that just flew past?"

"Ne, Torvald, I saw no bird at all. I have never seen an orange bird in all my life."

Or he might remark, "What a strong, icy wind that was," at a time when I'd not only felt no wind at all, but no nearby bush or tree had so much as rustled its leaves. It was not until after Torvald had seen or heard several times something that was imperceptible to me that I noticed something else about him. On each of these occasions, he would draw his thumbs so tightly against his palms that it seemed his hands had only four fingers apiece. Even more disturbing to me, at that moment and without another word, Torvald would go running off – it seemed very painfully so – and I would not see him again for the rest of the day. Then, when next we met, he never offered any explanation or apology for his odd behavior and his abrupt departure from my presence. Each time, he acted as if he had totally forgotten having behaved in that manner, and that was even more mystifying.

I discovered Torvald's terrible secret in a most unusual manner. It was a Sunday, and he and I had gone to a small hill overlooking Lake Constance for an idle picnic on an idle day. As we were companionably munching on our bread and cheese, Torvald suddenly said, "Listen, Martin. I hear an owl hooting."

I laughed. "An owl awake at midday? I do not think so."

And then Torvald got an anguished look on his face, and his thumbs curled tight against his palms. This time, just before he ran away from me, he uttered a gasping moan, a cry of ultimate pain. And this time, mayhap because of this dolorous cry, I chased after him.

Torvald was taller than me and could easily have outrun me, but I caught up with him not far from the lake, because he had fallen to the ground there. Clearly, he had run only far enough to find a place of concealment before he succumbed to the convulsion that now had him in its grip. He was not thrashing about. He lay on his back and his body was as rigid as a rock, but his head, arms, and legs were in spasm, all quivering at the same time. His face was so contorted that I would not have recognized it. His eyes were rolled back in his head so that only the whites showed. His tongue was thrust far out of his mouth, and excessive saliva spilled out around it. He also stank revoltingly, for he had voided both urine and feces.

I had never seen such a convulsion before, but I knew what it was – the falling sickness. Our infirmarian at Tours had told us what those fits were like, and he had given us the simplest instruction in what we could do to help someone if we should be nearby when he or she fell into such a state. So now I followed those instructions. I broke a twig from a nearby tree and, braving Torvald's horrible smell and appearance, went to him and thrust the twig between his upper teeth and his tongue, to prevent his biting it off. I had a small sack of salt in my waist wallet. I took a small pinch of it and sprinkled it on Torvald's outthrust tongue, since I'd been told that it would help if it somehow trickled down his throat. I took my short knife out of its sheath and wedged the cold blade under one of Torvald's clenched thumbs. The brother infirmarian had advised that cold metal pressed against the victim's hand would help the seizure pass. Finally – and this was the most difficult of all – breathing through my mouth to try to keep Torvald's abominable smell out of my nostrils, I pressed my hands on his abdomen and held the pressure there – another lesson I had been taught.

Eventually, Torvald's abdominal muscles relaxed under my hands. His arms and legs ceased their quivering, his eyes rolled into their normal position and wearily closed, his tongue retracted into his mouth, and his face was that of my friend Torvald once again. He lay there, breathing raggedly. Plucking a handful of grass, I wiped the spittle that had slimed his face, his chin, and his neck. I couldn't do anything about his other excretions, so I retreated to a tree some distance away, and found my own breathing was rather ragged as I inhaled deeply of the clean air around me.

Gradually, Torvald's breathing slowed to normal. He opened his eyes and looked up and down, then to either side, seemingly trying to determine where he was and how he had gotten there. Then, he raised himself to a sitting position and, looking further afield, he caught sight of me. I had rehearsed in my mind what I would say, for I fully expected him to grimace in embarrassment or distress at my having witnessed his seizure. Instead, astonishingly, he smiled brightly and called out to me, as if our mealtime conversation had never been interrupted, "Well, Martin, what were we just talking about? I seem to have forgotten –"

I had often wondered, when at other times we met again after one of his disappearances, whether he had forgotten having done so, or merely preferred to appear that he had forgotten. Now I knew that he truly had no remembrance of anything that had happened on those occasions, because it was clear to me that Torvald had no least recollection of his mention of that nonexistent owl, of his having cried out and dashed away, of the agonies he had gone through down by the lake, or of how much time had passed since we had sat on the hill and talked.

Torvald got to his feet stiffly, for his muscles must have been painfully cramped by their recent state, and started to trot over to me. But when he stood up, he must have gotten a whiff of his stench, and he stopped as if lightning had struck. His face crumpled with dismay and self-disgust, and he shut his eyes tightly and shook his head in ultimate sadness. He said, so quietly that I barely heard him, "You saw. Goodbye, Martin. I'm going to wash." He stalked stiffly off toward the lake, taking care to walk well away from me.

When he returned, he was dripping from his newly washed tunic, but at least he'd washed thoroughly, and there was no abiding odor. He saw me still sitting against the tree. He looked genuinely surprised. "Martin! You did not leave?"

"Why should I?"

"Everyone who has ever learned of my – learned about me – has stayed away from me. Surely you must have wondered why I have no friends. I used to have, from time to time, but I lost them all."

"Then I would hardly call them friends," I said. "Is that why you work in the mean occupations?"

He nodded. "No one else would hire a worker who might fall into a fit in public view. I don't know anyone where I work now, and if I drop, I run away and then my employer need not even pay me." He laughed bleakly. "Perhaps one day I shall drown in that ghastly liquid in the tannery pit. It would be a fitting end – never known, never seen, never loved."

I felt myself choking up. I said, "I once knew an infirmarian at a *schola* I attended in Aquitania. He told me that if one regularly drinks a concoction of darnel grass seeds, it supposedly makes one's attacks milder or less frequent."

"I tried that for awhile," Torvald said, "but one can never measure the dosage properly, and too heavy a dosage can be a lethal poison."

At that moment, I had a sudden flash of inspiration. Joan. Joan, who had learned early on of all manner of medicaments and brews and curatives. Of all the people who could possibly help my friend ... Why not?

Torvald was talking, albeit sadly. "I had not much success, and, monstrosity though I might be, I would prefer to be a live monster than a dead one."

"Don't say that!" I snapped. "Some of the greatest men in history have suffered from the falling sickness all their lives – Alexander, Julius Caesar, even Saint Paul. It did not hinder them being great men."

"Well," Torvald said with a sigh. "There is a remote chance that I may not have it for my entire life."

"How say you?" I said. I thought it was an incurable ailment.

"I have heard that for someone who has been afflicted since birth, as I have, ... well, they say that it will disappear when a girl has her first menstruum or a boy his ... his ... sexual initiation." Torvald blushed deeply. "Which I have not had."

"If that is true, why in the world have you remained a virgin for so long?"

"Do not mock me, Martin," he replied miserably. "Just what female could I have lain with? Every woman on the whole of Lake Constance must know about me. Parents warn their girl-children to keep away from me. No female would risk my impregnating her with a child that might inherit my affliction."

"Surely a woman of the night?"

"Not even that. Every prostitute has refused me, either from fear of catching my disease or for fear that I might go into convulsion in the middle of the act and somehow injure her."

God help me for my thoughts at that moment. Torvald was very comely, and he was doomed to a life of such tragedy as to me would be unimaginable. Yet I had found him to be kind and caring to every living soul, and he had been a real friend even in the brief time we'd known one another.

I have previously said that I had sated my own sexual appetites on this journey. My truly closest friend, Joan, had said, so long ago when we were leaving Angle-land for Aquitania that she could take care of her own needs. And, as time went on, she confided to me that she indeed had those needs.

CHAPTER 19

"You're asking me to shed my cassock as a man of God and become a whore?" she said, with surprising calm.

"*Ne*, Joan. You've heard the entire story. I would no more betray you than I would myself. He said 'a possible cure.' You've no idea in what agony this young man has lived his entire life. If nothing else, he would go to his death knowing … knowing …"

"Lest you forget, I am a *brother* in Christ. Or how would you explain that to your friend?"

"He must never know your, uh, other identity. Besides, it might even be a novelty to you. Have you ever dressed as a woman?"

At that, Joan became snappish. "A 'novelty?' How like a man to say such a stupid thing. You've no idea how a … how a woman thinks. Besides, my private activities are my business, not yours, and I'll trouble you not to ask me again."

"I meant no harm," I said, shuffling uncomfortably in the wooden chair, one of only three accoutrements – a bed, a chair, and a small desk – in her room. "Indeed, you need not minister to him in that way at all. You are wise in the way of roots and drugs and medicines and such. And if you are of God – be it as a man or a woman – surely you must have some compassion for the suffering of another."

"Is there any way I could see this ... this person? It's one thing for a man to say that another man is good-looking. A woman has a different perspective on such things."

"Aye, that is possible," I said. "Tomorrow afternoon, I will arrange for Torvald to meet me outside the inn. We will walk to the end of the street, then I will tell him I have forgotten something and return to my room for a few moments. That should give you a sufficiently close look at him."

And so it was, and so it went.

The next evening, when I returned to Joan's room to speak with her, she was so pale I thought she was ill. When she stood to embrace me, as friends embrace, she was wobbly and trembling. "Joan, are you all right?" I asked. "Shall I fetch a *medicus*?"

"*Ne*, Martin, I am not all right, and you must not fetch a *medicus*."

"What do you mean? You talk in riddles."

"Martin, I know your friend Torvald. I ... I have seen him before."

"What? Where? And does that mean that my friend is lying when he says he is virgin?"

"*Ne*, my friend. Listen, and as you have never betrayed my trust in the past, I ask that you not do so now. Anastasius was an aberration, a challenge, a dare, a child grasping at forbidden fruit, and in the end he used me like he's no doubt used many others. I have always thought of myself in complete control of my actions and my desires. I always thought I would rise high in the Church or in any other endeavor I wanted.

"But one evening, shortly before you came to Basilea, I was wandering through the streets of Basilea and noticed three men talking at a corner of a side street. Two of them were much older, but the third, who seemed to stand apart from them, was my age, and for the first time in my life, I felt faint with … with desire. I can't say it any other way. It was as though I'd had too much wine. I felt similar to the way I feel at this moment."

"Why do you need to tell me that, my friend?" I said, and in my knowledge of Joan I knew what she was going to say even before she half-whispered it.

"Your friend Torvald … he is the young man I saw that night."

~ ʃ ~

Of their introduction to one another, there is not much to say, and the years have dulled the memory. I had told Torvald that my cousin from Angle-land had lately come into town – on what pretext or other, I now forget.

I remember that Joan had abandoned her cassock, and when she came down to meet Torvald, she looked more stunning than I had ever seen her, before or since. She was wearing a woven blouse of fine material, with a rather low neckline. Somehow, an ingenious tailor or seamstress had cut the material so that it opened to a deep "v" far below her throat. Toward the top, two narrow leather thongs depended from each side of the neck. Joan had tied them together. Thus, while it was very easy to imagine what she looked like below her neck, you could not actually see her breasts. She wore a leather skirt and soft leather boots. Her short blonde hair framed her face well, and she wore a light fragrance.

For the barest instant, I suffered the pangs of harsh jealousy, for she had never, in all the time I'd known her, presented herself like that to me. But my better heart prevailed, as I realized that this might be the only opportunity Torvald would have for any small shred of happiness in his entire, blameless life.

No one in the world could possibly have confused this beauteous creature with the handsome, but unspectacular Brother Joannes Angliorum. After the brief introduction, Joan and Torvald, who was radiant, left the inn together in animated conversation.

Within moments of their departure, it being early afternoon, I left the inn for purposes of my own. Had I looked more carefully, I might have seen that Orestes had not yet left us.

~ ∫ ~

Joan did not return that night, nor the day after that, nor the day after that. Needless to say, I did not see Torvald at all during that time. When she finally returned to the inn, Joan looked nothing like she had looked when I had last seen her and she had traipsed out with Torvald. The blouse no longer had strings to mask the imagination. She looked flushed and she walked with a slight limp. When she greeted me, her voice was hoarse, a bit raw. Yet, if anything, she looked even more ravishing, even more desirable, than when I'd last seen her.

I have found through the years, and even now in my imprisonment, with my flesh mortifying and nothing to look forward to, I still find that a woman is at her absolute most beautiful after she has lain with a man, and has climaxed again and yet again. Joan looked that way now.

"Do you want to talk about it?"

"Tomorrow, Martin," she said. "If you please." She climbed the steps to her room gingerly, as if in exquisite pain.

~ ∫ ~

"It was wonderful, then?"

"You've no idea," she said dreamily. "We never left the bed except to eat and do the natural things for three whole days. It was … everything I've ever believed a woman could experience and more."

"I suppose I should be furious, jealous, all of those horrid feelings?"

"No more than I should be with you. Or do you think I was totally ignorant of your own dalliances?" I started to protest, but she laughed gaily. "Oh, don't worry, Martin, you'll always be my closest friend in the whole world."

"So you'd have me abandon my cassock and become your whore?" I mimicked her.

In answer, she took two pillows from her bed and hurled them at me. Before long, we were wrestling on the bed, like brother and sister, not like lovers, and I must admit it was fun, and we laughed and giggled, and rolled some more. After awhile, I lay back on the bed and she sat on the adjacent chair.

"Martin," she said seriously. "I've been giving a lot of thought to some things earlier this morning. Would it trouble you very much if I decided to settle in St. Gallen, as a woman?"

I felt a tension in the room. "You're serious?" I said. I felt a mixture of emotions, not the least of which were anger and betrayal. "After I changed my life to be with you, to be your protector, to watch you be everything you wanted to be?"

"I've thought of that," she said. "But should the decision of a child imprison the adult? I would never willingly hurt you, my Martin," she said. "But I've never known that my need to be what I truly am – a woman – could be so strong, so all-embracing."

"This after three days of bedroom activity?"

"Is that all you can think about? Torvald's different. You could never understand that. He needs me, and not just to fulfill his sexual needs, though they are voracious and never-ending. He is gentle, and sensitive to my needs, too."

"And you'd give up everything for him? Think of the life you can expect. And if there are children?"

"Martin," she said, standing and glaring at me. "I come to you for help, guidance, and comfort, and you give me lectures and morality lessons and jealous condemnation. Damn you, Martin! Damn you to hell!" She stomped out of the room, slamming the door behind her.

~ ∫ ~

An uncomfortable week went by. Joan and I avoided each other, but that did not take much effort, for Joan spent nearly her every waking hour with Torvald. When I saw them in the street together, I must acknowledge that I have rarely seen two people so much a part of each other that they were as one, oblivious to the rest of the world.

St. Gallen's streets and squares were perpetually thronged with people, but eventually I could recognize many of the permanent residents and distinguish them from the travelers and winter visitors like myself. I had reason to note two persons in particular. The street crows were usually unruly and unmannerly, pushing and shoving and elbowing each other, but they quieted immediately, bowed, scraped, indeed cringed, when a certain one of their citizens claimed passage. I did not catch sight of that person for a long time, because he always came through the streets in an immense, lavishly decorated, curtained *carruca*, its poles borne on the shoulders of eight sweating, trotting slaves, who shouted, "Make way for the Dominus Rosarius!" They made it clear that they would run over anyone who did not dodge.

When I inquired, I was told that Rosarius was the first among equals of St. Gallen, a combination of Mayor, Lord, and Master, whose status in comparison with Schweitzermann's was akin to Schweitzermann's status in comparison with Torvald's.

The second person I came to recognize was a heavyset, hulking young man with a slack, dull appearance. He was about my age. While I pondered that he must have been employed in some gainful activity, he seemed to amble about the city with no more to do than me. I never saw him do anything, except be as rude as possible to other citizens, shouldering them away, cursing and growling maliciously at them.

When I helped an elderly man whom he had rudely shoved aside so harshly that the man had fallen to the street, I asked, "Who is that lout, anyway?"

"That damnable brat is Rosariatus. He has no interest in the world besides stupid idleness and mindless brutality."

As the old fellow started to brush off the mud that had caked his tunic, I asked him, "Why don't the people band together and restrain him? I'd be willing to help, even though he be twice my size."

"Do not try, young man. None of us dares cross wills with him. He is the only child of the glorious Dominus Rosarius. Mind you, the Dominus is, himself, a modest and inoffensive man, not a tyrant. He is lenient with us, but, God help us, he is even more lenient with that misbegotten whelp. If only he had his father's mild temperament instead of that of his bitch-dragon mother. While I thank you for your assistance, the best advice I can give is for you to stay away from that devil-spawn."

And devil-spawn Rosariatus was, as I was soon to find out.

~ ʃ ~

Unknown to me, Rosariatus had developed a particular hatred of Torvald over the years, perhaps because he thought what Torvald had was catching, or perhaps because of an imagined slight. But I happened to be in the neighborhood when Rosariatus caught sight of Torvald and a very womanly Joan in the street together. I watched uncomfortably as Rosariatus' vapid eyes narrowed, then widened with a more malicious look than I had seen on any countenance save Anastasius' the night we had interrupted his attempted murder of that young girl-child.

I was more concerned when I saw the two lovers emerging from our inn one evening and walk leisurely in the direction of that hillock above the lake where I'd first learned of Torvald's affliction. Unknown to them, they were being followed by Rosariatus. On an instant, I followed them at a safe distance, if for no other reason than to protect Joan if matters came to that.

Joan and Torvald did nothing more than hold hands, lightly fondle one another, and talk of small, nothing things that lovers always talk about. Suddenly, there was a rustling in the brush nearby them, and a hoarse voice – Rosariatus' voice – roared, "You have had many a turn with that wench, Torvald, you stinking cripple. Now it's time for a *real* man to have a turn – *me*."

Rosariatus came out of his hiding place swinging a heavy wooden cudgel. I heard the simultaneous sounds of the cudgel's thud and Torvald's grunt, and my friend fairly flew off into the darkness to one side of Joan.

Next moment, I saw Joan pinned under Rosariatus' heavy, sweaty weight. He had disarranged his garments sufficiently to free his *fascinum*, and he ripped at Joan's clothing and began jabbing at her nether parts. Joan struggled and flailed, and cried out for help, but Rosariatus only laughed and lunged at her harder.

"You know you like this sport, little girl. And with me, you do not risk catching the falling sickness as you would from your freak friend, who certainly is in no position to help you. But you can help yourself to a real man. Just feel the size of my *fascinum*. Enough of your pretense. Let's get on with it."

As I shouted out and raced down the hill toward them, there was another loud thud and just as suddenly as Rosariatus had whisked Torvald away, Rosariatus himself was whisked away into the darkness. A very rattled Joan sat up and rubbed her eyes. Since I was, by now, very close, I saw her eyes widen in amazement. "Orestes! You?"

"Ah, yes, Brother Joannes," he said, his voice so gentle there was no hint of a smirk in it.

"You know?"

"I knew. Even before you and Torvald ... But I will never betray your secret, and since I am far closer to death than you, it will probably die with me ... or with our mutual friend Martin," he said, glancing in my direction.

"What of Torvald?" she asked.

"He will have a headache, but nothing worse. So will this other friend of yours. I did not bludgeon him hard enough to kill."

"Friend," Joan gasped. "That is the son of — "

"I know who he is," said Orestes. "You certainly have a talent for making unusual acquaintances. First Torvald, the city's laughingstock, now Rosariatus, the city's best-hated bastard."

As Joan rearranged her clothing, she said, contritely, "General, I never meant for you to see me thus."

"I am an old man and I have seen so much else that it would take more than anything you might do to scandalize me. Truly, I have not the slightest interest in whether you piss standing up or sitting down, or whatever else you choose to do with your private parts. Whether you are Brother Joannes or Joan the fishwife, or even, God be praised, the Pope himself, does not concern me one *ferta*."

"How did you happen to be here, Orestes? Just when we all needed your help?"

"I returned to St. Gallen a week ago. I have seen your comings and goings, and when I saw Rosariatus following you, and Martin following him, I decided there could be trouble, and something that was perhaps more than you young people could handle. What do you think we should do with the less-than-honorable Rosariatus?"

"Tie a large rock to him and sink him in the lake," Joan said hotly.

"Many people of St. Gallen would bless my efforts if I did that. But he is not your ordinary brute rapist. He is the son of the Dominus. While every inhabitant of St. Gallen, up to and including his father, might rejoice at his disappearance, there would be questions asked. And I daresay his mother's spies have almost certainly been watching him watch you, and that would lead to questions being asked of you. Not a good thing."

"So what should we do, seek justice in the courts?"

"*Ne*, Martin," he said. "A court is a place of law, not a place where you find justice. Only a weakling or a coward resorts to the law to resolve a problem involving personal honor. Rosariatus, being who he is, would instantly be acquitted." Orestes turned to Torvald and said, "You and this 'eminent personage,'" he fairly spat the words out, such was his contempt, "are of about the same age, and although he is bigger than you, he is also fatter and more slovenly. Would you agree to face Rosariatus in fair and equal and public trial by combat?"

Torvald did not hesitate. To protect the honor of his love, he would have risked anything.

"So be it," declared Orestes. "Let us escort him to the city and invoke the ancient law of ordeal by battle."

"What?" roared Rosariatus, now awake. "I, the son of Dominus Rosarius, fight hand to hand with a commoner? With the city's most contemptible simpleton? I absolutely reject such an outrageous —"

"Shut up," said Orestes, as indifferently as if he were talking to a dog. "Martin, bind his wrists with that kerchief of yours. His own belt will serve me for a leash to lead him along. Torvald, bring the cudgel that has already been used twice tonight. If our prisoner tries to escape, you know how to use it."

~ ∫ ~

That night, Joan stood in Tata Petrus' Basilica. Like most churches, that building served as a tribunal as well. She accused Rosariatus of assault and attempted rape, and asked that his guilt or innocence be adjudicated by the rite of ordeal. She asked the judges to allow Torvald to be her champion in that combat.

"I suggest, my lords," Orestes, in his full field marshal's regalia, suggested, "that the matter be settled in the city amphitheatre, so that all of St. Gallen may see justice done, and that the weapons be cudgels, since the cudgel appears to be the favorite implement of the accused."

There was considerable frowning and muttering among the judges, which was not surprising, because in addition to Joan, Torvald, Orestes, and myself, and the still kerchief-bound

Rosariatus, there was also present the Dominus Rosarius, his wife, and, of course, the church's priest, Schweitzermann / *Tata Petrus*. The Dominus' only objection to the proceedings was that Joan had gone out at night, at a time when no decent unmarried female would have done so, and thus her own morals were questionable.

The Dominus was interrupted by his wife, who barked ferociously, "And this wanton wench of a stranger dares to accuse a native citizen of our own St. Gallen, the son of our Dominus, a scion of an ancient house and the first among equals in this great city. I demand that this slanderous accusation be dismissed, that my son be absolved of all taint upon his reputation, and that this wayfaring little whore be publicly stripped naked and whipped beyond the city limits!"

There was another interruption, this time by the priest Schweitzermann, who said, silkily, "My lords, the Church does not interfere in purely civil matters, and neither will I, as a servant of the Church. But I was a St. Gallen merchant long before I became the city's priest. I beg leave to say a few words that may possibly be worth consideration in these proceedings."

I had expected the worst from this "priest," but Schweitzermann had clearly been inflated by his new position, and he astounded me by saying, "True, it is a mere and meager passing stranger who has made this grave accusation against a respected citizen of St. Gallen, but I remind you, my lords, that our St. Gallen derives its prosperity from the strangers who pass through our gates. Every citizen, from high to low, earns his profit from these strangers, the traveling merchants, the traders and purveyors. If the word were to go abroad that only St. Gallen's citizens are protected by its laws, that a stranger might here be the victim of injustice, even such a nonentity as this young vagrant whore, what, my lords, might happen to St. Gallen's prosperity? And that of yourselves? And of this, God's church? I recommend that you grant the petitioner's appeal for a trial by combat between Rosariatus and Torvald. It will relieve you of the onus of finding for or against either of the contending parties. In the rite of ordeal, it is the Lord who will be judge."

"How dare you?" screamed the bitch-dragon mother. Her husband simply stood silent. Her son began to perspire. "You frocked shopkeeper, who do you think you are, to force a member of the nobility into a vulgar public fight against an outcast and brainsick cripple, just for the sake of this worthless piece of female trash?"

"Clarissima, Your Highness." The priest addressed her respectfully but pointed a stern forefinger at her. "The duties and dignities of the nobility are truly weighty matters. But far weightier is the office of the priest, because, on the Divine Judgment Day, he must give account even for kings. Clarissima, should you excel all the rest of the human race in dignity, still your pride must bow before the stewards of Christian mysteries. When your priest speaks, it is for you to pay respect, not to dissent. I most solemnly warn you of this, and it is Christ who warns you through me."

The lady had gone quite ashen-faced and she said nothing further. Rosariatus was sweating more copiously than before. Finally, the Dominus laid his hand on his wife's arm and spoke in a mild voice. "Tata Petrus is right, my dear. Justice must be served, and in the ordeal it is God who will decide the right. Let us trust in God, and in our son's strong arm." He turned to the three judges. "My lords, I concur in the appeal. Let the combat take place tomorrow.

CHAPTER 20

Next morning, when Orestes, Joan, and I arrived at the amphitheatre, which, truth to tell, had seen much better days - *ne*, much better *centuries* – St. Gallen's entire population seemed to be at the gates, clamoring to buy tokens of admission.

The Church had long frowned on gladiatorial contests, and most of the Christian kings in the area had forbidden them. Today's combat, of course, was not being waged with the gladiator's sword or any other of the traditional weapons, but it promised to be a real blood contest, and that was certainly enough to draw a huge crowd. Those burghers would hardly have closed their markets and warehouses to mourn the death of a Dominus or Priest, but a spectacle such as this was different.

Every seat was filled. The common folk sat on the ledges of the upper tiers, now mostly crumbling or in ruins, but Orestes had paid a stiff price for the three of us to sit in the numbered seats of the second tier, usually accessible only to the noble or the wealthy. In the arena-level tier, reserved for the highest officials and dignitaries, the central podium was occupied by Dominus Rosarius, his lady, and the priest, Schweitzermann / Petrus, each of them sumptuously dressed. The Dominus was as expressionless as he had been the night before. His wife radiated white-hot fury. The priest looked as bland as cold gruel. Oily cold gruel.

It was not long before I heard a single trumpet's blast from the arena below. The crowd started to murmur and stir. Rosariatus and Torvald had emerged from gates on opposite sides of the perimeter wall. Each carried a stout ash cudgel, longer than he was tall and as thick as his wrist. Each wore only an athlete's loincloth and, over the rest of his body, a coating of oil to help slip the cudgels' blows. They approached one another in the center of the arena and then walked side by side to stand beneath the podium and raise their staffs in salute to the Dominus. Rosarius raised his right fist, in which he held a white cloth, to each of them impartially. Then, the trumpet blared again and the Dominus dropped the cloth.

Torvald and Rosariatus wheeled to face one another and took the fighting stance, each gripping his cudgel with one hand at its middle and the other hand halfway between the middle and the end. The two young men were well matched for combat. Torvald was taller and had a longer arm's reach, but Rosariatus was beefier, with more weight and muscle. Their skills with the staff also seemed to be about equal. While Torvald had never had a friend with whom to engage in mock cudgel fighting, he must have amused himself sometimes with solitary pretend-battles. Rosariatus had probably had many opportunities to compete against other young men, but since Rosariatus was who he was, those others had probably let him win easily.

Though neither of them could have stood up to a real, professional, experienced cudgel wielder, they were, to my inexperienced eyes, making a great show of swinging, parrying, thrusting, and dodging. This was not a bumbling novice performance. I looked over at Orestes, who was calmly observing the melee, no doubt with an eye far more expert than mine. He nodded as Rosariatus began to cringe and flinch and retreat.

The opponents had begun the fight by trying every stroke and move that is possible in cudgel combat, trying to find the other's courage and, more important, his weak points. Basically, the cudgel fighter's only offensive moves are the swing and the thrust, but they, too, can be delivered in different ways – a feint, for example, that suddenly becomes a thrust.

After Rosariatus and Torvald had battered at one another for some time, using all of the traditional offensive moves, and both had evidently decided on where the other was weakest, they began to concentrate on those points.

Rosariatus, whose arms were shorter, relied on swinging his cudgel rather than thrusting it, and he swung most often at Torvald's head. I think Rosariatus, who'd referred to Torvald as "brainsick," was hoping that even a glancing blow to the head would severely stun his adversary.

Torvald, for his part, soon realized that Rosariatus' squat, square body could hardly be moved by sidewise swings of the cudgel, so he began to rely on his longer reach, on lunging thrusts. He aimed alternately at the pit of Rosariatus' stomach, trying to ram the wind from his body, and at his enemy's hands, trying to break or weaken his grip on his own cudgel.

Torvald, leaner and quicker, was able to dodge or parry Rosariatus' swings toward his head, but the heavyset Rosariatus was not agile enough to avoid Torvald's thrusts. Several of Torvald's jabs to the stomach made Rosariatus utter an audible *whoosh* and stagger backward long enough to snatch a new gulp of air. Torvald also scored on his thrusts to his adversary's fingers, and once Rosariatus' right hand almost slipped from the cudgel. From then on, Rosariatus did not wield his cudgel offensively. Rather, he fought to prevent it being wrested from his grasp. He appeared to have abandoned hope of victory and tried merely to stave off defeat. Torvald pressed his advantage, forcing Rosariatus ever backward until the two of them were almost directly before the central podium.

"Look!" Joan shouted, even above the crowd. "That bastard Rosariatus is sweating the oil right off his body."

So he was. Where Rosariatus now stood, but shakily, shuffling his feet to keep his balance against Torvald's relentless pummeling, there was a stain spreading on the sand, and I do not think it consisted entirely of sweat and oil. Rosariatus was flicking his eyes frantically from side to side, seeking a refuge, or a rescue.

I glanced over to the center of the podium. The Dominus continued to sit impassively, but Rosariatus' bitch-queen mother would most willingly have swept down into the arena, belching flames at Torvald. The crowd was on its feet, most un-Helvetically screaming and jumping, and cheering and bawling.

"Well," Orestes said calmly. "It looks as though we have won. A brute bully is always a coward, and this one is publicly proving it. I am only pleased that it appears that right truly has prevailed."

Now a hefty shout went up from the crowd, "Torvald Tor-VALD! TOR-VALD!!" It echoed from one side of the stadium to the other, and in my excitement, I found myself jumping up, pummeling Orestes on the back, pounding Joan on the back.

All at once, the crowd stopped chanting in mid-word and a hush came over the throng.

Torvald stopped his battering of Rosariatus and stepped away from him. The spectators may have thought he was simply according his defeated opponent clemency, not killing him outright, not breaking his bones so he would be forever a cripple, not even beating Rosariatus until he lay prostrate on the sand and had to make a humiliating gesture of the lifted finger, pleading that his life be spared.

Of everyone assembled in that great amphitheatre, only the three of us knew the truth.

I knew it was not the thought of clemency that had motivated Torvald. He had ceased even to look at Rosariatus. His eyes slowly lifted above the arena, above the tiers of the amphitheatre, on up to the morning sky above, as if perhaps he had seen a strange orange bird fly over, or heard an owl hoot in daylight.

All through the battle, Torvald had shown no evidence of his affliction. But I had noticed that it oftenest came upon him not in moments of stress or duress, but when he was feeling happiest and most healthy. And so it did now, when he was on the verge of what would have been the culminating moment of his life. The cudgel dropped from his hands as his thumbs curled tightly into his palms. His hands were useless as hands. Rosariatus stood, staggering slightly, but his astonishment rendered him numb. Every other person in the amphitheatre was similarly stupefied, absolutely silent. Then, Torvald uttered the cry I had heard that day by the lake, and my blood turned cold. One other voice spoke, but so quietly no one but Rosariatus heard it. His mother had leaned over the balustrade and harshly whispered something to him.

Rosariatus had continued to stand bewildered, bleeding from his nose and from his almost crushed right hand, clearly unsure of what to do next, until his mother had told him. Now, suddenly, while Torvald still had his head far back and was still giving that unearthly wail, Rosariatus struck with all his strength. The cudgel caught Torvald in the throat, and he fell backward as stiffly as a tree going down under the cutter's axe.

The blow may not have killed Torvald. He might have risen to fight again, but the fit was upon him. He lay rigid and quivering as Rosariatus rained vicious blows all up and down his body. Torvald could still have made the plea for clemency, raising one forefinger, and the Dominus would have been obliged by law and tradition to halt the combat while he asked the crowd for its verdict. But poor Torvald could not even free one of his convulsion-clenched hands, not even to lift that single finger.

Torvald's quivering slowed and ceased. He was surely dead by then, but Rosariatus continued to flail at the shapeless corpse. The sight was so gruesome that the entire audience rose up, stamping their feet and chanting, "Clemency! Clemency!"

Rosariatus paused just long enough to glance toward the podium. The Dominus was about the make the traditional gesture, thumb downward, as a signal for the victor to drop his weapon, when the Clarissima boldly stepped in front of him and made the other traditional gesture – jabbing her thumb toward her breast – which, in the days of the ancient Roman Empire had meant, "Stab him!" Of course, Rosariatus obeyed his mother. While the crowd still bellowed, "Clemency!" he raised his cudgel and smashed his victim's head until it was nothing more than a pulpy mass.

At that, the crowd, which had previously been so bloodthirsty, began to bawl its sickened outrage, "Shame! Atrocity! Filthy slaughter! Bloody savage!" One more moment and I believe they would have poured out of the stands and ripped Rosariatus to pieces.

But the priest Schweitzermann was also on his feet and holding his arms high for attention. The crowd gradually quieted so he could be heard. "My people! Cease your impious protest and accept God's verdict. The Lord is just and wise and of righteous judgment. In Him there is no iniquity. God decreed that Torvald should be overcome and Rosariatus emerge victorious. Do not dare dispute the Lord's wisdom as He chose to reveal it to all of you this day. God's will be done, on earth as it is in heaven."

No one in the crowd was prepared to defy the priestly command, even though there was muttering and angry grumbling. I looked at Joan, my precious friend, who was silently, copiously weeping. And in that moment, ablaze with unbridled fury at the devil-spawn Rosariatus, the bitch-hound mother, and most of all at the unctuous, oily excuse for a priest, I conferred very quietly, very quickly, with Orestes. He nodded slowly, smiled, and got to his feet, arrayed in his full military regalia.

Orestes raised his arms high in a perfect parody of Tata Petrus' earlier motion. He did not wait for the muttering crowd to quieten any further, and those who were slowly exiting the amphitheatre were snapped back as though yanked by a strong cord. "SILENCE!" he thundered, and his voice and bearing reminded me of the prophets old. "This abomination shall not be allowed to stand!"

Schweitzermann turned a shade approaching purple. "How dare you defy Christ, you blasphemer, you — "

"But he got no further than stammering when Orestes roared yet louder, cutting him totally off. "Shut up, you pious hypocrite! You *upshtelte meisdreck!*"

The crowd, which had stood bug-eyed, staring at the two combatants, now broke into tumultuous laughter, totally unbelieving what they had heard Orestes say. Even Joan, whose lover had just been savagely killed, clapped her hand on her mouth. For Orestes had said the unthinkable and had, with one phrase, brought *Tata Petrus* down to what he truly was. The closest approximation I can give is that Orestes had called the *Tata* a piece of upraised mouse *skeit*. Literally, a piece of *skeit* who, elevated beyond his station, had assumed unwarranted airs.

"God will condemn —" the priest tried to interject, but now, for the first time ever, the crowd was not on their priest's side.

"*Ne*, unctuous merchant-risen-to-a-rank-he-bought," Orestes roared. "'Vengeance is mine,' saith the Lord. 'I will repay!'"

Now Rosariatus' bitch-mother joined the fray. "Who are you to insult St. Gallen's priest, you in your toy-soldier uniform, which you probably bought at pawn? Who are you to mock our city, you filthy, slimy foreigner? One who cavorted with that foreign whore and brought God's judgment down upon that brain-sick cripple? How dare you mock our Clarissimus, our Clarissima?"

"Listen, bitch-queen!" Orestes roared even louder, not for a moment letting his voice drop. "You have said your piece and frightened 'your' people so that they don't tell you to your face what they say behind your ugly back. In case you are neither worldly-wise nor disposed to even the rudest of manners, ask those in 'your' great city who have even the slightest knowledge of the outside world, who I am."

He was about to go on when a voice rang out from the crowd, almost as strong as Orestes' voice. "He tells the truth. I am the president-elect of the Merchants' Guild and I attest that this man is Orestes Gallianus, no less than Field Marshal to the late Karl der Grosse himself! His legions have brought wealth to our city sufficient to support it for the better part of a year!"

"But God gives no man the right to blaspheme!" shouted Schweitzermann, who would not relinquish his moral high ground without a battle.

"And no mere man has the right to assume he is equal either to God or to the Son of God," chided Orestes. "Are you going to hear what I have to say, or are you going to stand there and make yourself more of a buffoon than you already are?"

In the melee, the crowd seemed to have forgotten the bloodthirsty slaughter of only a few moments ago. This was something they had not bargained for, and they were getting double their money's worth this day. There was silence from the audience, but it was no longer shocked, scandalized, horrified silence. It was that silence that heralds interest in what is being said. The silence that comes before a revolution.

It was the Dominus who, in his quiet way, rescued the situation. When a verbal battle rages, it is invariably the man who stands at the center of the dais, silent, who attracts the attention of the crowd. And so it was. Even Orestes ceased his tirade as the Dominus spoke in a soft, clear voice. "Let the Marshal speak," Rosarius said, notably giving Orestes the respect of his honorific. "Say what you will, General."

"Thank you, Your Grace," Orestes said. "Thank you for being an island of courtesy in a storm of hypocrisy. I appeal to you and I appeal to the citizens of St. Gallen. What we have witnessed this morning was not God's will. It was savage butchery of the type that must not be inflicted on another human being, nor tolerated in any civilized society, be it St. Gallen or Constantinople, Rome or Aix la Chapelle. It was murder, plain and simple.

"By your leave, Dominus," he continued, "I am aware that Rosariatus is your son and heir, and that the words I am about to speak will torture you and potentially cause you great grief. But your duty, your *parens patria* to your subject citizens, is higher even than your desire to protect your blood.

"I accuse Rosariatus of unprovoked murder with malice aforethought. I demand trial by battle, not by cudgel, but as God intended, by hand-to-hand combat with no weapon but the human body. Of course, it would be an unfair fight were I to take on this whelp myself."

The crowd was thoroughly enjoying this show and started to laugh. For Orestes was, in appearance, an old man, one whose day, glorious as it may have been, had passed. Orestes continued. "Your Grace, there is no question that old age and treachery will always prevail over youth and vigor." The audience laughed louder, and a voice shouted, "You tell him, old fellow!"

Orestes quieted the crowd with a downward movement of his palms. "*Ne*, in order to make this fight absolutely fair, I propose that we wait one week hence to give your Rosariatus an opportunity to heal from his wounds, perhaps even to train himself. The young woman whom your Clarissima wife has now twice called a whore is my niece, and Torvald was her betrothed." There was a gasp that started on the podium and rolled through the crowd like a thunderclap.

"Her brother, my nephew, was witness to what befell the girl. He is shorter than Rosariatus by a head, lighter by a one-third measure, not possessed of your son's great musculature, and not even fully developed.

"Still, Your Grace, and my lords," he said, looking to where the three justices of the night before were seated, to the right of the Dominus, his wife, and the priest. "They say it is not the size of the dog in the fight, but the size of the fight in the dog. I propose to save Rosariatus his honor, if not his life, by asking that my nephew, Martin of Angle-land, serve as my champion."

Orestes motioned me to move to the center of the arena, near where Rosariatus stood. Our sizes were so disparate that more than a few observers snickered. One voice imitated that of a tiny dog, "Yip, yip, yip!" This was obviously the effect Orestes wanted, for now the insult was doubled. If Rosariatus declined the challenge, he would forever be a laughingstock throughout the city. My friend was obviously enjoying himself, and, at least in part, at my expense, for now he placed the capstone on his presentation.

"Your Grace, my lords, Tata Petrus, and my friends in the arena. One of your merchant kinsman said, and truly, that I have, in my small way, aided your worthy city from time to time. I will make this city and each of you a fair offer. If you reject my request for trial by ordeal, I promise you I will go direct to Louis Pius and to Ludwig his son, who holds supreme rule over the area that includes St. Gallen. I will ask, on my own recognizance, that they *order* St. Gallen to allow this trial to go forward."

Now the three Worthies – Dominus Rosarius, his bitch-wife, and the priest – glared at the three justices for assistance. They knew they were trapped. Although they had no idea how much influence Orestes might still have at the Royal Court, they could not deny that as the highest officer in Charlemagne's army, he certainly would be on closer speaking terms with his successors than would they.

"On the other hand, my friends," Orestes said. "I will wager from my own purse two thousand gold *solidi* that God is on the side of my champion, whether that wager be against one of you, the Church treasury, the Dominus and his Clarissima themselves, the Merchants' Guild, or the entire city."

Now the murmuring turned into an excited buzz. Two thousand gold *solidi* would have been a king's ransom five hundred years ago, when great wealth abounded. Now, in the poorer days, it was a sum almost beyond imagining. Even I thought that Orestes might have been a little off in the head, as buoyed up as I was with the thrill of what had happened.

"One week from today, Your Grace – the infamous Ides of March. You may choose to obey an Order from above and risk the scandal that goes with it, or you may choose to wager and, if you win, make your city far greater, and certainly wealthier, than it is now."

The Dominus, the priest, and the justices crowded around each other, and started talking in hushed whispers, ignoring the snarling and cursing, the hissing and caterwauling, of Rosarius' wife. The crowd was not so circumspect. They shouted and shook their fists in the air as one. "Trial! Trial!! Trial!!! Trial!!!!" they shouted, each time louder than the last.

The priest broke from the circle to invoke the name of God, but now the crowd took up a surlier, uglier chant, drowning out anything the priest might have said. "Meisdreck! Meisdreck!! Meisdreck!!!"

After what seemed forever, it was the Dominus who delivered the decision. By the glowering, scathing look his wife gave him, I knew what it was going to be. "Very well, Marshal Gallianus. As father not only to my son, but to my people as well, I must honor their wishes. Your request for trial by battle is granted. I trust you and your, ahem, niece will serve as seconds. By a rather unique and, er, highly unusual request, His Reverence, Tata Petrus, and my wife, the Clarissima, have asked to serve as my son's seconds. The battle will take place at the break of dawn, seven days hence, on the Ides of March. Hand to hand combat. Not here, but outside of the city, on the old Plain of Mars. Be it so."

And with that, the noble coterie quickly clambered into the Dominus' large carruca and departed the stadium.

CHAPTER 21

By the time I got back to my room, I was in a thorough state of agitation. My remaining lifespan might well be as little as seven days. Undoubtedly Rosariatus' mother, who had been humiliated in the arena, not only in front of a massive group of people, but, worse, in front of her son, her fondest possession, would react viciously. I'd heard the stories of her depravity and her almost insane lust for power and pride. It was not hard to imagine she would stoop to whatever it took to gain her own vengeance. And she had the power, the wealth, and the ear of that frocked fraud, *Tata Petrus*, to help her.

As the afternoon progressed, I became ever gloomier. The contest would be akin to the Biblical battle of David and Goliath, but only akin in one way – a very big, very strong man against a much smaller, slighter man, who, while by no means a weakling, had no sling-and-stone to rely on. A knock on my door brought me out of myself. Orestes entered, without so much as a by-your-leave.

"All right, champion, now you will have your chance," he said, much too gaily for my mood.

"Some chance, Orestes. For God's sake, I told you something in confidence. Why in heaven's name did you choose to bellow my rage to the entire city? What have I got to gain in this fiasco other than my death?"

"What a wonderful, optimistic outlook you have on life!" he continued in the same cheerful vein. "You could already have been dead, you know. Or have you forgotten our Hun friends back in the *Hrau Albos*?"

"For that I thank you, but I fear you have taken me out of the boiling pot in order to roast me over the flames."

" Not at all. Why do you think I wagered on you to *win*?"

"That's another thing. Two thousand gold *solidi*? As high-risen as you have been and as well-connected, I would wager you haven't seen half that much in your entire life."

"Well spoken, lad," Orestes rejoined heartily. "You are absolutely correct."

"Then how could you have made such an outrageous dare in the public arena?"

Orestes grasped me, not unkindly, and pulled me to my feet. "I think it might be a good idea for us to walk in the high road," he said. If nothing else, the exercise might do you some good and it might even lift your spirits."

"Where's Joan?"

"In her room, weeping and wailing, and doing what she has to do."

"Rather callous of you to say that," I said.

"And you, Martin?" he replied blandly enough. "I've spent the entire morning with the child, and I daresay you, her closest friend, have not so much as walked the few steps to her room to see if she is still alive."

Chastened, I walked into the street with Orestes with no further demur. We found our way down to the lake, and, as so often happens on Lake Constance, there was a mist and an uncomfortable wind. "I believe you mentioned the folly of my wagering two thousand gold solidi, just before we left the inn, and I congratulated you on your perceptiveness."

"How could anyone have believed you?"

"Because people will always believe what they want to believe. Do you think the Dominus is any different from the rest of the people in this town?"

"Well …" I pondered a moment before giving my answer. "He is certainly higher-born, certainly wealthier."

"How do you know?"

"That's easy. He rides about the town in an extravagant carruca, his clothing is of only the finest cut, the tales that are told about him — "

"Outward trappings. Do you not think he has debts to go with all of his show? And I'll wager he pays them more slowly than most, for he's learned that folk whom he considers beneath his station will vie for the privilege of claiming that the Dominus owes them money. Martin, a mouse may call himself a lion, and even his mice subjects may think of him as a lion and adore him as a lion, but to a real lion even that upraised mouse is no more than a morsel, not even fit to fill a hole in his tooth. Do you think our Dominus puts his pants on other than one leg at a time? Or that his skeit doesn't stink the same as any other man's?"

"I don't understand what you're trying to say, Orestes."

"People want to believe that I have two thousand gold solidi to spend. Therefore, in their minds, I must be a very wise and shrewd and powerful man, and I must know more than they. And if I am willing to wager such an astonishing sum on the claim that you will be successful in your vengeance against that bumbling ape, Rosariatus, and his even fouler mother, these common folk, the burghers, mayhap even some of the nobility, will wager their money that you will prevail. And they will bet one another on the outcome, for they will trust their own even more than they will risk the integrity of a stranger, even if their own are greedier, more avaricious, and more venal than the stranger."

I skimmed a smooth stone across the waters nearest the shoreline. "Meaning?"

"One wager I can make with absolute confidence is that, despite their gasping, their excitement, and their eagerness, not one hundredth of my claimed solidi will be put to risk. I will be more than surprised if any man, or any group, or any institution will wager so much as twenty solidi against me."

"Still," I murmured, "twenty solidi is a not insignificant sum."

"Aye, but it's far less than two thousand. And for the rest of my life, no one in St. Gallen will dare claim that I didn't have two thousand *solidi*." He chuckled.

I heard a commotion behind us, a loud crunching on the gravel walkway. Turning, I saw Rosariatus, heavily lunging in my direction, very red of face, loudly huffing and puffing. As I ducked to the side, it was as if he'd not even seen me. He passed within a man's height of me and never so much as looked to his left or his right.

"Faster, dolt! Move that heap of flab!" Two powerfully built men of about thirty shouted the insults at Rosariatus, and they were pursuing him with whips.

"I see the bitch-queen has started a training regimen for her baby boy," Orestes remarked caustically. "We'll have to do the same for you in a day or two, perhaps sooner, perhaps later."

Word was out throughout the city that the Dominus' wife had hired the best physical trainers and wrestlers in the area to subject Rosariatus to the sternest possible means of toughening him up. If such efforts had been arranged to frighten me yet more, they were doing a good job of it. One week may not seem like much to change a lifetime of sloth, but it is certainly enough to make a good start.

My mood darkened daily. I was barely able to keep my food down, but Orestes insisted that I eat well to maintain what strength I had. He also compelled me to walk, and even to jog long distances, so that my endurance increased. But, unlike the training inflicted on Rosariatus, he was neither unduly harsh nor unduly cruel. "You can shine a pig and make him momentarily leaner, but he's still a pig at heart."

Orestes and I spent hours each day with Joan. At least I had fear of my upcoming possible death to allay some of my grief, but Joan had nothing, and, as she remarked, she might well be rehearsing for more grief a week after her love had died. "If anything happens to you, Martin..." she said, but I didn't let her finish her sentence.

It was now three days before the ordeal of battle. I'd noticed Joan had taken to wearing her plain Brother Joannes garb once again, and she had ceased wearing any cosmetics, not that she had really needed any.

"Well," she said. "It seems as though God has made my decision for me. Perhaps He meant me to be a priest and a scholar after all." She walked over to the table near her bed, where she'd kept her vials of makeup and powders and greasepaint, and such. "I won't be needing these any longer."

"Joan, you're the one who's always known about medicines and drugs and curatives and such. God's oath, when I first met you and you were only a small child, you knew more about those things than any medicus I'd ever met. Surely you could find some small use for those things."

Joan looked at me, then looked at the assortment of astringents and unguents and other things on her table. I continued, "I wish I'd never made such a rash commitment. Perhaps one of your potions could make me disappear."

"You mean turn you into a woman?" she asked.

"Well, not exactly, although you seem to have done a remarkable job shifting from man to woman and back again." She looked at me thoughtfully, and I felt comforted that Joan was starting to show some of her old fire.

"Your hair is too short. Of course, we could find you a wig and dress you in skirts, but somehow I feel you'd never get over your guilt at having run away. Still ..." I looked at her questioningly. "Oh, nothing, nothing. Have you done any training for your upcoming battle?"

"Orestes said it wouldn't make much difference," I said, dismally.

Shortly thereafter, Orestes came to the door. "Time for another brisk walk," he said.

"May I speak with you for a moment, Orestes?" Joan said.

"Of course." They retired to a far corner of the room and whispered among themselves. Orestes handed her a tiny sack of coins.

I thought nothing of it until later that afternoon, when Orestes and I were returning from what he called our "stroll." Two blocks from our inn, I saw Joan emerge from a pharmaceutium. "Is that what she and you were talking about?" I asked.

"Aye. The poor child is having her menstruum and, I fear, a rather painful one at that, no doubt because of the events of the past week. She asked for some money to purchase a mild potion to assuage her pain somewhat.

The evening before the battle I was so agitated that I was trembling and having difficulty falling asleep. The last thing I expected was to be confronted by Orestes and Joan in my room, but that is what happened. When they told me of their plan, I was so incredulous as to totally disbelieve them at first. What they were proposing was monstrous. It was outrageous. It was beyond anything I could comprehend. And it just might work. When we had talked and experimented and worked until long after the sun had gone down, I fell into an exhausted sleep.

~ ∫ ~

Dawn. The Dominus had chosen the time and the place of the battle wisely. He did not want to risk a second jeering, perhaps this time a true revolt, when his scion mauled me as he had butchered Torvald. No matter how excited St. Gallen's citizens had been, hardly any of them would risk discomfort and the loss of two more hours of sleep to come to a lonely, desolate, usually windy, abandoned battlefield at a truly ungodly hour.

Aside from the participants, their seconds, the three judges, and a few hundred onlookers, the vast field was empty. Rosariatus looked different. The largest part of his fat had given way to toughened muscle, and instead of the vapid, empty look I'd seen in his eyes before, there was a look of determination, of hatred, the look of a bully and a murderer. By any measure, it looked like an unfair match up.

No wind was blowing, but as the sun rose it drew from the ground a clammy, gray-white mist that swirled thigh high. The place provided a properly gloomy and eerie setting for death.

Rosariatus and I stripped off our overcoats and our shirts, to bare our upper bodies. The seconds approached us to make sure that neither combatant was concealing a knife or other weapon in our waistbands or trouser pockets or boot tops.

"What's this?" the Clarissima screamed as she touched my flank. "This coward has applied a girl's makeup to his face and body! Trying to curry favor by appearing as a woman? What kind of freakish monster are you, anyway?" she hissed. "Are you trying to escape this battle you so earnestly wanted, you cheat? Or perhaps you've been screwing your miserable whore sister on your last night on earth?" Her outbreak drew muffled, derisive laughter from her small coterie.

"'Tis nothing, Honored Clarissima," Orestes said mildly. "The young man simply needed something to keep him warm on this chill morning, and, in his own way, he thought to wear something akin to the oil that wrestlers wore in the ancient days to make him more slippery. If you or the Dominus would like, I will happily assist in washing him off."

"Ne, that will not be necessary," said the Dominus. "If he chooses to look like a girl, it will simply take less embalmer's makeup when it's time to bury him. What say you, wife?"

She glared malevolently at me. "I say there's some trick here, but I cannot, for the life of me, determine what it is. I see he's wearing that goopy stuff all over his face and neck as well. I suppose if he has any balls – and we'll find that out after the contest has been decided – he's probably slathered them with cosmeta as well."

I was able to catch a snatch of conversation among the observers. "Look at them. One is slight and lithe, and perhaps he would be good at gentlemanly fisticuffs, but the other is as big and heavy and muscled as Hercules. It is a deplorable mismatch."

As we squared off, bare-breasted, I barely heard another observer saying, "Curious. This damnable cold has pimpled the invincible Rosariatus with gooseflesh all over. The little one is shivering but not otherwise showing chill. He must be fired with determination."

No sooner had we faced each other, then Rosariatus bellowed a mighty roar and drummed his big fists on his massive chest. I involuntarily took a step back. Rosariatus lunged forward and I threw my arms high in a protective reflex. That left my chest vulnerable, and Rosariatus instantly wrapped his mighty arms around me, either to squeeze me to a pulp or to break my back.

Flailing in apparent desperation, I made the only move I had freedom to make. I swiped one of my forearms, then the other, across Rosariatus' face. That only made Rosariatus lower his head and burrow it into the hollow between my neck and shoulder, where I could not reach to gouge at his eyes or do much else besides yank at his hair. While Rosariatus had his face protected there, and while he continued to crush my chest, he sank his teeth deep into the flesh at my collarbone. I screamed in utter pain. By now I was bent unnaturally backward. My eyes bulged from the pressure and I gasped for air, but my lungs were being crushed as well. I heard the unmistakable crack and felt the incredible pain of two of my ribs breaking. It was only a moment before my spine would snap and I would be relieved forever of that pain.

Then, suddenly, Rosariatus gave another cry – not warlike, but surprised, even distressed. He let go of me and reeled away, now using his hands to wipe furiously at his face, his eyes now shut tight and his mouth red with my blood. He also bore traces of my makeup. I was free but, for the moment, all I could do was crumple to my knees on the grass, gasping for breath and clutch my elbows against my broken and painful ribs, while blood trickled from my neck.

Rosariatus was still reeling about, but now he was clawing at his eyes and his mouth. Then he, too, went to his knees, and he began grabbing at the grass, scooping from it the mist-laden moisture to smear frantically on his face. I got shakily to my feet, stepped gingerly over to Rosariatus, and gave him a shove that toppled him over on his back. Rosariatus seemed unaware of his openness to attack. He was still rubbing his wet hands all over his face.

I barely heard the sound of commotion in the background. I knelt beside Rosariatus, drew back my right arm, extended my right hand with fingers straight and tight together, took calculating aim, and drove my hand like a spear into Rosariatus' solar plexus. Rosariatus gave another cry, this time of real pain, and he dropped his hands from his head to clutch at the pit of his stomach. I reared my rigid right hand back, then drove it into the Adam's apple of the writhing Rosariatus. He gave another, weaker, strangled cry, and his whole body convulsed. There was but one thing more to do. I used my stiffened hand like the flat blade of a knife. I swung it sideways, with all of my remaining strength, at the underside of Rosariatus' nose. Rosariatus made no further sound and no more movement, except a twitching and quivering from head to foot, and then he lay still. I again got shakily to my feet and, too breathless to speak, motioned for Orestes to fetch my clothes and help me into them.

The shock on the field was so palpable it rendered everyone speechless. Rosariatus' mother went screaming over to her dead child, and, when she found to her horror that he truly was dead, she uttered the most ululating, chilling, and fearsome wail I'd ever heard. The Dominus sat stony-faced on the chair that had been set for him. The priest trembled and shook. For once, he was speechless.

"Come Martin, Joan," Orestes said urgently. "We'd best depart, and right now, if we want to escape this city with our lives. The porters have already checked us out of the inn. We've only to pick up our horses and baggage and ride out of town."

"Wait, wait!" shouted four men who'd been watching the affray. "Pray let us accompany you, if only to give you what little protection we can."

"We accept, and gratefully," Joan said, before anyone else could stammer a protest.

"Let me go as well. I have room in my carriage for the injured young man and his sister." I was surprised to find it was one of the three justices.

It was a ragged, but triumphant gaggle that returned us to the inn. Our horses were already saddled.

"Not that it matters," said the justice, "but could you tell us how you did it? If you do, I promise it will go with me to my grave. I suspected something when I saw Rosariatus was covered with goosebumps and you were not."

Joan answered for us. "Martin was covered with goosebumps, too. You just couldn't see them. It occurred to me that if I could paint my face with my makeup, I could paint Martin's face and his upper body and arms, too. So I did, but with more than cosmetics. I purchased carbolic acid and calomel – corrosive sublimate – from a pharmaceutium. I powdered these chemicals and mixed them with the makeup."

"The carbolic and the calomel stung my skin a little," I said, "but I figured if I could get some in Rosariatus' eyes, it would sting a hell of a lot more, and it evidently did. But it was his own idea to take a bite of that stuff."

"I understand," the justice said. "But that other business – killing him just by poking him…?"

Orestes sat quietly, taking this all in as calmly as you please.

"Rosariatus' mother used every trainer and thug and bully that money could buy. I had only the Field Marshal, but that was more than enough. I had hoped, if I could blind

Rosariatus for a moment, I might get a headlock on him and break his neck, but Orestes told me to forget that. A neck like Rosariatus' is his strongest part. So the Marshal showed me that trick of using a stiff hand. He said you can kill a man by jamming it up under his breastbone and tearing his guts, or by smashing his Adam's apple so he strangles, or by hitting him hard under the nose. That breaks the bone at the bridge of his nose and drives the splinters up into his brain. But by Christ, it took all three to kill that big lout."

"Still, kill him you did," said Orestes. "I don't know when I've been more pleased and proud – or more surprised," he said.

"Well," I said. "I had some good advisers to help me do it."

"And I," said Orestes with pride, "had an enviable student."

~ ∫ ~

There remains little to tell of our stay in St. Gallen, since it ended later that morning. After I had been bound and strapped as tightly as possible to lessen the pounding pain in my ribs, and after I had been treated with various medicaments and ointments to stave off infection in my neck, Orestes, Joan, and I started off toward the east. Where the road forks at the edge of town, we bid farewell to one of the most glorious, by far the wisest, and perhaps the most memorable man in my life, who turned northwest toward Aachen.

Joan was still grieving, but now that seven days had passed, and she had truly been avenged, she held her head high – as Brother Joannes Angliorum once again – as we rode forward, unafraid, to see what awaited us in Bavaria and beyond.

BOOK IV.
THE DANUVIUS

Chapter 22

We left Brigantium at the end of March, 832, and continued eastward into Bavaria. Although that province was pleasant, there were few vestiges of "civilization" – nary a city or a village or a fortress, and very few churches of any significance. After some days, we came to the market town of Landeck, which was new and very clean. We took lodgings in the town's church, and Father Alessandro, a wise, gentle, and humorous man of the people – the antithesis of the pretentious Tata Petrus – waxed rapturous about places we'd see on our way east.

"On your journeys you will come to and see and ride upon many rivers until you might wish for a change of scenery, no matter how pleasant it seems at first. Might I suggest you consider going into the Salzkammergut – the land of salt?"

"The land of salt?" Joan asked incredulously. "Like a desert or a beach?"

"*Ne*, not quite like that." He would say no more, but only smiled noncommittally, and quickly changed the subject.

Of course, Father Alessandro"s refusal to speak further about the Salzkammergut only worked like a worm from within and further enticed us to the point that we determined to explore this strange area, if only for a day. My ribs were now giving me only occasional pain, and I was pleased to see that Joan's heart was giving her only occasional pain, and so it was that, armed with an eagerness to see the mysterious land of salt, we headed east once again.

A few days later, we crossed an invisible boundary line in the forest, passing eastward from Bavaria into the province which, in Roman days, had been called Noricum and which was variously described both by its old name, and by its newer name, Tirol. There were many more settlements here than we had seen in Bavaria, for colonists had come from Italia hundreds of years ago to mine the plentiful iron in the ground and create the fine Noric steel that had been used in the manufacture of weapons for Rome's legions.

When Joan and I reached the Aenus River, we at last came to a real road, much wider than a footpath. It was the old Roman road that traverses the Alps by way of the Brennerius, probably the most traveled pass through the entire Alps because it is the lowest. It was kept in fine repair, for that road bore a heavy traffic of persons, animals, wagons, and carts going to or coming from or beyond the cities of Tridentium in Italia to the south, and Castra Regina on the great river Danuvius to the north. That road crosses the Aenus on a well-constructed ancient bridge – a *brücke* in the German tongue – and at the eastern end of that bridge is the large and very wealthy city of Aenus Brücke.

Aenus Brücke is quite scenic, for the Aenus is a rapidly running and noisy river, the place is surrounded by Alps, and the high road through the Brennerius is everywhere intersected by smaller roads leading in many directions. Finding an inn was easy. The meal was delicious – Aenus fish, mountain-raised mutton and beef, and, of course, endless tankards of beer or mugs of delicate white wine. We were particularly attracted to a man of thirty, who was talking with two other men about the salt trade. I calculated, from the way he talked, he must have come from that land of salt Father Alessandro had so vaguely described. Joan and I positioned ourselves near to the fellow and listened as he spoke.

We soon found that the man, Gregorius Knapp, was the second son of the elderly director of a salt mine in a town called Hausstadt in the Salzkammergut. His elder brother had been the heir apparent and had managed those mines until his untimely death a year before, in a mining accident. Gregorius had been trained as a priest, for usually the second son was relegated to the priesthood, but now he found himself engaged in the business of his father's mines.

Herr Knapp was politically astute, a good listener and a man of sharp intellect. Even though he had never functioned as an active priest, he maintained his friendships with many priests and acolytes with whom he had gone to school in years past. Gregorius would never have donned the cassock or *stola* if he'd had to take a vow of chastity and abandon his taste for attractive women. Now that he was a businessman-trader, he didn't even have to pretend to a philosophy with which he did not agree.

After we had listened politely to the man for about an hour, Joan and I introduced ourselves and entered into the conversation. "Brothers?" Gregorius said. "You've taken the vow of chastity then?"

"Isn't that the way of all priests?" Joan asked.

"*Nein*," he replied equably. "The farther east and the farther south one goes, the less important it becomes. The whole idea of life without sex is an unnatural affront to the species."

"But surely Saint Augustine…" I interjected.

"Augustine screwed his brains out during his younger days. Indeed, there was hardly anything he didn't try. He became ascetic only when he became burned out and there was nothing more to do," Gregorius said. "And, as has so often been said, those who no longer can do, teach, or, in his case, preach."

"So you don't think it was a miraculous conversion? A vision? A ray of light?"

"Hardly," our new acquaintance rejoined. "Have you ever noticed it is the unhappiest man or the one who led the most miserable and friendless childhood, who becomes the greatest moralist? Find me a happy man and I will find you one who is tolerant of others' faults and foibles and beliefs."

"You said you came from Hausstadt in the land of salt. Why would anyone want to live in such a dry and dreary place?"

At that, Gregorius' face screwed up into a funny look. "A dry and dreary place," he said. It was a comment, not a question. "You've traveled far?" he asked.

"Quite far," said Joan. "From Angle-land to Aquitania, thence across Aquitania to Basilea and St. Gallen, and now here."

"I see," said Gregorius. "And where might you be heading from here?"

"To Athens," Joan said proudly. "Where we hope to complete our studies."

"You're no doubt going up the Aenus to the Danuvius, then?"

"We had thought to do so, but a most congenial priest suggested we might traverse the Salzkammergut instead of going straight to the Danuvius."

"Well," said Gregorius. "You young men seem convivial enough, and there's always safety, not to mention companionship, in numbers. I, myself, am going back to Hausstadt, and that is in the very center of the land of salt. Would you be averse to traveling with me through that 'dry and dreary land?'"

When we left Aenus Brücke a few days later, we went farther down the ever-widening Aenus, and then, when that river bent northward, away from it, over lands that were watered by only small streams. We traveled faster now, because it was late spring, and the countryside was lush with lovely meadows and snowcapped mountains. We came to the provincial capital which, in Roman times, had been known as Juvavum, and was now known by its older name, Salzburg. That city was anything but dry and dreary. In the very middle of the city, there is a huge, flat hill, several hundred feet above the town. We climbed to the top of that hill and from there, in every direction, we could see great, green fields stretching far to distant Alps. There is another river, the Salzach, which runs speedily through the town, bisecting it almost in two.

Gregorius avoided the main roads leading out of Salzburg. Instead, we traveled southeast through the gradually rising forelands of that range known to locals as the Roofstone Alps.

After a day of easy riding, we were in the heart of the Salzkammergut – the place of much salt. I had been waiting to come to the dry and dreary land I had imagined. As we rode on and on, we still did not come to such a place. Far from it. I soon learned that the region is amply supplied with salt mines, but they are all deep underground, and the entrances to those caverns only infrequently can be seen from the countryside. The rest of the landscape was truly grand – the loveliest country I had yet traveled through. Lush alpine meadows of wildflowers and sweet grasses alternated with forests that were different from all those we had earlier traversed. These forests were much like the parklands I would eventually see on rich men's great estates: not clogged with underbrush, the trees standing fastidiously apart, so that every one had room to spread its crown most bountifully, and between the trees were flowering shrubs and grass as carefully tailored and groomed as on a large estate.

I thought I had already seen enough beauty on our way, but all of that paled in my memory when I saw our destination. Shortly before noon one day, we rode around the shoulder of a high Alp. Gregorius reined his horse to a halt, and made a sweeping gesture of his arm to show me what lay below, and the sight made me catch my breath. "Hausstadt," Gregorius said proudly. "The Place of Echoes. My home."

~ ∫ ~

In my lifetime I have seen much and been to more places than most men have forgotten. I say, and not with false modesty, that I have probably seen more of the world than most people ever will. But still I remember Hausstadt as the most ravishingly beautiful and beguiling piece of earth I have ever beheld.

From the mountain whence Gregorius and Joan and I gazed down, the Place of Echoes was very like an oblong bowl made all of alps. There are four mountains, and where they come together, there is a lake, and it had to be a tremendously deep one, for the mountains' flanks went almost straight down into it, to meet conjoined somewhere far, far below. Only at intervals between the flanks, at lakeside, were there small patches of land sloping down to the water, and there were a few shelf-like meadows visible on some of the mountainsides. Several of the Alps on the farther side of the bowl – and they marched back from the lake one after the other like a stately dozen sentries – were so tall that their peaks, even now in late spring, were still white with snow. Here and there, the mountains also showed crags and cliffs of bare brown rock. But the bulk of them were clad in green forests, which climbed all the way up to the snow line.

The lake, Hausstadt-See, was a miniature compared to Lake Constance, but it was incomparably more radiant and inviting. The blue of the lake was indescribable, a precious blue gem nestled among the mountains' folds of green, fleecy forest. Not until long afterward did I have the opportunity to see a dark-yet-glowing blue sapphire, but when I did, I was instantly reminded of the color of that lake. Floating about on the water were some objects unidentifiably tiny from this distance, and directly below us – so far below us that it appeared to be one of those tiny toy villages that woodcarvers make for children – was the town of Hausstadt, occupying the whole of one of the few meager patches of lakeside land. I could see only the roofs of the town, every one steep-pitched to shed the snow in winter, and an open market square among the roofs, and some piers jutting out into the water. But there were many roofs, so many that I could not imagine how the houses under them all huddled together in a space so constricted.

We rode down from our alp, along a trail that ran close beside a wide stream bounding down a series of cataracts toward the lake. As we got nearer to Hausstadt, I could see how the town was built. There was very little flat land alongside the lake, so only a few of the houses, as well as a sizable church and the town square, with shops and *tabernae* and *deversoria* all around it, stood on level ground. The other houses and establishments of the town were stacked almost one atop the other, halfway up the steep mountainside. They were separated not by crosswise streets, but by tiny alleyways, and up and down that hill ran not streets, but stone staircases. The houses were so cramped and crowded that some were very narrow, but those compensated for the squeeze by being two or even three stories high.

At first sight, Hausstadt looked precariously perched, but it had undoubtedly been there for a very long time. All the buildings were solidly constructed of stout timbers or stone, with roofs of slate or tiles or thick shingles. Almost every one had its front plastered white and then brightly decorated, some with scrollwork designs painted in many colors, some with a flowering vine, or even a flowering tree, artfully trained to grow up flat against the housefront and around its door and window openings. The market square contained a fountain with four spouts continuously gushing water, and all the shops around that square were gaily adorned with tubs or boxes of flowers set about their sills.

I had never seen a community, from the smallest village to the biggest city that went to so great an effort to look so cheerful. It must have been the heart-stopping loveliness of its surroundings that inspired the people to make their town worthy of its setting. I learned from Gregorius that the townfolk could well afford these comely embellishments of their buildings, for on one of the Alps high above Hausstadt is a vast salt mine. I was told it was the oldest in the world. That mine, which was owned by Gregorius' father, and which he stood to inherit, was, at the time I visited, still inexhaustibly rich in the purest grade of salt.

We descended to the lake level at the outskirts of the town, dismounted our horses, paid for their board in a nearby stable, and strolled along Hausstadt's one wide street, the lakeside promenade. I could now make out what the objects in the water were. Those closest to us were gray herons and purple herons wading in the shallows or standing purposefully on one leg. A little farther out were gorgeous white swans drifting serenely about. Farthest out were the fishing boats, and strange but appealing they were to look at. Each is shaped exactly like a piece of melon chopped in half at the middle. Its prow curves high out of the water and its stern, where the boatman stands to row it, is flat and abrupt. No one could tell me the reason for their shape.

Gregorius insisted we accompany him to his favorite *taberna*, one of those facing the town square. The building's front was painted with curlicues and its door was flanked by flower boxes, but its rear wall, which was right on the lake, was actually laid away during mild weather, so we ate delicious grilled slabs of pike-perch caught only an hour or so earlier, and we had a fine, full view of the Hausstadt-See at twilight, and the still sun-tipped mountains beyond. We tossed bits of bread to the swans that glided below our terrace, and several times we shouted loudly over the water to hear our voices echo faintly and ever more faintly back to us from one far black peak after another. When we were done, Gregorius departed and Joan and I stayed in the *deversorium*. Alone in my room, I lay long awake with my head turned to the window, watching the moon come over a mountain to frost that blue, blue lake with glints of silver; and when my eyes closed at last, they closed on what I still remember as one of the most peacefully happy days of all my life.

Chapter 23

Gregorius came by shortly after breakfast and invited us to explore the region from the top down, so to speak. We set off on foot up a rigorous streamside trail. Since it was steep and, in places, rocky, I paused at numerous intervals to regain my wind and relax my muscles. I leisurely examined and appreciated the view from ever-higher altitudes. At last, we came to the Knapp family's salt mine, the primary reason for Hausstadt's existence.

The mine was the center of a whole community and a considerable factory. There was a quite grand house for the mine's director, less grand ones for his immediate subordinates, and an entire village of rude huts and small gardens for the workers. Wherever there was a shelf-like meadow on the mountain slopes, its borders were diked and the meadow was filled with water. The rock salt from the mines was dissolved in these pools, leached of any impurities and discoloration, then dried and re-created as granular, pure-white salt, ready for use. There was a shed for bagging the salt, an immense shed used for storing the bags, and stockades for the mules used to haul the bags over the Alps to their various destinations.

The miners who worked underground and the teamsters and drovers who moved the salt from one place to another, whether across the meadow or across half the continent of Europe, were all men. The above-ground work was, for the most part, done by their wives and children. The laborers, descendants of slaves who'd worked the mines hundreds of years ago, were now all freemen who continued in the same drudgery since it was the only work they knew how to do.

"Are you seeking work stranger? Are you a free laborer or someone's slave?"

I turned and beheld a little girl about eight or nine years old, brown-haired, brown-eyed, light fawn-skinned, and very pretty.

"I am neither," I said. "I merely came up to see what the salt works looks like."

"Then you must be a traveler from beyond these mountains. Everyone hereabouts is wearily familiar with this place." She sighed dramatically. "God knows I am, and I've only been here three months."

"And what might you be?" I asked, smiling because she was finely dressed in a well-tailored cloak, like a little lady. "Laborer or slave?"

"I," she said haughtily, "am the niece of Cardinal Sergius, who has just been appointed first Archbishop of Hamburg. My name is Aegina. Who are you?"

"Martin Paschal." We chatted for some time. She seemed quite pleased to have someone new to talk to, and she pointed out to me various features of the salt works, told me the names of various alpine peaks around the lake, and advised me which merchants in town were least likely to cheat strangers.

"And who might you be, Sir?" Aegina addressed an approaching figure.

"Joannes Angliorum, late a scholar at Tours abbey."

"How old are you?" she asked.

"Nineteen."

"And you've not yet a beard?"

"I'm afraid not," Joan said easily. "When I was quite young, about your age – ten? – "

"I'll be nine in August," Aegina said. Like any child over the age of six, she felt proud when someone *over*estimated her age.

"Anyway," Joan continued, "when I was ten I suffered some kind of rash from a plant in Angle-land, from whence I come. The *medicus* said I'd be fine, but, alas, I'd never grow much of a beard – and I haven't. But come now, a man is more than just a beard, is he not?"

"Well …" Aegina said in girlish mock anticipation of the teasing that would go on between she and some young man only a few years hence, "There are other differences as well."

Odd, I thought. *The young of every species seem innately to know who is male and who is female, regardless of the outer trappings. Yet, this young one accepts Joan as a male.*

"Have either of you ever seen the inside of a salt mine?" Aegina asked. "No? The inside is much more worth seeing than anything outside. I will ask Herr Knapp's permission to let me escort you."

"Gregorius?" Joan asked. "He's a friend of ours. I'm sure he will assent."

"I don't mean young Gregorius," she snapped. "I mean the *director* of the mine."

The elder Herr Knapp was a slight man with gray-white hair, not especially prepossessing, who must have spent a great deal of time in the mine, for his skin was almost colorless. Aegina told me the elder Herr Knapp was one of the few citizens in Hausstadt whose family had descended from Roman colonists. Four hundred years later, he was still a purebred Roman. I chuckled as I thought about how we regularly applied the term to purebred horses and purebred dogs and, for all I know, purebred cattle. But Herr Knapp never let anyone forget that he was Roman. When he signed any least document, he always added the Roman numeral designating his generation of the family. As I remember, Caius Julius Knapp was the XXIII or XXIVth of his line. Even though Rome was now a faded shadow of its once great glory, he had actually imported a woman from Rome to be his wife. She had died some years after giving birth, first to Caius Julius the XXIVth or XXVth, thence to Gregorius, but the elder Herr Knapp showed no great signs of bereavement. He was married to the mine.

The Hausstadt council of elders had appointed him, like his XXII or XXIII forefathers, to the directorship. He was a pleasant enough old fellow, who obviously adored his Cardinal's little niece, and would have granted her anything she asked, whether because he fancied himself worthy to keep company with a high prince of the Church, or because he truly treasured her. He indulgently gave Aegina leave to take us underground, and said he hoped we would enjoy touring the establishment of which he was so proud.

Inside the great dark entrance, the ingoing and outcoming miners deferentially made way for Aegina, Joan, and me. She picked a leather apron for each of us from one of five or six racks. I started to tie mine around my waist, but she laughed and said, "Not that way. Put it on hindside to the front. Here, turn around."

Puzzled, I turned my back to her, so I was facing the blackness of the mine's interior, and she arranged the apron to drape its long flap over my backside. "Now tie the thongs in front," she said, "pull the flap up between your legs and hold on to it with both hands."

I did so. With a giggle, Aegina gave me a violent shove that propelled me into the darkness. My feet instantly slid out from under me and I found myself breathlessly hurtling on my own apron down a steep chute worn in the solid salt, polished by perhaps millions of such slidings, so that it was as slippery as ice. For what seemed like a long time, but was probably only a few heartbeats, I plunged through utter blackness. The whole thing went much too quickly for me to even work up a commendable fear. Then, the chute's incline became less and less acute until it was almost level, and I saw a light ahead of me. I was still moving at great speed, however, when the chute abruptly came to an end, and I was tossed into the air for an instant before landing on a pile of cloth pillows and sweet-smelling, springy pine sprigs.

I sat stunned for a moment. Then I was really knocked breathless as Joan's feet slammed into my back, and then Aegina's feet slammed into her back, and the three of us tumbled off the pile of cushions.

"Quick, fellows! Move out, or you'll have a whole heap of miners on top of you before you know it!"

I rolled well away from the chute, and not a moment too soon. A gaggle of miners, each holding an empty basket, came shooting from out of the darkness into the torch-lit, salt-walled corridor where we had landed. Each man spryly sprang to his feet to make way for the rest, and then less eagerly plodded on along the hall. Beyond this procession, I saw another file of miners coming from inside the mine, bent under their baskets, being waved on in or briefly halted by a foreman who stood at the bottom of an exceptionally tall ladder, built of very thick beams and rungs, up which the miners toiled into the darkness above.

Aegina proceeded to lead us along the corridor, around various corners, and along other halls that branched off one another. Each was brightly lit and required torches only at distant intervals because the translucent salt walls diffracted and diffused light for a long way in either direction. In some manner I could not discern, every part of the mine was vented and the vents were interconnecting, reaching clear to the outside of the mountain. Thus, everywhere inside there was a faint but perceptible breeze that not only supplied fresh air at even the deepest reaches, but also whisked away the torches' smoke and prevented them from discoloring the salt at all. In almost every hallway there was a constant traffic of heavily-laden men going in one direction and empty-basketed men going in the other.

Joan asked Aegina, "How come, if there is so much traffic, some of the side corridors are totally empty?"

"They lead to places where the salt has been worked down to bare rock," she replied. "I won't take you to where the salt is presently being worked, for there's always the danger of a cave-in. However, there is one particular place I want to show you. It's a long way, both in and down."

Aegina gestured, and once again we stood at the head of another dark chute. This time, I found the swooping ride on my apron rather exhilarating. But as we wound our way through several corridors, then down another chute, and more corridors, and more chutes, I began to feel nauseous and squeamish, knowing there was a whole, huge, high Alp bulking over my head, held up only by walls and ceilings of salt.

The miners passing us, however, showed no sign of fear, and little Aegina went blithely along, so I gulped down my discomfort and followed where she led. Now, she turned off the main corridor into an empty, but torch-lit one, which got wider and wider as we progressed. Suddenly, it opened out altogether and we stood on the edge of a vast cavern. There were no people, but the cavern was more brightly lit than any of the busy walkways had been.

I had seen caverns before, but unlike the limestone caves I'd been in, everything here was fashioned of salt. I beheld fluted columns between floor and ceiling, lacework and draperies, motionless waterfalls around the walls, spires and steeples and pinnacles up-thrust from the floor, and icicle-like pendants dangling from the ceiling. Everything was made of salt, and so marvelous were the salt sculptures that in all the centuries the mine had been worked, those things had been preserved untouched.

The miners had gone to a great deal of trouble to illuminate the place. It must have been harder work than mining to affix torches all around, and up the arching walls to the very roof of the vault, as they had done. The resultant firelight, diffused throughout the salt shapes, reflected back and forth inside the soaring dome of salt, almost like echoes made visible.

"All this was made by nature," Aegina said softly. "But the miners added some man-made things so long ago that no one can remember when."

She beckoned us to one side of the cavern, where nature had somehow neglected to do its work. Here, miners had carved a small but entire Christian chapel, hollowed out, then furnished with an ambo table built of salt blocks and slab, and on the ambo stood a tall cross and a tall chalice, both sculpted from rock salt.

"Hausstadt has been a good Christian town for centuries," she said. "But there are still pagans in our midst."

Directly across from the chapel, another group of men, who professed a different religious belief, had carved a much simpler temple. The hollowed-out space contained only a man-sized salt statue, crudely done. Its interior was caked with soot and smelt of smoke – the only place in the mine that looked blemished. I asked Aegina how it had come to be.

"The pagan miners made sacrifices here," she said. "They brought the animal here, laid a fire, slew the animal in the name of some god, then cooked it and ate the meat." She laughed merrily and, I might add, quite musically. "The gods only got the smoke."

"And the Christian directors allowed the pagans to do that?" asked Joan.

"The Christian elders of Hausstadt made sure the director let them do it. It kept the workers contented and it cost the mine nothing. Now, Joannes and Martin, are you well-rested? It's a long way back, and we cannot slide up."

I grinned and said, "I believe I can climb the ladders with ease. Would you like me to carry you, little girl?"

"Carry me?" she said scornfully. "Better you should try to catch me." With that, she scampered off along the corridor that had brought us here.

We did not have to strain unduly hard to keep up with Aegina, but we made sure to keep up with her or we would surely have gotten lost along the way. I do admit, though, that when we climbed the last ladder and emerged from the mine's entrance, I was panting and perspiring, but she was not. But then, I had climbed that mountain *twice* that day, once on the outside of it, and once on the inside.

~ ∫ ~

What has never ceased to amaze me is the inconstancy of man. One can live in a place such as Hausstadt, which is wealthy without being opulent, scenically spellbinding in every direction you look, quiet and peaceful, with no hint of war or anger or bloodshed, or even excess drunkenness or debauchery anywhere – a veritable paradise on the face of the earth – and yet, as Aegina had said, even that becomes boring after a while to someone with an adventurous spirit.

By our fourth evening in Hausstadt, Joan and I were chafing to be once again on our way. We'd seen the mine, we'd seen the town, we'd clambered to the top of two Alps fronting the western side of the lake, and we'd eaten our fill of the town's delicious edibles and drank our share of its fine, sweet white wine.

"It is an interesting coincidence that you have recently come, and a still greater coincidence that you intend so soon to be going," Gregorius said. Would you feel offended if I asked you to dine at my father's home tonight? I promise you will not be bored."

The Director's residence was a grand house from without. It was an elegantly furnished manor within, with exposed beams and a capacious fireplace in which there burned a substantial log fire, even in the late spring. Aegina greeted us at the door. I had taken a great liking her, and the only thing I would regret about leaving Hausstadt would be my leaving that sparkling little imp behind.

A tall man of middle age, about thirty-five, stood behind her. He was an imposing figure, with a thick shock of black hair, beetling eyebrows, and intelligent, perceptive eyes. He took us in without a word, as though measuring us, for some time before he spoke. When he did, he spoke in a deep, rich bass voice. "Gentlemen, I see you've charmed not only young Knapp, but also my niece. The Herr and his son are dealing with some minor problem at the mine. They asked me to greet you. Until recently, my name was Stephen, but I am now called Sergius because the Holy Father, our Pope Gregory, wanted it that way."

I was tongue-tied. Even though I'd been a confidant and friend to a Bishop, I had never before met a true prince of the Church. Oh, I had heard of Cardinal Alcinorius, of course, who'd been elevated by Pope Paschal many years before, and I had learned from Bishop Numenior that Rome was a place of vicious politics within the body of Mother Church. But to meet and speak with a cardinal, someone only one step below the Holy Father, was a truly humbling experience.

Joan was not in the least intimidated or awed by Cardinal Sergius, either at our first meeting or thereafter. As she would say to me later, and then again much later, on a far more propitious occasion, "He puts his undergarments on like any other man, one leg at a time." It was not long before the four of us divided into two groups. I gravitated toward Aegina, while Joan entered into instant conversation with the Cardinal.

Aegina was a chameleon. One moment, she was showing me her dolls and her jewelry, which were of the highest quality, and what seemed like a moment later, she took me into a nearby alcove where there was a board game on a table, and taught me the game of chess, newly imported from Persia.

Joan and Cardinal Sergius sat in the large room adjacent to the alcove, and I picked up snatches of their spirited conversation. "Indeed I do feel honored, Johannes. Ansgar only founded the Bishopric a year ago, and already it's been raised to an Archbishopric. Gregory needed someone he felt he could trust to bring Christianity to the farthest northern reaches of Europe, and since I was the youngest and most expendable member of the *Collegia*, I was the lucky one."

"What about Alcinorius?" Joan asked, as if it were a

matter of only minor interest to her.

"That sneaky old bastard? Er, perhaps I should be more circumspect when I talk about a fellow Eminence, but that seems to be the prevailing opinion of him at the Holy See. He was assigned to Sarmatia, the very armpit of Christendom." He chuckled and Joan joined him in laughter.

"So you must have heard about the problems he caused us at Tours?"

"Oh, yes. Your Numenior is a political survivor in Mother Church. He's also a genuinely fine human being. Did you by any chance meet John Scotus Erigena when you were at Tours?"

Joan brightened. "Aye, I did. He, Martin, a priest named Nicola and I were quite close."

Sergius and Joan launched into what, to me, sounded very learned and scholarly discourse, while Aegina cajoled me to pay more attention to what I was doing at the chessboard.

We greeted Herr Knapp and Gregorius when they came in later. Sergius and Joan virtually ignored us and continued their discussion. The room was filled with hypnotic sparks, the more because they were not trying to compete with one another or overawe one another, but because it was clear they were trying to express their thoughts rather than impress either themselves or the rest of us. At last, perhaps from a surfeit of elegant viands or from the mellowing effect of fine wines, their conversation finally wound down to more mundane talk. By that time, Aegina had excused herself and gone upstairs to her bedroom to sleep. Herr Knapp finally reached the point of the evening's business.

"Joannes and Martin, you came at an auspicious time and you propose to leave at an auspicious time. Cardinal Sergius is bound for Hamburg, and he'll have precious little time to attend to Aegina. Aegina's mother died of consumption three years ago, and her father has been serving at a diplomatic post in Persia. She was left in Sergius' charge, a responsibility he happily assumed, but she has been shunted from pillar to post for the past year, and she has become homesick and longs to return to her home in Vindobona – *Wien* in modern parlance."

"Does she have relatives in Vindobona?"

"She does," Cardinal Sergius took up the conversation. "Her father will be there to greet her, as will my sister, Berenice, and another niece, Aegina's cousin Eva, who is twenty and, as yet, unmarried."

"Why, we're headed direct to Vindobona in the next two days," Joan said.

"So Gregorius has told me. I would be much beholden to you if you could take Aegina with you and protect her until she gets to Vindobona. I am obviously impressed with Joannes and it has not escaped my notice that little Aegina adores you, Martin. Would you consider doing this personal favor for me?"

"It would be my great honor," said Joan.

"I would, of course, provide a stipend for her care and sustenance."

"*Ne*, Eminence," I said. "My father's death many years ago left me well and fortunately provided-for. It would be no trouble. Indeed, it would be my great pleasure to accompany her, Eminence."

Two days after that, we three young travelers set out for Lentia, from whence we would take passage down the great and wide Danuvius, of which I had heard so much, to that great and glorious and elegant city, Vindobona, or, as it was now more commonly known, *Wien*.

CHAPTER 24

Aegina was a delightful, spirited, albeit impatient, companion on the road. Although her eagerness to rejoin her father was palpable, she maintained her interest in everything around her.

There were few roads in the area other than cart tracks or cattle trails, so we followed anything in the forest or in the interspersed meadows that headed in a general northeasterly direction. It was now late spring, and sunny days were the norm. Thus, it was easy to find our way. Because we had the child with us, Joan and I, who would otherwise have camped out, tried to find villages or other places of human habitation that might have a deversorium – they were more frequently called *gasthaus* in Germanic lands – or a private home where we could take lodging for the night.

"How come you're so easily able to tell when we're coming to a village?" Aegina asked on our second day out.

"We look for white storks and black-and-white magpies," I replied. "White storks nest on rooftops and black-and-white magpies live by theft, so anywhere I see either of these birds, I know that people live nearby."

The terrain for the most part consisted of great stretches of dense forests, interrupted at distant intervals by cleared pastures and peasant huts, clustered together for mutual protection as well as sociability. None was big enough to be called a town. The villages and hamlets offered little attraction to a wayfarer, for they were all squalid or impoverished and their residents were uniformly peasant-ignorant, peasant-slovenly, and peasant-ugly.

Most of those inhabitants we encountered did not know much about the world beyond their immediate homeplaces, and did not care to know about the greater world. When I asked one man for news of happenings more momentous than the marriage of local nonentities, he spoke vaguely of having heard rumors of wars and battles "somewhere yonder" – where, he could not say, except that nothing of the sort had lately happened near here. When I inquired of another man where the trail we were traveling led, he could only say, "I have heard that eventually you can get from this province to another, and that there is a great river somewhere around there, and on that river you might find a city of some size."

"What is the next province? What is the name of the river? The city?"

"*Ach*, stranger, if they have names I could not tell them to you."

At last, we came to a village that seemed substantially larger than the others we'd traversed in the last few days, and it was there that we finally got some useful information. We came upon a man who, though dressed in the country-bumpkin style of his compatriots, seemed more alert than the others. "Excuse me, sir," Joan said. "Have you heard of the city of Vindobona? Wien?" She pronounced it "*Veen*" in the German manner.

"Aye."

"Might you tell us how to get there?"

"I have never been there," said the man. "But there is an old Roman road due east of here. It will take you north to the Danuvius and the city. The road is twenty-five Roman miles distant. From there to Vindobona, perhaps another twenty-five."

Only one day's steady ride, dawn to dusk, to reach the road, and another two days to reach our goal. However, before we reached the old Roman road, we suffered a misadventure. In the late afternoon of the next day, we paused at a sparkling streamlet, dismounted to let our horses drink, and knelt a little way upstream to drink some of the water ourselves. I watched as little Aegina steadied herself with her right hand against a blackish rock mottled with green. Suddenly, those colors squirmed violently and Aegina screamed. I saw a large, full-grown serpent, a venomous adder, strike the child, sinking its fangs into her forearm.

I snarled a curse and smashed the reptile's head with another rock, but after that I had no idea what to do. I had had no experience whatever in dealing with snakebite, but I knew Aegina's life could be at stake. She was growing pale, breathing in and out rapidly and shallowly, and she was clearly in pain.

"Whatever you do, do not move," Joan commanded. She reached for a knife in her belt. Aegina started to shrink away in horror. "I said do not move!" Joan barked, and strode rapidly toward Aegina. "You must not move, not even to stop the pain. Any movement makes the venom course more quickly through your veins." By this time, Aegina was starting to whimper pitifully. Kneeling down beside Aegina, Joan slashed the right sleeve of her tunic and bared her arm, where, near the elbow, the twin punctures were bright red.

"Grit your teeth, Aegina. Bite down and don't be afraid. This will hurt." The child nodded dumbly. Joan pinched Aegina's skin at the point of the bite, between her thumb and forefinger. Then she carefully positioned the blade to cut the child.

"Will I bleed to death?" she asked calmly.

"*Ne*, bleeding is what you need, but you will not bleed overmuch. Thank God the adder was a large one and bit you where it did. If it were a baby, you'd be in real trouble. Any part of the body's flesh than can be pinched up between two fingers can be safely cut without the risk of cutting into any vital blood vessel. All right, darling, grit your teeth and look elsewhere."

She did, and she gave only a stifled whimper at what must have been the fierce pain of Joan's slashing away a walnut-sized piece of the child's skin and flesh. The little girl swallowed back tears. "Will I be all right?"

"I can't tell," Joan said truthfully, "but that will help. So will this." She whipped off her belt and wound it around Aegina's upper arm and cinched it tight. "Now put your arm under the cold water. Hold it there and let it bleed. I'll go tether our horses. We'll be here for some time."

I held the trembling child to me while she dutifully soaked her arm as Joan has directed. Soon, the bleeding slowed to a small trickle and almost stopped. When Joan returned, she looked at the wound, nodded, and said, "Aegina, you must now be braver than you ever have been. The good news is that you will survive. The bad news is that you may wish you could die when the snake's poison takes effect. I tell you this so you know I will always tell you the truth and will never lie to you."

Aegina nodded seriously.

"Here, drink this." Joan had plucked and brought back with her some stalks of the common spurge plant, and now she squeezed their milky, sticky sap into her flask, added water from the stream, briskly shook the mixture, and handed the flask to Aegina.

While the child struggled to drink the bitter potion without gagging on it, Joan spoke to her. "That adder was kinder than it wanted to be. It was lying coiled on its own best antidote." She scraped a quantity of the green moss off the black rock, lifted Aegina's gashed arm from the water – the bleeding was now only a thin ooze – plastered the moss against the wound, and tied it on with a strip of cloth which she had torn from the hem of her own tunic. She also loosened, then tightened again, the belt around Aegina's upper arm.

Joan talked quietly, comfortingly, to the child, who was alternately shivering and complaining of the bestial heat. I sat back, allowing Joan to handle the situation, as she was clearly far more competent than me. "Are you sure I'll live?" the child asked piteously.

"Yes, darling, I'm sure you will."

"And you say I'll be better?" Suddenly, Aegina gagged and there was a rush of bile into her throat. "I'm going, I'm going to —" she gasped, suddenly breathing in and out, growing paler each moment.

"Go ahead, honey, lean over the water and vomit," Joan said. "You may as well start getting used to it. Let me just loosen and tighten your belt again. Then I will lay a fire and spread out our blankets."

Joan beckoned me tend the fire and boil some water in a pot. I was thankful for the opportunity to do something. During the night, Joan and I would sleep off and on in shifts, for we spent all our time tending to Aegina. During the next three days and nights, we did not travel at all. At times, Aegina complained of seeing two of everything about her, including us. At other times, she talked so confusedly we could not understand a word she said.

We cooked warm broth and porridge for Aegina. Sometimes she kept it down, most times she did not, because she told us the smell of any cooking food violently nauseated her. Most of the time, Aegina seemed to be in excruciating pain. She screamed at the sharp cramps in her stomach, and she moaned that every muscle in her body ached until she wanted to bang her body against nearby rocks to stop the pain. Joan loosened or tightened the belt around the child's right arm periodically. Mostly, though, Joan and I had to restrain Aegina, sometimes even waking her from her sleep, to prevent her clawing the moss poultice off her forearm because the scab forming on the gash itched so maddeningly.

On many occasions, Aegina would go lurching off into the woods to spew her bowels empty. Each time, one of us would go with her and undress her to keep her from soiling her clothes, and we would carry her back to the water and wash her nether parts, to keep her as comfortable as possible, to inhibit infection, and to reduce the disgusting smell. On the morning of the fourth day after the bite, Aegina told us her head didn't ache nearly as much and that her stomach cramps had diminished. She continued to grab at her arm, but by this time we were familiar enough with the itching to anticipate her movement before she actually moved. On those occasions, she glared balefully, although weakly, at us.

"Well, my dear," Joan finally pronounced. "You've survived the snake's venom and you'll now get better rapidly."

"I feel as weak as a baby," she mumbled.

"Yes, and you'll continue to feel weak for a couple more days. We'll get some warm food into you and it will make you stronger. Do you think you can hold any food down?"

"Oh, yes," she said. "What smells so good?"

"Hot oatmeal," I said. "Would that we had some milk to make it creamier, but I have a bit of sugar to sweeten it."

"Oh, that would be lovely," she said, perking up a bit. "I am so hungry I could eat a whole sheep —" Suddenly, she gagged again, and vomited – very little this time, and even her dry heaves were not quite so pronounced – into the stream. "Well," she smiled ruefully, but with an indication her indomitable spirit was returning, "maybe not *quite* a sheep. Perhaps a small lamb."

"*Ne*, young lady," Joan rejoined. "We'll get a little tea into you and then a little oatmeal. We'll do it several times today and tomorrow until you decide you're strong enough."

Once Aegina realized both that she was going to survive and that she was going to get better, she was an ideal patient. Joan's talent as a *medicus* was better than any I'd ever seen. Aegina was my friend, but now she absolutely idolized "My healer Joannes," who, we were both certain, had saved her life.

On the morning of the sixth day, Aegina felt strong enough to travel, and we did so, albeit very slowly and very gently. We never urged the horses on to more than a leisurely walk. Joan compelled us to stop at least twice during the day to insist that the child take a nap.

Next day, we reached the Danuvius at Lentia. I'd heard that the Rhenus was a great river, but my first view of the Danuvius convinced me that any river in Europe would be a distant second when compared with this great, broad and exceedingly lovely river. We rode alongside the river, rather than take passage on it, for we were concerned that any different movement would alter Aegina's delicate condition and cause a relapse.

As it turns out, we need not have worried, for Aegina had the constitution of a young female ox. Still, our traverse down the river turned out to be not much slower than the rivergoing vessels that regularly passed us, for in places the water traffic was so congested that boats had to slow down in order not to collide with other skiffs, or barges, or small ships.

Around every bend of the river there were wealthy farming villages and towns, and fields filled with wheat and millet, hops and barley, onions and garlic, and sunflowers. The villages were colorful, and the inhabitants wore colorful, layered garbs. Along the way, we stopped to watch groups of dancers swaying and stomping, and jumping and skipping to folk dances of the region. We found ourselves clapping in rhythm as the musicians pulled bows across fiddles, or pounded on cymbals, drums, or gongs, or tooted through small and larger trumpets.

We were now entering early summer, and the inhabitants seemed to know they'd have to treasure and remember and live for these warm times on those days at year's end when cold winter winds would blast their villages for weeks on end. There were solid, two- and three-story buildings at strategic viewpoints and greater bends on the river, some dating back to ancient Roman days by the looks of them.

That we were traversing a Europe in the throes of change was evident from the names of the settlements and villages and towns through which we passed. In the old days, the Danuvius had been the northern border of Pannonia, and, in some places, the very edge of the grand old Roman Empire. Germanic tribes, once viewed by cultured Romans as "barbarian," had settled and imposed their own ideas of culture, including beer, one of the world's great inventions, and the German-Saxon language on the region.

Thus, between Lentia, which still retained its Roman name on the southern bank of the Danuvius, but was called Linz on the *Donau's* northern bank, and Vindobona / Wien, where we would decamp, we passed through familiarly Latin-named towns such as St. Valentinius, Amstedia, and Melikus, as well as settlements with German names, Krems, Klosterneuburg, and such. As we traveled farther east and came closer and closer to our destination, the thoroughfare became ever wider, ever more crowded, ever more carefully tended, and, of course, ever noisier. On our thirteenth day out of Hausstadt, we came at last to the metropolis of Vindobona, the largest and most impressive city I had yet seen.

Even now, in the lowly state to which I have sunk, I remember that charming center, once the northeasternmost outpost of the Roman Empire, and even now so well reputed and beloved that its inhabitants, and indeed a substantial part of Europe, proudly claim that the end of European civilization and the beginning of the oriental lands extending all the way to the Empire of the Seres, meet at the eastern gates of Vindobona.

CHAPTER 25

Even though it is commonly called Wien today, I still remember the place as Vindobona, and will refer to it by its old Latin name, if nothing else so that my readers, whoever they may be, will not become unnecessarily confused.

Vindobona grew up around a garrison that guarded the Roman Empire's frontier. But it was infinitely larger and busier and more populous and grander than Basilea or St. Gallen, or even London or Rome, because it stands where several ancient Roman roads converge and also alongside the most heavily traveled waterway in all of Europe. There were more than just barges and scows and fishing boats. There were freighting craft nearly as big as seagoing ships, propelled by many oarsmen, sometimes two or three banks of them, and when the wind was right, these oarsmen were aided by square sails held aloft on masts.

Most of Vindobona's buildings were stone or brick. Many of them were three- or four-stories high. These buildings included the usual amenities, inns, *restorans* or *cafés*, thermae and lupanares, riverside warehouses, extensive market arcades, and luxurious residences – but so many *more* and of such greater variety and diversity than I had seen elsewhere.

Tucked among the more imposing edifices were snug neighborhood *tabernae* and exquisite small shops vending jewels, perfumes, and other precious sorts of merchandise. Once, Vindobona was a modern, civilized, and refined city, and its culture was on a lesser scale only to Rome. Today, Vindobona has far surpassed Rome and is still second in the world, but second only to Constantinople.

Unlike London and Constantinople, which seem to be laid out in a more or less simple grid pattern, and unlike Rome, which seems to be laid out in more or less *no* pattern, Vindobona consists of concentric circles, which spread from the center of the city outward. The northern frontier of the city limits is the faraway Vindobona forest, the *Wienerwald*. Since there are no high alps, or any alps, in the vicinity, the highest point is the *Wienerwald*. As the city meanders east, the land flattens out.

Sergius had given us directions to Aegina's father's home, as well as to the residence address of his sister, Berenice, and his older niece Eva. Aegina urged us to hurry toward the Vindobona forest. She was trembling with excitement as we turned up a paved street containing three-story high brick structures. "Here! Right here!" she said, squirming until I had to hand her down from my horse. Once on the ground, she ran up to the front door of one of those structures and banged on the heavy wooden door with both of her small fists, shouting, "Papa! Papa! Papa!" in an unrelenting rhythm.

The door was promptly opened, and a slightly shorter, immaculately-dressed version of Sergius grabbed her as she literally jumped into his arms, and swung her round and round, plastering kisses on her forehead and her face. It took fully a hundred-count until Aegina's father saw us and beckoned us into his home.

"Papa! Joannes saved my life! I was bitten by a snake and I almost died. I would have died, but Brother Joannes saved my life. And I love Brother Martin so much! Perhaps I shall marry him when I'm grown!"

At the mention of the snake-bite, Aegina's father whitened, glanced at us questioningly, then appeared to warm and brighten once he knew his only daughter truly was safe and well. "Come in, gentlemen. I am Tacitus. Be assured of my undying thanks, not to mention the run of my home, and more than ample board for as long as you plan to be here."

The house was patrician, tasteful, and solid, but somehow much more alive than any residences I'd seen in Vesontio, Basilea, or St. Gallen. Its front and doorway were decorated almost as colorfully as those in Hausstadt. Its broad, hospitable forecourt was square and filled with bright green bushes and shrubs and flowering plants. The court was surrounded by four perimeter walls, and there were more than fifty windows that looked down onto it.

"There are separate quarters for your horses," Tacitus remarked. "Since they are within the walls of this house, in the adjoining wing, they are warm, safe, and secure in any weather." Tacitus had most tactfully supplied each stall with its own small goat to keep the horses from becoming bored.

When I returned, Joan was giving Tacitus a detailed description of our misadventure in the forest. Tacitus nodded thoughtfully as Joan mentioned the various ointments and plants and purgatives and medicaments. "I've been in Persia for more than two years last past. I am intrigued by what you say, since I studied Persian medical practices in my spare time there."

"Are those practices much different from ours?" Joan asked.

"Aye."

"More advanced or behind us?"

"Much more advanced."

Joan sighed. "There is so much to learn in this great world. How can anyone ever hope to glean more than a hairsbreadth of the knowledge that abounds?"

"I can't answer that question for you, young Johannes. All I can suggest is that you learn as much about the world as you can, apply your own reasoning as best you can, and remember a lesson I was once taught by a very old man in Persia: "There will always be a hundred men, perhaps more, who know exactly how a thing works, or how it is designed, or how it is built – and they will always be working for that man who knows *why*."

"A wise statement, Herr Tacitus," I said. "I understand there's more to see in Vindobona than almost any city in the world."

"True, but you don't need an old fellow like me to guide you about. I think you'd best consider people closer to your own age. Besides, rude though it may seem, I wish to spend as much time with my Aegina as possible."

"I, for one, will miss Aegina terribly. Brother Joannes and I are only lately come to town. Who would know of such younger people?"

"Well," Tacitus said, smiling enigmatically and somewhat slyly. "Perhaps we might ask my sister Berenice's daughter, Eva. We'll dine and rest tonight, then meet my kinfolk tomorrow morning."

Shortly after breakfast, Tacitus took us in his carriage about one-quarter of the distance through town, until we came to a street where there were smaller, still elegant, houses.

We stopped in front of one such house, two stories high, and alighted from the carriage.

The woman who opened the door was certainly handsome. We made our greetings, Aegina told her story about how Joan had saved her life, and we had just sat down to hot ale and puff pastries, when I heard a rustling on the floor above us. As I glanced up toward the source of the sound, Berenice said, "Not to worry. That's simply my daughter who, for some unknown reason, has decided to sleep in late this morning. She'll be down in a few moments and I'll introduce you to her then."

Several minutes later, Berenice's daughter Eva came into the room.

And my heart stopped.

It was the summer of 832, and it was mid-morning on the 17th of June, and I had finished two puff pastries and was sipping a cup of ale and listening politely to my elders. Now that I have lived so long, been raised high and cast low, and have seen and heard and experienced so much more than most of the world about me, I have discovered how totally little I knew of life on that morning.

I was twenty-three that day and thought myself wise beyond my years, schooled in Church law and Church lore, seasoned by Orestes, and I'd had dalliances.

How does one paint a verbal portrait of Eva, for no one can describe or portray a dream. I can tell the world that at twenty years of age, to me Eva was the most breathtakingly beautiful creature that ever lived, but who would know or believe that now? No one. If Eva was beautiful, it was because I willed it to be so, because she was my dream, because her beauty was cast from my eye. I cannot tell you, even now, how the rest of the world saw her. None of her relatives had spoken in rapture about her, none had said she was excessively – or even moderately – attractive. Aegina viewed her as an older playmate. So I was unprepared for what befell me.

When I said my heart stopped, I am certain, given the great passage of time since that morning, it may not really have stopped for any appreciable length of time, but perhaps only lurched in my chest.

Joan was nearly as tall as I, full-bodied and robust. Eva was tiny, almost elfin. She came up to my shoulders. She was blonde, as were so many Vindobonese, and wore her hair in plaits that came well below her shoulders, again typically Vindobonese. Her eyes were a very light, almost grayish, blue. Her gently curved body was not overly or overtly sensual, and she gave off an aura of white gardenias.

Could she possibly have felt the same way I did at that moment? I saw the black pupils in her eyes widen perceptibly when she looked at me. She smiled, somewhat uncertainly – fearful? Knowing? Foreshadowing what was to come?

Through a fog, I heard the introductions being made.

"Brother Martin Paschal, this is my niece, *Fräulein* Eva June Hunsecker."

I took her tiny hand in mine and bowed my head slightly. We were both trembling.

"I am pleased to make your acquaintance, *Herr* Paschal." Her voice was the tinkle of tiny, silver bells and it skittered over my rapidly beating heart. It was as if there were open wires between our own hearts. *With you and I together, there will be no Church – only church bells.*

"You don't smile very much, do you, *Herr* Paschal?"

"You do it so much better, Miss Eva. I'd like you to do the smiling for both of us, for the rest of our lives." For a moment that was silent but richly reverberant, we looked at one another. Then she gave a small, come-awake shake of her head, as if she were seeing the room and the rest of the people in it for the first time. Our eyes remained locked together and neither of us let go the other's hand until Eva's mother coughed gently. "It's well past time for your breakfast, dear. Would you at least like some ale?"

"Yes, mama, thank you. I apologize to you, Uncle Tacitus, Aegina, and Brother Joannes. I fear I have totally forgotten my manners. You see, I went to bed with rather a dreadful headache last night, and I slept longer than I ever do."

"No matter," Tacitus said. "I'm pleased to find you here, darling niece. Martin and Joannes have come to Vindobona for a brief stay. They're world travelers, having come all the way from Angle-land, and they are going east and south, Joannes to Athens and Martin to — "

"To wherever you would have me be and whenever you want me to be there," I said very softly to Eva. Aloud, I said, "We've been on the road for six months now, and we've learned many things."

"How exciting!" Eva said gaily. "I've always wanted to travel. I envy my young cousin, Aegina, who's already been to so many places, and I envy the two of you your journeys."

"Martin and Joannes need someone," Tacitus continued, "someone younger than I, to squire them around Vindobona and show them the sights of our fair city."

"Oh, Uncle," Eva said, the musical tinkle playing against my heart and across the inside of my ribcage, "of course I would be delighted to be with two such handsome and articulate gentlemen. Would you mind horribly if I asked a friend to come with us?"

"What about me?" pouted Aegina, intuiting, like all females young or old, that she had lost me to another, older woman, but sanguine about it nonetheless.

"What about me?" echoed Tacitus. "Or have you forgotten that a girl's greatest love is always her father?"

"Oh, Papa," she giggled, squeezing his hand and pulling at his chinwhiskers, "you'll always be my first love. Always and forever."

Without words, I looked directly at Eva and I'm certain she caught the echo of those words in my eyes. She dipped her head in a small nod.

"I feel ever so much better this morning," Eva said. "My headache's gone and I'm hungrier than ever."

"Wonderful," her mother said. "Our Eva's had these headaches for the past month. They come and go, undoubtedly caused by the stresses and strains of youth."

It was now nearing midday. Joan, Eva, and I begged our farewells to explore the city. We emerged into a Vindobona bathed in glory – or was it simply that any place in the world would have seemed glorious to me that day? The sky was a deep, cerulean blue, and small, puffy clouds drifted by, driven no doubt by a gentle breeze.

"My friend Victor lives nearby. He'll be so happy to meet you. He's always wanted to be a scholar or a priest, even since his youngest days, and you'll be his idols in no time."

Victor was Joan's age, nineteen, and although the four of us started out together, Victor and Joan were eager to walk faster than Eva and I. Soon, they were a good block ahead of us. They looked back every so often, more out of politeness than anything else.

Had they looked very closely, they might have been surprised, even scandalized, for we were discreetly nuzzling and fondling one another, oblivious to the world around us. Still, we managed to talk, and I learned much about Vindobona, and much more about the young woman who had totally captivated me from the first moment I'd seen her.

Eva had been born in Aquincum, the next large city to the east. Her father had been descended from the peoples of Attila, who had stormed across the *puszta*, the endless plains of Eastern Hungaria, three hundred years ago. He'd been a harbormaster at Aquincum until ten years ago, when he'd been killed in a boating accident. Mama was descended from Roman nobility of sorts. Her love affair with her husband had been fiery and dramatic, yet, crushed as she'd been when he died, she was not one to jump into the grave with him. Berenice had moved with her only daughter to Vindobona nine years before. She had prospered because of a settlement reached with her late husband's employer, two brothers who'd done remarkably well in their chosen professions, and her skills as a master seamstress to the premier sartors and sutors of the city.

Eva had been raised in a comfortable middle-class household. She remarked that for several years now, her mother had had a "special friend," Gyula, whom she entertained regularly. As delicate and seemingly sheltered as she appeared, Eva was not unaware of what was going on. Once or twice a week, she would sleep over at girlfriends' homes. Other times, that was not even necessary, because she and her mother had developed a close bonding that allowed for mutual understanding. Mama's room was far down the hall from Eva's, and "Uncle Gyula" had an accustomed cot downstairs, where he often spent the night.

Eva had read prodigiously. She wanted to travel, but, other than that, she had no idea what she wanted to do with the rest of her life. In that direct, yet charming, manner possessed of all Vindobonese women, young or old, Eva told me that although she'd had many proposals and opportunities and propositions, she was still a virgin. "And God knows how long I would have been one, until you came along."

I'm sure I must have turned pale, or, worse, very red, for Eva said, brightly, "Don't worry, my dear. I won't seduce you. That is, unless you want to be seduced."

"No, Eva," I said seriously. "I won't pretend I don't want you in that way. Any man would be a fool or a blind man not to want you. But I want so much more. I want you as my wife and my mate, for now and for ever."

Now it was Eva's turn to blush pink, and cast her eyes down. But she did not let go my hand for even a moment. When she looked up again, I saw her eyes were very bright, and tears were starting to form. "I – "

"Shhh," I said, squeezing her hand harder. "I know this seems to have come like a bolt of lightning. I hope you'll not take offense at my speaking the truth."

"*Ne*, it's not that, Martin. We've only met this morning. You don't know me – you can't know me – and how can I know you?"

"Would we be better suited to each other's souls, more comfortable in talking to one another, if we waited a year or two or three?"

"No," she said softly, not knowing whether to smile or give vent to her tears. "I've no doubt we'll never know one another better than we do now. And who knows how long this love – or any love – will last? So, while we live — "

"While we live? For God's sake, Eva, you're barely out of childhood. Twenty years old. You're only at the very beginning of your life. Tell me these things when we're both old and watching our grandchildren's children playing in the yard in back of our home."

"Somehow I never quite believed I would grow old," she replied. "Even when I was a child, I thought how wonderful it would be for me to drift away up to heaven before I got old and crippled and ugly and bitter. But now that there's you, I want to grow old on the same pillow as you." Of an instant, she reached out to me and I to her. I took her in my arms, gently, gently, so very gently, and simply held her close to me, felt the beat of her heart against mine, felt the light rise and fall of her small breasts against my chest, felt the mutual warmth and luster of love soak into our pores, and said nothing.

~ ∫ ~

Well, we did see Vindobona during the ensuing days, and there was much of it to see. On one such day, Victor had a course he needed to attend in his schola, and Eva told us she was a bit tired. She'd had a headache the day before, which, she said, was an ordinary occurrence during the week before her *menstruum*.

Neither Joan nor I minded that it was just the two of us. We stopped at a sartor's haberdashery to gaze at the latest styles of clothing worn by the city's swells. One of the shop's two partners came up to us with numerous patterns of garments and bolts of cloth: cottons from Egypt and Kos, linens from Camaracum, woolens from España, and even goose down from Gaza. But there was one fabric, an incredibly fine, soft, lovely, almost fluid fabric the likes of which I had never seen before.

"Silk," said the sartor. "It is spun and woven by the Seres. I am told they make it from a kind of fleece, or perhaps a down that they comb from the leaves of a certain tree that grows only in their land. I do not even know where their land lies, except it is far away to the east. This textile is so rare and precious that only the wealthiest can afford to wear it."

Then, he told me the price. It was not measured by the yard, which was the standard cloth measure, not even by the foot, but by the *uncia*. When he said how much this silk was per *uncia*, I tried not to look stunned, but I thought, *Holy Christ, spun gold would cost less!* I mumbled that the silk appeared too frail for the use to which I would put it.

"Frail?! I'll have you know, young sirs, that a silk tunic will outlast armor!"

I was by no means poverty-stricken. Indeed, when last I had heard from the Jew back in Angle-land, the value of my holdings had trebled. What was money for if not to spend? And whether or not I could make myself happy by the expenditure of money, I might make someone else very happy.

"Do you, *Herr* Sartor, have any measure of this silk in a light blue, almost gray, color?"

"Indeed, we have several measures. What's more, we can dye what we have to any color of the rainbow."

I selected a unit of this treasured fabric, one yard long by one and one-half feet wide. Joan gasped when she heard the price, for it represented a full month's worth of the allowance I had set for myself. To the sartor, I simply said, "Can the ends of this piece of silk be bound and reinforced to avoid fraying?"

"Of course, sir, and at no extra charge, and with any material you desire." With that, he summoned a sutor from next door, and that man came with an assortment of felt and leather and every kind of hide, from soft roebuck to garish crocodilus. When I saw what he had to offer, I not only accepted a buff-colored strand of roebuck, but also asked what it would cost to have a pair of soft boots made of matching roebuck hide, inset with soft lamb's wool for warmth and comfort. The price was not too high for my budget, so I commissioned a pair to be finished. Both the sartor and the sutor told me that the silk and the boots would be ready by midday.

While Joan and I were waiting, we stopped at a third shop, that of an unguentarius. I saw a basket full of vials, which the proprietor opened one after another to let me sample the scents of the perfumes they contained. "This one is the essence of flowers from the plain of Enna, where even the hounds are confounded in their hunting by the ambient aroma of so many fragrant blossoms. And here, Sir, is pure attar imported from the valley of the Roses in the eastern foothills of the Haemus Mountains of the Bulgars. In that valley, the inhabitants allow not a single other plant of any kind to grow, lest it pollute the impeccability of the roses. I have another attar of roses, less expensive because it comes from Paestum, where roses bloom twice a year."

"Have you any essence of white gardenia?"

"Ah, yes. Not very expensive, but light and lovely."

Afterward, we walked up the street for several blocks.

"You're seriously thinking of quitting the priesthood?" Joan said.

"Aye."

"For Eva?"

"Aye again. You were with Torvald. You know what it is like."

"Yes," she said, a bit sadly. "We did not have much time, and that's what made it so very, very precious. I, too, vowed to leave the Church – I would still leave the Church would it have brought him back. So I fear I must go to Athens on my own?"

"Why do you say that?

"You want to be with Eva."

"Always and forever, my friend."

"She lives here in Vindobona."

"Yes, but she's said her life's ambition is to travel, I imagine like her uncle Tacitus, who's no doubt filled her head with visions."

At that, Joan brightened. "So we could still travel together?"

"I would certainly hope so! I cannot think of a better traveling companion."

"Have you given any thought to what you would do?"

"Every man or woman has a talent to do whatever it takes to stay alive. Had you left the arms of Mother Church, you could have been anything from a *medicus* to a necromancer, and with your mind you could have challenged anyone. I have funds of my own. Over the years, I've become conversant in more than one language, which would make my services of some value to someone engaged in international ventures. I've kept diaries, since we left London, even though I've sent most of them back to Wessex for safekeeping, so I'm capable of writing down that which I observe. Somehow I'll manage," I said.

"And Eva?"

"I'll be there to protect her, and if, God forbid, anything should befall me, I would expect my closest friend in the world to protect her as well."

"Have you been together?" She asked with such directness, without artifice or guile or salacious interest, that I was not offended by the question.

"*Ne*, Joan, we have not. And not because she doesn't attract me. No human being has ever attracted me as much – except, in an earlier time, you – but I want it to be holy. When I take her to bed, it will be to our marriage bed, not before."

"Have you spoken of marriage?"

"I shall."

"When do you plan to do so?"

"That, my friend, is the surprise I have in store for everyone. I've told you how much she has always dreamed of traveling."

"Yes."

"Suppose we were to get married at sunrise or sunset on the Acropolis in Athens?"

"You're joking," Joan said.

"Never more serious in my life."

"God make your dearest wish come true, my friend."

"Amen. But it's the highest point of midday, and I've some gifts to retrieve."

~ ∫ ~

A fortnight later, I asked Eva's Uncle Tacitus, her mother Berenice, Gyula, Aegina, Joan, and, of course, Eva, to be present at Tacitus' home. I had arranged to have a many-course meal brought in by a caterer I'd found in a nearby district. We had just finished dining. The caterer had, at my insistence, procured an amphora of well-aged Falernian red wine. I stood to address the group, and my voice betrayed none of the nervousness I felt.

"I am sure all of this will come as a great shock to each of you, coming as it does so soon after Joannes and I arrived at your fair city. I have always been told not to repay kindness with evil, nor to steal, but I have a confession to make, one that will affect all of your lives."

Every eye in the room was on me. What kind of great sin was I going to confess? What kind of embarrassment would I bring to this kind and hospitable family?

"Since Eva has no living father, I ask and beg all of you for your consent to marry Eva, and Eva, I ask of you that you take the first step in allowing us to spend eternity together."

"That's not stealing," Tacitus broke out, grinning widely. "That's joining our family. Of course you have my consent. More than that, you have my blessing."

"And mine," rejoined each of the older folk in turn.

"And mine, I guess," said Aegina, not a little sourly.

"Eva?" I asked, looking deep into her eyes. I was pleased to see she was wearing the scarf and the slippers I'd purchased two weeks before, for it made her, if anything, yet more beautiful.

By this time, her eyes were brimming with tears. She managed to blurt out, "Before I give you my answer, which I think you already know, please tell us – tell me – what you mean by 'stealing?'"

"Well, my darling, I propose we not marry in Vindobona."

"Where then?"

"I propose we marry atop the Acropolis."

"In Athens?" she gasped.

"Unless you know of a better place. Uncle Tacitus, I would be so very honored if you could arrange for your brother, the Cardinal Sergius, to officiate at the ceremony. "

"And then?" Eva continued in a soft voice.

"And then, my love, we will begin our lives together. Mayhap in Vindobona, mayhap in Constantinople, mayhap in Persia," I answered, giving Tacitus a sidelong smile of my own. "Now, then, my beloved. I have asked and received the blessing of this wonderful, fine family, which I hope they do not now revoke having heard my plans. But I have not heard your answer."

"Martin," she said, "you've known my answer from the moment I first laid eyes on you. Were you ever in any doubt?

Of course I shall marry you, and proudly and gladly, and may we have many children, both sons and daughters, to carry on for us when our lives are done. Oh, Martin," she said, breaking down and crying copiously. "I love you so much. I love you so very, very much."

I felt a lump the size of an apple in my throat as she covered my face with gentle kisses.

"There is one more thing," I said, clearing my throat, "and I hope it will somehow allay your tears." I fished in my waist wallet for the small box and handed it to her. Inside was a small, perfectly cut diamond embedded in a white gold ring. On each side of the stone, the initials "M" and "E" were interlocked.

I remember that day as the happiest in my life.

CHAPTER 26

"Might I suggest the following, and before you say *ne*, listen to the reasoning of an old man." The three of us smiled. Tacitus was anything but old, but he was very experienced. "Martin, you wish to marry our Eva and you'll be taking her to places she's never been. I suggest that before you do that, you visit the place where she was born."

"Aquincum," Eva said.

"Aye, and the rest of northeastern Pannonia. You should not miss Lake Balatonea. Then, I suggest you proceed south and west to Laibach and thence to the head of the Hadriatic Sea at Tridentium. It should be quite close to winter by then, but you'll be south of the Alps. Here, let me show you."

He went into another room and emerged with a thick, heavy book of codexes. Placing it on the largest table in the room, he summoned us to look.

"The coast of Dalmatia is usually quite peaceful because it is usually warm, and balmy weather is not conducive to pitched battles. Although it rains in the winter, the climate is far more clement than in the Alps or the Haemus. Continue south as far as you can go, making sure always to keep the

Hadriatic Sea in sight. You'll pass through many smaller nations, none of them particularly hostile, and after you travel beyond the Illyrian frontier, you'll arrive in Hellas. From there, it's an easy trip over not very high mountains, to Athens." His plan sounded eminently sensible to me, and, by the way Joan nodded, it obviously sounded sensible to her.

"Meanwhile, I shall make arrangements for our entire family, and for several of our close friends to attend the wedding in Athens. Your journey through the Haemus Peninsula, even the western Haemus Peninsula, will be vigorous and adventuresome, and I realize young folk enjoy such excitement. By your leave – or not by your leave, I care not," he said, chuckling, "we ancients and my not-so-adventurous friends will take the easier route. We'll embark from Tridentium or Venetia and ply the Hadriatic in comfort and style. If we left at the same time you did, we'd still be there months ahead of you. That way, we can remain in Vindobona until spring, and still be there in time to celebrate with you."

"Marvelous, marvelous city, Athens," Tacitus sighed. "They say it was a new city at the time of the gods. I'm letting my imagination take me on ancient journeys."

"*Ne*, Uncle," Eva said. "You're letting the wine take you on ancient journeys."

"I don't know about the rest of you," Eva continued. "But it's getting late, and I feel a slight headache coming upon me. Would you mind terribly if I excused myself and went up to bed?" We didn't and she did, and we continued talking and planning for half the night.

~ ∫ ~

The voyage downriver from Vindobona was lazily pleasant. The Danuvius flowed eastward and we were bathed in the warm sun of high summer. The river's banks on both sides were thickly and monotonously forested, except where those green walls were interrupted, here and there, by a logging camp, a small farmstead, or a fishing village. That land itself was unspectacular, with gentle rolling hills, interrupted by somewhat higher ridges, as far as the eye could see. The barge on which we had taken passage was well equipped and the entire journey to Obuda took less than three days, so it was unnecessary for us to purchase additional provisions.

On the morning of the third day, the river made a great, sweeping turn to the south. By early afternoon, Eva excitedly pointed out the ruins of Roman Aquincum on a hill to our right.

"There's the northeastern edge of Pannonia," she cried. "The Romans planted the first vineyards ever seen in Hungaria just up that hill, They had all kinds of *thermae* all about the town. And there – just ahead on your right, about halfway up the hill – that's where I used to live! We must go there, oh, please, Martin, my dearest?"

"Of course, darling. That's the very first place we'll go tomorrow morning."

We made landing at Obuda, on the right bank of the Danuvius, about an hour later. While I was not enchanted by what I saw, I became enraptured simply watching Eva relive her past.

Although there was a grand view up and down the Danuvius from the heights of Obuda, the town was not impressive. The once proud Roman garrison at Aquincum had never recovered from its annihilation by Attila and some two hundred thousand Huns, who'd invaded from the east nearly four hundred years ago. A second reason for the town's current backwater status was that after the fall of Aquincum, it had been settled and sacked progressively by Goths, Lombards, and Avars, until Charlemagne had subdued the warring tribes some thirty-five years ago. Even then, the Great Charles had trouble finding anyone who really wanted to settle in Hungaria. As a result, the town was smaller than Basilea or Vesontio, with ten thousand inhabitants at most.

Looking east from the heights of Obuda, we could see land as flat as a table, all the way to the horizon, and, from what I have learned, well beyond that. The Great Plain of Hungaria extends far into the land of the *Rus*, and I am told men and women and even animals go mad from the monotony, and the never-ending harsh winds, and the driving rains that perpetually flood the place.

We took shelter in a *gasthaus* up the hill from the landing pier, for those lodgings in the immediate area of the dock were disreputable and filthy. Although very cheap by Vindobonese standards, the *gasthaus* where we stayed was moderately comfortable. What I remember best was the supper we had that night, which took place in a dark, smoky, communal dining room. There was no menu from which to order. A handsome, plump waitress simply fetched the meal of the day. The first course was Drunkard's Soup, a tasty, tart dish made from a base of pickled cabbage. Next came Robber's Meat, chunks of lamb, onions, mushrooms, tomatoes and green peppers alternated on a skewer and cooked over an open fire.

"That's perhaps the only decent thing the Huns brought to Hungaria," Eva remarked.

The Robber's Meat was accompanied by little pinched dumplings and potatoes served in a red pepper sauce. Only eight people took supper that evening, and we all shared two large jugs of Hungaria's wines, a straw-yellow Tokaji and the dark red wine called Bull's Blood.

Next morning, Eva was up earlier than either of us, dressed in a light summer dress that accentuated the curves of her slender body and the beautiful smoothness of her skin. She had not lived in Obuda for some years, but she seemed to know every stone and every ruin. She insisted we walk up the hill toward the ruins of Aquincum, and while there were a number of scattered stones from what had been the garrison walls, an old Roman bath, and even a small theatre, these ruins were not well attended-to. There was a forlorn, abandoned feel to the place.

To make conversation, I asked, "Eva, has this place changed since you were last here?"

"Oh, yes," she replied. "It's gotten so much larger in only ten years. Our house was at the southern end of town when we moved to Vindobona. Now, the city spreads down almost to Margaret Island. There are even warehouses and new buildings on the other side of the river."

I dared not say that if it was now so much larger, this place must *really* have been the end of the civilized world when Eva was born. I tried to concentrate on Margaret Island. That large and forested boat-shaped piece of land occupied an area almost as wide as the Danuvius itself.

"Were most of the *thermae* situated on that island?" Joan asked.

"Yes, they were." Eva sighed. "Of course, I've never seen a *thermae* in Aquincum. We can only trust that they did exist once."

The home where Eva had spent her first years was on a narrow street of several similar residences. It was smaller than her home in Vindobona, so I concluded that her mother had done rather better in closer proximity to her brothers than she had done in Obuda. The three of us were able to charm the building's current owner into letting us see what had become of the house. "It's so much smaller than I remembered it," Eva said.

"That's because *you* are so much larger than you were when you left it."

As we left, Eva looked back wistfully. "What a shame we have to grow up. I used to think we had the biggest house in the whole world, and that made me feel so secure. I think sometimes it's best not to go home again. Everything seems so changed. I'd hoped the house would at least have remained the same, but it has somehow shrunk." Eva's mood remained subdued for the rest of the day.

Next morning we left for Lake Balatonea, ninety Roman miles southwest of Obuda. Tacitus had thoughtfully provided Eva with a gentle mare of her own, and our pace was quite leisurely. It was not hard to find a welcoming inn enroute. Meals were ample, and there was never any choosing or ordering of the meal: it was always and ever kettle stew, a vast iron kettle kept perpetually simmering on the hearth, perpetually being topped up with whatever meat and vegetables came to hand. It was invariably hearty and invigorating. Both of the *gasthauses* where we stayed during our two nights on the road had a fat, ruddy-faced innkeeper, his equally fat, ruddy-faced wife, and at least three fat, ruddy-faced children. They seemed to have few worries, and their humor was of the broad peasant variety.

"Oh, we villagers are clever, all right," one innkeeper said. "Like the time when one of our prairie farmers owed fifty *nummus* to the local *arandar*, the region's richest man, and couldn't pay. When the great noble kept pressuring him, the farmer offered to sell his cow and hand over the proceeds in full settlement. The cow was easily worth one hundred fifty nummus, so the *arandar* agreed. They went together to the market, and the farmer took along a chicken, as well. A man came up and asked, "How much for the chicken?" The farmer said, "fifty *nummus*." The man said, "Good God! I could buy a cow for that much!" "I'll tell you what. Give me fifty *nummus* for the chicken and I'll let you have the cow for just half a *nummus*." So the deal was struck. The farmer pocketed the fifty *nummus* and paid off the rich man with the half a *nummus* he'd gotten for the cow. Just as agreed."

This brought a roar of laughter from the small assembly gathered at dinner, and, since we were all seated in close proximity and all apparently headed in one direction or another, we introduced ourselves to each other. The most interesting man we met that night was a man of middle-age, one Amalric, a broker in various merchandise, who regularly traveled from Vindobona to Singidunum and from there to Dacia, all the way Constantiana, which sat astride the western shore of the Black Sea.

Joan engaged him in lively converse immediately. "What, exactly, do you *do* as a traveling broker?"

"Ah," Amalric chuckled. "That depends on the season and the need. Many folk would say I deal in air – the Jews, who seem to live everywhere I travel and often seem to engage in the same trade – call it a *luftmensch* in their polyglot Jewish language. I find a need and try to fill it, profiting from the transaction on both sides. Near the Black Sea, there is a particularly smelly mud, probably the result of all the muck and detritus that gathers when the Danuvius finally comes to its end. Now, anyone would think there is little one can do with such a foul-smelling commodity, but, in truth, and somewhat because of my efforts, it is as valuable as gold."

"Why is that?" Eva asked.

"Young lady," Amalric replied, turning to face her. "You are obviously youthful and very beautiful, and you would never purchase such a thing at your age. But as young women of wealth, culture, and sophistication become older, they always have – and always will – try to keep the ravages of time at bay for as long as possible. They wish to erase the slightest hint of wrinkle from their faces and to keep the dewy, moist look of youth at any price. For more than a thousand years, women have used what unguents and creams they can to help them in their struggle. Since the Romans became masters of Dacia, half a millennium ago, opportunistic merchants and manufacturers have bottled this stinky, useless mud in tiny vials and sold it as beauty mud. Ladies at the Roman court concluded that if something smelt that bad, it must be as magically potent as it was represented to be, and purveyors purchased this mud in huge lots, at ever increasing prices, until it made Constantiana a wealthy town."

"And your job?" I asked.

"I travel to Constantiana independently or at the behest of a merchant in, say, Vindobona. I visit a purveyor who wants to sell the ghastly muck at the highest price he can get. Foreign markets, particularly wealthy foreign markets, afford that best price. I purchase a quantity of mud from him at one price, payable on delivery of the stuff in Vindobona. Because he has dealt with me before, the purveyor knows I won't cheat him. The mud costs him very little to produce and, since the buyer will pay immediately on delivery, he makes a goodly profit for the very small risk of transporting the goods.

"Meanwhile, I have either already lined up my purchaser in Vindobona or I know of several merchants to whom I can sell the mud. I sell the mud for far less than a single, unknowing merchant from Vindobona would have to pay, were he to travel to Constantiana, because I purchase much larger quantities from the purveyor in Constantiana than a single customer would purchase.

"I charge the purveyor a small fee for arranging transportation of the goods to Vindobona. I charge the teamster a small commission for the purveyor to hire that particular teamster to transport the mud. I charge the purveyor another small fee for arranging to have the goods picked up in Vindobona and distributed to the customer, and for ensuring that the purveyor is promptly paid. And finally, I charge my merchant in Vindobona a small premium over the price I paid the purveyor to get the goods into the merchant's hands in that Pannonian city."

"Clever," Joan remarked. "You're really out no money from your own pocket, no one feels cheated at the amount you receive, and by putting all those "small" fees together, you emerge with a rather tidy profit."

"Aye," Amalric responded, "but for the occasional cheat or theft or other casualty, and when that happens, I still make sure my client is paid, usually out of my own pocket. That's a small price to pay for the loyalty I generate in both the purveyor and the customer."

Because nights, even summer nights, were windy and often cold on the great plain of Hungaria, there was a huge log fire burning in the dining-and-gathering room of the inn, one that provided some heat and some light, but not very much of either.

"Could not the purveyor and the merchant and the drover arrange to deal with one another and thus save having to pay your fees?" Eva asked.

"They could, and, indeed, sometimes they try to do just that. I simply accept that with good grace, for I know that after one or two such exchanges, something will go wrong somewhere, the merchant and the drover and the manufacturer will all detest one another, or they will try to cheat one another, or they will simply tire of the extra effort involved for the small amount of savings on a transaction. You see, each one wants to make the most money with the least effort. So, before long, each returns to me, begging forgiveness, and offering me a higher commission. But enough of me. Whither goest the three of you?"

"To Athens," I said. "My fiancée was born in Aquincum and I thought to take her through her native Hungaria on the way to our wedding."

"How thoughtful!" Amalric exclaimed. "I wish you both a long and happy life, filled with the joys that children bring. Ah, that's the one thing I miss. Because of my travels, I have never settled down with a wife, never had any children. I suppose my line will die out with me, but, perhaps, there's still time. And you, young man?" he said, pointing to Joan. "How come you to be with these two?"

"I'm going to the *schola* at Athens to learn what I can of the world."

I squeezed Eva's hand gently and she smiled indulgently at me.

"I suppose you're going to spend a few days at Balatonea?" Amalric reached over and poured himself a large draught of the local red wine.

"Aye," I said.

"That lake is one of the strangest phenomena in Europe."

"Why say you that?" Joan asked.

"You'll soon notice," he said, "that it's always windy around Lake Balatonea. It's the biggest lake in all central Europe. It's oddly shaped – eighty Roman miles long and only eight miles wide – but even stranger than that, its bed is shaped like an underwater hill. Down at Balatonea's southern end, the bottom shelves so very gradually that you can wade out for a whole mile before the water reaches your chin. But it keeps on shelving down like an eighty-mile ramp, until, at the north end, it is fifty feet deep. I don't know why Lake Balatonea's unique characteristics should create a wind, but there always is a wind, and the water is always choppy."

"It seems to me, Herr Amalric, there's always a wind on this unending great plain," I said.

"That, too, but when a real storm comes up – and it generally comes from the south – it scrapes the water up from the southern end of the lake and tries to pile it on top of the deep water to the north. You'll see waves and billows and breakers as vicious as any sea could offer."

"That sounds frightening," Joan said, and I could see from the look on her face that she was recalling that long-ago passage we had taken from Angle-land to St.Valery.

"Not as frightening as you might think. There have been fishermen and ferrymen on the lake for generations. They've developed a knack for sensing any major storm in the offing. When they do, they've learned to stay off the lake, or, if they're upon it, to get off the lake as quickly as possible, and everyone runs for cover. They have a wonderful pike-perch, the *fogas*, that's a specialty of Balatonea. It is very profitable for me, since I often broker trades between Vindobona and that godforsaken Sarmatia to the north. Dried *fogas* for long-dried animal *skeit* which, when polished, becomes amber." Joan and I smiled at one another. Cardinal Alcinorius' See was at Sarmatia, and to hear it being called god-*forsaken* was an interesting twist of the phrase.

CHAPTER 27

Next day, as we got closer to Lake Balatonea, we noticed that the road was bordered by meadows of strange, limp, wild grasses that writhed and whipped like seaweed in just the mild stirring of the air. We passed vineyards in which long ribbons of bright-colored cloth were hung to blow and shake in the wind, probably to keep the birds in the area from snapping up the young grapes. By this time, we were already bored with the monotony of the landscape, and were gratified to find that we were very gradually ascending even a slight rise.

When we got to the top of this incline, we finally got our first view of Lake Balatonea. Its color was a milky turquoise, dotted with whitecaps of chop. There seemed to be bright green reed beds everywhere, and, in the sky above those beds, large numbers of steel-blue swallows and black-headed gulls. Poplar trees seemed to line every bank. Even in late summer they were still shedding their snowfall of white fluffs. Now and then, there would be a visible splash in the water as a fish lunged for one of them. Most traffic on the lake consisted of fishing dories and ferrymen's unwieldy big rowboats. As Amalric had predicted, the lake was, indeed, *very* large – it was impossible to see from the north to the south end or from the south to the north end, even from our less-than-impressive "height" above it, and it was very windy.

We elected to go first to the deep, north end of the lake. On the way to Almádi, which Amalric had told us was the largest settlement on that shore, we passed through a wonderfully aromatic place, where we saw hundreds of hectares of lavender, and more than fifty gardeners harvesting its blossoms. I glanced over to my lovely Eva, who was dreamily enjoying the sweet aroma. "I've heard of this place," she sighed. "Tihany. I'm told it supplies lavender to every perfume purveyor, *unguentarius*, and *pharmaceutium* in Europe."

"I'll wager you could detect this fragrance all the way across the lake," Joan said.

We reached Almádi at sunset, and that place, too, was perfumed, but by the more subtle aroma of limes. After storing our belongings in our small but surprisingly luxurious rooms, we descended to a large taproom, which seemed nearly half again as big as the inn. Even at this relatively early hour, its many tables were filled with men, and a few women, convivially drinking, loudly talking, and laughing.

"You're new here," piped the innkeeper's wife, whose name we never learned. "I'm sure you're wondering why we're so busy. Well, let me tell you, we are always packed here, even when there are no guests at the inn."

"Why is that?" asked Joan.

"It's our unique location, and, fortuitous it is, for my husband and I never thought about it when we built the inn. At that time, all we knew was that we had purchased a small patch of cleared land between two large farmsteads. Soon after, we learned our land was located exactly on the border, in the no-man's land between two provinces, the old Roman

Pannonian province of Vespremium, and the gothic county of Fejepis. My husband very wisely erected the taproom where it is because the county line runs right through the middle of that large room.

"As a result," she continued, "this inn is always patronized by highwaymen, outlaws, fugitives, and law enforcement officers, for the jurisdiction of each province or county ends at the county line. If, as often happens, the police of one county come in to take a look around, or just to have a drink, the rogues simply move to the other side of the room. That longest table in the center actually straddles the county line. I can tell you that at least once every evening you'll find detectives sitting on one side of the table and bandits sitting on the other side, all drinking amicably together."

The taproom was also a dining room. Instead of the kettle stew so common throughout the region, that night we enjoyed first a cold parsley soup, followed by the delicate, flaky, melt-in-the-mouth *fogas* in caper sauce, garnished with asparagus and potatoes roasted with red peppers of the kinds we had enjoyed in Aquincum. The wine we were served with our meal was among the best I'd ever tasted. "This is the best wine in Hungaria," our loquacious innkeeper's wife said. "That's because the vines always see their own reflection in Lake Balatonea. The sunlight reflects off the lake waters, so the vines get the sun on both sides of their leaves."

I don't know how it happened. Perhaps it was the wine, or the lingering aroma of lavender, or the present aroma of citrus, but that night I found myself in the same room as my Eva, while Joan spent the night in a different room. There was a capacious matrimonial bed in Eva's room, and, as naturally as though we were already married, we lay down upon it together.

Mingled among the aromas I'd experienced that day, I felt the warm, gardenia-sweet essence of Eva next to me. She shivered slightly, and I held her to me, both of us still clothed. Then, she slipped under the covers. I heard a slight, wispy sound. Daringly, I slipped under the covers with her and doffed my own tunic.

It was the first time we'd ever experienced the other's body without clothing, and I was both amazed and confused by the whirling emotions inside me. This woman was my betrothed and would be my wife within the span of a year – we would be companions, lovers, parents, and, God willing, even grandparents. Yet she was beautiful beyond anything I'd ever imagined and now, without clothes, I could not believe how soft and womanly she was, and I was stirred in my nether parts.

Eva made herself small in the bed, pulled the covers almost up to her eyes, and trembled visibly. Finally she said, in the voice of a small child, "Hold me. Only hold me, Martin. I want to feel you all over me."

I did. Her breasts were maidenly slight and cone-shaped, with small, girlish nipples. I clasped her to me, her back to my front, and held both of her breasts in my hand. I was able to hold her close and safe and warm, and we drifted off to sleep, and all that night I held her so, and that is all the loving we ever did, or ever needed to do.

~ ∫ ~

Next morning, Joan privately asked me what had occurred between Eva and me last night. I smiled, content to answer my oldest and closest friend, that I had loved Eva all night, but that we had not made love.

"If you can withstand such a test, you are destined for a long and happy life together."

The day was disappointingly overcast and gray, but the lakeside vineyards were turning red and gold and seemed to radiate a sunshine of their own,. The air was still scented with a clean, tart, citric aroma. "Lime trees," said the innkeeper. "We plant more than ten varieties around here, and they bloom at different times throughout the year, so the air here is almost always perfumed, except in winter.

Almádi was circled on two sides by hills, and the three of us wandered about those hills, admiring the simple peasant cottages, every one of which was adorned by climbing roses. Joan pointed out the highest hill in the vicinity, which was shaped like a lopsided cone.

"Yonder is the Great Nose," she said. "Our innkeeper told me last night after the two of you had gone to bed, that according to Almádi legend, the very last remaining giant on earth died here. The people respectfully buried him, but they could not scrape up enough soil to cover his nose. Let's climb it and see."

We did, and when we arrived there, we found it was a protrusion of solid rock, with no trace of vegetation anywhere on it except for splotches of varicolored lichen.

"The Nose has always served an even more important function than mere legend," Joan said. "From up here, you can see down through the surface glare on the water. Usually a fisherman from around here will direct one of his children to climb this hill. When the child sees a shoal of fish, he signals its location to the fisherman out on the water."

By late afternoon, it was warm, gray, and muggy. When we returned to the lakeside, our innkeeper, his wife, and two young boys were busily hauling tables and chairs inside the taproom. The sky, previously a featureless, lead-colored dome, was now bulging into pouches of bruise-colored cloud. "Is it likely to be a bad one?" I shouted to the innkeeper, through the rising wind.

"The storms are always bad on Balatonea."

We quickly retired to our upstairs room and sat together, gazing out the window onto the lake. Those few ferries braving the storm were tossing and lunging and yawing and the air was so thick with water that I wondered how the crew aboard those boats could possibly be keeping on course, or even if they were. The sky lit up every few seconds with forks and jags of blue-white lightning, which were immediately followed by mind-numbing, bone-shaking booms of thunder.

Eva trembled, partly with fear and partly with cold. She ensconced herself under the covers, and was soon asleep, and whimpering softly in her sleep. I noticed her complexion was paler than usual, and I attributed it to the day and its events. At dinnertime, she told Joan and me that she was feeling a bit dizzy, and asked if we would mind terribly if she didn't join us. She asked that we bring her a small tureen of soup when we'd finished our meal.

Now, with no demur from Joan, our sleeping arrangements were somewhat permanently rearranged. That night, and for several nights to come, I slept with Eva as though we were two spoons stacked sidewise, holding her tiny breasts and keeping her warm. Yet, we still did not engage each other sexually, and perhaps that was for the best.

The rain stopped shortly before dawn, and the wind dropped to no more than its usual brisk velocity. The lake subsided to its normal chop, and the last clouds trailed off northward in time for there really to be a dawn. The sun came up and set the whole wet world in clear glory. I saw striking little rainbows from every raindrop on every tree leaf, and in the land about the inn.

After breakfast, we bade farewell to our hosts and engaged a ferry to take us across the water to the southern end of the lake. The sky was still blue and the sun was bright when, some three hours later, we made landfall at Kettelius on the southern shore of the lake. To recover our "land legs," and those of our horses, we walked through the main area of the town. Some time later, at one corner, we came to a small, dark, closed-in building with a rather garish sign, "Fortune Teller."

I looked questioningly at both my companions. Eva said, "The *Rom* are the vagabonds of Hungaria, and who knows where else. They supposedly come from the east and the south, but no one can really say for certain where they originated. There are great numbers of them in Hungaria and Dacia. They never stay in one place very long."

"Gypsies," I muttered.

"Yes, they're called that, too. Mysterious and strange folks. People avoid them from fear. They set up fortune-telling shops wherever they go. Some people, even educated people, place great store in what they say. Why don't we try it and see what lies in our future?" Joan said.

"Maybe not," Eva said. "It could be frightening."

"Don't worry, darling," I said. "It can't be more than hocus-pocus entertainment, of no more accuracy than someone telling us what the weather is going to be like next week."

"Well —" she still sounded unsure. "If you say so, Martin."

We entered the small shop and found it very dark, for there were no windows to the outside. Three candles were burning on a table and there were three chairs grouped around that table. No sooner we'd entered, a curtain at the far end parted and a dark-haired woman of indeterminate age appeared. She wore a multi-colored peasant blouse and a long, black skirt. There was a cotton shawl around her neck. She stood apart from us and said, "Good afternoon, my young pilgrims from Vindobona, bound as you are to the south. I've been expecting you."

I was startled for a moment, then realized there are any number of tricks that would have enabled her to know whence we came from and whither we were bound."

Joan asked the woman how much she charged for each of us to have our fortune told. "Fifty *nummus* each." This seemed a trifling sum, but none of us mentioned how inexpensive it was. Still, Joan handed the woman two hundred *nummus* and did not demand change. The woman murmured thanks for the substantial bonus.

"As you can see, I've arranged the three chairs, one for each of you. Please sit down, in whatever arrangement you wish."

We did, and she sat before us. She took each of our hands in turn, stroked our arms gently, and looked deep into our eyes. She handed each of us a half lime and asked us to squeeze the juice into separate cups. She spat into each of the cups and put them aside. She then looked into the light of the three candles and rubbed her head with her fist, as if she had a headache.

After what seemed a very long time, she spoke in a soft, well-modulated, but somehow other-worldly voice, as though it were disembodied from her. "You are traveling together to the south. There are three of you, two women and one man, and you are headed to the far end of the Haemus Peninsula."

Eva cleared her throat, nervously. I felt a cold clamminess. Joan betrayed no emotion.

The *Rom* woman looked directly at Joan. "You will achieve unimaginable things, something no one of your kind has ever achieved before. You will be raised almost as high as your Jesus Christ, and then —"

"Yes?" Joan urged.

"I cannot see more than that right now. The air is foggy and my vision is blurred."

"What about us?" I asked.

The fortune teller coughed and looked uncomfortable. "You will love her for the rest of your life. She will love you for six months."

I gasped, involuntarily.

"Surely you speak of someone else," I said.

"*Ne*, I speak truly. Now I must close my shop. I foresee nothing else. Thank you for your generosity." She quickly escorted us out.

I felt numb, shocked at what the woman had said, and fearful.

"Oh, Martin," Eva said gaily. "She was so wrong, even from the very first, when she said there were two women and one man traveling together. Anyone can see we are one woman and two men. I'll admit, of course, that I was unnerved when she said I would only love you for six months. Martin, I can promise you on my life that I will not run off with another man. So you see, my darling, she was absolutely wrong in two of her predictions. And as for the third, anyone charging money to tell someone else's fortune wants to make a great prediction about the one who pays for her predictions. Joannes treated her kindly and paid her well, so of course she was duty-bound to tell him how brilliantly he'd succeed."

"I guess you're right, my angel," I said, holding her close to me. "Do you still feel that dizziness you felt last night?" I asked, wanting to change the subject.

"Only a little. It seems much better today, though. It was probably all the excitement of the storm and, and," she whispered, hugging me so that the upper part of my arm rested against her breast, "lying with a man." She giggled girlishly, as if she'd done something very naughty. "Even if I haven't exactly *lain* with my man."

I pretended to be comforted, but I was not. That night, in bed with Eva, I stayed awake a long time after she had descended into a peaceful sleep. Others than the gypsy had already predicted great things for Joan. And, although Eva had not the slightest reason to believe the gypsy's statement about two women and one man traveling together, of course the fortune-teller was deadly accurate. That left her third prediction. And that was the reason I found myself trembling uncontrollably and unable to sleep for most of the night.

CHAPTER 28

From Balatonea, we headed south and west, through the well-watered Podravinius Plain toward the Croatian heartland. Three days out, we crossed the Dravus River. On the fourth morning, Eva complained of severe pains in her head. They started when she first awakened in the morning, seemed to get somewhat better during the day, then worsened as evening approached. Although she had, from time to time, complained of headaches during the time I had known her, they had never, in my experience, sapped her of her strength or spirit. Eva looked pale and wan that evening, and Joan and I decided we should stay in the nearest town of any size, which turned out to be the Slavic town of Varazhdin, for a couple of nights, as a brief respite from our travel might ease Eva's discomfort.

That night, Joan told me, "Your fiancée is undoubtedly suffering from the *migraneus*. I am told that an unfortunately large number of people, both young and old, occasionally experience the great and vicious pain of that malady. It comes and it goes, and there is little one can do about it except try to stave off the greatest pain until it dies down in a day or two."

"What about *mandragoras* root?" I asked Joan, remembering how, so many years ago, she had told me about the Satan's apple that is today called mandrake.

"*Ne*, my friend," Joan replied. "Mandragoras and its stronger companion, *morphium*, are best saved for far more serious and substantial pain, that pain which heralds approaching death. There are far less drastic plants and medicines that are almost equally effective. Acetyl acid, for example."

"Do you have any with you?"

"Aye," she responded. "I'll administer some of that powder to your love tonight. Hopefully she'll feel much better in the morning."

We did, and she did, and two days later, we resumed our journey. However, as I soon learned, when one's greatest love is experiencing pain of any kind, one cannot avoid being concerned, and that I was, for Eva's headaches seemed extraordinarily frequent in the time I'd known her.

In those days, there were messenger services, which, for a fairly nominal price, carried messages back and forth throughout Europe. One horseman, riding at high speed, would travel to the nearest town of any significance, and then back from whence he'd come. A second horseman would travel to the next city and back, and so forth. These messengers plied the high roads, and since they traveled at maximum speed and carried little except those messages, highwaymen did not prey upon them. After discussing the increasing frequency of Eva's headaches with Joan, I retained one such service to deliver a message to Vindobona. Eva's uncle Tacitus was a wise and sophisticated man of the world. I explained the situation as best I could and asked if he could guide me to trustworthy *medicia* and *pharmaceutia* along our route of travel.

Within a month thereafter, when we arrived and were staying in Fiumius at the Croatian head of the Hadriatic Sea, I received a response from Tacitus. He advised me there were several *pharmaceutia* in virtually any town of size throughout our journey, but only in Spalatius and Athens itself would we find reasonably expert *medicia*. He gave us two choices in Spalatius.

"The first and better known is the clinic of Saints Peter and Paul on the main street of town. They are well-versed in the current Western medical practices and techniques. The second is a Jew named David ben-Halevi, who trained in Khurasan in Persia during the time of Caliph al-Ma'amun. When the military seized Khurasan ten years ago, Halevi moved on to Baghdad. He was extraordinarily well-reputed as a diagnostician and surgeon, both in Persia and in the Abassid capital. I'm told that Saints Peter and Paul refer cases to Doctor Halevi when they cannot – or do not want to – deal with the situation. In Athens, I frankly recommend my old friend, Vasilios Kakis, who always took good care of me."

Meanwhile, Joan had scoured Fiumius and secured a substantial cache of medicines from *pharmaceutia* in that town. "Acetyl acid as well as numerous plants and chemicals, which I can mix together into a more potent concoction, should that be necessary."

"And *mandragoras*?" I asked. "Mind, I am not trying to take issue with you in any way, but Eva is my love, and I don't relish her suffering even the most gentle pain."

"*Mandragoras* is very hard to obtain here. I'm told the farther south we go, and the closer we get to Constantinople, the more available it becomes, but, yes, I have put by a bit of the root. Very, very dear, of course."

When, later that day, and without disclosing any of the information imparted to me by Tacitus, I asked my bride-to-be how she was feeling, she said, "Oh, ever so much better today, my darling. Indeed, I would love to go out for dinner with you and Joannes if that's possible."

Fiumius was a scrofulous seaport, which reminded me of nothing so much as a many-times larger Gull's Landing. Joan and I found the least disreputable-looking eating establishment we could, and were conversing with one another when a man's voice spoke up behind us.

"Do I hear the Latin of educated folk?"

I turned and saw a man of thirty-five, shorter than me, who had a luxuriant, bushy moustache, earlocks that blended into a dark beard, and clear, friendly brown eyes. "Please excuse my forwardness, but ever since I've come to Fiumius three months ago, all I've heard is raucous gutter talk, and without an introduction it's very hard to find my way, particularly given my, ah, status in the community."

"You are Jewish?" Joan said. That was not hard to decipher, given the man was wearing a kippah, the small round hat worn by Jews, and we could see the fringes of a ritual prayer shawl, the tallit, emerging from under his coat.

"Indeed, but pray don't let that disturb you. As a wandering Jew, I manage eventually to accommodate to wherever I go. But I've still not introduced myself. I am Michael ben-Halevi."

"I've heard that name somewhere before," I said. "Have you any relatives in Dalmatia?"

"My older brother David, who's managed to make inroads in Spalatius. He's the doctor in the family, I'm the lawyer."

"You're from Khurasan?"

"Yes. How could you possibly know?"

"A friend of mine and the uncle of my fiancée, a diplomat by the name of Tacitus — "

"Ah, he was in Khurasan just before I left. A marvelous man, worldly, not so taken with himself that he viewed the Roman Church as the only religion."

Fortunately, Eva had no idea of how I'd really come to know the name ben-Halevi, although Joan glanced knowingly at me. Eva was only surprised at the alacrity with which Joan and I seemed to make acquaintances everywhere we went.

"I'm honored to meet you, Mister ben-Halevi," I said. "May I invite you to be our guest at dinner?"

The view from the restaurant's window was probably the best in the city. From this distance, the boisterous saloons cast bright, flickering lights over the oily water. The sound was just far enough away to be both exciting and harmless. "How come you didn't join your brother in Spalatius?" Joan asked.

"I intend to, eventually," said ben-Halevi. "It's just that as the younger of two brothers, I'd rather not have it said I was a success because of my brother's influence. When he moved to Baghdad, I stayed in Khurasan for awhile. But, of course, we remained very close. When do you and my friend Tacitus' lovely niece intend to marry?"

"June of this coming year – nine months hence, in Athens."

"I wish you the very best. You are indeed a fortunate man. And Eva, I must say you are fortunate as well, traveling in the company of two such sturdy young men. How old are you, if I may insult you by asking?"

"Twenty, Sir."

"Ah, such a young, glorious age – an entire life ahead of you, marriage, children ... You're truly at the beginning of your time. You're headed to Athens, did you say?"

"Yes." This from Joan.

"Will you, by any chance, be going through Spalatius?"

"Aye," I said.

"Then you must see my brother! I've not heard from him in two months and I miss him. Is there any chance you could deliver a message from me to him? I would be most beholden to you. Even though I have some money put by, I would sooner trust someone I know – even if it's someone I just met – rather than leave it to a messenger service."

"Certainly." This was a critical point in our conversation. How could I possibly tell Michael ben-Halevi about my concern for Eva with her sitting right at the table with us? In a casual tone that I hope did not betray my concern, I said, "You said your brother is a doctor – a medicus?"

"Yes, they call it that in the West. Of course, he was not trained in the Holy Roman Empire, and his medical practice may seem a bit different to those schooled in the Roman world."

"What do you mean?" Joan asked.

"Well," our new acquaintance said, "David practices medicine in a way that is sometimes viewed with fear and distrust in the West. He takes on cases no one else wants or would consider. He performs surgery when the patients are strongly anaesthetized, in places where other surgeons dare not venture. Many of his patients do not survive, but they would not have survived in any event."

When I heard this, I felt queasy, but Joan pursued her questioning. "What kind of surgery?"

"In addition to the usual kind – broken bones and the like – he pursues neural surgery – that's something they regularly teach in Persia, in India, and in the land of the Seres, even farther to the east, but Western medicine refuses to acknowledge the existence of such things."

"Neural surgery?" Eva asked.

"Surgery involving the nerves – the pain receptors. He will not hesitate to cut into the body if he believes it will cure the patient's disease. In some instances, he even opens the skull to reveal the brain. Like I said, his type of practice is largely unheard-of in the West."

"You said he deals in cases that other physicians won't touch?"

"Yes. Much of his practice is devoted to fighting the most dreaded of all diseases – kreps, the crab disease. Of course, since the death rate involving that disease is nine out of every ten patients, David believes that if he can save one in every hundred cases, he has succeeded."

"What does he use as an anaesthetic?" Joan asked.

"Mixtures of everything, plants, hashish, the most fortified draughts of wine, even mandragoras root and morphium in extreme cases. My brother insists the patient be rendered fully unconscious, totally out of the realm of pain, before he starts any surgery."

I did not enjoy hearing this talk – perhaps I am squeamish by nature, but at that moment I was hearing things I was not accustomed to hearing, spoken as directly and casually as if one were announcing the arrival of an expected guest at a social event. I tried to change the subject.

"What of your own work, Mister ben-Halevi?"

"We lawyers do not engage in such dramatic adventures. Rather, we supposedly solve problems between people and their government, or between people and other people. We can, and do, make mistakes, but at least no one's life is at stake. Just one's fortune or freedom," he said seriously.

"Have you found employment in Fiumius?"

"Yes. Fiumius is a great shipping port, which means most of the business in and out of here is international. I am familiar with the laws of the Byzantine Empire, the Abbasid Empire, and the Persian satrapy, as well as those of Egypt. This makes me a rather valuable – I daresay costly – adjunct to a major legal firm, and I have found that the law is one profession in which my religion or race or culture, call it what you will, makes little difference. We Jews were successful lawyers in the days of the Roman Empire, and law is something that simply doesn't go away. Now, if you don't mind, and if you truly would do me the favor of carrying a letter to my brother, I should like, at least, to write that letter. When were you planning on leaving Fiumius?"

"Within the next week," I replied.

"Good. I should have the letter ready within the next day or two."

I asked him to come by early in the morning when the letter was ready, knowing that if Eva was having another of her headaches, she would remain in her room, in bed, until almost noon. This would enable me to express some of my concerns to Michael ben-Halevi and to request of him an introduction to his brother the physician. True to his word, Michael appeared shortly after cockcrow the second morning after our meeting. When I told him what was on my mind, he expressed sympathy and the hopes that his brother would be able to relieve my beloved's pain. "It's most likely migraneus, surprisingly common in young girls of your fiancée's age. I'm almost certain my brother can concoct a mixture more powerful than the acetyl acid Joannes has provided. But there's no sense in speculating. It's best that Eva visit him when you're in Spalatius."

"How does your brother achieve his diagnosis?" I asked.

"There are numerous tests he performs, virtually none of which are recognized in the West, some of which are viewed as quite arcane or even the work of the devil. I'm told his diagnoses are very rarely wrong. But enough of such thoughts. Here, I'll write a referral to my brother this instant."

Michael ben-Halevi's note set forth in amazing detail everything I'd told him, including every symptom Eva had told me about when I'd questioned her during her most pronounced moments of pain and weakness. I asked that he not seal the envelope until I could have Joan look at it. "He's my dearest and wisest friend," I told Michael. "Would you mind my showing it to him?"

"Of course not," Michael replied. "As a lawyer, I would sooner err on the side of completeness than otherwise. We lawyers deal in evidence to make a point, and the more evidence, the more complete the picture we paint of an event."

After he left, I showed the letter to Joan, who confirmed it was indeed what Eva had related to her. Joan made other suggestions as to the degree of success or failure she'd experienced in her own medicinal mixtures, and I noted those on another piece of rough parchment. I then sealed the letter and placed it in my horse's saddlebag. That afternoon, Eva complained of the worst headache she'd yet experienced, and we were delayed three more days until she was once again able to travel. It was now October 833, a year after I'd left Tours. Due to Eva's condition, I spent my twenty-fourth birthday ministering to Eva – and, for the first time since we'd started, sleeping alone in a small cot next to her bed.

~ ʃ ~

Meanwhile, ensnared in my own world and almost oblivious to the world outside Eva's small room, a momentous event had taken place in that other, outside world. Lothar, Louis the Pious' eldest son, had led his two brothers in rebellion against their father – and succeeded! Louis, deserted by his army on the Field of Lies near Colmar in northern Aquitania, was defeated and imprisoned, and Lothar took over as sole ruler of the Holy Roman Empire.

CHAPTER 29

In the second week of October, Eva felt well enough to ride, and we turned south to descend that part of the land known as Dalmatia. The land abutting the Gulf of Kvarner turns steep and undulating, and its color is that of sunbleached bone. It's a barren, rocky place with little vegetation and an abundance of limestone, while the Hadriatic Sea is remarkably clean and clear, alternately colored rich green and, farther offshore, deep blue, reflecting the cloudless sky that formed a dome over our heads. The fierce heat we'd encountered when we had first arrived in Fiumius had abated.

I was quite concerned with Eva's less-than-robust health, and the anticipation, *ne*, the dread, that her malady could overwhelm her at any given moment, and with precious little notice. I determined – and Joan concurred – that when we arrived at Spalatius, I would take Eva to the Clinic of Saints Peter and Paul for a complete physical evaluation. It went unsaid between us that our fondest wish was that we need see Doctor ben-Halevi solely on a social basis.

Spalatius, the largest city we had encountered since Fiumius, was built around a crescent-shaped harbor on the south side of a high peninsula, sheltered from the open sea by many islands. Here we found a vast wooded area, limestone quarries, and, behind the city, high coastal mountains. More than five hundred years ago, the Roman emperor, Diocletianus, who had persecuted early adherents of Mother Church, built a massive retirement palace here. Joan told me that Diocletianus' successors, even unto the end of the Roman empire in the West, had used this palace as a retreat, and, in fact, when nearby Salona had been abandoned two hundred years ago, Roman Christians had barricaded themselves inside the walls of the palace and maintained a cautious kind of immunity from attacks by Byzantine Orthodox and Mouammedan religionists, and from regularly warring Bulgar, Illyrian, South Slavic, and other polyglot tribes.

We found an inn, and it was just as well we did so quickly, since Eva told us that evening that she felt the onset of pains in her head and dizziness. Although this was the very news I'd dreaded, it gave me the excuse I needed to tell her that I would obtain an appointment with the medical doctors at the Clinic of Saints Peter and Paul for the next day.

"But darling, why go there when we already have a personal introduction to Doctor ben-Halevi?"

I looked at Joan, who interpreted my mien immediately. She answered Eva smoothly. "Of course we'll go to Doctor ben-Halevi if the clinic doctors cannot help, but just in case anything happened to any of us, I asked your Uncle Tacitus for recommended *medicia* throughout Dalmatia and Greece, and the Clinic was his first recommendation." Which was not entirely a lie.

Eva spent an uncomfortable night, and next morning I sought out the clinic. It was situated on a hill just east of the center of town. It was as large as a hospitium, and, indeed, it functioned as such. The *medicia* walked about with a businesslike attitude. The bustle within the place – and the prices the clinic charged – gave me a sense of comfort and competence. Eva saw Doctor Fithianus, an intake physician and diagnostician, that very afternoon. By then, her headache had diminished and her dizziness had disappeared. She made light of my urgency, but agreed to go with Joan and me to the clinic.

Doctor Fithianus seemed very thorough. He asked a number of questions – where the headaches originated, how frequently they came on, how long they lasted, was the pain a stabbing pain, a shooting pain, a well-sited pain, or a generalized pain – things like that. He palpated the area of her left wrist and placed a metal scopus in the area between Eva's left shoulder and her left breast. Then he touched a metal speculum to her head in numerous places. He grunted noncommittally a few times, frowned occasionally, then grunted again. Finally he was finished with his examination.

"Migraneus," he pronounced. "While we have no cure for it, we can certainly alleviate its symptoms. You have been blending acetyl acid?" he asked Joan.

"Aye."

"Although that's a good analgesic for minor headaches, as you may have noticed, the young lady does not suffer from ordinary pain." Turning back to Eva, he said, "You said you suffered dizziness when you have these pains?"

"Not all the time," Eva said calmly.

"Another sign of migraneus. Sometimes when the pain is almost too great to bear, the body compensates by misdirecting a sense of dizziness to mask the worst of the aches. I will write you a prescription for medication that should alleviate much of the pain." He did, and directed us to fill the prescription at a nearby *pharmaceutium.* "Come by next week and we'll simply assure that the medicine is working properly."

We filled the prescription and by next morning Eva was in high spirits. "I've had a completely pain-free night. I can't remember when I've slept as well or felt so refreshed. Might we visit Diocletianus' Palace today?"

Relieved as I was in seeing her in this condition, I would have done anything she asked. My own spirits had lightened immeasurably when I saw how lovely she looked that morning. The day was bright and warm. Joan eagerly embraced the idea.

The palace was situated one street back from the center of Spalatius' harbor, and was surrounded by many remains from ancient Roman times. Even in its semi-ruined state, the palace was impressive. Rectangular in shape, its walls were significantly more than two hundred yards long and nearly two hundred wide. It was reinforced by towers along the perimeters of the wall. Diocletianus' mausoleum had been converted to a cathedral, and the only reminder of the once-great emperor was a sculpture of his head in a circular stone wreath below the dome, directly above the altar.

Although it was every bit as busy as Fiumius, Spalatius seemed more relaxed than its more northerly neighbor on the Hadriatic. The market was certainly as hectic, but somehow the warmth, the ever-present green trees, the layout of the town, and the fact that we were dealing with southern Romans, made Spalatius a happier place. Perhaps my feeling of well-being was a result of my learning that my Eva was not seriously ill, as I had dreaded.

We spent the better part of the day exploring the ancient Roman structures, some in ruins, others in a state of recognizable survival, if by no means complete and in use. I learned that Spalatius was much frequented in the summer because of its many music, dramatic, and other outdoor festivals, and also because of its wonderful beaches to the south of the harbor, beaches which afforded access to the clear, warm Hadriatic.

By this time of the year, many of those festivals were shut down, and since the days were shorter and cooler, one could only see a few solitary souls walking up and down the southern beaches. We dined on succulent *calamaria* stuffed with chopped fish, parsley, onions, and other green herbs, and we enjoyed the white wine of the region. Perhaps that is why what happened later than night happened.

When Eva and I returned to our room that night, she was ebullient, almost giggling – a combination of her first day in over a month of relief from her pain, and the softening influence of the wine we'd had at dinner. I was more excited than ever at the sight of her, and all that evening I had wrestled with my promise that we would not come together until after we were married in June. Certainly her illness had focused my mind on being as gentle and caring to her as one human being could be to another.

As I embraced her, Eva said, "I feel a bit sticky from our long and adventurous day. Would you mind if I took a bath before we go to sleep?"

She entered the bathing room, and I watched, not a little regretfully, as she closed the door behind her. I pictured in my mind what it would be like to be with her for the rest of my life. Our wedding was now only eight months away. I settled onto the bed and closed my eyes.

I heard a faint sound and felt a presence in the room. I looked up. Eva was standing at the foot of the bed wearing a white, filmy nightdress. I rose quickly, went to where she was standing, and held her. There were no words. I buried my face in her hair, breathing in the sweet, fresh smell of her. I kissed her brow, her cheek. Eva was so tiny, so delicate. My hand moved to one of her breasts. She put her own hand over mine and hugged me harder still.

It was Eva who broke the embrace. "Darling," she said huskily, "I know we promised not to ... do anything like that ... until after we were married, but somehow tonight is ... We've got our lives ahead of us, however long that might be, but ..." She smiled, a combination of the Madonna and the eternal woman. "Would it really trouble you so much if ...?"

My own voice was hoarse. "What if something happened?"

"I've always wanted your child, since the day I fell in love with you. If it happens earlier than we expected, well ... I guess you'll think of me as a fallen woman." She smiled teasingly and, I thought, just a little wickedly.

I looked into her beautiful, beautiful gray-blue eyes. I took her hand, as gently as I've ever done anything in my life, and silently led her to the bed. Moments later, we lay in each other's arms, lovers at last, grasping for one another, straining to reach beyond the limits of earthly love. Yet, we were as gentle as two fawns frolicking in a field. When, after a long time, it was over, I lay awake, feeling her gentle breath as she lay curled about my body. Moments later, soft tears flowed down my own cheeks as I drifted into the sleep of the blessed.

~ ∫ ~

"You two could have kept the noise level down a little, unless you intended to discomfit those of us who don't have the luxury of a lover at the moment," Joan teased next morning.

Eva was momentarily embarrassed, but quickly recovered. "Joannes, as good-looking and charming a man as you are, I somehow have no doubt you could have your pick of any maiden – or almost maiden – you wanted." She clucked her tongue. "What a shame so much charm is wasted on a priest."

"Hold, woman," Joan said mock seriously. "I'm not yet a priest. That's the nice thing about being a scholar – no commitment one way or the other, and no responsibility. Of course, my friend Martin ended up with Vindobona's loveliest woman, so whatever befalls me, I'm afraid I'll have to make do with second best."

I squeezed Eva's hand and she squeezed back. Her eyes, even in the morning light, were radiant, filled with the brightness of love fulfilled and lust satisfied.

"Didn't we promise to take our friend Michael's letter to his brother, the doctor?" Joan asked. "November is upon us, and very soon it will be time to move south. I thought today might be as good as any ... oh, I see the two of you are so involved in each other that today would not be the appropriate day for you to visit anyone. Very well, then, the three of us have been traveling together for nearly four months. While you two lovebirds obviously don't want to be apart, I think perhaps I'll visit the estimable Doctor ben-Halevi this morning and leave the two of you to your own ... diversions. You don't have to tell me where it is or how to get there. I already asked one of the staff at the clinic two days back."

That suited us fine. I went to our room, extracted the envelope, and brought it back down to Joan. Eva and I were at least courteous enough to see her on her way, even though, as Joan had truly spoken, we had other diversions on our minds. Some hours later, about midday, we had a light meal at our inn and asked the innkeeper what there was of interest to see beyond the city of Spalatius.

"Many things," the congenial fellow replied. "Old Diocletianus didn't choose this area of the world for his retirement simply because of its harbor. Looking at the two of you, I'm reminded of a time many years ago, when I was about your age and frisky, a fellow who was then as old as I am now, told me about a secret place at the top of Forest Hill, where, in a copse well hidden from prying eyes, there was a small waterfall surrounded by a warm, flat area where one could walk in privacy and peace…"

~ ∫ ~

Eva shouted joyously. Her voice echoed down the mountainside. She called out again and again. My name, her own, childish gibberish. There was not another human being in sight.

"Oh, Martin, I can't wait to dive into this lovely pool!" With that, she stripped off her tunic, posed like a small Aphrodite, ran to one of the terraces, and jumped into the water, immersing herself. "Martin, if you don't come in this minute, I'm going to drag you in here!"

I needed no second invitation. I shed my own garment and joined her. We jabbered nonsense, jumped up and down among the pool's cascades, and submersed one another, touching, feeling, electrifying ourselves with intimacy. We could not grasp each other tight enough, hold the other close enough. Afterward, we alighted into the afternoon sunlight and found a small patch of grass surrounded by a wall that blocked any wind from swirling around us.

We made love in the grass, then we made love again, and yet again until we collapsed with fatigue. Afterward, we lay quietly, hidden from view, drifting into and out of a light sleep.

We returned to the inn in time for our evening meal, and found Joan waiting for us. She seemed quite serious, almost withdrawn, and in my exuberant happiness I did not think to ask her why she appeared morose. Surely it couldn't be jealousy. While Eva and I ate ravenously, Joan picked delicately at her meal, and did not consume much.

We retired early that night after a day in heaven, too exhausted to do anything but sleep in one another's arms.

Our time in love-made heaven lasted less than a week.

CHAPTER 30

"We must go through a series of tests to determine if my theory is correct." Doctor ben-Halevi was a slightly taller, older version of his brother. His hair was brown, interspersed with gray, as was his beard. It was his eyes I remember now. They were dark brown and the kindest eyes I had ever seen. His look was one of concern. "When did she start experiencing these new pains?"

"Yesterday morning, doctor," I said. "I can't understand it. She's taken the medication Doctor Fithianus prescribed every day, and she told me she's felt healthier than she'd ever remembered."

"Hmmm." He scratched his chin thoughtfully. "Fithianus' prescription was certainly appropriate by western standards for the treatment of migraneus. Although I might have suggested a different regimen, I cannot quarrel with him."

"Why, then, did the pains return with such a vengeance?"

"Did she engage in any unusual activities during the past few days?" he asked. I blushed deeply. "Ne, Martin," he said, completely ignoring my embarrassment. "Engaging in sex, even for the first time, is not the type of unusual activity I had in mind. I am a physician, not a moralist. I leave that sort of thing to priests and such. In any event, I have never known sexual pleasure to cause head pain such as your friend Joannes described to me."

"Other than that I can think of nothing."

"Strange foods? Perhaps she may have been allergic?"

"Calamaria."

"Possible, but hardly likely. Proximity to plants?"

"We went to Forest Hill."

"I've never known anyone to come down with such head pains from umbrella pines or cedars." He sat on a couch nearby and bade Joan and I do the same. "I want to make certain I have everything correct. Can you describe exactly what happened?"

"Yes, Doctor," I said. My hands had taken on a slight tremor. "Yesterday morning, she awoke just before cockcrow and complained of what felt like a large lump inside her head. She said it was different from what she'd experienced in the past, and a little bit frightening. Even though Eva is young, she is not given to attacks of panic or anxiety. She fell asleep for another small while. When next she awoke, she said that she could not see clearly – she felt there were tiny air bubbles in front of her eyes and that there was a red-colored halo around the bubbles. When she tried to get up from the bed to make her morning toilet, she complained of tremendous dizziness, and I had to help her to the necessaria."

"Any pain?" he asked.

"At first it was not great. As the morning wore on, it got worse, and she asked that I take her back to the clinic. Joannes told me he had spoken with you the day before."

"Yes, he did."

"Joannes felt Eva and I should attend you. You were kind enough to see us yesterday, and you know the story from there."

"I may, or I may not, as you say, 'know the story.' I spoke with her for a short while, but felt it best that I give her a mild sedative, then a somewhat heavier sedative, to allow her to rest without feeling the worst of the symptoms."

"How is she now?" Joan asked.

"Still drowsy, Brother Joannes. That's to be expected. I hope she will suffer far less pain today, since it's best I perform the tests I spoke about with you when she is not suffering from an acute onset of the headaches and dizzy spells. Would you prefer to be present when I conduct these tests?"

"Absolutely," Joan and I answered as one.

"Good. The presence of familiar friends will put young Eva at her ease."

I found myself feeling faint and a little ill. "Doctor … do you have any thought as to what it might be?"

"Honestly, Martin, I cannot make a diagnosis at this moment. I won't pretend you shouldn't be concerned. Let us hope that we can clarify my preliminary thoughts."

As perfect an answer as I might have received from the ancient oracle at Delphi, I thought. It did not lessen my worry, but then again, it did not portend that Eva was in imminent peril either. Unlike Doctor Fithinaus, Doctor ben-Halevi impressed me as someone who was genuinely interested in the health and well being, not only of his patient, but of his patient's loved ones as well. He did not appear to be waiting for his next patient, or impatient to get on with his business. Rather, he took as much time as necessary. His examination, his physical tests, his probing questions were done calmly and kindly. Eschewing the prevalent Western methods, he insisted that Eva undress fully, after drawing a curtain around her so that we could not see. I heard his questions from behind the curtain.

"Does this hurt? And this? Which is the greater pain? Where is it centered?" and similar questions.

After Eva had clothed herself once again, Doctor ben-Halevi continued his palpations of her neck, her skull, the back of her head, and the front of her head. At one point, he picked up a small mallet with a blunt, pointed end, and tapped her skull gently in several places. He did not ask any questions, but rather listened with full concentration on the sounds that emanated from these taps. His examination lasted longer than any I'd experienced and the sun was starting to set when he concluded.

"You've been a brave and patient girl, Eva, my dear," he finally said solicitously. "I'd like to speak with Martin and Joannes while you rest awhile."

"Can I not hear what you have to say?" she asked.

"Very well. Let us all sit down together."

If Eva had been sentenced to death at that moment, I could not have been more horrified. As it was, during part of Doctor ben-Halevi's explanation, I had to excuse myself, and when I had left his office, I vomited profusely into a pot that had thoughtfully been provided in the outside office. When I returned, I tried to concentrate on his words.

"The tests confirm what I had thought, and, I must be candid, what I had feared. There is evidence of a tumor of some sort inside your skull. Although the lump you believe you felt inside your head yesterday morning would certainly not confirm my opinion, a number of other tests, and a number of your answers to my questions, have confirmed that opinion. Let us sit around the table in my office, so I can show you what I believe is happening and how I believe we can deal with it."

Doctor ben-Halevi's office was filled with codices and carpets, but was otherwise Spartan. He withdrew one of the codices from a cabinet and brought it over to an oval table where we were seated. The codex contained various drawings of a man's skull, including a top view and a side view of an open skull. He described in a dry, quiet voice the method by which he would shave Eva's head, put her under a deep anaesthetic, and, as gently as possible, with the assistance of his son Moses, invade the cavity of her head, exposing the brain. He would then attempt to locate the suspected tumor, and, if it were there, to excise it, replace that part of the skull where he had entered her brain, and stitch it back the way it had been.

Eva was remarkably calm throughout his explanation, although her face was paler than usual. It was she who initiated a series of questions, which Doctor ben-Halevi answered directly.

"Why can't you simply leave the tumor where it is and treat it with medication?"

"If there is a tumor, it will be one of two kinds. Hopefully, the tumor will be benign. That means there are no kreps growths. Even so, a benign tumor can turn malignant at any time, and even if it were not to do so, it could expand, impacting on the brain and pushing against it from the inside. That could create unbelievable pain and even lead to death."

"What if the tumor has these crab growths you mention?"

"One can only pray we've caught the malignancy in time and, more important, that we take out every possible bit of the kreps we find. More important, let's hope it is not a malignant growth."

Once again, I left the room, and once again I voided was what left inside of me. When I returned, Joan had taken up the questioning of Doctor ben-Halevi, and her voice was remarkably calm – as quiet and direct as his was – and her questions were as penetrating.

"Have you done this type of operation before?"

"Yes, in Khurasan and in Baghdad several times. Here, twice."

"What has your success rate been?"

Doctor ben-Halevi drew in a deep breath. "Truthfully, not great. If you're asking whether I have saved lives, the answer is yes. In a non-malignant tumor, of the twenty operations in which I've participated, four patients survived."

"And in malignant tumors."

"None."

Eva gasped. Joan continued.

"What if you left things simply as they are?"

"If the tumor is benign, the patient might live anywhere from one to five years. If the tumor is malignant, that is entirely in God's hands. I would estimate from six months to a year. But I choose to view the quality of life rather than the time left as a better measurement."

"What do you mean?" I asked weakly.

"Left alone, the tumor, if there is a tumor, might enlarge or it might not. If it stays the same, the pain will remain and perhaps become more frequent, of longer duration, and harsher. If the tumor grows, it would become infinitely worse."

"And if you are wrong in your opinion and there's no tumor?" Joan asked.

"There would be no harm done from the incision and the restitching, except that Eva might have a very sore head – on the outside – for a month or two, and she would learn what it would feel like to be a bald woman," Doctor ben-Halevi said, with an entirely straight face.

"When would you want to operate?" Joan continued.

"As soon as possible. We don't know what causes a tumor to occur, but we do know that if the tumor is malignant, it spreads its poison daily. For some reason, kreps has a tendency to spread and grow more rapidly than normal organs in the body."

"We need time to think about it, Doctor," I said, blinking my eyes very rapidly to keep the tears from flowing.

"I understand," ben-Halevi said. "It will be painful, but I believe I can help mask the pain."

"Mandragoras?" Joan asked.

"Precisely," the doctor replied. "If the pain is as you describe it, Eva, it will help you through the next few days until you decide."

~ ∫ ~

That night, Eva ate little and we retired very early to our bed. She made herself small and fragile, a desperate, hopeless child, and the worst of it was there was nothing I could do to aid or comfort her. Have you ever felt the misery of watching someone you love with all your heart shrivel before your very eyes? Even as I sit here writing all this, so many years later, I can feel my heart shedding bitter tears. Joan came in and administered a portion of the ground mandragoras root Doctor ben-Halevi had given us, and I held poor, trembling Eva until she fell into a fitful sleep. Afterward, Joan and I sat and spoke quietly, she holding my hand in hers, listening to me sob, and stroking my back gently, until I could articulate what I felt.

"Is this what the rom fortune teller meant when she said I would love Eva all my life and she would only love me for six months? How much better would it have been had she left me for another? At least she would be well and alive, and with a future. For God's sake, she's only twenty years old."

"Are you feeling sorry for yourself as well?"

"Of course, Joan. How could I not? You remember Torvald."

"Yes. There were times when I wished my heart would simply have stopped beating and I would have stopped breathing, but it is not given to us to decide what is going to happen in our lives. And unless we wish to condemn and blaspheme every law and rule and commandment of God, suicide is out of the question."

"So what must I do?"

"Live, my friend. A part of you will surely die if Eva dies, but, if nothing else, you must feel the exquisite pain of your loss and have the courage to survive it. You must live not for one person, but for the two of you that might have become one. And you must pray. While Eva breathes, she lives, and where there is life, there is hope. That's yet another gift given to us by God. Now, Martin, you will not be strong for Eva if you remain awake all night and the next day and the next night. I propose to give you the smallest grains of mandragoras this night, for your own benefit."

"But …"

"Ne, Martin, it's not for the relief of any physical pain, but it is for the relief of pain nonetheless."

I did, and somehow I managed to sleep – and deeply – until well beyond cockcrow the next morning.

~ ∫ ~

At the end, there really was no choice. Joan and Eva and I knew this. We had to trust someone, and each of us agreed

Doctor ben-Halevi was our greatest, ne, our only hope. If Eva had a chance of one in a hundred, or one in a thousand, or even one chance out of an infinity, the only thing for certain is that if she did not allow Doctor ben-Halevi to operate, she had no chance, except that of submitting to worsening pain for whatever time was left to her.

Joan went to Doctor ben-Halevi's office the next afternoon and advised him that Eva would undergo the operation. Joan told me later that she and Doctor ben-Halevi had prayed together, each in their own way, for two hours after she had conveyed our decision.

"I would never have believed he'd do that," she said. "A man of science and a man of God. All of us could learn from him, and he, a Jew. He's asked that we come to his offices this evening and spend the night there. He believes the operation will take most of the day, so he would like to start just after sunrise. He told me his son Moses would assist him, and he asked if we wanted to be in the operating theatre."

"Ne," I said miserably. "You saw how I performed when we discussed the matter in Doctor ben-Halevi's offices. I think it would only interfere with the doctor's concentration."

"I agree," Joan said gently. "I hope you do not feel hurt, but I asked Doctor ben-Halevi if I could be in the operating room, and he said I could."

That afternoon, Doctor ben-Halevi explained once again how he would perform the operation. "I will administer a measured dose of mandragoras to you three hours after dinner, and you will sleep very deeply. This will enable your body to relax and be strong. During that time, I will shave your head and bathe it thoroughly. Tomorrow morning, I will apply a quite large dose of mandragoras morphium, a much more powerful mixture. You will not be conscious of anything that happens until, God willing, you awaken with an uncomfortable, but hopefully not too severe, headache, for which I will apply increasingly lesser doses of medication."

"Is there anything I can do, Doctor?" I asked.

"Yes. Your job will be to pray the hardest, for all of us."

~ ∫ ~

They emerged from that room late in the afternoon.

The looks on all their faces were grim, and I didn't even have the courage to ask.

The three of them silently washed their hands, which I saw were bloodied, in soap and hot water. Then Doctor ben-Halevi approached me. "It was a large tumor and located in a very sensitive place. Had it expanded even half a thumbnail in any direction, she would long ago have been dead. As it is, God-be-thanked, it was benign, so far as I can tell. And what there was of it, and the area immediately around it, has been excised. She is alive. We have stitched her up. She is now in God's hands."

CHAPTER 31

Eva's recovery was long and slow and very painful. The three of us moved into a residence owned by Doctor ben-Halevi, which was situated directly behind his offices. Joan provided me with details concerning the operation, which I did not wish to hear, and yet, now that Eva was alive and that formerly living thing in her head had been removed, I was eager to hear. Joan was pleased that the doctor had allowed her into the operating room and that he had told her she'd actually been of some assistance, monitoring Eva's vital signs to ensure that she had not succumbed on the operating table.

Doctor ben-Halevi had placed Joan in charge of providing the convalescing Eva with medication sufficient to dull her pain, but not enough to harm her. The scar from the incision at the top of Eva's head was much smaller and finer than I had expected it would be, and already there was a sparse regrowth of hair, a shade darker than it had been. Eva slept most of the day and all of the night, and, thank God, I was allowed to participate in her hoped-for recovery by spooning food – mostly soup and finely ground vegetables and meat – into my Eva during those times she was awake.

November became December. Slowly, then more rapidly, Eva continued her recovery. By the end of December, her hair was still short and sparse, but there was a luster in her eyes which told me, even more than her words, that she was no longer experiencing headaches, pain, or dizziness. She was now walking about the residence and eating on her own and she was rapidly gaining strength. One day, early in January, she asked if we could take a brief journey into town.

Doctor ben-Halevi approved and my heart leapt inside my chest as I squired my beloved around the city. She could have asked for anything, and I'd have purchased it for her, regardless of the cost and regardless whether I could afford it or not.

Shortly thereafter, Doctor ben-Halevi, as proud as a new father at the birth of his first child, pronounced Eva not only cured, but fit to travel as well. He presented a bill that was so astonishingly minimal for all he had done that Joan and I couldn't even speak. "All I ask in return," he said, "is that I be invited to the wedding, since I've never been to Athens but always wanted to go there."

That afternoon, I purchased the finest horse that could be found in Spalatius, and a small carriage to boot, and that evening, after I was certain Doctor ben-Halevi had gone to bed, I left the horse and carriage in a small enclosure behind his own residence, with a brief note, "So you might come to our wedding in style."

Next morning, at sunrise, six months to the day after the *rom* fortune teller had foretold such a gloomy future, Eva awoke to a roomful of fresh, fragrant flowers and to me sitting next to her, smiling at her, as she slowly opened her eyes and came once again into the world of life. Joan entered the room moments later.

"I suggest we resume our journey tomorrow morning. Since the two of you are in the majority, I have to convince one of you that this is a good idea."

"Of course it is, Joannes," Eva laughingly replied. "The sooner the better. I can't wait to utter my marriage vows in Athens."

"That makes it unanimous," I joined in. "I suggest we invite Doctor ben-Halevi and his family to a celebratory dinner tonight."

"My goodness, Martin, I just noticed all these flowers. For me, darling?"

"Of course. Certainly not for Joannes. This is the six month anniversary of the fortune teller's dire predictions, and here we are, all of us, healthy, safe, and once again sound."

"Yes," Eva said, dreamily. "Healthy, safe, sound, and fulfilled."

I didn't ask what she meant by that last statement, but I assumed it tied in with her eagerness to be on her way to Athens and to our wedding.

"I feel so wonderful," she continued. "What remains to be done today?"

"Even though we're going to be journeying into the spring, and it will meet us as we travel south and it travels north, I suggest we purchase sufficient provender for our needs, including woolen coats, scarves, sturdy boots with felt linings, and, most important, warm head coverings," Joan said.

We spent the early part of the morning inviting the ben-Halevi family to celebrate our departure, the latter part of the morning expanding our wardrobe, and our afternoon napping.

No sooner we were in our room, Eva pulled me onto the bed, fully clothed, and hugged me, squealing, laughing, and mussing my hair with her fingers. "Darling, I've got something to tell you. I couldn't wait any longer."

"What is it, my love?"

"I've just missed my second *menstruum*."

I turned white with shock, then red with unexpected joy at the magnitude of what Eva had just said. "You mean you're — ?"

"Yes, my angel. It might be wise for us to advance the wedding date to May, or even, if we can make it to Athens more quickly, April. I've heard of a blushing bride, but it would be rather embarrassing to be a *bulging* bride, wouldn't you say?" She giggled happily. "My God, darling, isn't it wonderful? It's such a miracle! First God and Doctor ben-Halevi save my life and now I'm repaying God by bringing another life – our own child – into the world. And what an auspicious moment for me to tell you. I wish the fortune teller were here now so she could see what really happened."

That afternoon was a revelation for me. A child – *my* child – in the womb of the one I loved most. Could there be any greater happiness? I drifted off to sleep.

I don't know how much time elapsed before I felt Eva shoving me, rather harder than necessary. "Darling," she whispered harshly. "Wake up. Please wake up, Martin."

"Mnnnn, what is it?"

"Martin, please. Something's wrong. I hurt. And I'm bleeding ... down there."

"What?" I was instantly awake, and fully so. "When did it start?"

"While I was asleep. The pain woke me up. Oh, Martin, it hurts, it hurts so badly. Please, please do something." She had paled and was now in tears. She clutched at her abdomen and her legs were drawn up tightly, rigidly, to her body. I tried to get her to relax, but she couldn't. Now her face was turning ashen, and her breathing came in shallow rasps.

"Stay here, darling," I said, instantly realizing how stupid and helpless my words sounded. "I'll get Joannes."

Joan said we must seek out Doctor ben-Halevi immediately. "At least it has nothing to do with her brain surgery," Joan said. "Let us hope it's not food poisoning or something else that strikes quickly." Joan was off in a moment, after telling me to stay with Eva and fill our leather canteen pouch with hot water and apply it to Eva's abdomen, where the cramps seemed most severe.

Doctor ben-Halevi took one look at Eva and said, "We must get her to my clinic immediately. We've not a moment to lose. I've already arranged for a *carruca*. Martin, you and Joannes sit with her. Eva was, by this time, moaning incoherently, sobbing, her body rigid with pain.

"Mandragoras?" Joan asked the doctor.

"*Ne, morphium* – as substantial dose as she can stand. I brought it with me."

"D-do you have any thoughts, any thoughts at all?" I stammered in my shock.

"Pray God it is not what I think it is," he replied.

"Oh, God! Food poisoning? Water poisoning?" I said, feeling myself moan with fear and dread.

"I have no answer yet. Let us get her to my clinic – and rapidly."

~ ∫ ~

What is there to say? What started as the happiest day of my life turned into the most hellish night of my existence. Even now, even in my imprisonment, I think back to that night and I shake with revulsion and bitterness, and, yes, violent and uncontrollable anger at a God who would allow such a thing to happen.

Eva continued to moan, but she was unconscious. Her body remained tightly rigid, until, just before we arrived at Doctor ben-Halevi's clinic, less than two Roman miles away, Eva gave an immense convulsive shudder, her body fell limp, and she stopped breathing.

Doctor ben-Halevi tried everything in his arsenal of medical skills to bring her back to life. He lunged and pushed at the area of her heart and her rib cage. He cut into the tube below her throat to try to force air into her. All to no avail. Eva was dead. In an instant, my world had collapsed.

I sat in a corner of the operating theatre, on a low seat, and cried as I had never cried before. I mumbled and I shouted and I screamed until my throat was raw and sore beyond imagining. Through it all, Joan sat on a stool next to me, gently rubbing my upper back, mostly just rocking me and saying nothing. What was there to say?

Even now, I have no idea of how long it was before Doctor ben-Halevi came to us. His eyes were as full of tears as mine, and all he could say was, "So young, so very young. It should not have been at all, and it should not have been her."

I somehow managed to blubber, through my roughened voice, "Oh, God, Oh, God, Oh, God. She – she – she t-t-told me this afternoon she was pregnant with our child. H-how? W-why? Oh, my God!" and I collapsed into bitter tears once again.

Now it was Doctor ben-Halevi who held me in his arms. When I had quieted down so that my sobbing and harsh gasps were slower and more measurable, he said, "Yes, I found out she was with child when I examined her. It was as I had feared."

"What do you mean?" Joan asked.

"The *fetus* was not in the womb."

"Explain." Joan's voice was direct, demanding, but not insulting.

"In medical terms, we call it *ectopius* – a strange occurrence that happens very, very infrequently, but it does happen. Normally conception takes place in the womb. When it does not …" He coughed to stifle back his own incipient tears. "In every case I've seen but one, the mother had no chance. No chance at all. It is almost impossible to diagnose. In my entire medical career, I've known of only one instance where they were able to treat the mother in time, slice open the tube and scrape what was there out. The woman never came near her husband again, and she went insane with grief."

"God's punishment!" I shouted, insensibly. "I have the curse of Cain on me and I must live with it the rest of my life. I'd sooner die!" I babbled. "We should have been married first. We promised one another — "

"Nonsense," said the doctor, sharply, cutting me off in mid-voice. "This is not God's curse. This is one of nature's tragic and ghastly accidents. I have seen this happen to young brides and to mothers who'd borne half a dozen perfectly healthy children. I've seen it happen to the most endearing and innocent young women – and I count your Eva as lovely as though she were my own daughter – and I've seen it happen to harridans whose very tongues polluted the earth on which they walked. It had nothing to do with you and it had nothing to do with her. If it hadn't have happened now, who knows but that it might have happened six months, a year, a decade after you'd married? Ours is not to question God's – or Nature's – ways."

"And the baby?" I whispered softly.

"The *fetus* was barely two months since conception," he said. "At that age, the baby is not even fully formed, and was certainly not breathing. Tragically, there was no way he could have survived."

"He?" Joan asked.

"*Aye*, it was a boy."

At that, I burst into a new round of tears, uncontrolled and uncontrollable.

"Martin, Joannes, you are both of the Church?"

"Of course, Doctor ben-Halevi," Joan replied. "As was Eva."

"I am not," he said. "But might I beg a favor of you? One that I feel might be of some help to you in your hour of need?"

"What would that be?" Joan asked.

"Please stay in my home tonight and for a few nights thereafter. I have sent my son to advise his mother you will be coming."

I nodded numbly, but said nothing.

Joan said, "There is no harm to be done by what you ask. We must remain here until Martin – until we – feel we can travel once again."

A week later, a messenger arrived with a letter sent from Tacitus. "Dear Martin and Joannes. My brother, my sister, and I share your incalculable loss. Doctor ben-Halevi wrote to us and told us. How dreadful that one so young would die so suddenly of food poisoning. Martin, you must be devastated beyond devastation. My uncle died that way, but he was an old man of forty-five, and full of years. Doctor ben-Halevi also wrote of how you were with her when she suffered the tumor, and how loyal and loving you were to her throughout your time together. At least you have the privilege of knowing that you brought another human being the greatest happiness one could bring another. We are forever in yours – and Joannes' – debt, and one never knows how – or when – it can, or will, be repaid. Your most affectionate friend, Tacitus."

BOOK V.
THE WHITE SEA

CHAPTER 32

As I have earlier related, my Jewish agent in Portsmouth had been true to his word and furnished me with a passbook that I could show other Jewish moneylenders and agents anywhere in Europe. Although I had spent what, to me, were profligate sums in the eighteen months since I'd left Tours, I received information from my agent that truly astonished me on the day we left Spalatius. A counter-rebellion in the Holy Roman Empire had restored Louis Pious to the throne. What's more, he had forgiven his rebellious sons and restored them to their lands and honors. The Danes had invaded Angle-land. Emperor Theophilus in Constantinople had expelled all painters and artists from the Byzantine Empire as part of his bloody drive against icons. What amazed me was the effect these events had had on my holdings.

Through the unification of Southern Angle-land under Egbert, land values in Wessex had soared. My agent had sold more than half of those lands and reinvested the proceeds in real estate in London and Aquitania. As a result of Louis' reaccession to the throne, those holdings, in turn, had tripled in value. Since instability anywhere chases investors to reliable

– and transferable currency – the one-third of my holdings in the hands of the Jewish agent, instead of producing a return of three percent per annum, had, during the past two years, produced the unheard-of return of ten percent per annum. The only "disappointment," if one wanted to call it that, was that the managers of the lord's manor where my father had earned – and buried – his treasure, had made "only" six percent per year on the minuscule percentage of my fortune I had left with them for safekeeping.

My holdings were regenerating themselves and growing much faster than I was spending.

Without being asked to do so, I sent money to Tacitus to insure that Eva's mother was well-provided for, for the remainder of her days. I withdrew only enough funds to get as far as Dyrrachium, since I knew we would be traversing the untamed lands of bandits, clashes between Rome and Byzantium, and battles and warlets among various Avar and Slavic tribes

In May 834, Joan and I, who now had no timetable when we must be in Athens, departed Spalatius and started south once again. The weather was clement. Heartbroken as I was, the landscape to our right and to our left, was lovely. There were no less than a dozen quite large islands immediately off the coast – forest-clad or bone-dry lands of great size in the middle of the shimmering Hadriatic Sea. Beyond the narrow strip of coastal lands on which we traveled, to the east, but not far away, were hills and sharply etched peaks. Small rivers descended from those peaks to the sea at the small settlement of Plocius.

By the time we reached the new and thoroughly modern city of Ragusa, a place that had been settled by Greeks less than a century before, we disposed of most of our heavy woolen garb, reserving only leather jackets, boots, and headgear for those few nights we anticipated we'd be in the cold mountains of Illyria or northern Greece without benefit of a suitable inn.

"If you like, we could take passage on a ship to Patras," Joan said, before we left Ragusa.

"Ne, ne, we both promised each other we'd go the overland route."

"When we leave Ragusa, we'll leave the 'civilized' world for a bit. Neither Rome nor Byzantium claims any control over the land of the Black Mountains, nor of that part of Illyria east of the Hadriatic coast. No one has much say about what goes on in those mountains. It's been a land of blood feuds since time out of mind."

"Have you given any thought to what we're going to do once we get to Athens?"

What were we going to do indeed? Money was not a concern, but money was just a means to an end, and without any idea of what that end might be, we were nothing more than vagabond drifters, of no value whatever to the world in which we lived. Descending from Ragusa on a narrow strip between Lake Scutari and the Sea, we continued our discussion. "Do you remember what I said the first moment you met me, after you'd almost ridden over me on your horse?"

"Aye, Joan, as though it were yesterday," I said, smiling for the first time since Eva's death, "'I am Joan, and one day I shall be famous throughout the world. Perhaps you shall be of some service to me when I attain my calling.'"

"I've never lost that belief, Martin, and you have certainly been more than 'of some service to me.' You've been here for me before there was Torvald and before there was Eva. You've been, and you are, my closest friend in the entire world, the one person I will always trust, no matter what happens. I'll be twenty-one years old in two months, and you're nearly twenty-five, surely not an age where we are ready to be old and buried, but it is time for us to start living our future."

"What would you suggest?"

"We've finished our courses at Tours and have been truly credentialed. We no longer need those fraudulent documents we brought with us when we came to Tours. We've made some powerful friends along the way. I think when we arrive in Athens, we should take the stola of priesthood."

"Like Tata Petrus?" I said, seeing if I could get a rise from my companion.

"No, you dolt. We won't need to serve as pastoral ministers, but we'll be qualified to teach and to request of the Holy See that we be given an appointment no one else wants. That way, we'll be noticed by those in positions of power."

"Go on."

"When we get to Athens, I intend to apply to serve as an associate at the Academy of Saint Gaius Petronius, the premier center of learning. Both Roman and Byzantine Christians attend that academy, and notables of both divisions frequently meet there. Bishop Numenior was kind enough to write us real letters of commendation that can be affirmed by anyone. Cardinal Sergius was so thankful to me for the way we treated his niece that he wrote a commendation letter for each of us as well. Those documents alone should be more than sufficient to gain us an interview at the Academy."

"That's all well and good for you, since you are probably already known for your disputations with John Scotus Erigena, but once in the Academy, how would I survive?"

"Martin, you are a superb writer. Some are called brilliant, visionary, men of great ideas and learning. But those ideas would die after a single lifetime without the equally, ne, even more important work of those who chronicle those ideas so they might be remembered after the death of those brilliant and visionary men. You, Martin, are this latter kind of scholar – a recaller, a recorder, and a scribe."

"That sounds rather self-important and pretentious, don't you think?"

"Not at all," Joan rejoined. "Who would have known of the existence of the ancients, but for the writings of Herodotus or Pliny? Theodoric would have been nothing more than a forgotten Ostrogoth, but for Boethius. You have an unerring eye for seeing what goes on about you, and a simple, direct way of writing about what goes on around you. If you think I am exaggerating, ask our friend Nicola."

"Ha!" I barked. "We'd have to find him first."

"Why, he's in Rome, of course."

"Of course," I said. "As if any fool would know that. The last I heard, he was proceeding to Ravenna to act as a parish priest, just about the time we were leaving Tours."

"Well, my friend, you may be able to observe and write about what you see before your eyes, but, with the exception of writing to your Jewish financial agent, for which I am very grateful, by the way, you don't seem to know much about what is going on in the Church."

"What is Nicola doing these days?" I asked.

"The Pope came through Ravenna and saw that our Nicola had founded an institution for the care of the poor and the needy, widows and orphans. Far from disdaining them from on high, Nicola lived among them, and amassed a marvelous reputation among his poor constituents. Gregory elevated him to Monsignor. Even now there's talk that when a Bishopric becomes available, Nicola may well be next in line for that position if Gregory is still pope."

"So our friend has been elevated? A favorite of the Pope himself?"

"Yes, but Nicola, being Nicola, doesn't see it that way. They say he lives as simply as ever and has no pretensions of rising in the Church."

"Where did you get your information?"

"From Sergius and from Tacitus."

"And Anastasius?" I asked, surprisingly devoid of bitterness.

"He is still in Sarmatia. He hitched his fortune to Alcinorius, and since that old cardinal is very much out of favor with Gregory, Anastasius' supposed influence has not availed him."

"I'm glad we're only a day or two out of Dyrrachium," I said, changing the subject. "As wealthy as I supposedly am, I'll need to secure more as soon as we get to that port city."

"But you've spent hardly anything."

"I withdrew hardly anything. I figured the journey from Spalatius would not be a long one, and given my mood at the time, I wasn't about to spend much. What can you tell me about Dyrrachium, my learned friend?"

"Not much. If Athens is a backwater, Dyrrachium is a mud puddle. It does have one of the best ports on the Hadriatic. It was actually a bishopric at one time, but no more."

"Why do you call it a mud puddle?"

"Times change, people change. Earthquakes come. That same Theodoric of whom we spoke earlier today, sacked the city. Today it's mostly Byzantine."

"Well, if it produces wine as good as Scutari, it might not be that bad," I said. And on that note, we adjourned to our rooms for the night.

~ ʃ ~

Dyrrachium was quite old, but not without charm. It was the western terminus of the Via Egnatia, a famous Roman high road, which went all the way to Constantinople, and the Via Egnatia was the oversea extension of the even more ancient, and much more famous, Via Appia, which traversed Italia from Brindisi to Rome itself. The Brindisi-to-Dyrrachium sea route was ancient. As we walked up and through narrow streets, almost to the city walls, we came to a fifteen thousand-seat amphitheatre built in the days of Hadrian. Even in its partially ruined state, I was given to understand that it was still used for the largest events, such as they were, in Dyrrachium.

Although much smaller than that of Spalatius and infinitely smaller than that of Fiumius, Dyrrhachium's port was still a lively and bustling place. We took lodging halfway between the port and the amphitheatre. On our second evening in Dyrrachium, the full orb of the moon made the city almost as bright as day. "What a night to see the amphitheatre!" Joan said. "It should be magnificent!"

I agreed, and after a filling dinner, we were on our way. The arena was as thrilling as Joan had foretold, and it was easy to imagine the ancient games that must have entertained the throngs at a time when Rome still owned the known world.

"Let's climb to the top," I said. We were both a bit breathless when we got there. From that height, the raised stage off to one side of the theatre was bathed in both the natural light of the moon, and that light reflected off a hundred rows of ascending seats. Overwhelmed by this stirring sight, we descended down the aisles until we had reached the arena level.

Suddenly, I felt myself grabbed from behind. I was about to shout to Joan that she should not pull such a prank, when a ball of cloth was rudely shoved into my mouth. Looking around in panic, I found that Joan had been similarly grappled and gagged. We looked at one another and try to signal each other with our eyes, but it was only a moment before I felt a dark scarf tied about my head and eyes, blinding me. I struggled valiantly, but as uselessly as a fish hopelessly caught in a net, and I heard muffled movement from where I envisioned Joan would be.

My panic turned to dread as I saw, in my mind's eye, our captors unsheathing knives to plunge into our necks, or hauling a cudgel over to beat us senseless before killing us. But nothing of the sort happened. I was held in a viselike grip that neither tightened nor loosened. When I found I was not being punched or pummeled, but merely being held, I ceased my struggle and concentrated on breathing.

Not too long afterward, one of our captors said, "Please listen for a moment. We don't intend to harm you and we aren't interested in your money. We have been told to bring you to a secret meeting place. Someone wants to talk to you. The blindfolds are necessary so you cannot see where we're going or say where you've been. The gags are for more obvious reasons. Now, please step as we guide you. There won't be any steep climbs or descents, and we'll steer you clear of impediments." We had no choice but to do as they said. Moments later, our other captor said, in a deeper voice, "We've come to a carruca. We'll help you into it." Once we were ensconced in the covered carriage, our captors took the gags out of our mouths, but left us blindfolded. "There's no need for you to be further discomfited," the first man said. "We're beyond the city and there's no danger of you being heard."

"Thank you," Joan said calmly. "Do we know the people to whom you're taking us?"

"One of them, no," the second captor said. "As to the others, who knows? Which of you is Joannes?"

Stunned as I was that our captors knew our names, I started to stammer out that I was, hoping to protect Joan, but she beat me to the words. "I am," she said.

"Then you must be Martin. Have you eaten?"

"If you were following us, you'd know we had dinner little more than an hour ago."

"Good," said the first man. "No one likes to attend an important meeting on an empty stomach." He laughed heartily at his heavy humor.

"How long will it take us to get there?" I asked.

"Not long. You may as well relax and enjoy the ride.

When the carruca stopped, our captors removed our blindfolds. Joan's captor was not much older than Joan. He was tall and slender. Had he not surprised us, I could easily have taken him in a fair fight. My attendant was just as tall, but more burly. Whoever wanted to see us had planned our kidnap quite carefully. Both of these men had mild faces, hardly the type I would have expected to be kidnappers. We were on a sere, dusty steppe, well beyond the city walls, but not yet up into the mountains. There was a building several yards away, a dimly lit, solid, unprepossessing farmhouse. A tall figure approached the area between the carriage and the building. The man looked older and more careworn than he had the year before, but I recognized him easily. "Your Eminence?"

"Good evening, Martin, Joannes. Thank you for coming on such short notice." He chuckled and the lines in his face relaxed. "You needn't make any comment. It's been a difficult year for you, and it has been a difficult year for me as well. I share your pain."

"Thank you, Eminence. The archbishopric in Hamburg is difficult, then?"

"Very, and thankless as well."

A second voice that I recognized immediately said, "It was very kind of you to send such a beneficence, unnecessary as it was, to our sister, but we thank you nonetheless. It is an indication of your character."

"Thank you, Herr Tacitus," I said. "We are, uh, surprised at the time and place you picked for a … reunion?"

"Sometimes diplomacy requires a bit of tact, other times a bit of subterfuge," he said.

"How did you find us?" This from Joan.

Sergius answered, "Mother Church is not without her eyes and ears. And her friends. You knew Doctor ben-Halevi advised us that Eva had died from a sudden onset of food poisoning?"

"Aye," Joan said.

"The good doctor has been a great ally of Mother Church, one of hundreds of pairs of eyes and ears throughout the Haemus Peninsula. Before that, it was a messenger in Fiumius, a boatman at Balatonea, numerous others. Even your financial agent, whom you only met this morning when you withdrew some money, told us you were in Dyrrhachium shortly after you'd left. Your agent in Angle-land made us promise that Mother Church would watch over you and protect you from any harm on the Continent."

"You could have intercepted us at any point in our journey," Joan said.

"Well, of course, you expected to see us at the wedding and we expected to see you at the wedding, but there was no need for such a meeting until now."

"And I wouldn't have been able to attend because I wasn't even invited to the wedding."

"Nicola!" Joan ran over and hugged him with joy. I was not far behind.

"In the living flesh."

"But why you?"

"They didn't have to kidnap me, but they thought I would give them greater credibility."

"Them? But we already know them," I said.

"There are a couple you don't know," Nicola replied. "Come." He led us into a room where a number of candles gave off a soft light. Seated inside was a man as tall as Sergius, of medium girth. The top of his pate was bald, but he had a full head of white hair and a beard and moustache. He had a long face and a gentle but impressive manner. As I became accustomed to the dim light, I saw the white stola, a cross on each side, and the red robe. I had seen paintings of the man at Tours and in most major cathedrals where I'd traveled.

Without waiting for introductions, Joan and I prostrated ourselves before Gregory IV, Archbishop of Rome, successor to the Fisherman, Pope of all Western Christendom. He signaled us to rise by holding out his right hand and raising his index and middle finger. "Brother Joannes, Brother Martin, welcome. Peace be unto you."

"And Unto You, Your Holiness," we responded in unison.

Without waiting for us to say more, Pope Gregory, whose voice was deceptively soft said, "Thank you so much for coming on such short notice." His eyes glimmered with bright humor, yet with an edge of steel. "Joannes Angliorum, I'm told you are one of the brightest young minds in the Roman Church, and Martin Paschal, I have been impressed by what I've seen of your writing. I have a special fondness for your last name, for it was Saint Paschal who first ordained me many years ago."

"Thank you, Holiness," Joan replied evenly. "You wished to meet with us?"

"I did," the Pope responded. "You are indeed as direct as I was told. I have a small favor to ask of you two."

"Of course, Holiness, you know your wish is more than our command," I said.

"Since my accession to the papacy seven years ago, Europe has entered a period of darkness and agony. You know of the schism between Louis and his sons, particularly Lothar?"

"Aye," said Joan.

"You are aware of my role in that ongoing feud?"

"I am, Holiness," said Joan. "Lothar asked you to come across the Alps and mediate between the sons and the father."

"That is true," Gregory said. "No sooner had I reached eastern France, the bishops favorable to Emperor Louis protested my attempts. Although I told them in no uncertain terms that the government of souls, which belongs to the supreme pontiff, is greater than the imperial power, which is temporal, they rejected my pleas. Alas, my attempt at mediation was unsuccessful."

"But they seem to have worked things out," I ventured.

"For the time being, perhaps, but I fear when Louis dies, as he inevitably must, there will be a yet greater schism between the brothers. I could live in peace if those were the only problems in and around the papal domains. There are more."

Nicola continued. "The Norsemen are scouring the western coasts and stabbing up the rivers of Europe. The Saracens dominate the White Sea coasts, tearing Sicily away from the Byzantine Empire. There's rumor they might even attack Italia."

"And both Empires are too weak or don't care to deal with the problem?"

"Unfortunately true, Martin" Tacitus said.

"Theophilus, the Byzantine emperor, concerns us," the Pope said. "He's prohibited all religious art and has made life difficult for the holy artists. We've got enough of a schism between the Roman Church and the Orthodox Church without that malcontent adding fuel to the fire. That's where each of you can do us a small service."

"What is that, Holiness?" Joan asked.

"You two plan to attend the Academy of Saint Gaius Petronius," he said, "one of the few areas where we Romans and our Eastern Brothers are able to quietly meet and converse in camera; where we can enter into honest dialogue in the knowledge that nothing will leak out to those who would do our efforts harm."

"What would you wish of us, Holiness?" I asked.

"Simply that the two of you act as my private eyes and ears whenever and wherever that needs to take place. Sit in the councils and listen – simply listen. Martin, you will record what is said, and Joannes, you will interpret the meaning behind what is said. Each of you will send letters to me by special messenger. The Holy See may occasionally request that you pass private letters to certain people in Our Name." He stopped and chuckled, before continuing, "Regardless of who the Patriarch of Constantinople may believe is the supreme pontiff."

"Spies, Holiness?" Joan asked.

The Pope arched his eyebrows. "There is nothing immoral about having as accurate information as possible, recorded by unimpeachable sources. If you want to call it 'spying,' that's your choice of words. I prefer to call it intelligence gathering.

Of course, I expect you will both be associates in the Academy, but that will be your public face. Several important men, including numerous visitors to the Academy from without, will know who you are and for what purpose you are there. Many times they will contact you."

"Why are we meeting here, Holiness?" Joan asked. "You could easily have summoned us to the Holy See, to Avignon, to wherever you wished within the Holy Roman Empire."

"Sometimes even the Holy Father himself must show himself where he would not be expected. You are aware that Dyrrachium is under Theophilus' temporal rule?"

"I am," Joan said.

"But this is not exactly a substantial center of his empire." At that we all laughed. "Joannes called it a mud puddle, Holiness," I said.

"Aptly put." Gregory's eyes glinted with humor once again. "I very much doubt if Theophilus has even come within a hundred miles of it in the five years he's been on the Purple Throne. It's probably wise he does not do so, for there is a substantial Roman minority here. It's unlikely he'd be met with Hosannahs in the streets, since no one in Dyrrachium is pleased with his policies."

"The Patriarch John goes along with his heresies," Sergius remarked, archly.

"Aye," the Pope replied. "That's because his sinecure is more important to him than his integrity."

"Why Dyrrachium?" Joan asked again.

"Perhaps I can answer that, Brother Joannes." A medium-sized man with piercing brown eyes and a heavy black beard, no more than five or six years my senior, entered the room briskly, and sat in the only empty chair. "I am Ignatius. Forgive me for joining the conversation in so rude a manner."

"Not at all," the Pope said. Turning to Joan and me, he continued, "As you know, we are doctrinally at odds with our Christian brethren in Byzantium. The Patriarch at Constantinople claims he is the true – and only – vicar of Christ on earth and that Rome is subordinate. Naturally, for the consumption of our adherents, Rome publicly proclaims that we are the true – and only – vicar of Christ on earth, and that the Byzantine Patriarch is nothing more than a fraud and a pretender. So, of course, there is no communication between the leaders of Christendom at all – at least so far as the mass of Christianity believes. Since John has become Patriarch, what private communications there have always been have broken down still farther."

"As a practical, human reality, it really doesn't matter who is the predominant leader of Christendom, or who is Christ's vicar on earth, so long as each of us holds foremost in our heart that we are Christ's spokesman to the multitudes who live within our domains," Ignatius said.

"Well spoken," Cardinal Sergius said. He'd been listening in silence to the exchange.

I rose, walked over to a nearby table where there were several small earthenware cups and a pot of hot water, poured a cup for myself, and went back to my seat. Despite my interest in the conversation, I felt my eyelids starting to get heavy.

"Might I fetch you a cup of hot water, Holiness?" I asked.

"Ne, Martin, thank you," Gregory replied. He continued speaking, primarily to Joan and me. "Ignatius is as important to Rome – and I daresay to Byzantium – as anyone in the Byzantine Empire. Unfortunately, he is, at present, somewhat out of favor with the powers at Constantinople because he has publicly decried Theophilus' iconoclasm as heresy. While my friend and I may disagree on dogma, we are certainly in agreement that good Christians everywhere need the icons, the relics of the Faith, to remind them how ancient our religious beliefs are and from whence they came. Joannes, that may be a roundabout way of answering your earlier enquiry about why we are meeting in Dyrrachium. For Ignatius to be seen at the Holy See or, for that matter, anywhere within the Holy Roman Empire, would have the effect of branding him a traitor to his patriarch and his own emperor. Likewise, if anyone of consequence knew we were in communication with Ignatius, who enjoys a rank similar to that of cardinal in the Roman Church, Byzantium would immediately let the Christian world know we were interfering in the internal affairs of the Orthodox Church and Ignatius would be highly suspect."

"That's why I arranged for everyone to meet in one of the few places in Christendom that would not be of concern to anyone of importance," Tacitus said. "Dyrrachium, by its very anonymity, makes it a precious meeting point for East and West, and this nondescript building, situated as it is well off the Via Egnatia and in the hills above Dyrrachium, is even more anonymous than the town itself."

"But we cannot meet here much longer. There are suspicions. I trust each of us knows why we are communicating with Ignatius?"

No one answered the implied question, but, yes, it was rather easy to see why. Our great and glorious Holiness, Pope Gregory IV, was as political as any other human being in a position of leadership. He was eager to make sure exactly who the next Patriarch of Byzantium would be if – hopefully when – the icon-rejecting Patriarch John was replaced.

"So you'll be using us to continue your contacts with one another," Joan said. It was a statement, not a question.

"And others, of course," replied His Holiness. "One last thing remains," the Pope said. "I intend to bestow the stola of priest on each of you tonight, as well as the official title of Monsignor. Sometimes you may be called upon to act as my personal emissaries or even to negotiate at a high level. Although I cannot formally designate you as bishops due to your youth and, more important, your unfamiliarity with the diplomatic terrain, each of you will have the pro tempore title of Bishop at Large, which will give you a certain degree of influence at any important meetings you might attend. You will not commit Mother Church to any significant position on your own. Rather, you are to temporize, consult with us or our designee, and then provide your response in accordance with the wishes of the Holy See."

I was trembling with excitement at this unbelievable turn of our fortunes. Joan was calm.

We bowed our heads, and after pouring a few drops of oil from a tiny cup onto our heads, the Pope himself placed a stola around each of our shoulders.

"You may now arise, Monsignor Joannes Angliorum and Monsignor Martin Paschal. It is my pleasure to welcome you to, shall we say, a 'higher' brotherhood. Peace be with you."

"And with you, Holiness," we replied.

"For your own safety, would you mind if our two 'helpers' blindfold you once again? It is perhaps best that you truly not know the exact place where we 'did not meet' tonight."

"As I said before, Your Holiness, your wish is our command."

~ ∫ ~

Later that night, when the magnitude of what had happened finally replaced our initial shock, Joan and I could not stop talking. We had been handed our futures on a golden platter, without even applying, because of the simple "request" of the Holy Father.

God puts everything in balance. I had only recently lost the love of my life. When I was cast down into the bitterest void, I had suddenly been upraised and elevated. I only prayed that I would be able to fulfill my new duties with responsibility and a reasonable degree of success.

Chapter 33

Vindobona was a refined city, which wore its age like a queen. Athens was an old bawd, and gave no pretense of being anything more. Rude shacks stood cheek-by-jowl with ancient ruins, which, in turn, stood next to impressive public buildings and all manner of churches. There were daily open-air markets, weekly open-air markets, and open-air hawkers, purveyors of every imaginable comestible and souvenir, in every segment of the city. Vindobona danced gracefully to the music of wheeled carriages and elegantly-dressed gentlefolk. Athens was raucous, noisy, and rambunctious, day and night.

The city is situated in a bowl, with mountains on three sides, almost at the southern end of a long peninsula. Like Rome, Athens is not located directly on the sea, but is located less than a day's journey from the water. As Ostia is to Rome, so the port of Piraeus is to Athens. Eight hills rise from Athens' low plain, all of them close to the city center. From pine-covered Lykavittus Hill, the highest point in Athens, we could see all there was to see, even to Piraeus. During the years we were in Athens, Joan and I spent many hours near its summit, because it is the kind of place that allows one to dream, to plan, and to find solitude and peace.

The Academy of Saint Gaius Petronius was southwest of Lykavittus Hill, halfway up Philipoppus Hill. The summit of that hill commanded as fine a view of the city as Lykavittus, but because of its proximity to Athens, and to Athens' most famous series of monuments atop Acropolis Hill, it was invariably crowded with tourist and traveler, Churchman and whore, family man and thief. During our time in Athens, we traveled extensively to many areas of both the Roman and the Byzantine Empire. In all that time, indeed, in all my life, and to this very day, I remember one thing about Athens that I have never seen, before or since, in any other place on earth. That something was the presence during every sunny day, and even during some days that were not sunny, and even during moonlit nights, of a unique brightness I'd never experienced before. In other places, when the sun goes down it descends in a great ball of red fire. But in Athens, it descends in a light that turns from a definable pink through the spectrum of colors to violet, magenta, and purple, before it bids good night to the world.

The Academy of Saint Gaius Petronius was one of several similarly situated institutions in the city where learned men of every age, from youth to whitebeard, gathered and discussed and evaluated and disputed wisdom from every sphere of knowledge. It was invariably full of intellectual challenge. It was an unwritten rule that any man could espouse any philosophy, no matter how arcane or seemingly insane, with complete impunity. It was housed in a series of three long buildings in the shape of the letter "U." We did not celebrate the Orders of service at midnight or early morning. We did not deliberately violate any tenets of the Church, but the rules were quite relaxed at Saint Gaius Petronius.

The army of Christ was similar to a real army. The foot soldiers – acolytes and postulants and monks, and such, did the dirty work and engaged in true warfare for the soul of the Church. Joan and I were officers in the Army. We were expected to – and did – live as befits officers. We were commanders, and as such we were expected to be strong and well-prepared, and that meant well-rested and well-fed. It was not for us to arise at midnight, or even, for that matter, six hours later, nor were we expected to take a vow of poverty, silence, or celibacy, provided we did not rub such luxuries in the faces of the infantrymen in our army. To my knowledge, experience, and observation, the lower one is in the echelon of any organization, the more such a person wants, *ne, needs* to see his bishop, his king, or his leader able to meet with other bishops, kings, or leaders, as an equal.

While I missed Eva perhaps more than I had loved her, memories fade as time marches inexorably toward the future. Truly, time is the greatest thief of all. By day, Joan taught and I recorded many discussions and arguments and proceedings, both in and out of the Academy. Several days each week I served as *magister*, chronicler, and teacher. Although Joan was invariably courteous and diplomatic, I witnessed several incidents where, without braggadocio or disdain, she bested every teacher or student in any dispute, to the extent that they walked away mumbling that there had never been as clever or brilliant a person as Joannes Angliorum. Joan never consciously tried to make a reputation for herself. It just came naturally.

Often, Joan and I frequented *tabernae* and lectures, concerts and plays in the nearby Herodes Atticus theatre, or we would climb to the top of the Acropolis, enter the Beuleus Gate, and simply gaze in awe at the Propylaeia, the Temple of Athena Nike, the Erechtheion, and the splendid Parthenon. "Can you believe that building is over thirteen hundred years old?" Joan gasped, the first time she saw it. "How absolutely perfect it is from every side," she said in rapt admiration.

When one has a daily routine and, as one grows older, each day passes more quickly than the last. Before I knew it, three years had passed. It was the Year of Our Lord 838, and I'd passed my twenty-eighth birthday. Joan was twenty-four, and, since she did not – indeed could not – grow a beard, she looked even younger than her years. Charlemagne's son and his grandsons continued their drive to destroy what their glorious ancestor had struggled so hard to create. When Louis the Pious' son Pepin, died that year, the elderly and all-too-forgiving Louis divided the Empire among his sons once again. Ludwig the German refused to accept the division, particularly since his brother Lothar had been designated Holy Roman Emperor-presumptive at such time as the old emperor died. When Lothar tried to reduce Louis' two remaining sons to vassal kings, Ludwig invaded Saxony. Old Louis repelled the invasion, but he was clearly weakening in body and spirit.

Once again, the old emperor forgave Ludwig. Now, he appealed to Lothar to protect his second wife, Judith, and the child of his advanced age, Charles, now known as "the Bald."

Angle-land was even worse off. The Danes were at war with Wessex, and Kenneth MacAlpin, formerly the self-styled king of Kintyre, was now king of all of the Scots. His territory extended to the northern borders of Angle-land.

Meanwhile, Joan and I continued to serve as trusted messengers between East and West. Joan was the more visible, public face of diplomacy. I acted as recorder and transcriber. While we were at Athens, we had increased our store of languages so that we now spoke fluent Latin and Greek, as well as the offshoot languages of the Goths, German and Angle-ish, and the new French language, which was derived from Latin. This fluency enabled us to easily travel through the lands of the Eastern and Western Churches, understanding and, more important, making ourselves understood without the need of a translator, in the councils of both Byzantium and Rome.

The volume of our messages, both incoming and outgoing, increased as the Holy Roman Empire started fragmenting further. Poor, exhausted Louis Pius fell ill on the way back to Aix la Chapelle and died near Ingelheim. Lothar succeeded to the title of Holy Roman Emperor. Charles and Ludwig immediately rebelled against their brother. A minor kinglet, Moimir, formed a confederation of Slavs in Bohemia, Moravia, Slovakia, Hungaria, and Transylvania, on the Empire's eastern flank. Pope Gregory tried to intervene and mediate. Once again, his efforts were rebuffed. Gregory's gaze then turned eastward, to try to achieve some modicum of success in his prelacy. Athens, as the safe meeting ground of East and West, offered the most likely place to achieve that success.

In 842, Emperor Theophilus died and his wife, Theodora, became regent for her infant son Michael III. One of her first acts was to renounce the persecution of the iconographers and to declare iconoclasm at an end. By that time, I was in my thirty-third year and Joan was nearly twenty-nine. That year, Pope Gregory sent both of us to the very seat of the Byzantine Empire on a mission that would provide immense and lasting consequences for each of us.

~ ∫ ~

"Can you believe it?" Joan squealed in delight. "Nicola – our Nicola – has been invested with the red *stola*! A cardinal!

And he's only what – thirty-seven years old?" She held up the letter we'd just received like it was a holy relic.

"That is so marvelous," I responded with equal excitement. "Remember when he was a postulant in London? He's the one who said he wasn't particularly bright and had no connections anywhere, and, as we both know, he certainly did not have the type of purse that would buy him an appointment anywhere."

"It goes to show," Joan said. "Sometimes God provides that sheer goodness carries the day over brilliance or connections or money."

"Unquestionably he was in the right place at the right time, but still, his innate likeability and hard work were recognized and he got what he deserved."

"There's more news," Joan said. "The Holy Father is sending Nicola to Constantinople to discuss 'matters of some importance' with the new Patriarch Ignatius and Empress Theodora. Nicola has requested – and Pope Gregory has commanded – that you and I accompany him to the seat of the Byzantine Empire to be part of the conclave."

Now, both of us were really excited. Although we'd been to just about every place in the empire but Constantinople, neither of us had ever been to Rome-of-the-East, which was said to be the greatest city in the world at that time.

"When does he expect us there?" I asked Joan.

"A month from now."

"Then we'd best take passage by ship."

"I agree," Joan said.

In distance, it was roughly the same whether we went over the Via Egnatia or traveled the Aegean by ship, but since we were coming as personages and as official emissaries of the Holy See, it would seem more appropriate if we arrived in the style befitting our stations.

~ ∫ ~

One can come to Constantinople over the Via Egnatia from Greece, through the wild Bulgar lands in the Haemus Peninsula, by way of Hadrianopolis, from the Black Sea by traveling south through the Bosphorous, or from the wilds of Asia.

But of all the ways I have ever arrived at the Queen of all cities – and in my life I have come to Constantinople from each of these directions – there is truly only one way to really be exposed to the sheer magnificence of Rome-in-the-East, and that is to arrive by sea from the south, coming upon that astounding metropolis where the northern reaches of the Sea of Marmara touch the southern extremity of the Bosphorous. That sight is surely unforgettable.

It was the latter part of June when we traversed the White Sea, passing between hundreds of rocky islands with square, whitewashed buildings, blindingly white, sandy beaches, and tree-topped hills. The very names of these islands reflected the Homeric and Virgilian odes of antiquity – Kea and Andros, Evstratios and Lesvos, Limnos and Samothraki. Just after coming within sight of the western coast of Asia Minor, we entered the Dardanelles. Less than one Roman mile to the east was the site believed to be that of Troy itself. To our left, the hilly peninsula of the Gallipoli almost crushed against mainland Asia Minor. As suddenly as the waterway had narrowed, it widened once again into the gentle Sea of Marmara. Straight ahead, we saw the seven majestic hills of European Constantinople, heart of the Byzantine Empire, the only city in the world to sit astride two continents.

As we came closer to the city, Justinian's huge and massive Church of the Holy Wisdom, Haghia Sophia, dominated the hill closest to the sea – or, to be more accurate, the *seas*, for as we entered the Bosphorous, that thirty-mile-long strait that separates Europe from Asia and the Black Sea from the Sea of Marmara, we saw that Constantinople is made up of three parts land and three parts water.

We were entering the city from the largest body of water, the Sea of Marmara. As we rounded the tip of the peninsula that marked the Old City, we entered a place where the Bosphorous forked straight and slightly to the right, and a third body of water, that inlet known as the Golden Horn – perhaps because during many sunsets we were there, its waters truly looked as if they were liquid gold – led off to the west. The two parts of European Constantinople, one to our left and one straight ahead, were equidistant from Asiatic Constantinople, less than a Roman mile to our right.

Everywhere we looked, we encountered visually stunning sights – gigantic, colorful buildings atop sharply defined hills, more churches than we'd ever seen in any city, markets descending to the ports – and there were many ports and harbors, not just a single port. Bridges crossed between the old and new parts of town. Hundreds of ferries crossed the Bosphorous each hour. Each of these had to beware of the several hundred small fishing boats plying the waters that surrounded the city.

Fish were plentiful, and the boatmen had a unique manner of supplying fresh fish to their customers. When a fishing boat had caught its fill, its masters moved their skiff toward the nearest dock, while grilling freshly-caught fish on metal braziers aboard their craft. By the time they arrived at dock or port or even a spit of land, the fish were browned and sizzling, and the crowds waited to purchase a fillet or two of such fish, stuffed between two pieces of thick bread. The boat was emptied of fish within a few moments after it made landfall.

We debarked at a landing just below the hill on which Haghia Sophia stood, and were met at the landing by the equivalent of cardinals in the Eastern Church. We ignored them, because we saw our Nico trotting, almost running, toward us.

"Nico!" Joan shouted. "Over here, Nico!" She forgot who she was and whom she represented, so eager was she to hug our friend in a tight embrace. Less than a moment later, I was part of the hugging trio, and we all babbled at one another at the same time. The conservative Orthodox churchmen looked at us with something akin to amazement, for we of the Roman Church were not renowned for such outbursts of enthusiastic passion as we displayed.

Nico managed to draw us away from the others just long enough to say, "To them I'm known as Cardinal Nicholas. Of course, we'll be Joan – oops, Joannes Angliorum, Martin, and Nicola for so long as we live. God, but it's good to see you! Joan, you've not aged a moment, and if you become any more beautiful, no one will believe you're a man and a Monsignor."

"And you, Nico, you silver-tongued rogue," I said. Do I detect a slight bit of salt in the rather sparse and peppery black beard you're wearing?"

"Shush," Nicola said, laughing. "I've only recently grown this to make my hosts feel more at ease with me. Not a good job, you say?"

"Must I be sworn to tell the truth, or would you rather I just commented on how well you look, Nico?"

"What about you, Martin? You're what now, thirty-five? Forty?"

"The devil take you," I said, clapping him on the back. "I'm not yet thirty-three."

"You could have fooled me. I'd have thought fifty at least. I was trying to be kind. Seriously, I've arranged that we take lodging together before we confer with our hosts. I'm sure you'll want to know what all this is about, but we've three days before the first session meets, and we've got so much to talk about, I don't know where to begin. Let's at least make some show of appreciation to our hosts for their impressive welcome, so they don't think we've totally lost our manners or our sanity."

Nico introduced us to three Orthodox Churchmen who replicated our precise stations within the Roman Church. Fathers Julianus and Justinius were Joan's and my age, whereas Methodius was clearly the leader of our welcoming delegation.

We found out that evening that no matter the Church affiliation, young men of good will – and one woman, although no one but Nicola and I knew this – can shed the cassock and have a fine time in a city, particularly one such as Constantinople.

Within a block or two of the Royal Road were narrow streets filled with every imaginable daytime and nighttime entertainment. Wine was cheap and plentiful, food was abundant, and, if one was so disposed, women of all ages, sizes, and prices were readily available. Trinkets and gifts proliferated everywhere. In open markets throughout the city, spices from Egypt and the Far East jostled adjoining bins of silk, cotton, and ramie. Extravagantly filigreed metalwork was in astonishing supply. I even found a cheap piece of amber imported from Sarmatia, and thought, momentarily, about sending it anonymously to old Cardinal Alcinorius.

"How would you like to be one of those merchants?" Nicola asked me. "Or, in your case, you could be a letter writer and make a fortune."

"What do you mean?"

"Even though this is the heart of Empire, the vast majority of people can't read Greek or Latin. When I was last here, day and night I saw the lines in front of the scribes' stands. They write the same flowing, overdone love poetry, or ridiculous, overstated requests for the emperor's assistance every day. So often have they done this, they can most likely do it in their sleep. Each precious young girl thinks the poetry was written for her ears alone. Occasionally, the petition to the emperor finds its way to one of the emperor's petty bureaucrats. Even charging the smallest nummus for each piece of work, the scribes make a fortune."

"Clever, but a complete waste of Martin's talents," Joan said.

While we were dining that night, Justinius pounded so hard on the plank table at which we were seated that two goblets fell over, spilling wine across the table onto my trousers and Methodius' robe. Methodius stood, lifted his arms like an Old Testament prophet, and commanded, "You have three ways of paying for your misdeed. You may personally wash this cassock, you may buy me a new one, or," he paused, "you may show our new friends that Eastern priests can dance as well as a wild man from the plains of *Rus*."

Taking up the challenge, Justinius went onto the square, wooden dance floor, tossed several coins to the corner where the musicians were playing, clapped his hands, shouted out the name of some tune, and waited for the musicians to begin. The song was obviously familiar to the multitudes in the taberna, for they started shouting and clapping and stamping their feet in time to the music. Justinius, alone in the center of the floor, began a sinuous, slow dance, weaving, snapping his fingers in rhythm to the music. He lost himself in the spirit of his movements, clapping his hands for the band to play faster. As they did, he performed acrobatic feats I'd never seen before.

Justinius jumped and squatted. As he squatted, he kicked one leg forward, then the other. He signaled for Julianus to join him. The whole crowd shouted encouragement. Then, each of them did what, to me, seemed impossible. Julianus jumped up, spread-eagled his feet and arms, so that his left foot flew all the way up to his left arm and his right arm connected with his right foot. While this was going on, Justinius somersaulted in the air and came down perfectly on his feet.

Now, Methodius approached the two of them, and sang in a loud, wonderful baritone voice. A taberna-maid brought a huge flagon of wine to our table, and after knocking back a draught of the heady stuff, each of us went onto the dance floor and joined a circle of patrons that had formed and was now doing a ragged circle dance around the two athlete-priest-dancers.

The loud, raucous fun continued for hours. I cannot tell you how many hours we danced and sang – and Joan and Julianus even tried their hand at playing a couple of the musical instruments – and I think they played them pretty well. Of course, I also cannot tell you how many cups of wine I had that night, but I vaguely remember staggering back to our quarters, which were only a few blocks away, across from the Haghia Eirene church.

Chapter 34

When I awoke, it was already midday. My tongue was asleep and my teeth itched, if that is possible. My head weighed about the same as a large horse, which made it rather difficult to lift. I didn't know if I wanted to urinate first or retch first, or both at the same time. I heard a profoundly loud and jangling booming in my head. Looking through bleary, watering eyes, I saw Methodius. He tiptoed into my bedroom and handed me a cup of foul-smelling cloudy-white liquid.

"Horse piss," he said blithely.

I didn't get the humor and moaned heavily.

"All right, my friend, maybe not horse piss, but it will make you feel a bit better. Quaff it quickly, though, because you'll swear it is horse piss."

I did, and it tasted even viler than it smelt. Within an hour, however, whatever Methodius had given me started working, and by early evening I was feeling somewhat better. When I went down to eat at the communal table, I found a large tureen of cabbage soup, two spirited Orthodox dancers-turned-clergymen, and two very quiet, humbled friends.

"Well, where are we going tonight?" Julianus asked us.

"Straight upstairs and back to bed," Joan said. "Do your really do that every night?"

"Ne, not at all," Justinius replied. "We just thought you wanted to have a good time and that you pictured us as dour ascetics."

"Hardly," I said.

"Justinius, we're all members of the same family, and we all happen to suffer from the same disease – we're all human," Joan said. "Did you truly think we're somehow different than you?"

"I don't know how to answer that," Justinius said. "We're taught one set of values, one set of prejudices when we're young, and we grow into adulthood well-settled with those values."

"We're much the same," Nicola joined in. "We've always been told that you Orthodox Christians feel morally superior to us and that your Patriarch is the true and only leader of Christendom. We're also taught that we of the Roman Church were parent to the Eastern Church."

"But isn't it true that the Jews whom we both regard as lesser mortals, are the true members of the parent religion?" This from Methodius.

The waiter came to our table with an amphora of wine. Everyone at the table declined the libation. "Aren't these things we're going to be discussing at the formal meetings during the next few days?" I inquired.

"Aye, but there we'll be posturing. What goes on here tonight is between us and us alone," Methodius said. "Agreed?" We all assented. "Good," Methodius continued. "Then let us speak candidly of what is truly in our hearts. Perhaps if, in our very small conclave, we can make some headway, we might influence the larger body, so at least we can agree on some matters, and from there some larger matters, until, by God's will, we come closer to the brotherhood we each share." That night was far different from the night before, but each evening held its own value, and each activity cemented the commonality and brotherhood of man and the Fatherhood of God.

~ ʃ ~

Next morning, I was awakened by Justinius, who said, "We've got a full day before the conclave starts. How would you like to wander through our fair city and see what there is to see?"

I was instantly alert, and realized how much better I felt than the day before. "That would be wonderful, Justinius," I replied. "Are the others awake?"

"Aye, and breakfast awaits us downstairs as well."

We were staying in a dormitorium close to Haghia Eirene, the Church of Divine Peace, where the conclave would be held on the morrow, so naturally we started our perambulation there. That edifice had been the meeting place of the Second Ecumenical Council, four hundred fifty years ago, so it was, even then, a very old church. It was distinguished for its reddish roof.

"When we were approaching Constantinople, we saw a huge harbor on the south side of the city," Joan said. "Yet we sailed all the way around the cape to Eminence Harbor before we landed. Wouldn't it have made more sense to dock at the large port?"

"Ne," Methodius replied. "Let's walk there and I'll show you why."

It was not a far walk to the southern edge of the peninsula, and we passed the Hippodrome on the way. The Hippodrome is not so much a structure as it is a huge, open field that has been used since the days of Constantine, and is to this day still used, as a venue for parades and the races between the blues and the greens that excite the entire city, and for all manner of public events. Nearby are three large columns and obelisks. The highest of them is ninety feet high. It is said to have come from Heliopolis in Egypt, and to date back to the reign of Thutmose III, which was more than two thousand, five hundred years ago – one hundred generations back. A number beyond all imagining!

A little farther on, we came to the Serpent's Column, which is only a mere stump compared to the Egyptian obelisk, even if it is three times the height of an ordinary man. Atop that stump was a golden tripod of three intertwined snakes. The Serpent's Column is emblematic of the vast wealth of this Queen City, but there were gold-adorned buildings everywhere throughout the capital of Byzantium. Methodius told me the Serpent's Column had originally stood at Delphi in Graecia to commemorate the Greek victory over the Persians, and that took place "only" fifteen hundred years ago. The last of the three structures surrounding the Hippodrome was the Colossus, and it was not as impressive as the other two, for it was made of masonry and no one seemed to know how old it was.

To the north – and behind us – stood the most magnificent structure in all Christendom, but Methodius had told us he was saving this building – the Church of Holy Wisdom – for last, "since it is not only grander than the ancient Temple of Solomon, but also because it is so close to our dormitorium. By the time we return we will, all of us, need a rest."

Soon we came to the harbor – two harbors, actually – on the south side of the peninsula. The first was the commercial wharf, Theodosius' harbor, and it was filled with small merchantmen and fishing vessels. East of that port was the Proklianean Harbor, and that was the reason we had not debarked at Theodosius' harbor. Proklianean Harbor was the Empire's largest naval base. There were well over a hundred dromons – warships – in the harbor, and Methodius told us there were hundreds more at sea at any one time. Even though the Byzantine Empire had lately suffered more devastating defeats than glorious victories, the dromons were impressive to behold. They were long and lean. Some had two banks of oars, others only one. The bronze rams of these ships were pitted and scarred and blackened from constant immersion in salt water. Gray, black, and red-purple barnacles graced the prows and the sterns of these ships. There was a tower amidships in each of the vessels, and from these towers, archers could loose their arrows down to the decks of opposing ships. In front of and behind each tower were holes for sailing masts, but only one or two of the dromons in port had their masts up now. Despite the fact that the ships were at rest and none seemed to be moving, the port resounded with the constant activity of men were scurrying about, scraping barnacles, painting and scrubbing decks, hammering, sawing, and shouting.

These seamen were clad in short wool or linen tunics that stopped above their knees, or, in many cases, they wore only a cloth to cover their loins, with sheathed knives on the right side. They were dark-skinned and their faces were deeply etched with lines carved by wind, sun, salt air, and harsh weather. The Greek they shouted or grunted was clipped, almost incomprehensible.

"Sailor Greek," Justinius remarked. "They're not highly educated, often there's little time in the heat of battle to go into long soliloquies. They say what they have to say, as briefly as possible."

From the heights above the harbor, I looked to my left. I could see all the way to Eminence Landing, where we'd docked two nights before. As far as I could see, there was a huge, high, thick stone wall encircling the peninsula. Every hundred yards or so, there was a square stone tower overlooking the walls.

"Those walls are more than seven thousand yards from end to end," Methodius remarked.

"Do they truly provide protection for the City?" Joan asked.

"They have withstood fires for hundreds of years," Julianus replied.

"Mayhap," Joan persisted. "But that is the right answer to a different question. My question was whether or not the walls have provided protection."

"Well, umm …" Julianus colored slightly. "They've never really been tested."

We continued our journey west all the way to Hadrian's Gate. Turning north, we came to a huge, two-story aqueduct. "The Aqueduct of Valens," Justinius said, to no one in particular. "It was built five hundred years ago, during the reign of that ancient Roman emperor, and it still provides the city with fresh, clean water. Look yonder! There's one of the Empress' palaces!"

"One of them?" I asked, gazing in rapt attention at the large, marble structure.

"Oh, yes," Justinius replied. "There are several throughout the city on both sides of the Golden Horn and across the Bosphorous as well.

We passed the jewel-like little monastery called Saint Savior in Chora and came to the Royal Highway. Turning east, we passed into a busy industrial neighborhood, filled with workers' shacks, manufactories, open air markets, and what appeared to be the dregs of humanity and the cesspits of the Byzantine Empire.

"Time to eat," said Methodius gaily.

We'd been walking for some hours by that time. I was quite foot-weary and hungry as well, but I thought Methodius was joking. "Excuse me, Your Worship," I said, "but where would one find a decent eatery around here? This is by no means a wealthy area."

"Ah, but you are wrong, my friend," Methodius responded equably. "Some of the wealthiest merchants, traders, and industrialists make their fortunes from this very quarter. They need to eat at midday, and those who work so hard at virtual slave wages are voracious eaters as well. This is the best place in the city to eat precisely because of that combination."

Julianus continued. "You don't get a choice of what to eat at these places. You get what the cooks feel like making that day, as much as you want, and at an astonishingly low price."

We did not eat in grand style, but we enjoyed a grand meal. There seems to be one food that unites and bonds human beings everywhere, which makes me wonder why they fight to preserve their imagined differences between one another. That food is made in the simplest way imaginable. One starts with a huge pot containing various amounts of water. To that is added whatever vegetables and meats, fish, or fowl are available, various spices depending on the cook's taste, and a fire under the kettle to cook the mixture. The huge cauldron is never rinsed or cleaned – at least I have never seen it rinsed or cleaned – but rather, it is constantly refilled, winter or summer, with whatever comestibles are at that moment readily and cheaply available.

Huge mounds of boiled rice accompanied our fare, and there were massive loaves of bread to dip into the saucers and crockery from which we ate. All around us, workmen and bosses, masters and slaves, belched and then filled their dishes with more food.

Bishop Methodius had told us he'd save the best for last, and he was right. From the outside, Haghia Sophia – the Church of Holy Wisdom – was the most magnificent edifice I'd ever seen, and even in Rome there is not a structure that surpasses it. And what a history it has had! The first church on this site, built by Constantine the Great in 326, was burned down, and a later church was destroyed during the long-ago Nike insurrection. But it was left to the great Justinian to create the mammoth structure I saw that day.

To demonstrate her knowledge, Joan politely interrupted, "And when Justinian laid eyes on the Church in 537, he cried out, 'Oh, Solomon, I have surpassed you!'"

"That may well be," Nicola said mildly, "but thanks to the wicked Babylonians we'll never have a chance to compare Solomon's Temple to the Church of the Holy Wisdom."

"*Aye*, you are right," Justinius said. "Are any of you familiar with cubits, so we can do some comparisons?"

"Biblical, Greek, or Roman cubits?" Joan asked. Justinius thought she was joking. I knew better.

"Is there a difference?" he asked.

"Of course," Joan replied. "Shall we compare them with our Roman yard measurement?"

Justinian was caught in what had started as a joke, and said, "That's fine with me."

"Very well," said Joan. "One yard equals 1.65 Biblical cubits, or 1.967 Greek cubits, or 2.057 Roman cubits."

"Of course," Methodius said, chuckling. "I'm sure you're well aware of that, Justinius."

The younger man looked befuddled, so Bishop Methodius rescued him. "Let's use Biblical cubits, Monsignor Joannes, since we want to compare like with like. Haghia Sophia is 82 yards long, by 77 yards wide, by 63 yards high."

"All right," said Joan, performing the mathematical calculations in her head. "Using Biblical terms, that's 134.86 cubits long by 126.6 cubits wide, by 104.587 cubits high. Now, does anyone know the Biblical measurements of Solomon's Temple so we can compare?"

Justinius was scrupulously studying something on the ground. Julianus was scratching his head in obvious confusion. Only Methodius seemed to have followed Joan's display of brilliance. Nicola smiled and clapped his hands softly. I simply said, "Solomon's Temple was smaller."

"Can we see the inside now?" I asked Methodius.

"Of course, but only if Monsignor Joannes observes it for what it is, not for its Biblical dimensions," he said, smiling broadly.

Inside, it was easy to see why the great emperor Justinian boasted of having bested the ancient King Solomon. There were windows on every level of the monstrous building. Some were clear, allowing light to flow through the great hall, and some were of glass stained in every color of the rainbow, adding a warmth and resonance to the place. The huge dome was so light and airy, it seemed to float above the building, marking a separation between earth and heaven. Everywhere there were icons and illuminations, all in gold leaf, rich blues, reds, greens, yellows, purples, blacks, and whites, far more intense than any colors I had yet seen. I trembled with the sheer excitement of being in such a hallowed place, completely overwhelmed by the magnificence of every cubit of Haghia Sophia.

The sun was halfway between the zenith and the horizon when we finally left that great and incredible place. "Time for a little relaxation?" Methodius asked.

I replied, "Is there something more to experience in this city that overwhelms the senses?"

"There is," he said. We followed in Methodius' footsteps to a large, marble-faced building between the Haghia Sophia and the hippodrome. "These are the Baths of Zeuxippos. They were built by the Western Roman emperor Septimius Severus, more than a hundred years before Constantine the Great accepted Christianity and transformed Byzantium into Constantinople. I tell you this because I don't want you to be shocked. The baths were ornamented in pagan style, with eighty statues of philosophers and poets, and even figures from their false mythology."

Nicola crossed himself, more as a gesture of peace than as one intended to turn aside evil spirits. "They are but memories," he said.

"Shall we go in?" Methodius urged.

All of us except Joan assented. Joan said, "I should so like to enjoy these baths, but I feel a bit ill from the dinner a few hours ago."

"Nonsense," said Julianus. "You've more likely addled your brains by telling so many details about cubits."

"Well, that too," Joan rejoined. "Either way, would you mind terribly if I excused myself and returned to the dormitorium?"

So Joan left us, and I was treated to my first Byzantine public bath.

Methodius led our small group into the baths. As I entered, the brick and marble facing on the outside gave way to cheerful blue tiles. There was a fountain in the entry hall, which continually sprayed water into a round, tile-covered fish pond. Fat, orange carp swam lazily about, oblivious to men who lounged about the pond, nursing a glass of ale or, perhaps, stronger stuff. I watched Methodius and followed his example. I removed my shoes and received a pair of wooden clogs. An attendant pointed to a private cubicle, told me to undress completely, and handed me a piece of white cloth to wrap around my waist.

I stepped out of the dressing room and rejoined Methodius, Nicola, Justinius, and Julianus. Another attendant showed us to a room that contained a sink, warm water, and soap. I washed away the grime of the day's walk, then rinsed myself and toweled dry. When I emerged from the washing room, I entered the first of the steam rooms and sat on a wooden bench, becoming accustomed to the wet heat that enveloped me.

A few minutes later, we moved on to the hottest steam room. At first, I felt uncomfortable. Soon, I got used to the baking heat. There were marble platforms all around, with wooden palettes on top of them. I stretched out and relaxed, as I saw the others doing, closed my eyes, and let the heat penetrate my body. I felt a slight nudge, opened my eyes, and saw another attendant standing over me. I looked over toward Methodius, who nodded, then closed my eyes again.

The masseur started at the bottom of my feet and worked his way up to my head, kneading, thumping, rubbing. At one point, he walked on my body. I felt every muscle slacken and go limp. All tension disappeared. When the massage was finished, I could hardly move.

Afterward, we returned to the wash room, soaped and rinsed with warm water, then emerged into the central area of a huge, square room covered by a vaulted dome. There was a large pool in the center, heated by wood-burning brick ovens which surrounded the central hall and recirculated the water from wall to tank and back. I stepped into the water and luxuriated in its warmth. All about me several other men swam or paddled slowly about. I closed my eyes once again, and inhaled the wonderful wet steam. After half an hour, the five of us emerged and entered a small room where we were greeted by more attendants. I lay on another bench. An aide poured buckets of warm water over me, then rubbed and scraped my body with a coarse sponge. Although I felt the sandy scratch of the material against my body and saw areas of my skin flaking off, it was not uncomfortable.

When the attendant was done, he poured more hot water over me, then soaped my body with a horsehair brush, working it up into a rich lather. There was more hot water, followed by buckets of cooler, tepid water. "Finished," the aide said, handing me a thick white robe.

When I returned to my cubicle, I found my clothes washed, dried, and softened. As I alighted from the dressing room, I found my four friends waiting at a nearby table with two small cups of steaming mead. Our group returned to the dormitorium shortly thereafter. I climbed the stairs to my room, lay down on my bed for a moment, and it was well after sunrise the next morning before I next awoke. I was totally refreshed, mentally and physically alert, and ready and eager to attend the Conclave in which we were to engage our Orthodox Brethren at midday.

CHAPTER 35

During the Ninth Ecumenical Conclave, which subsequently led to the Ninth Ecumenical Synod, I developed several beliefs which may sound heretical to Mother Church, but they remain my feelings to this very day.

My first belief is that a man will believe in whatever God or dogma he chooses, and that any attempt to force him to believe in his heart something he does not believe, is doomed to failure. He may profess whatever idea is at that moment popular, so he may gain for himself personal and political station and satisfaction. Some men change religious beliefs as often as they change tunics or togas or loincloths. But in his heart, if he has a belief, he will hardly be disabused of it by the words of a noble, a priest, a pope, or a patriarch.

I have come as well to believe that one "religion" is every bit as valid and valuable, or as useless and meaningless, as any other. Every man, woman, animal, and being for all I know, from the smallest ant to the elephant that abides in far-off Africa, has a basic need to feel he or she is part of a greater something – that he is put on earth for some purpose, and that he is a link in a chain that stretches to eternity. Religion fills such a need.

Now, I know that every practicing Christian purports to believe in Christ, but since every man somehow needs to feel his religion is superior to every other religion on earth, he needs to differentiate his professed beliefs so that *his* Christ is superior to his *neighbor's* Christ, or that *his* religious leader is paramount to any other religious leader. I feel this is shortsighted and stupid, because when it comes to religion, we are, all of us, children, and there is only one Adult. Thus, fighting a war in the name of religion or elevating one man over another because of religion, or casting a man down as a result of religious beliefs is no different from one child calling another names and throwing sand in the other's eyes. The analogy to sand is a good one, because when sand is thrown in your eyes, you cannot see clearly for the pain and the burning it causes.

So what is the real difference between one man's religion and another's? *None.* There is but one God in heaven and on earth, and there are many paths to that God. To say that one religion is the true religion is to say that one road to Rome or Constantinople or Jerusalem is the only true road, and that all other roads are nonexistent.

But supposedly intelligent people – Church leaders, emperors, philosophers, and senators – must aggrandize themselves or their power or their belief in some method, and thus it was that the First Ninth Ecumenical Conclave commenced in Constantinople, symbolically the heart of the Eastern Church, on September 14, 842, nine days after my thirty-third birthday. The Conclave was to lead to the Synod, which would last into 844, but neither Joan, Nicola, nor I knew it at the time.

There were four hundred sixty-seven bishops throughout Christendom, and some were much higher than others. For example, His Holiness, the pope, is actually another name for the Bishop of Rome, and the Patriarch Ignatius was, in reality, the Bishop of Constantinople. For that matter, Alcinorius was the Bishop of Sarmatia, not that that made much difference to the Church.

Thirty-six bishops and their retainers arrived in Constantinople to take part in the First Ninth Ecumenical Conclave, which convened at Haghia Eirene, a church of middling size that overlooks the Golden Horn. The proceedings began just after the midday meal, and I witnessed a ceremony even more impressive than the investiture of the Pope.

In those days, the Patriarch of Constantinople was subordinate to the emperor. On the day the Conclave commenced, there were actually two Supreme Byzantine emperors. The child Michael III was nominal ruler of the Byzantine Empire, but the Empress Theodora, widow of the late Theophilus, was the emperor in fact, serving as regent during her son's minority. The Byzantine Empire was one in which nothing succeeds like excess, and there was plenty of that in the great pomp with which the Conclave opened. Precisely one hour after we'd sat down to our meal, there was a thunder of drums and horns and pipes, as a band consisting of a hundred instrumentalists marched down the aisle of the Church. Because it was not that large of a church, those hundred players divided and went to the right and the left of the ceremonial pulpit, and immediately out the back doors of the Church.

The band was followed by a century of the emperor's Guards, each of whom wore the multicolored uniform of his unit. They, too, surrounded the pulpit, came to a halt, and stood quietly, in full battle dress. They were followed by Ignatius, Patriarch of Constantinople, who was clothed in a ceremonial gown of rich wools and linens and silk embroidered with gold thread. He wore a silver fox fur *stola* about his shoulders. A large, square Eastern cross depended from his neck. He bowed before the Altar of God, then turned and bowed to the entering Vicegerents of God on Earth. The son preceded the mother, and they were dressed exactly alike. Each wore full imperial regalia: a long red tunic, the *skaramangion;* over it, the cloak known in ancient days as the *chlamys*, in purple with gold-embroidered border, and ornamented with shimmering pearls; the long bejeweled scarf of the *loros* draped over their chests in the shape of the letter "X," symbolizing Christ's holy and victorious cross; and on their feet the *tzagia*, the red-purple boots permitted to the emperor alone.

Young Michael delivered the ceremonial oratory opening the Conclave in a clear, well-modulated voice. "In the name of the Father and the Son," – I noticed he did not include the words "Holy Ghost," for a dispute had been flaring for half a millennium over that issue – "we welcome you to our fair City and fervently hope it graces you with its hospitality. We open herewith the First Ninth Ecumenical Conclave and pray that your efforts are filled with the success they so richly deserve." He crossed himself. "In the name of the Father and the Son, we bless you and wish God's countenance to shine upon you and grant you peace."

Young Emperor Michael and his Emperor Mother turned as one, until they were facing the Narthex of the Church. Then, walking with slow, majestic gait, they departed, followed by their guards, themselves marching in that same slow, majestic pace.

Patriarch Ignatius addressed his opening remarks to us. They were filled with protestations of peace and love among all elements of Christ's Church everywhere, and cautiously avoided anything that could be construed as controversial. The controversies would, as we all knew, be addressed during the coming days, weeks, and months.

The conclave did not meet every day, for Ecclesiastical life in Constantinople was neither hurried nor bothered. Orthodox priests did not live a wholly contemplative existence. They were neither bound by vows of poverty nor vows of chastity. More often than not, the conclave broke into small working groups to address points of contention, conflict, and agreement, reporting back to the General Session of the Conclave sometimes once every fortnight, more often once a month, for Christ's numerous vicars on earth viewed their work as so awesome and serious that they needed respite from the magnitude of their works. Such respite, I found, consumed about four days out of every seven. During those days of respite, Joan, Nicola, and I prowled the Queen City, learning more about life here.

"I really enjoy the main streets in this city," Nicola exclaimed. "They're all cobble-stoned, so you can use them in any weather."

"Yes, they're lovely," Joan said, "but have you seen the alleys?"

"What do you mean?" Nicola asked.

"Not the surface or even the mud. The children."

"The children?" I asked.

"Yes. This city is filled with children three or four years old, running in the alleys with hardly any clothes and certainly no shoes. Many of them look like they're half starved."

"I've seen that," Nicola said softly. "Very like my parishioners in Ravenna and Rome. My heart goes out to them, but what can we do? We're of the Roman Church, not in the majority here."

"That may well be," Joan said, "but we can do something to help, even if it is to bring this tragedy to the attention of the conclave. They sit around, supposedly working on matters of great consequence, but in truth feeding their bellies and their equally capacious egos. They don't see what is going on around them, and what's more, they don't want to see what is going on around them."

"And you think you could break in on their grandiose dispute over whether there is monotheletism or the doctrine of dual will in Christ?"

"Yes, Martin, someone has to make the plight of these poor children public. They've been arguing over differences in theology, the world of the hereafter, when innocent children, who didn't ask to be brought into the world, are dying of hunger and cold in the streets of the wealthiest city in the world."

"Trust our Joan to cut into the deepest vein," Nicola said. Turning to her, he said more seriously, "Sometimes the few must do the moral thing, even in the face of the apathy of the many. Do you have any ideas?"

"Certainly, Nicola. Even if the Roman Church is in the minority of the Byzantine Empire, what is to stop us from begging Pope Gregory for some money – a piddling small amount for that matter – so we could set up a soup kitchen and a shelter for even a few of the homeless, the battered, and the unwanted? We could set it up in the poorest quarter of Constantinople, and if we reach even a few souls, perhaps the other Churchmen would join our small effort."

"Running this shelter would indeed be a thankless task."

"Thankless? How can it be thankless? To save even one life is to save the universe. I, for one, would consider it an honor and a privilege to serve in such a position." Neither of us said anything in response, because we knew that once Joan had her heart set on something, she would not be deterred from her goal. She would do it, she would do it right, and she would attract twenties, fifties, even hundreds of helpers in the process.

"Do you want me to mention it to our Eastern brethren?" Nicola asked.

"Yes, and Martin and I shall talk about it in our small working group, won't we Martin?"

"I ... uh ... that is ... certainly," I responded.

And so it came to pass that at the next small meeting between Nicola and Ignatius, and at the next small meeting of our working subcommittee, and at the next general meeting of the Ecumenical Conclave, and ultimately at general meetings of what eventually became the First Ninth Ecumenical Synod, the proposal for Joan's shelter and soup kitchen for homeless children was raised over and over again. Nicola urged Gregory to donate money from Peter's Pence and Gregory, in turn, prevailed upon Ignatius to match the papal donation of funds. Within a year there were three small, but successful, operations in the poorest sections of the wealthiest city in Christendom.

For days on end, Joan and I worked at the most menial jobs in one of the three shelters, or we would be cajoling rich and middle-class burghers to donate a pence here, a *nummus* there, a piece or two of used clothing – the rich man's cast-off clothing was never threadbare – a small cooking brazier, or any of a number of necessaries. We could not use all of the donations in the shelters, so we found poor families and gave them things they'd have otherwise gone without. We and our growing minions of loyal helpers, sought jobs for the able-bodied poor.

Once a week, Joan held a small church service in the shelters themselves, and one Sunday morning, when I invited Nicola to come and observe such a service, he was astonished to see well over a hundred people – men, women, and raggedy children – praying and singing as vigorously as – *ne*, more vigorously than – the high-and-mighty Churchmen who were, at that moment, attending services at Haghia Sophia, Saint Savior in Chora, Haghia Eirene, or any of several larger – and three hundred smaller – churches throughout the Queen City.

We by no means avoided the Conclave. Joan and I were well aware that Pope Gregory had bade us come to Constantinople to participate actively in the Conclave, and, if and when such should eventuate, the much larger Synod that would follow.

I have earlier remarked on a few of the differences that separate the two arms of the Church, and I have earlier commented – perhaps heretically – what I saw to be the absurdity of these so-called differences.

The Christian folk of what were, in ancient days, the provinces of the Roman East, Syria and Palestine and Egypt, emphasized Christ's divine nature at the expense of His humanity, claiming that after the Incarnation he had but one nature, the divine. The fourth holy ecumenical synod, that which was held at Chalcedon, condemned this as impious heresy, but the Syrians and Egyptians clung to this belief – called *monotheletism* – nonetheless.

The Roman Empire at Byzantium tried to root out what they called the monophysite heresy for almost two hundred years; but the Eastern leaders would not abandon their belief.

In the latter part of the Sixth Century, Harakleios of Constantinople sought a theological formula he hoped both the orthodox and the monophysites could accept, seeking to plaster over the differences between them rather than destroying monotheletism. This was the idea that, while Christ did indeed have two natures, the human and the divine, a single – divine – energy animated them.

The pope at Rome, Honorius, assented in the doctrine of one will, if not energy, in Christ. The monophysites rejoiced, but the patriarch of Jerusalem anathematized Herakleios' formula. So did many other theologians, but Herakleios wanted to maintain some degree of goodwill from the monophysites of

Syria and Egypt. But now, there was a new claimed heresy. Far from aiding Herakleios, the Syrians and Egyptians welcomed the new prophet, Mouammed, then erupting from Arabia. Worse yet, they welcomed the Arabians as liberators from the Roman rule!

Then, thinking he was doing something great, Herakleios put forth his statement of faith, forbidding discussion of whether Christ had one energy or two, and declaring that, as Pope Honorius had said, He had but a single will. The monophysites, once more, were pleased, and the orthodox were dismayed. The new doctrine prevailed in Constantinople, but was condemned in Jerusalem, in Carthage, in Numidia, in Mauretania, and in Italy, where all popes after Honorius rejected his formulation.

Then, there was yet another reversal of theology. Constantine IV convened the Sixth Ecumenical Synod at Constantinople in November, 680, the twelfth year of his reign. His brother – and co-emperor protested, "We'll be the laughingstock of all Christendom, east and west, if we turn our backs on beliefs we've supported these past fifty years."

To which Constantine, who was the senior emperor, responded, "And what have we got for all that support? Will the monophysites in Syria and Egypt rise up for us against the Arabs because we confess Christ's two natures have but one will? It doesn't look that way to me. By the Virgin, they're even starting to go over to the creed of the false prophet. And the popes at Rome have been throwing anathemas at us ever since Honorius dropped dead."

A dispute ensued between Constantine and his patriarch, Theodore, and that prelate was removed from the patriarchal throne on the following day. Now, more than one hundred fifty years later, the very same schism was being argued, and the potentates of East and West were no closer to resolution of the issue than they had been nearly five hundred years before.

Now, if you can understand that difference, if you can understand why grown men, intelligent men, educated theological leaders dispute this issue with such verve and vigor and bitter condemnation of those who do not accept their view of the cosmos, that they excommunicate and anathematize those who don't agree with them, then you are a better, wiser man than I shall ever be. While I contemplated what I believed to be the absurdity of man's intolerance of another man's belief, I held my thoughts intact and silent, other than to talk about them with Joan. She added her own responses. "I cannot believe others don't share your views, my friend – at least inside themselves. However, we function in a society of church politics and there must be a more indirect way of helping our church fathers to come to a saner conclusion."

Meanwhile, although Constantinople dominated our thoughts, Europe changed once again. Louis Pious' three surviving sons, Lothar, Ludwig, and Charles, met at Verdun in August, 843, and agreed to partition the Empire. Ludwig succeeded to Bavaria and the eastern lands; Charles acquired dominance over much of what had been Gaul in the ancient days and was now being called France; and Lothar retained the title of emperor and took the territory between the other two, from the Channel coast to Italy. Lothar remained in charge of Aix-la-Chappelle and Rome.

Joan told me she'd heard that our old friend, John Scotus Erigena, had become scholar in residence at the court of Charles the Bald. A month later, in September 843, the conclave was greatly enlarged when the Byzantine emperors called for an Ecumenical Synod, to be held at Haghia Sophia, the greatest church in Christendom, on November first.

The Holy Father designated Cardinal Sergius and our Nicola to head the Roman delegation, which would consist of one hundred fifty bishops of the western Church. I was delighted at the appointment of Sergius, whom I'd not seen for more than nine years, for since his brother Tacitus had died two years before, he was my last direct link to Eva. My God, I thought. Has it been a full decade since she's been gone? How did the time go by so quickly?

At my first sight of that senior cardinal, I was shocked at the ravages time had wrought. The once dapper Sergius had become an old man. He walked stiffly, obviously in great pain, leaning on a sturdy cane. His left leg was heavily bandaged, from knee to foot, and he was assisted by two younger men. When I greeted him, his voice was also that of an old man, wheezy and scratchy.

"Martin, Joannes, I realize you are shocked at how I look. I should have written you. The gout has taken a terrible toll, and I'm in the midst of an attack, even as we speak. Last year, it was a kidney stone. I fear the excesses of my youth have caught up with me."

I hugged the older man, carefully avoiding his bandaged extremity. "What can I do to make you more comfortable my Lord Eminence?" I asked, and sincerely.

"For now, precious little, I'm afraid," he responded. "The damnable gout seems to wander about my body. It always starts at the big toe, and from there it seems to poison every one of my joints. When I lie down at night, it feels somewhat better, but when I awaken in the morning, or when I must pass water, it is worst. I pray you never experience such pain."

Joan looked at Sergius directly. She, too, was concerned. "Are you seeing a *medicus* for your symptoms, Eminence?" she asked.

"Several, Joannes," the cardinal responded grimly, "and their views all differ. Some prescribe wine, which eases the pain for awhile. Others say the wine will make it worse, which I find is also true. I've taken ten different kinds of powders and potions, and they've rubbed me with a like number of ointments and salves. Nothing really seems to help."

Sergius was taken to his quarters in a sedan chair, held aloft by six hefty men. Joan, Nicola, and I walked alongside the sedan chair, speaking of minor and forgettable things, trying to divert Sergius from thinking of his pain. When we had gotten him to his luxurious suite of rooms and placed him in his commodious bed, Sergius said, "Joannes, I recall you were a miracle worker when you saved my niece Aegina's life after the snakebite. I also heard from my late brother that your diagnosis of Eva's condition was more accurate than that of the Roman *medicus* in Spalatius. Do you know anything about gout, anything at all that could help me."

"Aye, Eminence," Joan said. "But I must ask you questions that may seem personal."

"If it will relieve my pain, you may ask anything."

"What kinds of food do you indulge in?"

"Food? All kinds of food, Joannes. I have always loved the rich, tasty fare of the northern lands – roast duck, duck liver paste, calves' liver, and the wonderful sauces that go with them."

Joan nodded. "And wine? Beer?"

"Wine has always been necessary to wash the food down."

Joan murmured something to herself. "Have any of the *medici* prescribed acetyl acid for your pain?"

"Aye," Sergius said. "For short periods, that seems to be the only thing that helps."

"And," said Joan sternly, "if I may be blunt, Your Eminence, that is probably the worst thing you can take for the gout."

The cardinal's eyes widened. "Say you so?"

"Yes. Your Eminence, I believe I can tell you what might ease your pain somewhat, but I am not sure you will appreciate what I say, and you must promise me I will not lose my head if I tell you what I think."

At that, Sergius laughed heartily, despite his pain, and it was the first time since he'd arrived that I saw vestiges of his old self. "*Ne, medicus* Joannes. Your head will remain united with the rest of your body."

"All right, then. I will ask you to follow my advice for a fortnight. Will you promise me to do that?"

"Aye, anything," he said.

"Very well, then. For the next fortnight, you will eat no meat or fish or fowl of any kind, and especially not the liver or heart. No sauces. Absolutely no wine or, for that matter, anything with alcohol in it. No acetyl acid, no acid of any kind. As little honey as possible. You will eat plain, dark bread, and you will drink water, as much water as you can tolerate. For variety, you may eat beans and rice, and you may spice them with peppers. Nothing more."

The cardinal paled. "You may as well kill me now, Joannes," he said. "How can I possibly exist on such a bland diet? I would as soon die first."

"In some matters, Eminence, regardless of what the high churchmen seem to be disputing at this very moment, you do have free will. You can continue as you have been, and suffer from gout, and I can promise you the attacks will become worse, or you can ingest what you call 'a bland diet,' and it may help you. That is your choice."

Sergius grumbled and carried on further, but ultimately he said, "I will try what you say for a fortnight, no more. I should not have promised you your head would stay on your shoulders."

Two weeks passed. During that time we saw nothing more of Sergius. Truth to tell, Joan and I were too busy running the shelter, for as September passed into October, the weather was becoming cooler and it was important that we collect as much warm clothing as possible.

During the second week of October, we received word that Cardinal Sergius wanted to meet with us. When we arrived in his chambers, Sergius still looked pale and a bit pasty, but his leg was no longer bandaged and he stood to greet us, without a cane. His smile was broad and genuine.

"Monsignor Joannes," he commenced, "I don't know who taught you this black magic you practiced, but obviously it has worked wonders. I am not totally without pain at all hours, but you have performed a miracle. Thanks to you and your, ah, cure, I can now sleep the entire night, and although I wake with some stiffness in my joints, it is no longer so intolerable. I've not felt so well in five years at least. Tell me, how much longer must I abstain from everything I so enjoy?"

"For the rest of your life, Eminence," Joan said dryly.

What little color there was in his cheeks drained from them. "For … the … rest … of … my … life?"

"Aye, Eminence. But, as I said, you have free will."

"Cannot I stay on this diet for one week, then take a week off, then go back on?"

"Aye," Joan replied. "Then you will have one week of excruciating pain and one week of relatively minor relief, followed by a period of even more excruciating pain."

"Ah, then you are the devil, Joannes," Cardinal Sergius remarked sadly.

"*Ne*, Eminence," Joan said. "You may work within your own body. I don't mean this in an unsympathetic way, but these things can, and do, happen."

"Well," Sergius said resignedly, "I will have to adjust and, as you say, decide what I need to do. I'm told that you and Martin have set up a series of soup kitchens and shelters in the poorest sections of Constantinople. Perhaps you might tell me of your work …"

CHAPTER 36

Rather than tell Sergius of our work, Joan and I chose to show him what we were doing. He seemed well pleased because he could now perambulate on his own, and without pain, but Joan and I noticed that each time he would pass a restaurant or eatery, he would sigh at the aroma of roasted meat or fried fish, or he would gaze longingly at heaping platters of duck or goose or chicken, slathered with butter and sauces. Cardinal he may have been, but our friend had suffered the sin of gluttony, and, of late, he was now *suffering* from the sin of gluttony.

The shelters were operating smoothly. While Joan and I still oversaw them, it was no longer necessary for us to work in them daily. Since there was still a month before the commencement of the Ecumenical Synod, we squired Sergius around the city so he could take in its wonders. The three centers of life in Constantinople were the Palaces, the racecourse, and the Cathedral. If Haghia Sophia belonged to God, and the Palaces belonged to the emperor, the Hippodrome belonged to the people. If the baths were shut and the Hippodrome closed, life for the Byzantine populace became stale, flat, and unprofitable.

The circus parties of the Blues and Greens were organized much like a city militia, and even the emperor realized that the taunts across the race-course, and the cheers and jeers that issued from the throats of a hundred thousand people, were escape valves for evil humors that might otherwise have threatened the Purple Throne. The Hippodrome employed an army of folk – guards, trainers, stablemen, charioteers, and more. Between the morning and afternoon chariot races, there were exhibitions given by pantomimists and acrobats, by rope-walkers who dressed and undressed on the tight rope, and by those who balanced a pole on their foreheads, up which boys climbed and postured at its top. There were fights with wild beasts in the Circus, so that a staff of keepers was a necessity. Acacius, the father of that long-ago Empress Theodora – not the present Empress, but the wife of the great Justinian – was a bear warden, and Theodora herself had been a pantomime actress.

The charioteers lived in a world where pagan superstitions flourished. They sought to bind their competitors by magic charms and amulets, and thus guarantee their defeat. Before the races, drivers were searched to see that they did not carry some magical mascot that might unfairly secure them victory. Curses upon the heads of hated rivals were frequently written on small lead tablets.

On one occasion, a fortnight before the Synod, Joan, Nicola, Sergius and I actually witnessed one of these events, and I can still picture the scene: the Greens and Blues numbered in the thousands. Patricians, senators, and even esteemed Churchmen, clothed in gorgeous robes of silk and flashing jewels on their fingers and from their necks, sat on the terrace reserved for them. High above the course, connected to the

Palace and cut off from the Circus itself, was the emperor's box.

Just before the games, everyone went silent, as if a plague had decimated the city. Then, after the suspense became almost too great to bear, Emperor Michael and his Emperor Regent Mother, Theodora, entered the box. Michael raised his mantle and made the sign of the cross. Huge choirs erupted into song, and under the melodious sounds of praises to Christ and the Virgin, we also heard the passionate supplications for the victory of this or that charioteer. Then the chariots burst away and the tumultuous sound rocked an entire quarter of the Queen City.

The Hippodrome was more than just a race-course. It truly served as the last asylum of the liberties of the ancient *Populus Romanus*. Here, the people could call the emperor to account, or demand the dismissal of a hated minister, or even a bishop of the Eastern Church. Indeed, despite the shouts of "*Tu vincas Michaelis!*" the citizenry of Constantinople had only two real heroes: the winner in the chariot race and the ascetic saint. The people raised pictures and statues to the charioteer, and he received special privileges. But pilgrims came to the ascetic from every side, longing to see the saint on his pillar, to gain a benediction, or to carry off one of those little images of the holy man that were manufactured wholesale for the needs of the pious.

~ ∫ ~

The First Ninth Ecumenical Synod commenced with even greater fanfare and panoply than had the Conclave, on the first day of November 843. There were hundreds of bishops and thousand of retainers, bowers, scrapers, and shrewd merchantmen who made money out of any such event.

Sergius and Nicola, as cardinals of the Western Church, were afforded special seating close to the speakers' rostrum. Because Joan and I were closely affiliated with those two high-and-mighties, we observed the proceedings from much closer than most participants.

The Byzantine emperor greeted the thronged assembly briefly in Greek, and then left the huge central hall of Haghia Sophia, giving more than a little truth to my earlier statement that the Palaces belonged to the emperor and Haghia Sophia belonged to the Church. Ignatius gave his opening remarks, also in Greek, and invited Sergius, as senior representative of the Roman Church to speak to the multitude. Sergius spoke in crisp, clear Latin. And so it went for the rest of the day and for several days after that. Each member of the Orthodox delegation spoke in Greek, and a translator repeated his words in Latin. Conversely, each Roman Churchman spoke in Latin, and these words were translated into Greek.

It didn't take long before Joan recognized – and so told Nicola and Sergius – that the translations on each side were not quite accurate, and, in some instances, they were most *in*accurate. "It's plain to see that no one is really listening to what the other side is saying. If they are listening, heaven help them if they don't understand the other's language, for they'll get no aid from the interpreters."

"That's part of the problem," Nicola said. "The two Churches have not really spoken one another's language for two hundred fifty years, and each insists that its language is paramount, even as each church contends that its leader is *primus inter pares*."

"But I thought the Synod was to discuss differences between monotheletism and orthodoxy," I said.

"The Churches aren't even clear on that. If one Church says one thing, the other Church, as a matter of principle, speaks its reverse."

After a fortnight, the patience of the participants was starting to wear thin. At first, the speakers had all spoken in glowing terms about their confraternity and how wonderful it was that brothers could meet as comrades-at-arms in the Army of Christ. But as time went by, and the points made by first one, then the other, arm of Christendom became bogged down in minutiae and posturing, tempers started to fray. Since Joan and I were fluent in both Latin and Greek, we were able to hear the murmurings and angry undertones, spoken by the audience, and spoken in such low and quiet voices they could not be readily heard.

"Do you understand what Pelagius is saying about monophysites and orthodox?"

"Hell, no."

"Why can't these stupid Italian farmers learn to speak a civilized language?" I heard from a section of the audience that was almost uniformly Byzantine.

"Those folks were raised in the sties with the farm animals," his friend said. "No wonder their speech sounds like a bunch of pigs grunting in a farmyard."

Neither Joan nor I participated in these secondary conversations, but we listened to everything and we heard, and, more important, we understood the meanings and the under-meanings of what was said. On the thirteenth night after the Synod had convened, Joan and I went to visit Sergius in his chambers. Although he was eating a piece of broiled chicken, for the most part he had abstained from his prior gluttony, and he walked with a vigorous gait like the Sergius we had known at Hausstadt.

"Joannes, Martin," he greeted us warmly. "Coming to check up on me, *medicus*?" he addressed Joan, winking. "As you can see, I am eating rather grimly."

"Indeed, Eminence. No pain, I take it?"

"Hardly any. By the way, Martin, I very much appreciate your recommendation of the baths. I've been going there every evening after the day's work, and it has helped tremendously."

"Thank you, Eminence. How do you feel the Synod is going?"

"I've heard grumbling in the audience, but from where I sit, it sounds like a bored hum."

"It's more than boring, Eminence. There's a feeling of disgust in the air. They've heard it all before and they don't understand it better now than they did at the Eighth Synod, or, for that matter, the Seventh or the Fifth or the Third Synod. The translations are less accurate than any Church convention I've yet attended. These Churchmen are speaking to impress their own, and not to express anything to anyone else, or even to try to bridge the chasm that separates the Churches."

"*Aye*," Sergius said, a bit sadly I thought. "This Synod is going nowhere rapidly. I expect that fist-fights will break out shortly if we do not break this pattern."

"Your Eminence, Martin, I have an idea. If you or any other highly placed Churchman speaks, you risk angering the Pope, and you risk offending our host, the Patriarch. On the other hand, if Martin or I, or someone of relatively low station and presumptuous youth be given the opportunity to address the assembly, and if what we say offends anyone, they will simply clear us off the stage with boos and catcalls, as a minor annoyance with no real power to bind anyone."

"Hmmmm," the cardinal said, savoring the idea for a few moments.

"Eminence," I encouraged, "we'd be akin to a scout or a stalking horse, or the lowest private in the Army of Christ."

"Yes, I see the ingenuity of your plan. The higher Churchmen take no risk whatever, since we can dissociate ourselves from any of your ideas that may be too forward. Have you thought of which of you should give this oration?"

"Yes, Your Eminence," said Joan. "We have decided that since you are much our senior in wisdom, if not in age – the cardinal liked that statement – we would ask that you flip a *nummus* coin – either Roman or Byzantine, your choice – and we will be bound by the outcome."

So the coin was flipped – a Roman coin, of course – and God or the gods decreed that Joan should deliver the talk. We discussed what Joan was going to say with both Nicola and Sergius, so there would be no surprises insofar as they were concerned.

Next morning, on what was to have been the last day of the *First* Ninth Ecumenical Synod – the Second was to be held in Constantinople in March of the following year, Sergius stood to address the speakers and the audience. "My most worthy Lord Bishops," he said. "We have, all of us, heard great and wondrous things at this synod." There was a loud groan as the audience foresaw yet another droning, rambling discourse. "But," he continued, "most speeches have come from our past and our present – cardinals, the Patriarch, and various bishops. We have not heard from our future – the priests and the monsignors and the junior clerics and the *schola* – we don't know what they are thinking, but I can tell all of you that from the pained expressions on so many faces, the loud groaning I just heard when you thought I was going to proceed in much the same vein. I concluded that none of us was getting our message across.

"Last evening, I spoke earnestly with two young Monsignors who come from Angle-land, and I asked them what they thought. To my surprise, and to my delight, they asked to be allowed to address this august gathering for but a few moments. I beg that the next speaker cede his place in line for those few moments so that Monsignor Joannes Angliorum be allowed to speak." Since the next man scheduled to speak was a Roman churchman, and since he well knew where his bread was buttered, he readily yielded the floor to Joan. I have recorded Joan's speech verbatim, since it was to have such a profound effect on our own careers.

"My brothers in Christ," she began, and I noticed for the first time that she was able to do some trick or the like with her voice, so that it sounded very much that of a man – a tenor, but there would be no mistaking that she was anything but a man. "Everyone representing the Orthodox Church has spoken in Greek and everyone speaking on behalf of the Roman Church has used Latin – and, with all due respect, the translations have been inexact at best, not due to the fault of the interpreters, but because there are some things that are distinctly *Greek* in the Greek language and their meaning can never be translated exactly, and there are turns of a phrase, hidden meanings, and idiosyncrasies in *Latin* that can only be known to someone who's lived in Italia all his life." There was an interested half-chuckle in the audience, and when Joan repeated exactly the same thing in Greek, the laughter, although still sparse, was appreciative.

"Therefore," she continued, "so that there may be no mistake, no hidden meaning, and no thoughts that do not come from my heart, I will speak in both Latin and Greek, and if I falter in any of my words, my brother, Monsignor Martin Paschal, also of Angle-land, will assist me in either language. I ask that no translator or interpreter accompany us, for I believe that each language is absolutely equal in dignity, absolutely equal in beauty, and absolutely equal in importance to all of us, and one of the purposes of my talk is to urge that there must be full understanding of each language, and the inflections and meanings and nuances of each language if we want simply to talk with one another, face to face, without pretense, and if we are truly to be brothers in Christ."

As she was speaking, the immense hall had gone silent, attentive for the first time since the Synod had begun. When she got to the last phrase, there was applause from both sides of the room, also the first I'd heard in the past two weeks.

"Gentlemen," she intoned. "I don't speak to you as a Monsignor and I don't speak to you as a representative of the Divinity we all share. I speak to you as one of you, a common man, and one who accepts – and loves – each of you in this room as my brother. We have been through hundreds of years of Synods, and still we are without resolution of our problems. The Pope excommunicates Orthodox Christians who don't share his views, and the Patriarch anathematizes Roman Christians who don't share his views. And at the end of the day, these excommunications and anathemas are meaningless, except in the forum where they were pronounced."

"Hear! Hear!" a voice called from the audience.

"Will the Roman be any less a Roman or a dignitary at Rome because he was anathematized by the Patriarch? Will the Byzantine or a dignitary at Constantinople, which was once called New Rome, be *persona non grata* in his home city because a Pope a thousand Roman miles away has excommunicated him?" The answer to each question is, "Of course not."

More, deeper applause.

"Can any of you really, truly relate to the differences in doctrine that separate our two Churches? Can any of you truthfully say you understand the divine spirit when you have never – and could never – experience such a spirit while you, like me, like all of us, inhabit the human climes of the earth? Both our Churches have embraced each of the underlying concepts that now separate us. On each occasion where there has been a reversal of belief or philosophy or concept, it has been a reaction to the other Church embracing a formerly shunned belief or philosophy or concept, and usually for one reason and one reason alone: to achieve preeminence over the other head of the Christian Church, whether that be the Eastern Church or the Western Church.

"I say this, and I beg that you listen and consider it, my brothers in Christ. We are all Christians, every one of us, no better nor worse than any other Christian on the face of the earth, and while we compete for the hearts, the souls, and, let us be brutally frank, the donations of men in every corner of the earth, if we are to be brothers in Christ, then let us be brothers in Christ, not mortal combatants.

"Why must it be necessary for one Pope or one Patriarch to claim worldwide hegemony over all Christendom, when such a proclamation is an impossible dream? Why can we not simply dwell in peace as brothers and as equal neighbors with equal claims to supremacy, but supremacy only within the domain of each house? God the Father said, 'There are many mansions in my house.' Why must one try to dominate another? Does a good neighbor try to seize his neighbor's home or his property or his sheep, or his dog? No. If he is a good neighbor, he respects his neighbor and protects his neighbor's home, his property, his sheep, and his dog.

"Hear me, my friends, my brothers, and my neighbors …" she paused for a moment to let the weight of the silence sink in, and you could have heard a coin drop in that entire huge hall. Then she thundered – literally thundered, and the depth and carriage of her voice surprised even me, *"FOR OUR BRETHREN TO CONSTANTLY ARGUE ABOUT WHO SHOULD PREDOMINATE OVER ANYONE ELSE IS EXACTLY THE SAME AS TWO FLEAS ARGUING ABOUT WHICH ONE OWNS THE DOG!"*

Now there was greater thunder – the thunderous applause of the entire assembly that stood up as a single body, cheering, clapping, stamping their feet – and that unified applause continued for the better part of a minute, perhaps even more.

When the last of the noise had died down, Joan concluded in a quiet, but carrying, tone. "Can this work? If you think it can't, I urge only that you go down to the poorest parts of Constantinople, where you'll find that anonymous Roman Christians, living in the midst of the greatest Orthodox city in Christendom, have started three small, but flourishing, shelters, which provide food, clothing, and shelter to all downtrodden, regardless of what they profess to believe. The Romans take no credit for this small venture, for it is not important who started it. What is important is that it got started and it grows day-by-day, week-by-week. I ask that each of you, my Brothers in Christ, simply go and look at these shelters and draw your own conclusions – and that, if you find it in the goodness of your hearts, you consider donating a *nummus* here, an old piece of clothing there, even a crust of bread. And if you do that, you will prove what the underlying concept of Christianity *is*, whatever it is *called*. I thank you."

Joan stepped quickly away from the rostrum, amid a tumult that threatened to erupt into a happy, approving, loving riot. She glanced momentarily over at Sergius and Nicola, who were positively beaming, clapping and stamping harder than anyone else in the room.

Next day, Sergius demanded to see my transcript of Joan's speech. Indeed, he demanded that I write out a new, fresh copy for him. He said he wanted the Holy Father to see what Joan had said, and he wanted to tell Gregory himself how the speech had electrified the entire assembly.

Alas, it was not to be. Shortly after Sergius and Nicola had departed for Rome, we heard the sad news that Pope Gregory had died in January, 844. But as momentous as this news was, there were two events that far overshadowed the death of Gregory IV.

The first was that Sergius was elected Pope.

The second was that, as one his first official acts, Pope Sergius elevated Joan and me to the rank of bishops.

BOOK VI.
ASCENT

CHAPTER 37

It was necessary for us to travel to Rome to be invested with the Bishop's miter. Nicola had told us not to be too disappointed at what we saw, and not to have any expectation that Rome would be a pleasant surprise. It had been sacked so many times in the last four hundred years that its population had been decimated until no one quite knew if the once supreme city was inhabited by twenty thousand souls or fifty thousand. He said that at most it was one-twentieth the size it had been in its glory days.

What had caused the precipitous decline of the Eternal City? Many things. Of the seventy million souls in the Roman Empire at the beginning of the fifth century, less than ten percent were Italians. Once, Rome had lived on its conquests and its colonies to the East, but by the Year of Our Lord 400, the conquests had ended and the slow retreat had begun. Italia was forced to depend on its own human and material resources, and these had been dangerously reduced by family limitation, famine, epidemics, taxation, waste, and war. Now that its markets were being lost in the East and in Gaul, Rome could no longer support the urban population that had eked out its living in shops and homes. The middle classes, once the mainstay of empire, were weakened by economic decline and the ravages of that most pernicious of vermin, the tax collector.

Meanwhile, the cost of slave labor had risen to where it was economically unsound. The rich deserted the city for country villas. Even though Rome was no longer a capital, and seldom even saw an emperor, it remained the social and intellectual focus of what was still called the "Roman" Empire.

But the real reason why the city of Rome collapsed was that people prefer to live their lives in quiet, relatively safe, anonymity. If a city becomes known as an unsafe place, people start moving away, slowly at first, but as the exodus gathers force, people leave in droves.

The beginning of the end of Rome occurred four hundred thirty-six years ago. The Goth Alaric, who had nearly attacked Rome before, had gone north, beyond the Alps, when he'd been promised four thousand pounds of gold. In 408, Alaric complained about nonpayment of the promised debt and demanded it be paid immediately. When the emperor Honorius refused, Alaric marched over the Alps, pillaged Aquilea and Cremona, raised thirty thousand mercenaries, and swept down the Flaminian Way to the very walls of Rome.

The Roman Senate suspected the widow of a former Roman leader as Alaric's accomplice and put her to death. Alaric responded by laying siege to Rome. Soon, the people began to starve, and the once proudest and most civilized city in the known world resorted to cannibalism for the first time in its glorious history.

The Roman Senate sent a delegation to Alaric, asking for terms. They warned Alaric that a million Romans were ready to resist. Alaric laughed and answered, disdainfully, "The thicker the grass, the more easily it is mowed." He offered to withdraw if Rome paid him all the gold and silver and valuable movable property in the city. The envoys asked, "What will be left to us?"

"Your lives," Alaric replied scornfully.

Rome chose further resistance. Only a few weeks later starvation motivated a new offer of surrender. In the end, Alaric accepted 5,000 pounds of gold, 30,000 pounds of silver, 4,000 silk tunics, 3,000 skins, and 3,000 pounds of pepper.

Meanwhile, a huge number of barbarian slaves escaped from their Roman masters and joined Alaric's army. A runaway slave opened the gates, the Goths poured in, and for the first time in more than eight hundred years, the Eternal City was taken by an enemy. What occurred to Roman citizens thereafter led to the first mass exodus from the City. Within a century, the last days of Rome marked the end of the world as it had been for more than a thousand years.

We took a swift merchantman from Constantinople to Athens to Patras, and thence across the Hadriatic Sea to Brindisium and the eastern terminus of the Via Appia. I have seen many maritime port cities in my day, but I was never so glad to get into *and out of* a city as I was Brindisium. People arrive here, stop only long enough to defecate anywhere they can find a pit, or, if they arrive late, to engage a well-worn hospitium or an equally well-worn woman, sometimes both. and to leave as quickly as they can. As it is the last city one sees in Italia – or the first, depending if you are arriving from the East or debarking to the East – street sellers constantly push themselves in your face, selling overpriced cheap souvenirs and every manner of jewelry and etchings made of paste, all of which are guaranteed to last at least one hour after you leave the place.

Ugly hostelries, inns, restaurants, and whores abound, and it is hard to tell which has the rankest odor or the greasiest and oiliest appearance. The waters of the usually crystal clear Hadriatic are here polluted and befouled, so much so that dead fish constantly float belly-up near the wooden ramparts that divide the land from the sea.

Even though the Church was paying for us to travel from Constantinople to Rome in grand style, Joan remarked, and I readily agreed, as we bumped over the bone-shattering old high road in a public *carruca*, that the term "grand style" was nonexistent as we skirted the filthy, decrepit, unutterably poor hill towns of Matera and Potenza. After a time we came to the last hill before the sea, and beheld the vast, crescent-shaped Bay of Neapolis.

From afar, there is no more beautiful juxtaposition of land and sea and dramatic mountains in the world than one's first view of Neapolis. "My God," Joan sighed. "Have you ever seen a more idyllic sight? That's Mount Vesuvius to the left. It's hard to conceive that beautiful cone, that perfect mountain, spewed such death and destruction over Pompeii seven hundred fifty years ago. And that bay! The waters are green and azure and blue. What an incredibly beautiful city Neapolis must be! I'd so love to stop there some day."

"Why not now, Bishop Joannes?"

"*Ne*, the time is not yet. We must arrive in Rome as soon as possible."

The Via Appia improved as we approached Rome. We came into the city from the south, and out of deference to those of our Faith who had gone before, we stopped and visited those terrestrial caves they call the catacombs – the Catacombs of Saint Calixtus and the Catacombs of Domitilla – where the bones of departed priests, bishops, saints, and martyrs are stacked four and sometimes five layers high. Seeing a dead person who has not been embalmed can be a gruesome sight, but viewing a pile of dry bones is like ... looking at a pile of dry bones. It's hard to imagine that upon these bones once hung the flesh of live human beings, who, like all of us, laughed, cried, ate, slept, and, as they grew older, experienced pain. As one grows older, so many parts of the human body hurt, or don't work, or sometimes both at the same time.

Despite what Nicola had told us, despite the decline of the Eternal City into a small shadow of its greatness, and despite everything else anyone said to discount or denigrate Rome, it was still Rome. As Joan and I came upon that City for the first time, I told Joan a beautiful and poignant story the wonderful Orestes had told me during the time we were together.

"As a very young Captain," he'd said, "during my service in Syria, I had occasion to be part of an honor guard that met with a delegation of Persian royalty in Damascus. It was full of pomp and pageantry as only Orientals can manage so well. I was so smitten with the Shah's young daughter, the Princess Moonlight, that I could think of nothing else for the entire two weeks we were in Damascus. I would have given five years off my life to be with that one. What incredibly beautiful children we might have produced. Her mother was a handsome woman of middle age, and her father was, of course, the Shah, tall and majestic.

"The only disappointment in my visit came during my last night in Syria, when I was present at a dinner in honor of the Dowager Princess Willow, a wrinkled, balding, mottled, shrunken, moldy, decrepit, unspeakably old grandmother, with bare and withered gray gums, a mossy tongue, and a granulated upper lip. So revolting was this ancient hag to me that it almost turned my stomach, and I found myself wondering how anyone this ugly could have risen to a position of honor within the royal family. Nevertheless, I was polite and deferential to the old woman, and she blessed me in a gravelly voice.

"I thought nothing more about this until, some time later, I found myself in Baghdad, and my General told me, 'Tonight, young Orestes, you will have a privilege accorded few others. The Persian army – the only army in the world that dates back to before there even *was* a Rome – is celebrating the retirement of its Marshal-General Moujan. His name is legend throughout the Byzantine Empire, the Abassid Empire, and even the newly-consecrated Holy Roman Empire. His battles are studied in every empire, kingdom or state. He is eighty-one years old, and the Shah has refused his requests to retire until now.'

"Marshal-General Moujan was tall and ramrod straight, with iron-gray hair and a commanding presence, even given his remarkable age. During the dinner, my General was seated at the same table as the Marshal, and since I was my general's aide-de-camp, I was seated to his immediate left, two chairs away from the Marshal-General. Dinner conversation was as one would have expected of two old military heroes, as each relived memories of old battles, comrades long dead, place names that meant almost nothing to me.

"Only when my General mentioned our recent visit to the Persian court did the old Marshal-General heave a great sigh of regret. 'The Dowager Princess Willow still lives then?' he asked. 'Why, she would be eighty years of age now, a year younger than me.'

"My ears perked up and I flinched slightly, remembering the old hag. The Marshal-General lifted a goblet of red wine, looked into it, and put it down without drinking. Then he said, 'Doubtless the Princess Willow no longer shows it – and I very much doubt you'd believe it – but that same Princess Willow was, in her youth, the most astonishingly beautiful woman in Persia, perhaps the most beautiful woman who ever lived.'

"My general murmured noncommittally. I thought back with revulsion to my meeting her.

"'Ah, when she and I and the world were young,' said old Marshal-General Moujan dreamily. 'The report of her loveliness brought me from Tabriz, and brought innumerable other princes and soldiers and governors from as far away as Kashmir, and not one of these suitors was disappointed when he saw her. I could tell you of that maiden's radiant eyes and her lips like roses, of her grace, but that would not begin to picture her for you. Why, just to look at her could heat a man to fever and yet refresh him at the same time.'

"Under my breath, I scoffed incredulity, but not loud enough for the Marshal-General to hear.

"'There was not a man in all Persia who would not have risked a beating from the Palace Guards, just to sneak near and steal a glimpse of the Princess Willow walking in her garden. To have seen her without her *chador* veil, a man would have given his very life. In the remote hope of a smile from her, why, a man would have relinquished his immortal soul. Any further intimacy would have been unthinkable, even for the multitude of princes hopelessly in love with her.'

"I sat staring at Moujan, amazed and unbelieving. The old hag I had seen at the Shah's banquet – a vision unattainable and inviolable? Impossible! Ludicrous!

"'There were so many suitors and all so anguished in their yearning that the tender-hearted Willow could not or would not choose from among them and thus blight the lives of all the rest. Any other maiden would have fretted at the passing of her springtime, as she had not yet wed, but Willow only grew more beautiful and graceful, and clover-sweet as time went on.'

"I stared at the Marshal-General. My skepticism was slowly giving way to wonder. The old crone had been all that? So exquisitely desirable to this world-renowned man and to other men in that long-gone time, so exquisitely memorable that she was not yet forgotten, by this one at least, even now as he approached the end of his life.

"'Honored and esteemed Marshal-General,' I said, clearing my throat, 'What was the eventual outcome of that crowded courtship?'

"'Ah, young Captain,' Moujan said, raising his wine goblet and sipping slowly, 'it had to come to a conclusion at last. Her father the Shah – with her approval, I'm sure – finally chose for her the Shahzadè of Shiraz. He and the Princess Willow were wed, and the whole Persian Empire – all but the rejected suitors – celebrated with joyous holiday. However, for a long time they had no children. I strongly suspect the bridegroom was so overwhelmed by his good fortune, and by the pure beauty of his bride, that it was a long time before he could consummate his marriage. It was not until his father died, and he succeeded as Shah in Shiraz, and Willow was thirty years or older, that she gave birth to their only child, and then only a daughter. The daughter was handsome, only nothing near the mother, and I have seen the latest in the line, the Princess Moonlight, who is well-named, for she is only a pale and lesser version of what the Princess Willow had been.'

"The dinner ended early, for as virile and strong as he seemed, the Marshal-General was by no means a young man. Later that night, I lay awake in my bedroll thinking, trying to reconcile in my mind the derelict old grandmother with she who had been the Princess Willow of such unsurpassable beauty. I was confused. If Marshal-General Moujan saw her now, would he see the aged and ugly crone, or would his eyes behold the glorious maiden she had once been? I found myself wrenching present time into past time, and past into present, and I wondered, *does immortality reside in memory?*

"And that, young Martin," Orestes had concluded, "is why the ancient, Eternal City of Rome is so like the ancient and gnarled Princess Willow. There are those who remember what she was once like, and they, in turn, tell their sons, who tell their sons what it was like, and as generations pass, the City takes on yet greater allure, even as it becomes old and shriveled and bald and scabrous."

I remembered that story as Joan and I entered what had, for eleven centuries, been *the City* and was now only a crumbling large village. I remember that story even more today, as I, myself, sit crumbling in Hadrian's Tower, imprisoned, cast low, and uncertain of my future, if any there is to be. I know one thing now that I did not know then.

It is that a man stays always the same age, somewhere down inside himself. Only the outside of him grows older – his body and its presentation to the temporal world. Inwardly, he attains to a certain age, and stays there throughout his whole remaining life. That perpetual inner age may vary, I suppose, with different individuals, but in general I suspect it gets fixed at early maturity, when the mind has reached adult awareness and acuity, but has not yet been calloused by habit and disillusion; when the body is newly full-grown and feeling the fires of life, but not yet any of life's ashes. The calendar and his mirror and the solicitude of his juniors may tell a man that he is old, and he can see for himself that the world and all about him have aged, but secretly he knows that he is still a youth of nineteen or twenty.

It must be even more true of a woman, to whom youth and beauty and vitality are so much more to be treasured and conserved. I am sure there is not anywhere a woman of advanced age who has not inside her a maiden of tender years.

Although I never met the Princess Willow of whom that long-deceased Marshal-General Moujan had spoken with such undying love, she having undoubtedly died more than a hundred years before I was born, I must believe that even in her ancient dotage, that long-ago woman could see in her mirror the radiant eyes and rose lips and willow grace that her suitor Moujan still could see, more than half a century after parting from her, and could smell the fragrance of clover after rain he had attributed to her, the sweetest-scented thing God ever put on this earth.

CHAPTER 38

When we arrived in the Year of our Lord 844, Rome was the center, but hardly the model, of Latin Christianity. No city in Christendom seemed to have less respect for religion, except as a vested interest. Make no mistake, there were religious souls in Rome, gentle spirits who aided pilgrims in maintaining the shrines, but their voices were seldom heard above the din of politics.

Aside from the papacy, Rome was a poor city. Despite its having shrunken to one-twentieth its size during the ancient days, it was still sacked from time to time, simply because it was Rome and simply because it was a symbol of something – whether that something was a past glory or a despised and threatening religion. The most recent unfriendly visitors had been – and still were, and still are to this day – the Saracens, those who follow the teachings of Mouammed in faraway Arabia.

The Eternal City was neither a hub of industry, nor of commerce. The so-called Papal States were based on small agrarian pursuits. Market gardens, vineyards, and cattle paddocks mingled with homes and ruins within the Aurelian walls. The lower classes lived half by handicraft and half by ecclesiastical charity. Surprisingly, there was still a middle class, and it was in the ascendant, much more so than it had been during the last days of the ancient empire. Merchants, lawyers, teachers, scholars, and resident or visiting priests often attended the city. The upper classes – and I accepted the fact that Joan and I were now of the upper class – consisted of the higher clergy and the landed nobility. The old Roman custom of owning an estate in the country and living in the city still prevailed.

Roman nobles were divided into factions led by rich and powerful families, who were opting to use more Italianized names than had obtained in the earlier days of the Roman Empire – Caetani, Annibaldi, Corsi, Fava, Conti, Orsini, Colonna, Pierleoni, and Frangipani. Each family made its Roman residence an armed fortress.

While we, as higher Churchmen, believed that as keepers of Christ's law we were paramount in the City and in the far-flung Holy Roman Empire, the truth was somewhat different. The Church was only one of four powers, the others being the autocracy of the Holy Roman emperors, the oligarchy of the nobles, and, last, and probably least, the democracy of the citizens. Relics of the Roman Forum kept Romans aware of the rights, responsibilities, and privileges of their ancient republic. Leading nobles were, incongruously, still called senators, even though the Roman Senate had, to all intents and purposes, disappeared with the first of the ancient emperors, Octavian, later called Augustus Caesar. Consuls were still chosen or appointed, although they wielded absolutely no power. From time to time, one would even come upon some old manuscripts that preserved half-forgotten edicts of Roman law.

Yet, in the midst of this now largely agrarian town, where poor laborers waited for the shield of nightfall to steal and pillage stones of marble and porphyry and granite and basalt, to prop up their own rude shacks, there was still much to be seen.

The ancient Flavian Amphitheatre, later known as the Colosseum, had been constructed three quarters of a millennium ago. It was still such a magnificent structure that only Haghia Sophia rivals it, and since they are so different from one another, one cannot truly compare with the other. The Amphitheatre stands where the Palatine, Caelian, and Oppian hills meet, on a spot where, I was told, there had been a swampy lake.

"Can you believe this place held fifty thousand people at one time?"

"I can easily accept that. What else can you tell me about this place?"

"Oh, Martin. Where can I start? You know of the gladiatorial contests, of course?"

"Of course," I said. In truth, I did know of this favorite entertainment of ancient Rome.

"The cruelest fights were those between men and animals." As we climbed to the upper tiers, still intact, she pointed to the vast arena below. "The Romans were very clever. They made the arena into a natural-looking forest, with hills and woods and caves, to make it look like there was going to be a hunt. They even called these kinds of shows 'hunts.' Nor did the technique and the imagination of the Romans stop there. They created an artificial lake in the middle of the arena and fought naval battles on that lake."

"Wasn't that where the early Christians were slaughtered and martyred?"

"*Aye*," Joan responded. "Even when the weather turned inclement, the events went on, since the Romans invented a device that spread a huge awning over the building."

The magnificent Colosseum was not the only legacy of ancient Rome. There were hundreds of magnificent edifices still standing when Joan and I walked through the City. Trajan's Column, erected to immortalize that emperor's achievements, stood 130 feet high with a 12-foot-high statue standing atop the column. The monstrous Mausoleum of Hadrian – Hadrian's Tower, located adjacent to the River Tiber, has served as a place where many important persons of old were imprisoned, or where they sought refuge, and it still functions as such. So I write, somewhat cynically, that I must be more important than I would otherwise have believed, if I am presently resident in so historical a place.

The Roman Forum – ah, what can anyone do but dream of the days that were, when one walks down its ruined avenue, with its pillars and columns and arches and statues, some still standing? – and the Baths of Caracalla, where they still stage entertainments and performances.

"Oh, look!" I said one day. "There's the Pantheon, the one building in Rome we absolutely must see!" Joan sighed good-naturedly, and we entered the vast building, which is smaller than Haghia Sophia, but far older. The Pantheon is not a ruin. It is the most perfectly kept, still-functioning ancient monument in the world. Built some nine hundred years ago, before the ancient Roman Empire, it was originally dedicated to many of the pagan Roman deities. It owes its preservation and present state to the fact that two hundred years ago, it was consecrated as a Church.

The following day, we were invested with our bishops' miters in that holiest of places, the seat of the Holy See. The ceremony was smaller and more private than I had imagined, for there were only three Churchmen beside us who were elevated that day. Having seen the panoply and gaudiness of the Eastern Orthodox ceremonies, I did not know whether to be envious of that Oriental splendor, or secretly proud that our elevation was so much more dignified, even businesslike.

Pope Sergius, who had gone off the diet Joan had prescribed, then on again, then off again, was in that halfway stage where he clearly exhibited some pain and walked with a cane, but when we asked about his condition, he remarked equably that it was "tolerable." The process of investment was simple and straightforward, and took less than half an hour. Afterward, we sat down at a single round table, and the Pope engaged each of us in pleasant banter. We introduced ourselves to one another.

One man in particular appealed to me greatly. He was a ruddy-faced, jovial Irishman. I guessed he was about five years older than me. "Padraigh, or, in Latin, Patrick, named after the Sainted father who brought Christianity to the wilds of the Hibernian Isle," he said, in a pronounced, charming brogue. "But, although 'tis bishop I now am, ye may call me 'Paddy' when it is just us high-risen folk together." We all laughed roundly at that.

Joan sat to my right, and introduced herself as Joannes Angliorum, late of Angle-land and Athens.

"Aye, then ye'll be knowin' of that fellow Erigena?" Patrick boomed.

"Indeed we do!" I cried, and joyfully. "We were together at Tours."

"Foyne man he is," Patrick continued. "Set himself up a great sinecure at King Charlie's court. He's just been made head of the king's school there!"

The Pope broke into our conversation. "He'll be elevated to bishop in a month or two, as soon as I get Emperor Lothar's imprimatur, which I should have by month's end."

"Wonderful!" I said. "I can't think of a more deserving soul, except Bishop Joannes."

"And yerself," Patrick said. "Papa Sergius tells me ye're the best man of letters in Roman Christendom, and that he relies on you for an accurate representation of what really goes on throughout the Western Church."

"That's a little overmuch," I said, blushing. I bowed to the Pope. "But I thank you and I am beholden to you for saying such wondrous things, even if they be not true."

"But they are true, Bishop Paschal," the Pope said. Bishop Paschal! I turned that over and over in my mind. My head was spinning with a combination of the wine and the realization that for some reason I could not comprehend, Nicola, Joan, and I, who had started out together from London with an uncertain future, had, in little more than twenty years, achieved more than I'd ever thought possible. Nicola – a prince of the Church, second in rank only to the Pope himself; and Joan and I, only one level down. It was hard to conceive that at thirty-five years of age, I was still a relatively young Churchman, whereas Joan, who was thirty, was at that time the youngest bishop, so far as I knew, in Western Christendom.

As we passed around the rest of the table, the two other new bishops introduced themselves. Caius Brancius, like Patrick, was only a few years older than me, serious, somewhat conservative in manner, but not entirely humorless. I imagine life would have been hard for him, as he came from the buffer lands of Moravia. I say the buffer lands, because although Prince Moimir had just united the Slav tribes of Bohemia, Moravia, Slovakia, and Pannonia into the federation only recently called Great Moravia, less than half of his Slavic constituency were Christianized. Even Moimir himself had only converted to the Church late in life, and then, once Frankish missionaries had brought Moravia into the fold, the Prince turned against them for supporting his neighbor and rival, Prince Pribina. In addition, poor Bishop Brancius had to do a balancing act among Moravia's neighbors, Bavaria, Sarmatia, the northern lands under Ludwig's domination, Pannonia, and Hungaria. Moravia was not protected by high mountains or established fortresses, for in ancient days it had been beyond the Danuvius and it lay open to periodic predations from the East.

The last of the new bishops, Horatius Bonacristus, was from Croatia, and he endeared himself to both Joan and me when he mentioned how much he admired the Jewish doctor, ben Halevi of Spalatius. He waxed eloquent on the doctor's unique and successful methods and his gentle and *Christian* manner, not knowing Joan and I had availed ourselves of the good works of that noble physician several years before.

As the afternoon wore on, the newly ordained bishops became comfortably companionable, motivated in large part by the gregarious Cardinal Nicola. Pope Sergius had meanwhile retired to his chambers, and Joan had had the gentle diplomacy not to mention that he was only half-obeying her anti-gout regimen.

~ ∫ ~

That evening, Pope Sergius seemed to feel a bit better, and we had a pleasant light supper. Midway through our conversation, he rapped on his goblet of wine, proposed a toast to each of us, and addressed us thus: "Gentlemen, Prince-

Bishops, welcome to our small brotherhood. This afternoon, I presented you with your miters and the accoutrements of your office. Now, I'd like to present each of you with a more tangible gift. I have already advised Padraigh," he said, using the Celtic name for the bluff Irishman, "that he will serve as Bishop in Ireland. Horatius, you deserve a larger See than Spalatius. What would you say to the eastern part of Hispania – near the border of old Gaul?"

"Aye, that would be my pleasure, Your Holiness," the new bishop replied, beaming. Indeed, it should have been his pleasure, since he would be close to Rome, still closer to Avignon, and close to Tours as well.

"Caius Brancius," the Holy Father continued, "you have distinguished yourself in one of the most difficult assignments the Church could hand out – probably second only to Sarmatia and our beloved Cardinal Alcinorius." All of us laughed, for Alcinorius had passed from a pestilence on the See to merely an embittered old man. "I think it's time for a somewhat more rewarding experience for you," Sergius continued. "How would you like the Veneto?"

Another wonderful assignment. The newly consecrated Bishop Brancius dropped his conservative demeanor and literally whooped with joy. That left the two of us. Needless to say, we were nervous. Obviously we'd been together so long, and Sergius knew we were the closest of friends. I could only hope we would not be separated for too long, or over too great a distance.

Sergius hesitated for several moments. I was certain he wanted the tension to build. Finally, he said, "Joannes Angliorum, you are one of the most brilliant scholars and voices the Church has had in many a year – it is not necessary, and it is rather unseemly of you to protest with false modesty. You have served Mother Church well in Athens and in Constantinople. But one cannot claim to have truly seen and experienced Christendom unless one has been to Jerusalem, the place where it all started." Joan went wide-eyed at that. Jerusalem may have been a downfallen city on the very edge of Christendom itself, bordered on every side by the emerging followers of Mouammed, but it had a longer and more glorious history than Rome itself.

"Finally, our chronicler, Bishop Martin."

My heart was pounding inside my chest. I was hoping against hope I would be sent to the Holy Land, or even to Antioch, so that Joan and I could at least see each other occasionally.

"Martin, I have precious little knowledge of the far reaches of our Church, and I would very much like to have an accurate observation of the whole of it. I would like you to travel to Hibernia."

"Eire?" I said, dumbfounded. "But Your Holiness — "

"You need not express such excitement. I know I've already appointed Patrick to a position there."

I hung my head. My God, I had never been far from Joan since she was a child and I was only a little older. Now, we would be so far removed from one another, we would be on opposite ends of the Church itself. It would take us months to communicate with one another, let alone visit. She was my closest friend in the world. I depended on her and she on me, and we were like two halves of a single soul. We had been with each other, comforted one another in tragedy, celebrated with each other in joy. I looked over and saw that Joan, too, was ashen-faced. Sergius knew how close we were – had known for many years. What had we done to so offend him that we would be separated by so cruel a distance? After allowing his words to sink in, our Prelate smiled gently and continued.

"I expect, Martin, that you will spend six months in Hibernia, and that Padraigh will be your guide. And you, young man," he said, turning to Joan, "will spend six months in the Holy Land, where I expect you will meet with our Brethren and you will meet with emissaries from the followers of Mouammed, and you will replicate your success in founding shelters for the poor in Constantinople. That's a lot to do in six months. Then, I expect both of you to return to Rome. I need both of you for your separate and very discrete talents at the Holy See itself. I'm sure we will find appropriate employment for your skills here."

The color returned to my cheeks and I heaved a huge, and very audible, sigh of relief. Joan nodded with dignity, but I could see how excited and pleased she was. Six months would be nothing more than a brief hiatus, almost a vacation from one another. Even couples who have been married for several years strengthen their relationship if they are, from time to time, away from one another for short interludes. Indeed, I reminisced back to my two months' travel from Tours to Basilea with no one but myself, and later with Orestes. It had been an exciting and adventurous time.

Orestes had told me that one of the hardest times in a young man's life is when he is enrolled in the army and going through the earliest training regimen, rising before cockcrow, running most of the day with heavy packs on his back, eating miserly rations, and crashing onto a cold, wet floor each night, shivering as if beset by fever, burning up as if beset by fever. Yet, years later, that same man will think back to his military days and talk about his exploits as though these were the happiest and most fulfilling moments of his life.

I was now thirty-five, middle-age, and I was being afforded an adventure normally reserved to those more youthful than me. I looked into my goblet of wine, which held exactly half its capacity. Was what I had been offered a goblet half full or a goblet half empty? Of a moment, I decided our Pope had blessed me with a *full* goblet of wine in extending me this opportunity, and I grinned.

"Your Holiness, it is my honor and my privilege to do your bidding."

"Excellent, Martin!" Sergius said, enthusiastically. "I think you will find Padraigh an excellent guide to the Green Island."

"*Aye*," the Irishman said. "And I believe Martin, who comes from a land not that far from mine, will make a boon companion indeed."

Chapter 39

"The first thing, ye'll have to find out something about the Irish," Paddy said. "Celts they are, but though they're descended from the same folk as the Gauls, they're different as can be. Somehow, the Irish are bigger than life, they've got more blood and piss and vinegar in their veins than any other folk I've ever known."

"You think I'll be able to learn about the country in six months?"

"Martin, ye'll find out enough about Eire in six *days* to last ye a lifetime, and then ye'll need the rest of your life to try to understand us. When do we leave, by the way?"

"End of November," I told him.

"It'll be rough sailing," Patrick replied. "Fortunately, we'll be journeying overland to France. We'll take a boat across the Channel to Portsmouth, ride to the west, and travel by boat across the Irish Sea."

"Two months' journey?"

"About," he said. "Ye might want to read a few things that'll give you some idea of my people."

"Such as?"

"If you truly want to know the soul of my people, you must read *Tain Bo Cooley*. In Latin, it translates as *The Cattle Raid of Cooley*."

"And that's how I'll find out everything I need to know about the Irish?" I said, turning my eye to watch a fly trying – and failing – to escape from the predatory efforts of a spider.

"Pay attention, now, you!" Patrick growled. "I'll have ye know that *The Cattle Raid of Cooley* is no sillier a name than the *Odyssey*, the *Iliad*, or the *Aeneid*," he continued. "Each is the national epic of a different civilization at a different time. Are you, by any remote chance, familiar with those other works?"

"I am," I replied. I did not know whether he was angry or playing at being angry. "I read the original of the *Iliad* and the *Odyssey* in Greek, and the *Aeneid* in Latin."

"Aren't you something, then?" he replied, slapping his knee and pouring both of us huge draughts of wine. "Tell me, Martin," he continued in a quieter, more confidential tone, "Ye're not a virgin, are ye?"

"*Ne*," I said equably.

"Good. I might have suggested ye not read the *Tain* if ye were."

"Oh?" Now, I was much more interested.

"Of course," he continued, "unless ye read Irish Celtic – Gaelic – it's be useless for you to try to read it. Gaelic is a noble language, but such a difficult one unless ye've been born to it."

"Oh." I was deflated.

"Never you mind, young Martin. I've spent the last year translating the *Tain* so it can be lodged in a monastery and not lost to the world. I've written a second copy in small letters for myself, so I could carry the codex with me. I'll loan it to you in the month before we leave."

~ ∫ ~

"Joan, can you believe this? Listen, here we have King Ailil and Queen Maeve of Connagh. They've just been frolicking in bed together, and all of a sudden they're challenging one another as to which is the wealthier."

"But they're married," Joan said. "Doesn't it all belong to the both of them together?"

"Apparently not. The Queen claims she came from better, richer stock than the King, and he is lucky to have her. He contests her boast, so they go about the countryside counting and inventorying every stick and stone and animal and possession they have. It turns out they are exactly equal except the king has one bull in his herd that had been a calf of one of Queen Maeve's cows. Refusing to be led by a woman, this great bull had gone over to the King's herd. Maeve couldn't find the equal of this bull in her herd, and her spirits dropped as though she hadn't a single penny."

"So?"

"Maeve calls for her chief messenger and demands that he find a bull even better than King Ailil's bull. The messenger finds such a bull, the Brown Bull of Cooley."

"I see," Joan said, uninterested.

"Wait, listen to what happens then. I'll read the translation exactly. 'Go there, MacRoth,' orders Maeve. 'Ask Daire to loan me the bull for a year. At the end of the year, he can have fifty yearling heifers in payment for the loan, and the Brown Bull of Cooley back. And you can offer him this too: If Daire himself comes with the bull, I'll give him a portion of the fine plain of Ai equal to his own lands, a chariot worth thrice seven bondmaids, and my own friendly thighs on top of that.'"

"*What?* Did I hear that correctly?"

"You did, my friend."

"That's … that's …" she started giggling uncontrollably. "That's outrageous!"

"And that, dearest Joan, is the national epic of the Irish people."

"Completely without scruple or moral straitjacket, wild men and wilder women!" Joan said. "They sound absolutely magnificent!"

"That's what I think, too," I said. "Listen to a poem Paddy wrote about them: 'For the great Gaels of Ireland are the men that God made mad, For all their wars are merry, And all their songs are sad.'"

"Martin, I'm about to go to the Holiest City in the world – the oldest, the most historical, and one said to be the most mysterious and beautiful. Yet, at this very moment, I am so envious of you I'd trade places with you in the time it takes to say, 'Yes, Your Holiness.'"

I grinned at that remark. "Come to think of it, Joan, I'm beginning to feel that way, too. You know what I'm most looking forward to?"

"No."

"Coming back and telling you all about it."

~ ∫ ~

"Saint Patrick was Roman-born," Paddy continued. "Kidnapped to Ireland, where he was a shepherd-slave for six years. Out in the fields, all alone, no one but sheep to talk to. His only companions were hunger and nakedness. I'd have gone crazy."

"How come he didn't?" I asked.

"For some reason, he began to pray. He'd never been a religious child. When you have absolutely no one else to talk to, you talk to God or you talk to yourself or you talk to your sheep, and those animals are stupid, let me tell you, so ye'd have no great conversation with them." He laughed the belly laugh I'd become so familiar with during the past month and a half.

"One night, so he tells, a mysterious voice came to him in a dream and said, 'You are going home. Look, your ship is ready.' Patrick walked two hundred Roman miles, through territory he had never been to before, without being stopped or followed, 'til he reached a southeastern inlet, where he saw a ship. Somehow or other, he was able to board the ship at the last possible moment. It took them three days to reach the Continent, and when they got there, the Captain and crew found nothing but devastation.

"They couldn't find a single human being or, more important, a meal. Finally, the captain taunted Patrick, 'How about it, Christian? You say your god is great and all-powerful, so why can't you pray for us? We're starving to death, and there's little chance of our ever seeing a living soul.' And you know what Patrick said?"

At that moment, the ship gave a lurch, and my stomach gave a lurch as well, as we entered a particularly choppy sea. "I don't know what he said, but this sounds like the story of the Biblical Jonah who was in the belly of a great fish for three days."

"Just about the same thing," Paddy said. "'From the bottom of your heart, turn trustingly to the Lord my God, for nothing is impossible to Him, and today He will send you food for your journey until you are filled, for His abundance is everywhere.' The men, who had nothing to lose, bowed their heads and tried a moment of faith. All of a sudden, they heard the sound of a stampede. Looking in the direction of the sound, they saw a herd of pigs trotting down the road in their direction – not just food, but the best food of all!"

"Bishop Padraigh," I said, "You are a bard worthy of Homer! We're only a fortnight from Ireland and you've kept me entertained every day of the journey. Are all Irishmen really as colorful as you?"

"Me, colorful? Hardly, lad."

I'd come to accept his affectation. He was, at most, five years my senior, yet he always called me "lad," or "young man," or "young fellow," or the like. If it made him happy, it didn't bother me, so why make an issue of it?

"I'm among the most uninteresting of the Celts," he continued. "That's why I went into the priesthood. No originality, no ambition."

"I certainly don't believe that."

"I am not joking, Martin," he said. "Every Irishman I've met truly believes he is the best storyteller who ever lived, that he can drink any man under the table, and that he can singlehandedly defeat one hundred thirty kings, just like the ancient lad Coohoolen."

"I'm not doubting you, Paddy," I responded. "I'm just saying if you consider yourself to be uninteresting, how can I possibly learn all there is to learn about Ireland in a lifetime?"

"As I told ye, Martin, you could spend a lifetime trying to learn. Ye'll either know in the first hour you're in Ireland or ye'll never know. *Aye*, 'tis a splendid, tragic land, and I fear it is as people say: Ireland is the land of the future – and Ireland will *always* be the land of the future. But what every man who says that forgets is that while we're waiting for the future, we, all of us, must live *in the present*."

It was now nearing the end of January, Anno Domini 845. The dreaded Norsemen had not bothered with southern

England or Ireland. They had been spending their energies destroying Hamburg, where Sergius had served as bishop, and penetrating into Germany. The See at Hamburg had been moved to Bremen.

There were five major divisions of Ireland: Munster in the south, Ulster in the north, and, squeezed between them, Connacht in the west, Meath in the middle, and Leinster in the east.

We made landfall at Dun Laoghaire, which the Celts pronounced "Dun Leary," the sorriest excuse for a port I'd ever seen. It wasn't so much a town as it was a collection of clans, each of which held a section of the landing, as its own little fortress. Since Padraigh was a familiar and welcome figure among all the clans, he was equally friendly to them all.

The greeting the inhabitants gave him was neither quiet nor peaceful. He was pummeled on the back, kissed on his cheeks, pinched, and pummeled again, by both men and women. Ireland had apparently never heard of the Roman custom, or, I might say, the Roman Christian custom, of separating the roles of females from that of males. The women I saw at Dun Laoghaire – indeed throughout Ireland during my tenure there – were every bit the equal of their men. Their attitude was, whatever a man can do, a woman can probably do better. The males were the warriors and the drinkers, but the women could, when the occasion arose, be every bit as warlike, could drink a man under the table, and were certainly as deceptive, or more so, than their male counterparts.

Even though Dun Laoghaire was not much of a port, it was a port, and that meant there were drinking establishments throughout the small settlement. Paddy and I were hustled and dragged and pushed and prodded to at least eight of them that first evening, and since, with only a couple exceptions, our hosts provided the beer or wine or honey mead for us at no cost, we were expected to match them drink for drink. My head can attest from my memory of the following morning that we did.

As Paddy had forewarned me, every Irishman – or Irishwoman, for that matter – thought himself or herself the greatest storyteller in the history of the world, and, after my first several draughts of their hearty beer, I came to believe they truly were the world's best tellers of tales.

"Paddy, m'lad, did y'ever tell your friend the fable of the Man and the Lion?"

"That I did not," replied my guide. "'Tis because you tell it so much better, O'Halloran. Why don't you tell the man, so I need not depart from my drink?" At that, my brother bishop belched loudly.

"Very well, then," O'Halloran began. "The Man once invited the Lion to be his guest and received him with wondrous hospitality. The Lion had the run of a magnificent palace, akin to that of Connor himself. There were paintings and sculptures everywhere, but what attracted the Lion most were depictions of the noble Lion and members of his tribe. There was, however, one remarkable feature common to all this artwork, and that was this: no matter how they were represented, the Man was always victorious and the Lion was always overcome. When the Lion had finished his tour of the mansion, his host asked him what he thought of the splendors of the place. The Lion, ever a gracious guest, gave a reply that did full justice to the riches of the Man and the wondrous skill of the artists, but he added, 'Lions would have fared better, had lions been the artists.'"

There was a loud roar from all assembled, even though they'd no doubt heard this story a hundred times or more, for what else was there to talk about? Indeed, I have found in my life that most men or women truly don't have much new or inspiring to say. Their habits are pretty much predictable. Left to their own devices, other than making war and making love, pursuing and conquering another man's mate and trying to avoid the consequences thereof, praying and preying, eating and drinking, sleeping, occasionally reading, writing, or painting, working, and, most important, listening to and spreading gossip, what else is there to do? Men and women race through life on a preordained race-course. In that respect, we are all similar, whether we inhabit Ireland or Arabia, Sarmatia or the land of the Ethiopes.

I was particularly fascinated by tales about the Wee Folk – the Little People – the faeries and leprechauns of Irish legend. Make no mistake, these were not kindly little folk. Their smiles invariably had a cast of evil to them, and if they were not downright malignant and evil, they were certainly to be avoided, unless, of course, one could steal something from them and frustrate their evil intent and their more evil character. I heard so many tales of them that night, and, indeed, those same tales were replicated all over Ireland in the following months, that I hesitate to write them down for fear there will be nothing else to write about. Indeed, I've no doubt the Wee Folk would entice me to write about them to divert me from writing the truth I am setting down here.

During the next two days, Paddy and I purchased two small geldings which were in fairly good shape – an Irishman would never sell a beast that could function as a warhorse or stud to a great line of progeny. We also bought a few traveling implements, and some salt pork. It was difficult to get out of bed on each of those days, because the nights following those days were invariably larded with hearty food, hearty drink, and rowdy company.

On the third day, we began roving through the Irish countryside. Indeed, the entire country was Irish countryside, for I never found any settlements or towns of any substance in Ireland. I have earlier remarked on what a poor little port Dun Laoghaire was – a rude collection of small huts and a few families. I was to find during the next half-year that Dun Laoghaire was one of the largest cities in Ireland. As we were riding north to Baile Átha Cliath, which Padraigh had boasted was the largest city on the island, and which turned out to have no more than twice as many families as Dun Laoghaire, I asked my host, "Paddy, how many kings are there in Ireland?"

"I'd imagine two hundred or so."

"Two hundred kings?"

"*Aye*, mayhap double that. Y'see, here we've a different concept of 'king' than they do on the Continent. The largest kingdom on the Island was that of the legendary Ailil and Maeve. They ruled the entire province of Connacht. A kingdom might be as small as a single hill, and its king might rule over as few as twenty families, but those families were warriors all, and they fought in the ancient tradition of the Celts."

"Which was?"

"They fought their battles absolutely naked, but for a sword, a spear, and a braided neckpiece of gold, silver, copper, or such other metal as they could find. You can imagine the impact that must have had on their enemies." He chuckled. "*Aye*, the Sainted Patrick himself found them thus. Behold, young Martin, look yonder."

I did, and was surprised to see a fairly substantial church, the largest building in Baile Átha Cliath by far.

"Saint Patrick's Church, probably the oldest one on the Island."

Ten or even twenty churches such as Saint Patrick's would have fit comfortably inside Haghia Sophia, but this was of small consequence to me. I have found that the temple of a man's soul is inside his heart, and that, in turn, can be larger than a score of Haghia Sophias. This Saint Patrick's was rough and crude, a square, stone building, but it was possessed of as much spirituality as any church or cathedral I've seen before or since. We passed through on a Sunday, and of course we attended the service. There were fully thirty Christians praying in that small church, and we were dressed in rude traveling habit, so as not to call attention to ourselves. You may well have imagined how flustered the local priest was, when he found out he had led two bishops in prayer that morning.

We left town not long after the church service and spent the night in Glendalough, a monastic community of saints and scholars. The monastery was walled off from the surrounding countryside by an encircling stone rampart. A tall stone tower stood as a lookout, close to the perimeter wall. At the center stood a church or worship hall, the place of assembly for the monks and scholars who lived here. There were five small buildings scattered throughout the grounds of the monastery. These served as classrooms, study rooms, storerooms, meeting halls, and dining rooms. The remainder of the monastery property included tiny, beehive-shaped structures that were sleeping areas. There were man-sized stone crosses strategically placed throughout the grounds, and a single gate served as a point of entry and exit for the monastic community. The monastery could have served as a fortress, for any of those same rooms could have been converted to barracks and facilities as fit for making war as for making illuminated books.

As we continued south and west, we entered what Padraigh told me was the high country – the "mountains" of Ireland. Not one of these soft, green hills was more than about a thousand feet high. It rained continually during my first two months in Ireland, and even after spring came there was some rain at least once a day, and when it did not rain, it was constantly damp and misty. Ah, but I've never seen so green a country in my life.

"Ye'll find we're welcome every place we go," Paddy said, a few days after we'd turned west, as we were riding through the hills and plains of Munster, "not because we're well known, or even known a' tall, but because this is a land of farmsteads and homesteads and little else. The visitor is always welcome to stay and take dinner and a bed for the night, for in a land such as this, we are the stuff of which news and gossip is made."

"Why do we stop at those places, Paddy?" I asked. "There must be several monasteries about the country."

"That's so, Martin, but when ye're the only source of news coming through, ye're always appreciated." Padraigh was certainly right. At each stop along the way, our arrival was heralded as a major event. The head of the local clan inevitably ordered a feast. Clansmen and clanswomen found the best room in the house for us. Paddy brought news from the outside world, a message from a loved one in a distant place, a source of fresh life.

Often, people asked Padraigh whether he knew so-and-so's relative in this homestead or that. Was he going to the Burren? Would he mind carrying a letter to this woman's cousin or that man's great uncle? I soon learned how lonely and tedious life in Ireland could be, and how great were distances that separated those who left their loved ones to depart their native communities for other places. Although they all seemed to know that Paddy had been elevated to bishop, he was no more a high-and-mighty than any of their petty kings or their neighbors, for he'd been born and raised on the Emerald Isle, and being a Churchman was no different from plying any other honest profession or calling.

As our Pope had asked me to observe and record as much as I could about the Irish, I set to with a vengeance, for I longed to prove myself worthy of my first assignment. I traveled in plain and unadorned clothes, the better to put my hosts at their ease. In the time I was there, thanks in great part to Padraigh's introductions, I learned much indeed.

What I found was mesmerizing. When the ancient Roman Empire was declining into a lawless morass, Ireland was in the ascendant. Until 590, women fought alongside their men. Even priests were only exempted from fighting forty years ago. A woman in Kenmare told me, "The underlying foundation of our society is the family. Several families make up a sept, and several septs make up a clan, and several clans make up a tribe. All members of a tribe were descended from a common ancestor. If someone's name was Mac-something, such as MacNeill, he was the son of Neill, and if he was named O'Neill, that meant he was a grandson of some tribal name, such as that of the Neills."

The woman's husband added, "Most of the land is owned in common by clans or septs, but that's starting to change, and one day, mayhap, families will own their own property."

A priest in Clonard was proud to tell me that monks and nuns had opened all kinds of schools throughout Ireland. "Ours was founded in the year 590 and has five hundred students."

"What courses are taught there?" I asked.

"We have a twelve year course leading to a doctorate in philosophy that includes Biblical studies, theology, Latin and Greek classics, Gaelic grammar and literature, mathematics, astronomy, history, music, medicine, and law." I was amazed. We'd not enjoyed that breadth of learning at Tours, and Tours was considered one of the premier places of learning in the Holy Roman Empire.

"Not only that," the priest told us. "If a bright, but poor, student comes to our attention, we support him from public funds, for most students are preparing for the priesthood, and we Irish make every sacrifice to further that vocation. Have you, by any chance, heard of John Scotus Erigena?" Hearing our friend's name on this outpost of the civilized world momentarily shocked me, and when I answered that not only had I heard of him, but I knew him as a friend, the priest proudly said, "He learned his Greek in Ireland."

For the most part, the Irish consumed themselves in legend and romance. Poets not only frequented every tavern on the island, they also served as teachers, lawyers, and historians. "Aye," Paddy said one day as we approached the southwest corner of Ireland, "we have our scientists and explorers, too, same as other lands, only better. Professor Fergil has me convinced the earth is spherical in shape. That becomes obvious when you see a ship on the horizon. Next time ye see one, look about ye. That ship will leave a nearby dock, and as it gains distance, ye'll see that it seems to go down. When ye see that same vessel returning, it seems to come from below and gradually rise up as it comes closer."

In the southwest, I saw for the first time what I would call real mountains – one was more than three thousand feet high – and the landscape was every bit as dramatic as that around Hausstadt, yet wholly different from that place. Passes slashed through the mountains. Dour lakes and bogs abounded everywhere. The great, wild sea was nearby, and the circuitous routes we took had romantic, Gaelic, and, I believe, pre-Christian names – the Ring of Kerry, Ballaghbeama Pass, the Dingle Peninsula. These places jutted out into the great Ocean, which was called in Latin the Atlanticus, and that Ocean was not calm or inviting, but vicious and noisy and frightening every hour of the day or night.

Here, there were few trees. The land was hilly, gray, rocky, and storm-beaten. Those few habitations here existed solely by stubbornness. The wind always blew, and mostly it blew in rain and storms and hail and sleet. It was, I thought, the end of the world. I was reminded of a fine, new, illuminated map I had seen of this place when I was back at Tours. Beyond the western peninsulas and land's end – in that part of Atlanticus that bounded the western edges of Ireland – was marked, "Here do be monsters."

"It's not really the end of the world, Martin," Padraigh assured me. Half a century ago, a group of monks set sail west from the Irish coast. They found a land to the west and north, which they call Iceland. Can you imagine what an inhospitable place that must be?"

A little later, I asked, "Why would anyone want to live in this part of Ireland, let alone fight over it?"

"Simply because it's there, and simply because it's land, and simply because it is the European mind and the Irish mindset that someone must, or should, own it."

"What can one do with such a land?"

"Well, m'young lad," Paddy replied, "there are rocks enough to build a thousand palaces, scrub enough to feed a thousand goats or sheep, cold wind enough to make one feel especially warm and loving on a chill night before a roaring fire, and crevasses enough to explore for a lifetime. And, if ye've not noticed, everywhere in Ireland we go, we see large, blonde, strong, buxom, and intensely independent women who need conquerin'. 'Tis a challenge is Ireland, so why not try to tame this part of the island as well as challenge its women?"

This was the attitude I found on what many Irishmen – and Irishwomen, too – called their "Emerald Isle."

Chapter 40

As we moved north, we were following the sun into spring, but spring in Ireland is not like spring in other lands. It is simply slightly less dour and cold and windy and bleak and dark than it is in the dead of winter. "Pay attention, Martin," Padraigh said one early April morning. Today we enter the Boireann – the Burren. Ye'll see land unlike any on earth, and ye'll feel what Ireland is truly all about."

I have previously written that the southwest peninsulas of Ireland constituted the end of the world. That was before I'd reached the land known as the Burren. It is the harshest, most inhospitable country I've ever seen – a country battered by the tumultuous ocean and filled with rocks. It was almost unbearably wracked with pain and sorrow even at first glance – there was neither water enough to drown a man, nor a tree to hang him, nor soil enough to bury him. I could not fathom how anyone would want to stay here for more than a few moments. Yet, as I looked about, I found there was something primitive, primordial, spiritual and utterly magnificent about this place. If there were gods, this is surely where they would live, for the land was haunting, unlike any other place on earth.

As if reading my thoughts, Paddy said, "This is the place where the Wee Folk ran to, and where the gods chased them and hunted them down, and where ancient man tried to tame them."

Riding through the Burren, we found ancient ring forts, round towers and high, stone crosses. We found more than one warm tavern that served up great and generous helpings of the great black beer of Ireland and the most intense, wondrously happy and terribly dolorous music I'd heard. We'd been in Ireland some three and one-half months, more than half the time allotted to me by Pope Sergius, on the day I truly came to the end of the world: the Cliffs of Moher.

The Cliffs are sheer rocks, without any trails or means to climb up or climb down. They drop straight down nearly a thousand feet to the sea. I tried on several occasions to look over the cliffs from several feet away. Each time, I was overcome by dizziness. Yet, I felt an intense combination of nausea and exhilaration. The angry sea, so far below, banged and bashed and clanged and clashed against the rock with an eerie sound that discomfited me yet further. On the day we arrived at the Cliffs, it was raining steadily and the wind was howling – literally howling – so that walking on the wet, rocky surface was dangerous enough.

I must have been lost in thought or inattentive, for I slipped and fell, and started rolling toward the sheer drop, unable to stop myself. I saw my life flash by in an instant, and knew with certainty that these were my last few moments on earth. As I was rolling and sliding, and grasping onto anything I could find to make purchase, and not making purchase anywhere – everything happened so fast that I didn't even have time to scream – I was suddenly yanked – yanked – back with a bone-cracking crunch and felt chains digging into my skin everywhere.

I was in that half blacked-out stage that accompanies unexpected salvation when I saw Padraigh and two large and burly men walk calmly up to where I lay writhing like a fish in a net – and I found that I was lying in a net.

"That's the seventh one this year, and we're only into April," one of the men said to my friend. "It's a rather easy way to be stood to a drink, and it does give us something to relieve the boredom."

"Aye, and it's a good and Christian thing to do, savin' a man's life and all. Ye know, fellas, this time ye've truly done the Lord's work. That be a regular bishop ye've saved."

The two men crossed themselves. "Saints be praised," intoned the second man, whether with profound reverence or profound irreverence I could not tell.

"Ye know, ye could open up a bit of a traveler's attraction on ye'r own? Charge a penny or so and guarantee a safe walk along the Cliffs. Where did ye get this idea?"

"'Twas my brother's actually. We done seen the local fisherfolk casting nets about, and we thought, 'There's at least two or three fools fall off these cliffs every year, break their heads and bodies and provide food for the monsters of the deep.' If ye live in the area, ye know where the path is most slippery and where it pitches down toward the cliff."

"So we figured out a way to nail some posts between the places where the rocks come together, and hitch some strong rope netting and lines to it," the second man said. "O'course, when someone's lookin' at the Cliffs or o'er the Cliffs, they don't pay any attention to netting or ropes what with the rain and the clouds and the wind and all. They think they're being cautious enough if they just watch out for their feet and keep their distance from the edge of the Cliffs."

"Me and Hrinc, our homes are on a little hill nearby and we can always see when anyone happens by, except if they come at night, and what fool's gonna' come here at night? It's become a game. We bang on one another's door, or sometimes the womenfolk bang on the door, and then we usually follow at a distance. Y'see, someone who's walkin' to the Cliffs, they want to see the Cliffs, and not some little worthless hill on the other side of the cliffs, so we just walk a bit inland from them. They don't see us, but we know where the ropes are and we know where the really dangerous places are, so when a visitor comes near those places, we take our positions and the moment we see 'em slip, like this fella here, we tug on the ropes and up comes the net."

"Verily, I thank you for my life," I finally piped up. I was still shaking, but I felt the least I could do was acknowledge what they'd done.

"Oh, it's practice for other things as well," the one called Hrinc said. "Ye can't ever be too watchful around these parts. We ain't got much, but there's them that's got less, and sometimes they come around from the Cliff-side, hoping to steal a stray sheep or goat. When we see that about to happen, we can also pull the ropes up so the rustler, who's lookin' for an animal not a rope, will trip, and we'll be on him in an instant."

"Or," said his brother, "we can pull the net all the way up and over that scalawag and teach him a lesson. It's time for the noon meal, and if ye'll be wantin' some food after ye'r experience, we'll be happy to provide some for ye."

We did and they did, and although they asked precious little for their fare, which was a pot of mutton stew with greens, we paid them handsomely, for, as they had said, they did not have much, and each had a wife and three wee ones to feed, and since we needed a place to stay for the night, we stayed with them and paid handsomely for that, too. Their homes were rough, rude structures, but built all of stone, and built well, for they kept out most of the wind and the cold, and there was a slow burning fire, not fueled by any wood I could see.

"Peat," said one of the women. "We find it in nearby bogs, since there's not a tree in sight. God's replacement burns well and long, and we cozy up with one another and make our own heat at night."

Next morning, we departed to the north, after taking breakfast with our hosts, paying handsomely for that yet again. It had been a fair exchange, I thought. Everywhere I'd gone in Ireland I'd found that people's hearts were as large as their bodies. Paddy told me we'd probably paid them more in a day and night than they were likely to see in two months.

"So I've given them two months' worth of money to save my own life? Rather a good bargain, I think."

"That's so," Paddy replied.

"Where are we going now?"

"Connacht – the land of the legendary Ailil and Maeve of the Tain and the land of Deirdre of the Sorrows."

~ ∫ ~

"And so it was that Deirdre was born to King Connor's favorite bard," Paddy began, as we rode across the border lowlands between Connacht and Ulster in the far north. "The king's Druid priest predicted she would bring many sorrows to her land of Ulster.

> *'High queens will ache with envy*
> *to see those lips of Parthian-red*
> *opening on her pearly teeth,*
> *and see her pure perfect body.'*

"The people cried out, 'Let her be slain!' but King Connor protected her, reared her, and planned to marry her. Deirdre grew more beautiful each day."

I thought back to the tale Orestes had told me about the Persian Princess Willow and I thought back, as well, to the pure love I'd had in my heart for Eva. I had an idea that although Deirdre would certainly be sister to Willow or Eva, there might be some difference in their outlooks and deeds and the way they would go about their lives.

"One morning," Paddy continued, "Deirdre saw the handsome Noyshu playing ball with other youths. She retrieved a misthrown ball and handed it to him, and he 'pressed her hand joyously.' Methinks he pressed something else as well," Paddy said, "for that very day she said to her handmaid, 'Take a message to him and tell him to come and talk with me secretly tonight.'

"Though Noyshu knew Deirdre was pledged to the old king and that there was a curse on her, he could not help himself.

"'That is a fine heifer going by,' he teased.

"'As well it might be,' Deirdre shot back. 'The heifers grow big where there are no bulls.'

"'You have the bull of this province all to yourself – the king of Ulster.'

"'Of the two, I'd pick a game young bull like you.'"

"I can guess what happens next," I said, blushing.

"*Aye*, that of course," said Paddy. "On the following night, Noyshu and his two brothers took the willing Deirdre out of the palace and across the sea to Scotland. A Scottish king fell in love with her, and the brothers hid her in the highlands.

"After some time, old King Connor sent a message he'd forgive them all if they came back to Ireland. Noyshu was homesick and eager to return to his native land, even though Deirdre warned him there'd be treachery. Nonetheless, she followed her love and his brothers back to Ireland, where they were tracked down and killed by the trickery and deceit of Ian MacDurtag, one of King Connor's allies.

"Deirdre, insane with grief, flung herself upon the ground and drank her dead lover's blood. Though she submitted to Connor, she never smiled again. King Connor, out of spite, decided to share her with MacDurtag. Next day, they set out for the fair at Macha. Deirdre was behind MacDurtag in the chariot, but she had sworn neither of these two men would ever have her.

"'That's a good one,' Connor said. 'Between me and Ian, you are a ewe eyeing two rams.'

"Deirdre saw a big block of stone coming up ahead of them. She hurled her head at the stone so that her skull burst, and she was dead."

I sat my horse, staring at the far horizon, aghast, entranced, hypnotized by the sheer imagery Padraigh portrayed.

The countryside in Ulster was no different than that of Connacht. Padraigh waited a day or so before he beguiled me with his next tale – this one much lighter fare than Deirdre of the Sorrows, but no less sensual. "Would ye like to hear another story about Coohoolen?"

"That Coohoolen who slew one hundred thirty kings when he was a lad of seventeen?"

"The same."

"*Aye*, that I would."

"One day, young Coohoolen came to woo an Irish girl named Emma. As he approached her, she greeted him, 'May your road be blessed!' to which he replied, 'May the apple of your eye see only good.' Then, peering down her dress, he said, 'I see a sweet country. I could rest my weapon there.'

"'No man will travel this country until he has killed a hundred men at every ford, from the River Ailbine to where the frothy Brea makes Fedelm leap.'

"'In that sweet country I'll rest my weapon,' he responded.

"'No man will travel this country until he has done the feat of the salmon-leap carrying twice his weight in gold, and struck down three groups of nine men with a single stroke, leaving the middle man of each nine unharmed,' Emma rejoined.

"'In that sweet country I'll rest my weapon.'

"'No man will travel this country who hasn't gone sleepless from Halloween until Groundhog Day, when the ewes are milked at spring's beginning.'

"'It is said and done.'"

"Was she worth it?" I asked, grinning.

"D'ye think someone who answered him tit-for-tat like that, so to speak, wouldn't be?" Paddy replied.

Each country has its beautiful areas and its ugly areas, and Ireland had many of both. In my time in Ireland, I saw a country without the pretty habits of Rome and Gaul, wetter by far than those lands bordering the White Sea, possessed of greater poverty and greater simplicity than I'd experienced anywhere. Oh, Ireland was different from any place I'd seen. It was a land whose inhabitants lived life in bold, brash, primitive colors, yet whose Christianity, steadfastness, and purity of belief were stronger than anywhere else I'd seen. The Irish were truly fearless foot soldiers in the Army of Christ – its bishops would be captains, but no higher, for they would, like Padraigh, remain one with the people regardless of how high they'd risen in the Church.

The difference between Padraigh, a true Christian and a true bishop, and Schweitzermann, that foppish and fraudulent pretender of a priest back in St. Gallen, was the difference between bright sunlight and dark shadow, between sheer beauty and rank ugliness, and I would recall with an inexplicable fondness and love, that harsh, green, terribly beautiful land for the rest of my days.

CHAPTER 41

Pope Sergius spent three days reading my chronology. At the end of that time he was most generous with his praise and said I had been of inestimable assistance to him in learning more about a hitherto mysterious place. He and I spoke for more than an hour, and although he seemed much older and in poorer health than I remembered him, his mind was as quick and perceptive as ever. Finally, I was unable to contain myself any longer. "Your Holiness," I asked, "might I enquire as to when we might expect the return of Brother, er, Bishop Joannes?"

"Indeed, he's stopped in Constantinople on his way back – another of those endless Synods, but I told him you'd probably want to meet him there, look in on the shelters you started, and have a bit of a holiday before your next assignment."

Joan and I had a joyous reunion with one another, and with our three Byzantine friends, Methodius, Justinius and Julianus. Our shelters were flourishing as never before, and the first five days were truly a holiday. Unfortunately, we'd been together only six days when we received a terse and tense message from the Holy See. "The Saracen deniers of

Christ are said to be massing for a strike on Rome later this
year. We have asked Louis, King of Italy, to intervene." Less
than a fortnight later, word spread through Constantinople like
wildfire. War! The Saracen fleet was at the mouth of the Tiber.
Ostia and Portus were under siege.

Joan quickly grasped the significance of what had
happened. "This afternoon, prices in Rome will double.
Tomorrow they'll double again. The Holy See will not have the
wherewithal to withstand next winter without food, clothing,
and other supplies. It's urgent we make it to Rome as quickly as
possible. But before we do, we must buy futures on everything
we can find here. The wheat and rice crops will be delivered
in about five months, the first olives will ripen in Anatolia and
Athens shortly thereafter. We can guarantee a low price by
purchasing and paying for as much of these commodities as
possible now, with a delivery date in six months at Rome or
wherever the Holy See directs."

"Ingenious!" I said. "Whether the Saracens successfully
invade Rome or are repulsed, Rome will need the protection
of an army, but the kings will want the Holy See to pay for
it. If the Arabs successfully attack, Rome will be starved by
that time, and its citizens will pay whatever they can. If, on
the other hand, Rome depends on the Holy Roman Empire to
protect it, the See can sell wheat and rice and olives and olive
oil to the north at a time when prices are traditionally at their
highest. Either way, the Church ensures its survival."

"We need to purchase these things now, for cash. It will
be months before the Church sends money, even if it has
sufficient money to spend."

"I can solve that," I said. "I have a great deal of wealth at
my disposal. Suppose I were to advance the necessary funds
on behalf of the Church — ?"

It was said and it was done. By the time we left Constantinople in June, we had secured an inestimable amount of the three commodities on which I had staked fully two-thirds of my fortune. Fortunately, Jewish agents in Byzantium had contacted the necessary factotums in Angle-land and in Moravia, where I had substantial additional holdings, and were able to arrange for advances of money by a very clever system.

Instead of selling the lands outright, I mortgaged them to lenders – Jews and, remarkably, even Arabs – with payment due on the whole, plus two percent interest – a vast sum indeed – one year from the date of receipt – the eighteenth day of June 847. The Jewish agents received an additional one percent of the entire deal. If I paid back on time and as promised, the lands would revert to me, but if I failed by so much as a day to redeem the properties, they would be quit to the mortgagees or their agents.

What gratified me most was I was using Saracen money – since the Arabs had no idea what I was going to use the proceeds of the loan for, only that I was a commodities trader – to defeat them in their attempts to destroy Rome. We commissioned ships of various nations and kingdoms and empires to deliver the commodities to us, when and where directed. To further protect the identity of the buyer, we placed title in the name of my Jewish agent in Angle-land.

We left Constantinople on June twentieth. Two weeks later we arrived at Piraeus. The news from Rome was devastating. The Saracens had taken Ostia and Portus, and had defeated all of the relief forces. Worse still, they had sacked the basilicas of St. Peter and St. Paul, and, to the horror of every good Christian, the Saracens had even started to dig up those sacred graves that housed Apostles' bodies. "Pray for us!" Sergius had sent the message to every bishopric within the jurisdiction of the Roman Church. "Help us, dear brother in Christ!" The Pope had sent a message to the Patriarch of Constantinople.

When we received a message from Sergius directing, "For your own safety, stay as far as possible from the Holy See until we can straighten this out!" Joan was adamant. "Sergius needs us now more than ever. We may be disobeying his directive, but I think the Holy Father will forgive us. However, we may have to go to Rome via a different route."

That very afternoon, we booked passage to Spalatius. We knew the Saracens would blockade Brindisium. "If we go north as far as Venezia, we'll be slowed down by numerous soldiers and pilgrims and just plain confused people, going to or coming from the Eternal City," Joan said. "I have an idea of how we can speed up our journey. Perhaps Doctor ben Halevi can help us put it into play."

When we got to that Hadriatic port, we had a fine, warm, albeit bittersweet reunion with that great and good man. "My, my, bishops! You fellows certainly have advanced."

We told ben-Halevi of Joan's plan. He was first amused, then amazed, then roundly congratulatory. "What a shame you were not born Jews," he said. "You would have added most dramatically to our good fortunes, and undoubtedly our purses as well."

"Yes, Doctor, but we haven't figured how to get back into Rome unseen," I said.

"Mmmmm. Yes, that presents a small problem. Not insurmountable, though. The Jews are known throughout the Christian strongholds and the Arab strongholds as 'hidden people' – nonentities. I have an idea …"

~ ∫ ~

The boat from Spalatius to Pescara in the very center of Italia's Hadriatic coast took little more than a day to make port. As we'd expected, Saracens guarded all entrances to the city, and while the six Christians who'd taken passage with us were checked and searched for what seemed like hours, Joan and I, very obviously Persian Jews, dressed in long, dark caftans, prayer shawls, and high, Oriental skullcaps, may as well have been invisible. After we had paid a small bribe in Persian coin to the guards, we were waved by, without so much as a cursory search.

"Jehudi," one guard mumbled, smirking at his companion and rolling his eyes in disgust. "They're so tight they'll hold onto the smallest coin until it bleeds! Can you believe Uncle Isaac and his friend actually gave us each a coin? When we get back to Arabia, we'd do well to frame them!" The other guard laughed out loud.

We continued into the small city. When we were far out of eyeshot of the port police, I nearly fell to the ground laughing. Joan looked so comical, with frizzy, iron gray hair, thanks to a wig ben-Halevi had secured for us, and an equally frizzy and kinky and curly full beard that matched the wig. "You are one ugly Yid," I said to my friend.

"And you think you are prettier?"

"Why do you say that?"

"Uncle Isaac, your nose is as long and hooked as a Syrian, and the mole on your cheek is absolutely revolting. As for your beard, it's marked with gray – real gray – since you are truly getting a bit long in the tooth."

"Nonsense!" I said. "That's not real gray. It's blended in and you know it. The nose only looks a bit unusual because of the added clay and the cosmetic Doctor ben-Halevi gave me."

"I don't think either one of us will attract a beautiful Christian maiden, or any maiden for that matter. One need only come within five feet of you and the smell will drive them away."

"I've noticed that myself. Can we not even bathe? It's five days over land to Rome, and I find it hard to live with myself."

"I'm sure there are places along the road where we can find water in which to bathe, but we must be careful not to be seen. Sometimes we'll have to take our baths at twilight, or mayhap even a quick dip in the dead of night."

The trip took five days and we did find places to bathe. I made certain not to wet my gray-streaked facial hair or my exquisitely constructed nose, and Joan carefully removed and reapplied her wig and beard after each bath. We did not go into the water at all during the last three days, because Jews were reputed to have a strong odor, and we did not want to betray our disguises.

We approached the Eternal City from the east. Although the basilicas of St.Peter and St. Paul, both of which were outside the walls, had been unmercifully pillaged, the high, thick walls of Rome had once again protected the city from complete devastation. There was panic everywhere, as Rome's inhabitants flocked to every marketplace in the city, trying to find rice, flour, oil, and honey, all of which were virtually nonexistent. Since we looked odd and Oriental, a few angry citizens threw eggs and tomatoes at us, but otherwise we were pretty much ignored – the invisible people.

When we asked where the Pope was staying these days, we were directed to a small, nondescript church in Palestrina, a half-day's walk away. It was now mid-October. When we asked to see His Holiness, a self-important and very officious official brushed us off. On the second day, we begged an audience again. That selfsame official started to close the door in our faces, when Nicola happened by.

Joan shouted, "Nicola! It's us!"

Of course he could not recognize the two Persian Jews, but he certainly recognized the voices. "Joa – Joannes? Martin? Monsignor, open that door immediately and open it right now!"

~ ∫ ~

Sergius looked older than ever, and grayer, too. He was clearly failing rapidly. The year had certainly taken its toll on him, and he presented as a very sick old man.

"Joannes? Martin? Is it really you?" His voice sounded reedy and wheezy, as old, weak people sometimes do.

"Aye, Holiness," I answered for both of us.

"Come closer, let me see you. I fear my eyes are failing along with the rest of my body." He touched our faces gently. Each of us bent to kiss the Papal ring. "Ah, it is you. One of the few pleasant things that has happened in this dreadful year, which I fear may be my last."

"Nonsense, Holiness," Joan said a bit too cheerily. "We would not have deserted you in any event, and you will, with God's help, remain in the shoes of the Fisherman for a long time."

"I wish it were so, but it's not," the Pope said. "I've seen the ravages the Papacy has wrought on me. More, I feel the ravages. I hope I can last out the year at least. I'm only holding on to see who may succeed me. Benedict? Leo? There's even talk of Anastasius, making a grab for the Holy See. Enough. What news have you brought us from Byzantium?"

Joan and I told Pope Sergius and Nicola, and the telling took two hours, and when we had explained everything to him, the Pontiff's face relaxed and he seemed to have lost fifteen years off his age. Only his voice remained feeble. "The Church will, of course, repay you, with ten percent interest. The Holy See can easily afford it. We can sell or trade your goods at three times what you paid for them. Why shouldn't you share in the benefit?"

When I told Sergius I would accept only the amount of my loans and my direct costs of interest and agency, and not one nummus more, he smiled, a slow, deep smile. "God bless you both!" he said. "The Roman Church owes you a greater debt than you may realize. You may, in your own way, have ensured the survival of Mother Church."

At the end of November, the Saracens withdrew from Rome. A frigid winter portended. But neither Joan nor I were the least disturbed by it, for a much more momentous and warming event occurred. We were invested with the red stola and tall hat of Cardinals, princes of the Church, second only to the Holy Father himself.

CHAPTER 42

Scarcely two months later, on January 27, 847, the noble Pope Sergius II who, to us, had always been a friend and benefactor, died. Almost simultaneously, Moimir of Moravia passed on. We learned, to our joy, that little Aegina's husband, Rostislav, had become the ruler of Moravia.

"Now there's one young lady who did as well for herself as she intended," Joan said to me early in February.

"Two," I murmured. Joan blushed, but said nothing.

"Who do you think will be the new Bishop of Rome?" she asked.

"I can't really speculate, but the Cardinals had better vote soon. With the Saracens not quite gone from our sea, the Church needs a strong spiritual leader, and quickly. I will, of course, do everything in my power to help Sergius' favorite, Leo, succeed to the throne."

"What about Benedict?" she said. "He's been cardinal-priest of St. Calixtus for a year, and many say he was Sergius' shadow, so close were they to one another."

"Perhaps, but he made Leo cardinal-priest of the Four Crowned Martyrs' Church."

"What about Anastasius?"

I glared. "If that slimy skeit is elected, we'd do better in Sarmatia than at the Holy See."

"But he's making a political run around the leading contenders. I'm concerned, Martin. After all, he knows —"

"But he swore many years ago — "

"An oath that means absolutely nothing to him. If he felt I was standing in his way, he would stop at nothing. Thank God he's been in Sarmatia all these years. He only came back to Rome after Sergius' death."

"Which is one of the reasons you grew the beard?" I smiled, realizing that she "grew" the beard anew every morning.

"Aye," she said. "Joannes is not an uncommon name. If he knows I've been elevated to cardinal, I hope he'd never surmise he'd lain with the bearded man behind the title."

"Which is all the more reason we must do everything in our power to make sure the vote is not split," I said. Any hint of a division among the Church leaders and Anastasius would seize power by any means."

"I'll do everything I can assist you in subverting Anastasius' efforts, but I must stay very much in the background, so as not to be noticed. I suggest it would be best if I were to absent myself during the Papal election."

"Where would you go?"

"Constantinople. But we've still got to defeat him. How?"

"Nicola!" I said. "He's had the ear of Sergius and Leo and Benedict. Perhaps if he and I approach Leo and Benedict and tell what we know. After all, it will be the word of two cardinals against one bishop."

Joan smiled and brotherly squeezed my hand. "I think I shall take passage to Constantinople Monday week."

The following Tuesday, I told my plan to Nicola. He responded he'd been thinking much the same thing, but had worried that if Joan's true identity were discovered it would bode ill for all of us. "After all, Sergius saw the two of you as alter egos of one another. Odd," he added, "Sergius thought that after Eva died there might have been a homosexual relationship between you two." He chuckled. "If he only knew the real truth."

Leo and Benedict were the leading contenders for the Papal throne, but each was an honorable and just man. Nicola, as one of Sergius' most trusted advisors, called a meeting between the four of us. He asked that we dress in ordinary tunics and meet among the ruins of St. Peter's outside the walls.

On the appointed day, Nicola, with a wry twist of humor, wore a cockfeather pinned to his hat, affecting a style now popular in Pannonia.

As we walked toward Trastevere, across the Tiber, we appeared to be three ordinary citizens and one foppish dandy out for a stroll. Nicola, keeping his voice low, talked about how, several years ago, he had come upon a young priest, who, under cover of night, had drugged a young girl whom he'd gotten pregnant. Leo and Benedict each frowned, keenly aware of what this meant to their campaigns if what Nicola said were true.

"Cardinal Nicholas," Benedict said, "it is all well and good what you say, but surely it is your word against his. He will undoubtedly deny his wrongdoing, perhaps even bring charges against you in the Ecclesiastical Court."

"Still, it's an interesting idea," Leo said, "even if there is a shred of truth to it. It is unfortunate these things take place when and where there are no corroborating witnesses."

"But there is such a witness," Nicola added. "And a cardinal, to boot."

"Martin?" Leo asked, gazing wide-eyed at me.

"Aye," I said, "and there is yet more." I told them about the conspiracy to destroy Bishop Numenior at Tours. "Numenior, if he's still alive, could certainly confirm it."

"He is," Benedict said. "He's still a bishop, albeit a very old man. I can certainly check out your story, but we may not have time to do it. Have you any witnesses to that event?"

"Several," I said. "Two investigators, a fellow who was a young monk at that time, Cardinal Nicholas, who was at Tours when I was there, and one other. I cannot, for very private reasons, disclose the identity of that witness, who is also a cardinal. But there is another man you may have heard of, and he would be manifestly credible, John Scotus Erigena."

"Erigena?" both candidates said as one, almost choking the word out. "The Erigena at Charles' court?"

"The same," I rejoined.

"The other witness you say you can't disclose, where is he now?" Leo asked.

"He is, alas, out of the realm at this moment. He has given me a signed affidavit allowing me to vote my conscience as his, for he cannot be in Rome for the vote." We'd become so engrossed in our conversation, we'd walked much farther than we'd intended, clear to the base of Monte Marius. We retraced our steps to the Tiber, then headed east along its banks.

"The problem is," Nicola said, "if the two of you continue to contest the election against one another, each of you is so respected and so beloved that any third candidate who offers a reasonable alternative to either would be voted in, if for no other reason than that the College of Cardinals would hesitate to offend either of you."

Leo and Benedict, old friends who had worked together in tandem with Sergius, requested that we excuse them to walk by themselves, and we did. The following day, Nicola and I received word that the two Papal candidates had decided Benedict would, at the last moment, withdraw his name from consideration, and if Leo were elected Pope, he had secretly promised Benedict any position in Roman Christendom he desired.

"Most likely Chancellor of the Exchequer," Nicola said sardonically. "That's where the power really lies."

A week later, I asked Nicola,

"What about Anastasius?"

"The Papal election is thirty days away. Cardinal Sixtus, the senior of all cardinals, who is sitting as Acting Bishop of Rome pro tempore, has initiated a private investigation of certain allegations. I'm told he has sent word to Angle-land and to Aquitania to confirm certain rumors he's heard about one of the announced candidates."

Less than a week prior to the convocation of the College of Cardinals, Cardinal Sixtus called Leo, Benedict, and Anastasius into the private Papal quarters for a chat. No one ever learned what was said during this meeting. Nicola, who'd been in the outer chambers at the time, later told me he'd seen Anastasius leave the Papal quarters ahead of the others. He looked neither left nor right. His face was very pale.

The next morning, Cardinal Sixtus and Bishop Anastasius appeared before a specially convened meeting of the Collegium. A trembling Anastasius unexpectedly announced, in a quiet monotone, that he was withdrawing his name as a Papal candidate. He cited extensive personal commitments and a lingering, but unspecified illness that would prevent him from attending to his duties were he elected Pope. He publicly asked that his supporters vote instead for Leo.

Cardinal Sixtus told the Collegium that he was deeply grieved that Anastasius was withdrawing from the race, and that he regretted the loss of someone of Anastasius' eminent stature, "someone who has so ably and nobly served Mother Church during his twelve year tenure in Sarmatia," but he understood Anastasius' devotion to duty and wished him well.

In the shocked silence that followed, Benedict announced, "My brothers in Christ, it is not well that two of us, Leo and I, who have been friends for the last thirty years, allow our perceived contest to force you to take a position for or against one of us and thereafter suffer heartache because of an unfounded feeling of favoritism or betrayal for or against one or the other of us." How different he sounded from the dry, crusty announcement of Anastasius. Benedict was a fine and emotional man, who spoke from the heart.

"Leo and I have discussed this dilemma at length, and we have come to concord, for the good of our colleagues and friends, and for the unity and greater good of the Church. Therefore, it is with a full and loving heart that I ask that my name, too, be withdrawn from consideration. I ask that I be given the honor and the privilege to cast the first vote for Leo, who will bring dignity, goodness, and much needed strength and confidence to the Holy See. I urge you to join me in a Hosanna for our next Holy Father, Leo IV."

There was a collective sigh of relief, as each cardinal present joined Benedict in hailing the man who was now certainly the Pope-elect. And it was so, and it was so by uniform approbation, and such was the feeling of the Collegium and the need of the Holy See that Leo was consecrated to fill the Shoes of the Fisherman without waiting for imperial confirmation. However, since it was politically and militarily necessary and astute, the Church sent a rapid messenger to Emperor Lothar to assure him that the investiture of Leo was in no way meant to lessen the emperor's prerogative to confirm Leo's succession.

Nor did Leo forget those who had helped him. To this day, I have never found out how Leo learned that Joan was the other witness to the events we'd disclosed to Benedict and Leo, although I suspect it was Nicola who told the Pope some time after the election.

Shortly after Leo's elevation, Benedict became, as expected, Chancellor of the Exchequer. Nicola, too, was raised very high, and became the Secretary of State to the Holy See. I was amazed and gratified when I was appointed as Scriptus Scriptorum – Secretary and Scribe to Nicola. Since Anastasius had been in Sarmatia so long and was presumed to be familiar with that frontier of Christendom, he was elevated to serve as Archbishop of that See, with the strongly stated order that he could do as he wished there – provided he was to return to the Holy See at Rome only when he was commanded by the Holy Father to do so.

But the biggest surprise of all was accorded Joan, for at the age of thirty-three, she was appointed Under Secretary of State, Roving Ambassador, and Personal Emissary of Pope Leo IV. Most stunning of all was the knowledge that the position to which Joan had been elevated was traditionally awarded to a person whom the Church considered a major candidate to become Pope at some time in the future.

CHAPTER 43

Leo's first job was to ensure that the sack of St. Peter's Basilica would not be repeated. He enlisted a thousand workers to start construction of a wall around the Vatican Hill and the immediately adjacent district. It was a great undertaking, for Rome was going through hard times, but the Pope's energy was unflagging. He obtained money from the emperor and workers from the agricultural estates. Even while the walls were rising, the Saracens were mounting a great fleet, such as the world had never seen before, and that fleet was being readied to sail against Rome, and finish the devastation they had inflicted on the Eternal City the year before.

This time, however, the Italians rallied around Leo and took measures to shore up the seat of the Roman Church. A combined military fleet from Neapolis, Amalfius, and Gaeta sailed into the Tiber. Since these three Southern Italian cities were nominally under the Eastern emperor, the Romans wondered whether the fleet had come to help them or to attack them.

Joan was dispatched to Constantinople to speak with the Byzantine Emperors Michael and his mother Theodora, who confirmed to her that notwithstanding Rome was not Orthodox, it was still Christian. Joan returned to Rome and presented Pope Leo with a letter bearing the purple seal of the Byzantine emperors pledging aid and support. Concurrently, Nicola received assurances from Admiral Caesarius of the triple alliance that the fleet was coming to protect Christianity against the deniers of Christ.

Leo himself led a Roman army to Ostia to join the fleet. He personally celebrated Mass and gave Holy Communion to all hands. The troops, spiritually fortified and ready with their arms, met the Saracens and engaged in vicious, but indecisive, preliminary battles. That night, Pope Leo once again led a huge Mass, praising and encouraging his legionnaires and sailors.

On the following morning, a strong wind blew up from the south, separated the fleets, and, by day's end, completely wrecked the Saracen fleet. Rome was saved, and the Pope celebrated a third Holy Mass, this one of great thanksgiving. He returned to Rome the following day and redoubled his effort to build what was now being popularly called the Leonine Walls.

I was responsible for chronicling the events taking place under our vigorous new Pope and for disseminating important news of the Church all over the Holy Roman Empire, and as far removed as Ireland, Germania, Pannonia, Sarmatia, the Haemus Peninsula, and, of course, to Athens and Constantinople. It would have been impossible for me to accomplish this without aid, so I was assigned some fifty assistants, who would instantly copy everything I wrote. These copies would be transmitted by ship or fast horse to other centers where other scribes and scriveners would copy the copy they received and messenger those copies to other, smaller churches and bishoprics and parishes.

In addition to publishing the news of the realm, the Official Scribe was responsible for publishing Ecclesiastical laws and precedent-making decisions, Papal Encyclical Bulls, and various other official records, including the Liber Pontificalis, the Chronicle of Popes. This latter required me to actually read the Chronicle, and to make changes or amendments, as the current Pope or Collegium of Cardinals deemed appropriate.

Earlier in my life, I had traveled much, but during my term as Scribe to the Secretary of State, I found myself far too busy to venture far beyond Rome. Joan, on the other hand, ranged far and wide throughout Christendom, and I kept abreast of her doings through private correspondence, which she sent me in ambassadorial pouches. She must have sent a dozen or more, but I have kept a portion of one such typical letter secreted in my personal effects even now, for they provide a memoir of what life was like in that exciting time.

~ ∫ ~

"March 2, 848

"My Dearest Martin:

"Last month, I finally saw Fulda, in northeastern Germany. It's a monstrously large, forbidding stone structure, located in a clearing, with dark forests on every side, and a few low, rolling hills. Between you and me, I'm glad I never came here, as it is more stifling than I would possibly have supposed. Recently, a monk named Gottschalk came up with a supposedly 'heretical' doctrine. He claims that everything is predetermined; that there is no free will in man, and that there is no such thing as divine redemption. That sounds as silly to me as the dispute between the Eastern and Western churches on the character of Christ. But it has caused a huge stir in religious circles, and Archbishop

Hincmar is leading the charge against what is being called 'predestinarianism,' which, to me, is a 17-letter word for more stupidity when one has nothing better to do.

"Much more enjoyable, I visited with our dear old friend Erigena at Compiègne. He's chief of Charles' Palace School, and travels between Compiègne and Laon at his leisure. Scotus is as brilliant and irascible as ever. He looks as though he has not missed many meals. ...

"Hincmar has asked Erigena to write a reply to Gottschalk's doctrine. John showed me the opening of his responsive treatise, which he calls *De divina praedestinatione*, and it is going to upset a lot of people. Here's how he starts:

"In earnestly investigating and attempting to discover the reason of all things, every means of attaining to a pious and perfect doctrine lies in that science and discipline which the Greeks call philosophy.

"There is no predestination. The will is free in both God and man; God does not know evil, for if He knew it, He would be the cause of it."

"As we both know, once Erigena gets an intellectual bone to chew, he will not stop until that bone is gnawed to powder."

~ ∫ ~

Joan was traveling and, more important, she was meeting and befriending all the great, and still more important, the influential minds of the time. I had always known Joan was brilliant. In Constantinople, she had proved how she could, by her common sense and balanced, pleasant manner, sway the multitudes. Now, for the first time, I was learning from many sources that Joan had become what the ancient Greeks had called a politician. It did not take a genius to realize that

Joannes Angliorum was rapidly becoming a first magnitude star, very much ascendant in the heavens of the Christian leadership.

One day in the middle of the year 849, Nicola approached me and murmured in a very quiet, very private voice, "Martin, does it seem to you that our Joan could possibly be angling for ... you know?"

"You're joking!" I said, shocked.

"You may think I am joking, and, for that matter, mayhap Joan herself would think I'm joking, but as Secretary of the Papal State, I hear many things from many sources, and I can tell you there is an incredible groundswell of interest in Joan's future at such time as Leo is no longer among us."

"You can't be serious!"

"Oh, but I am, my friend. You remember when she was twelve years old and I was a postulant and I told you she was the brightest human being I'd ever known? Remember when she told you she would be someone very important some day? Neither one of us scoffed then. It may not be propitious to scoff now."

"Nicola, you know as well as I that — "

Nicola shushed me quickly. "Every wall has several pairs of ears behind it. I think it's time my scribe and I visited some of the glorious new fountains they're building in the great Vatican Square."

As we walked toward the middle of that Square, Nicola said, sardonically, "I know exactly what you were going to say, and, believe me, I've thought the same thing myself. Who'd have to know? And what an incredible thing it would be if it actually worked!"

"Joan?" I ruminated over the matter for several moments before it struck me like a thunderclap. If anyone in the entire world could bring it off, Joan could do it! But, perhaps I was jumping ahead of myself. "Nicola, aren't we being premature? Leo's been on the Papal throne only two years. He's young for a pope, and very vigorous. His namesake, Leo III sat for twenty-one years. Gregory was pope for seventeen years."

"That's exactly two popes," Nicola replied. The ninth century has not been particularly kind to Holy Fathers: Stephen IV, one year, Paschal, seven years, Eugene, three years, Valentine, one month. Even Sergius lasted only three years. If we perform that same mathematical trick Joan did in Constantinople, the average pope has lasted seven years during this century. That means our present pope would, statistically at least, be expected to pass into heaven five years from now, some time in 854."

"That's ghoulish of you, Nicola."

"Perhaps, but how long have you and I been friends?"

"A quarter century."

"Then humor me."

~ ∫ ~

Later that year, Benedict, the Chancellor of the Exchequer, the second most powerful man in Roman Christendom and the presumptive pope when Leo ultimately died, approached me.

"Martin," he said, "what do you think of Cardinal Joannes?"

"He's a clever man, highly intelligent," I said guardedly. "He and I have been the closest of friends for twenty-five years."

"I know that. I think you know I respect both of you as well, and I certainly owe my present position to you. I don't quite know how to phrase this, but is he a moral man?"

"I've never known one more so," I said, and honestly. I proceeded to tell him about Joannes and the adder who'd attacked a small child; Joannes had saved the child's life, and now that child was the reigning princess of Moravia. I told Benedict about Joannes' sympathetic understanding when Eva had died.

Benedict said, "I find it very comfortable being Chancellor of the Exchequer. No one looks over my shoulders, I'm not responsible for momentous decisions, and," he chuckled, "no one has been known to murder the keeper of the Papal treasury."

"Surely you can't mean what I think you mean, Eminence," I said.

"Oh, but I do, Martin. Sergius told me many times that the Shoes of the Fisherman weigh heavily on the wearer, that they are tight and make for sore feet. Leo and I have been close friends for nearly as many years as you've been on earth, and he, too, has said, and more than once, that the Papal crown is often intolerably heavy. He confided in me that if he had to do it over again, he would have withdrawn in favor of me before I had a chance to open my mouth. Martin, would you take a light supper with me tonight?"

"If that is your wish, Eminence."

"It is. Shall we say just after sunset?"

~ ∫ ~

"Your Holiness?" It was an exclamation rather than a question.

"Good evening, Martin. I understand you and my friend Benedict have been talking."

"That is so," I said.

"He's made mention of certain ... things."

"Aye." I had no idea where this conversation was leading, or why the Holy Father himself had joined us in Benedict's chambers. I thought it best to listen rather than speak.

"The Holy See lasts beyond the life of any Pope," Leo began. "But sometimes a Pope can influence events beyond his own lifetime. I am certain, for example, that Benedict would carry out my wishes, were he to succeed me."

"Absolutely true, Holiness," Benedict said.

"And I think Benedict would make a superb Pope," Leo continued. In response, Benedict bowed his head modestly. "There are problems, however," the Fisherman said. "Anastasius associates his fall with Calixtus, may his memory be blessed, Benedict and myself. Whatever else this evil Anastasius may be, he is not without powerful friends. He is also a very clever man. I have no doubt he is, even as we speak, plotting my demise somewhere. Both Benedict and I are most concerned that if that were to happen, Benedict, his other perceived nemesis, would be the only one standing in the way of his accession to the Papal throne."

"God help us all and God help the Church if Anastasius succeeds!" I could not contain myself.

"I agree," the Holy Father said. "That is why, for the time being, we must deflect attention from Benedict, if – when – the inevitable happens."

"God willing, that will be many, many years, Your Holiness," I said, and earnestly.

"I hope you're right, Martin. Twenty years or so would be a goodly reign, although not a particularly comfortable one. The Shoes chafe. You have served Sergius and the Papacy loyally and nobly. You are a good man."

"Thank you, Holiness."

Benedict poured us goblets of the crisp, dry wine of that eastern region of Italia called Chianti. He brought out a bowl of pistachio nuts and one of pickled olives. By that time, we were all hungry and we happily and companionably nibbled on the nuts and olives, occasionally taking a draught of wine.

"I would prefer that my friend Benedict lead a long and comfortable life. The power and presence of Anastasius would not guarantee that, and if Anastasius succeeded to the Papal throne, the one thing you could count on, without fail, is that Anastasius would annul virtually everything we've done during our reign. The Church needs an intelligent, vibrant, young leader, one who could deflect attention from Benedict, while Benedict enjoyed the ability to guide and perhaps influence such a leader."

It slowly dawned on me what was happening here. The two highest leaders in all of Roman Christendom were plotting to place "their man" on the Papal throne if, and when, Leo was no longer around. Of course, if Leo lasted fifteen or twenty more years, none of this discussion would have any meaning. But if Leo's reign were somehow cut short —

My words were measured, and I tried to keep the trembling out of my voice. "And you are thinking of Joannes Angliorum." A statement, not a question.

The Pope actually roared out a hearty laugh. "You see, Benedict, he is not as stupid as he looks!" He winked at me to let me know this was not meant as an insult, but to cement a very private concordat – dare I say a conspiracy? – between the three of us.

"Why tell me these things?" I asked.

"You're Joannes' closest friend and confidant. There is no possible way we could bring this to his attention, not privately, and most certainly not publicly. This has to be handled with more tact and diplomacy than anyone else is capable of giving. You two are even closer than Benedict and me. No one except the Papal Secretary of State knows our Brother as well as you, and it would be unseemly for him to approach Joannes."

"Please, Your Holiness, Your Eminence, I beg you to confirm the direct meaning of what you say. You are asking me to confer with Cardinal Joannes Angliorum very privately, in a place as far from Rome as one can get, and determine whether he would be willing to stand for election as Pope if – and only if – Your Holiness were to pass from the scene within a very short period; that he would be a guarantor that Your Holiness' policies would not be disturbed; and that Benedict would serve as a 'senior guide' to Joannes."

"That is absolutely correct, Martin," Leo said. "And if we get a positive affirmation from Cardinal Joannes Angliorum that he would be willing to abide by the Holy Father's conditions, we would quietly start talking to certain, umm, important people."

CHAPTER 44

Joan and I met in Dyrrachium. I was surprised at the quiet confidence with which she greeted my news. "I have no vested interest in becoming the most powerful Papal leader or the greatest Pope who ever lived," she said. "I would happily welcome Benedict's wise counsel. I have come to believe the most successful leader is the one who delegates responsibility as widely as possible, and who doesn't need to salve his own ego."

"So you'd seriously consider it?"

"Yes. Don't look so shocked, Martin. You're thinking what everyone in the world would join you in thinking: a woman on the Papal throne? Impossible! Well, why is it impossible? I'll grant you I could never ascend to the Papacy if it were known that I was a woman. But I've publicly been a man for so long I probably wouldn't even know how to dress like a woman anymore."

"They say one person, and only one, can keep a secret. If two know — "

"Martin, are you saying I shouldn't trust you with my very life?"

"Of course not. But there are four who know. The third one, Nicola, I'd trust without reservation. The fourth one — "

"Aye, and what a bastard he'd be, especially if he perceived I was standing in his way."

Two fishing boats slid into the nearby dock. Each of us purchased a piece of grilled fish, stuffed into a half-loaf of bread.

"But he might not know," I said. "You weren't anywhere nearby during Calixtus' investigation. You've been out of Rome eleven out of every twelve months, so you're not someone he'd suspect of being a challenge to him, and every year that passes distances him more from you. You were a momentary plaything in a youth he'd as soon forget."

"So what am I supposed to do if I accept Leo's offer?"

"Exactly what you've been doing: good works, promoting schools and shelters and orphanages. Cardinals are spread all over Christendom, and each has a single vote in the Collegium. I hear tell you've made many friends. Make certain you make more friends."

~ ∫ ~

"He accepted?" Benedict asked.

"Aye, Eminence."

"And he'll keep his word?"

"I'd stake my life on it."

Benedict heaved a mighty sigh of relief. "The Holy Father will be well pleased."

~ ∫ ~

In the year 850, the aging Lothar asked the Holy See to invest his son, Louis II, with the Papal Imprimatur and diadem of the Holy Roman Emperor. Pope Leo agreed to do this. So grateful was Lothar that he, himself led the ass on which His Holiness rode to the place where young Louis was crowned.

Indeed, many things of consequence took place in the Christian world that year. The Bulgars created their own empire on the faraway Volga River. Rurik, a Norseman, advanced as far south as Kiev, where he became ruler. For the first time ever, those dreaded men from the North, some of them Danes, began to trade with Constantinople and the Khazars.

I was delighted to receive correspondence from Doctor David ben-Halevi, who wrote that large groups of Jews were settling in the German lands, and, what's more, they had stopped using only Hebrew in their conversations and had developed a common language of their own, which they called Yiddish, which was fast becoming the language of their international commerce.

In November of that year, an Arabian goatherd was amazed to find that when his goats ate a certain kind of red berry, which grew on nearby bushes, they developed amazing energy and stamina. By some accident, these berries fell into a roasting pan one day at dusk, and they turned brown, brittle and hard. When he ate these roasted berries, he found himself possessed of more energy than ever before, although he found if he chewed these berries at night it was hard for him to sleep. It is now common knowledge, of course, that he called the berries khafi, and that that drink has spread far and wide already, from Arabia to Hibernia.

No matter how far and how frequently I had traveled in my life, Angle-land had been, and always would be, my home. In my forty-second year, my thoughts strayed back to my native land. Mayhap it was because my father had died in his forty-second year, or it may have been because the dry land around Rome so little resembled the island on which I'd been born. My heart hurt for my homeland when, in 851, Danish forces entered the Thames estuary. As high as I had risen in the Church, there was not a thing I could do about it.

I felt especial joy when Ethelwulf defeated the Danes at Oakley, but that joy gave way to desolation when, later that year, the Danes sacked and destroyed that most magnificent of edifices, Canterbury Cathedral. I thought, if only the Angle-ish had used that new French invention, the crossbow, they might have saved the mighty Church fortress.

In France, John Scotus Erigena actually published his De Divina Praedestinatione, and many Christian clerics were demanding his head, but his adoring ruler, Charles, protected him.

By June 852, Leo's wall was completed and the Pope himself was the first to stroll around, then on top of it. He looked hale and hearty, and it seemed he truly would sit on the Papal throne for another fifteen or twenty years. Notwithstanding the See's secret plans for Joan should anything prematurely cut short his reign, Joan was both cultivating friends and truly doing good deeds, which I duly reported in the news-letter I published each month.

She cajoled bishops to part with ten percent of their annual incomes to strengthen those institutions of which she was so proud – the shelters, the orphanages, and the providers for the poor. But now, she had a new idea. The concept of the Hotel de Dieu – literally the "Inn of God" – in Angle-ish the "Hospital" – was not Joan's original concept. A Hotel de Dieu had been established in Paris. The idea of saving lives physically as well as spiritually, appealed mightily to her. The Hotel de Dieu was not simply a place that people went to die, but one that might enable them to be cured and to live productive lives once again. I remembered when Doctor ben-Halevi had told us there were many such institutions in Persia.

Joan was quick to give credit, not to herself, but to those bishops and priests and monks who supported these Hotels de Dieu and who often worked in them as medici, orderlies, and food providers. By doing these things so selflessly, her reputation grew yet greater.

Joan ran into more difficulty, however, when she tried to stem a tide that had begun to take hold in Angle-land, Ireland, and France. In those days, armies – and I don't mean large armies – often engaged in petty wars. When a man went off to war – usually he was a small farmer or landholder – he worried for the welfare of his wife and children left at home, for who would there be to care for and manage the land, pay the taxes thereon to the local thane, and protect the land from depredation by others?

There were many little wars and many little soldiers. The Church, grand and trusted institution that it was, offered such men a solution that seemed kind and wonderful: "We, the Church, will take control of your land in trust while you are away campaigning. At our expense, we will bring in and pay for competent managers, who will run the farm. We will divide the proceeds, so that your wife and children will have fully one-half of all profits from the crops, animals, and whatever other husbandry is useful to the farm. Since the farm will nominally be Church land, you will have the full power of the Church to defend your land. The Church will even pay what taxes there are on your land. When you come back from the wars, we will restore your land to you, and you may take back the land as if you had never gone off to war."

In theory, this was selfless and noble. But what the Church conveniently forgot or neglected to tell the soldier was, first, that the Church was immune from taxation, so the land was never taxed, and, much more important, that the only condition for the farmer-soldier reclaiming his land was that he must come back, in person, to claim his land.

Now, it does not take a great mind to figure out that no war is fought but that some men die, usually one out of every five who enter such a fray, usually foot soldiers rather than officers. The Church could count on the fact that those men who were killed would not come back to claim their land. When that happened, the Church acquired full title to the land. Thus, the Church had a vested interest, not in the outcome of any war, but rather in the war itself. The largest profiteer in any war was Mother Church.

Joan's attempt to move Church leaders to amend this practice so that the farmer-soldier or, in the event of his death, his surviving family could claim the land back, fell on deaf ears. Mind you, Joan was neither more nor less human than anyone else, and, since she was a political being and an arm of Mother Church, she did not push the issue too hard. But even if one Cardinal or bishop approved of the idea, or gave lip service to it, it would ensure that some of the brighter small landholders might figure they could do much better by eliminating the middleman by simply hiring a farm manager on their own.

Even though she was a Cardinal, Joan did not hesitate to fraternize with the so-called "common folk." When she did, she constantly urged them to band together to help themselves, whether by way of cooperative farm groups, cooperative marketing arrangements, cooperative schools, cooperative shelters, orphanages, and even hospitals.

In addition to the small landholders who went off to war, the wealthier, larger landholders, confident of buying heaven after enjoying lives of polygamy, murder, and every sin imaginable, bequeathed the Church large plots of land. So did penitent magnates and devout heiresses. In all the countries through which I traveled, I found one thing to be common: in each country: Christianity took on the qualities of the national temperament. In Ireland, for example, it became mystic, sentimental, individualistic, and passionate. It adopted the fairies, the little people.

What made Joan even more politically astute was that, for the greatest portion of the year, she remained out of Rome. Since all of the infighting for high position within the Church took place at Rome, it soon became apparent to anyone in the Eternal City that Joan was outside of the inner circle of power, that she had no pretensions to greater office, and thus she was not to be considered a threat to their turf. What these same climbers neglected to consider was that each Cardinal had one vote when it came to choosing a Pope. The Cardinal in the cold, damp bogs of Ireland had exactly the same vote as Benedict.

Meanwhile, in Rome itself, Leo reconsecrated former pagan temples to Christian use and care. The Pantheon was dedicated to the Virgin Mary and All Martyrs. The temple of Janus became the church of St. Dionysius. The temple of Saturn was converted to the church of the Savior. Leo renewed and embellished St. Peter's Basilica, and through the growth of the papacy and the coming of pilgrims, a busy suburb grew up around that group of ecclesiastical buildings which took its name from the ancient Vatican Hill.

On the first day of spring 853, Ethelwulf, king of the West Saxons, sent his young son to be crowned by Pope Leo. The Pope, eager to cement relations with all of Christianity, agreed. The child was formally baptized and given the name Alfred. As I watched and duly recorded the baptism and coronation, I could not help but think that the Holy Father looked more tired than usual. For the first time, I noticed that his usually spry step was halting.

As spring gave way to summer that year, I thought back to a conversation Nicola and I had had four years before. My friend had suggested that, statistically at least, there was a good probability Leo would die the following year. August marked a time of some slight relaxation in my duties. Rome was always hot at that time of year. Heat breeds lethargy, long afternoon naps, and a search for the coolest place in the vicinity. I'd always found that except for the catacombs – and who in their right mind would want to spend days on end in the company of the long dead? – one such cooling place was the Papal library in the basement of the State offices. One day I chanced to be leafing through the Catalogue of Popes, I suppose to test Nicola's theory of the length of their respective reigns.

I found that during the last three centuries, most popes reigned for only two or three years. As I delved deeper into the puzzle of why these men ruled for such a brief period, it became clear to me that most popes were chosen as a reward for services rendered, so most of them were elderly and infirm when they ascended the Papal throne. Pope Sissinius, for example, was consecrated on January 15, Anno Domini 708. He was so crippled by arthritis, he could not even find his mouth to feed himself. He died twenty days later. A century ago, Pope Stephen II lasted only four days, the shortest reign ever recorded.

Was I consumed with foreboding because of Nicola's words? Or because of the agreement reached between Leo and Benedict concerning the succession if – if – our Holy Father were to pass earlier than I anticipated?

In January 854, I asked Nicola how old Pope Leo was. "Seventy-four. Why do you ask? Ah, Martin, you must be thinking about our conversation of four years ago."

"I'll not deny that. I suppose I'm feeling my own age. September last, I was forty-four."

"Ah, you young lads are all alike," Nicola said, playfully pinching my arm. "One day, you may get to be an old ferta like me. I'm a hale and hearty forty-seven." He turned serious and sighed. "Where did the time ago? It seems we only met Joan a couple years ago, and it was just a blink of an eye ago we were at Tours together."

"Is it just me, or does it seem to you that the older you get, the faster every year goes by?"

"You're right about that. But don't worry, my friend, you don't look anywhere near forty-four. I'd easily mistake you for not a day over forty-three."

"Rascal! Seriously, how is His Holiness' health? When I saw him at Alfred's coronation, he seemed less energetic than usual. I haven't seen him much since then."

"I really don't know. He and Benedict have been spending a lot of time together, mostly in the Pope's private quarters. He seems to rally when he speaks publicly, but he does seem to be less out in public than I've known him to be in years past."

Seventy-four! My God, that was a very great age! Why, Leo had been twenty years old and already a priest in the year Charlemagne had been crowned Holy Roman Emperor – nine years before I was born! If he were to reign even ten more years, he would be positively ancient.

In the spring of 854, I saw Leo at Easter Mass. He had aged much more noticeably this time, and there was a severe palsy in his hand as he administered the sacrament. Truth to tell, I had made a conscious effort to avoid thinking about the hitherto distant and impossible possibility that Joan – my Joan – could be elevated to Pope, but as I saw Leo at Easter, the reality of the situation hit me like a blow to my stomach.

Then, only two months later, the impossible happened. The Pope took to his bed on June 17 and never recovered. He died peacefully in his sleep three days later, on June 20, 854.

CHAPTER 45

The populace of Rome assumed that Benedict would succeed to the papacy and that the transition would be orderly. Inside the college of cardinals, the mood was tense. Anastasius, though still only bishop, and hence not part of the collegium and not entitled to vote, had nevertheless cajoled or bullied his way into the chamber and asked to address his scarlet-robed brethren before they voted.

Once inside, Anastasius, in his smooth, oily way, made it clear that he had substantial evidence of fraud and chicanery on the part of Benedict and Leo during the latter's reign. He was hooted down when he implied there was something a little too close about their friendship, but the same group of cardinals listened more attentively when he told them he had ample proof that he had been forced by lies and trickery and demonstrably false accusations to withdraw from the papal race before Leo had been elected. He created near havoc when he threatened to take his case directly to the people of Rome. "After all," he said, "it is the people and not the cardinals who have traditionally elected the Pope, and it would not be hard to convince them that they still have that power, even if the 'old men in red' have tried to steal that power from them."

Anastasius knew, and the cardinals knew, that this upstart bishop could – and I had not the slightest doubt that he would – precipitate a Papal crisis were he to carry out his threat. From long acquaintance with Anastasius, I knew he was capable of anything, fair or foul, to accomplish his ends, even it meant taking the Church down with him.

Joan was not at Rome that day. She had been in Constantinople, in serious negotiations with the Patriarch and the Emperor Michael on matters of mutual defense in the event of further Saracen attacks. She'd been unable to leave the Byzantine capital, even on hearing of Leo's death, until two weeks ago, and she was, even now, enroute to the Eternal City.

Benedict, a cunning old veteran of many internecine Church battles, "played his cards," as they say, with consummate skill, for after all, he and Leo – and, for that matter Nicola and I – were not the least surprised by Anastasius' unseemly outburst and had planned for this very thing to occur. Looking very sad, somewhat confused, and certainly bedraggled, he addressed his colleagues while Anastasius was still in the room. "My friends and my brothers, of course I deny any of the false accusations made by Bishop Anastasius. It appears he has a problem with me, and not with you. Nevertheless, because of the position of responsibility you have given me, I must think first of Mother Church, not of myself. For me to aspire to the mantle of blessed Peter is something I have thought about for many, many years. But if, by doing so I create an unbearable schism in the Church at this moment of crisis, I am less than a Christian. Therefore, it with the heaviest of hearts that I make my choice. The

Church's good must be paramount to my own. I ask that you not consider me for the position of the Holy Father."

"No, no!" rang out a chorus of horrified voices. There was a sense of great anger against Anastasius, and now Benedict seized upon the moment.

"I am willing to withdraw only if my brother Anastasius likewise says he does not aspire to Peter's mantle."

This, I thought, was a pure political ploy on the part of Benedict. He knew for certain there was no way the cardinals, who were angrier than I'd ever seen them, would dare elect Anastasius Pope, even if Anastasius were Saint Peter himself. By issuing this challenge, which he knew the proud Anastasius would not accept, he was ensuring that it would be a miracle if that evil opportunist received even a handful of votes.

"I accept no such challenge!" Anastasius replied loftily. "They stole the Papacy from me in 847, and I will not tolerate their underhanded attempt to steal it from me now. I will go to the people within the next week!"

Benedict was ready for the gauntlet to be thrown, and this time he responded. "And I, sir, call for an immediate vote of the collegium of cardinals to declare you *anathematized* this instant, and by acclamation of the entire collegium. And upon such vote, I will have Cardinal Paschal publish immediately, and for the widest possible dissemination to the people of Rome and throughout Christianity, that you have been anathematized, excommunicated, and stripped of all Churchly positions."

"*Aye! Aye!* A vote now!" shouted the assembled throng, as one.

"You have but one chance, Anastasius," Benedict roared. "Recant your threats now! Recant your slanders now! Swear in the name of the Holy of Holies, in front of the Holy College of

Cardinals now, this instant, that you will withdraw your name from consideration – and I will do the same – and that you will, under no circumstances, go to the populace of Rome."

Anastasius turned pale. He swallowed so hard that his Adam's apple was bobbing, almost humorously. I was sitting near to him and saw him break out in a thin sheen of perspiration.

"If I succumb to this monstrous threat, Eminence," he said, spitting out the word "Eminence" as though it were poison, "will you then revoke your call for the vote you proposed?"

"*Aye*," said Benedict. "But only if, in addition, you leave the Holy See and depart back to Sarmatia from whence you came, under Papal guard, within the hour."

"And I shall keep my rank and position?"

"That, too."

"And you will not serve as the next Pope?"

"True."

Anastasius knew when he was defeated – humiliated publicly before his Church superiors – but he was making the most of the opportunity to, as the Seres people say, "save face." I noted that not once did he withdraw his accusations or vilification of Benedict, and, in that way, he had won a portion of the day for himself, for the man he assumed to be his nemesis would be denied the right to wear the Shoes of Peter.

"Very well, then. We will both step down from consideration."

Anastasius turned on his heel and quickly left the chamber, escorted by Papal guards.

After the tumult, which rose in his wake, quieted down, Benedict addressed the cardinals once again, this time in a much quieter voice. "My brothers," he said. "Let us confer together quietly as friends, so we might determine what qualities we seek in the man we propose to elect as the new Holy Father. I propose that after we do so, we think on the matter for ten days."

What a sly old fox he was. It would take at least another week for Joan to arrive at the Holy See and for Anastasius to be well out of range where he might do further harm. I suspect Benedict had privately conversed with several of his colleagues for months about the person he thought would most appropriately be consecrated to the highest office in all of Christendom. Joan had been featured in every news-letter sent out to the cardinals during the past year, and this was not by design, but because she was truly the most news-worthy personality in the Roman Church. Unless I was truly mistaken in my assessment of the situation, there was only one realistic competitor for the Papacy – Nicola, the second man in power and prestige after Benedict.

Nicola was his usual sanguine, humorous self when we spoke in private two days after the firestorm in the cardinals' chamber. "*Ne*, Martin, if my time is meant to come, it will come. But it would be so much more fun to see — "

"Sshhh!" I admonished him, grinning. We hugged then, a great bear hug, and laughed at the sheer lunacy of what we both believed was about to happen.

In the end, it was anticlimactic. As expected, five cardinal supporters of Anastasius, rather than face the opprobrium of their brothers – and probably embarrassed at the mess the Bishop of Sarmatia had made of things ten days before – simply abstained from voting.

Nicola quickly disabused the remaining cardinals of their desire to vote for him, but spoke up loftily of one who, he said, deserved the Papacy far more than he. Indeed, he was the one who nominated Joan, saying, "During the past ten days we have, all of us, discussed and unanimously agreed on what we wanted in a Holy Father: a relatively young man, untarnished by Church politics, a leader who is viewed with favor throughout the Christian world, both East and West, a man so intelligent he can hold his own with any of the current spate of brilliant scholars and philosophers, and a man of proven good works. Can there be any doubt there is but one man within our brethren who fulfills every one of these qualifications and more? It is, therefore, with consummate pride – and if pride is a sin in this instance, I happily confess to it – that I put in nomination the name of Joannes Angliorum."

There was no other name placed in nomination.

The vote was swift and decisive – and unanimous.

Moments later, a steady, self-confident, bearded Joan stepped to the podium, amid thunderous acclamation. Her first words, and the way she delivered them, were as plain spoken as when I first met her so many years ago.

"My brothers and my friends. I stand humbly before you at this moment. Although you have accorded me the greatest honor anyone can achieve in this world, and although you have designated me the Holy Father, in my heart and soul, you will always be my brothers and my friends. It is with awe and gratefulness beyond measure that I accept, in great humility, the stewardship of the Holy See. I have chosen for myself, with, I hope, your blessing and prayers, to serve as Pope John VIII. Please join me in a prayer of thanksgiving."

We all did, and vigorously and with whole hearts.

And thus began the reign of John VIII – *who was a woman*, and who would sit on the Papal throne for two years, five months, and four days.

BOOK VII.
POPE JOAN

Chapter 46

Joan was consecrated as Pope John VIII on July 21, 854, one month and one day after Leo's death. The usual pomp and pageantry accompanied her ordination. Cardinals, each accompanied by his secretary and his *caudatario*, a priest who held the train of his ceremonial mantle, formed a papal cortege as they prepared to enter the chamber hall of St. Peter's. Each cardinal was grouped according to his rank and function. Next came the bishops, in white ceremonial robes, each with *his caudatario*. Anastasius was conspicuously absent.

The new Pope announced Papal appointments the following week. True to her promise, Benedict was appointed Chancellor of the Exchequer and to the newly-designated position of Deputy Pope and *Papa pro tempore* – acting Pope when Joan would be absent from Rome. Nicola maintained his position as Secretary of the Papal State, but he, too, was rewarded with the position of Second Deputy Pope and *Papa secondaria pro tempore* – acting Pope when, if it ever happened, Joan and Benedict would be absent from the Holy See at the same time. To my old job of *Scriptus Scriptorum* was added that of *Scriptus Scriptorum per Il Papa*, personal secretary to the Pope. Such duties compelled me to accompany the Pope, wherever in the world the Pope went.

Joan held strictly to her part of the bargain. As a result, although Joan was the public face of the Papacy, to all intents and purposes Benedict was the real Pope in everything but name. It was much the same as we had earlier seen in Constantinople, where Michael was the emperor, but his mother, the Regent Theodora, was "emperor in charge of the emperor."

The first year of Joan's papacy was one of extraordinary peace, contentment, and outstanding management within the Church. Joan listened carefully to her "Deputy," and I took down all of their conversations. Benedict was scrupulously polite, *ne*, warm toward Joan, treating her like a favorite son, and Joan was respectful, loving, and completely deferential to her mentor. Each of them had informally determined exactly how this papacy was to operate. Joan traveled that first year, more and farther afield than any other pope in the past several centuries. She gave speeches or talks everywhere she went. If I must confess the sin of pride in my own work, I thought they were quite well-written. I know they were well-received.

Joan's talent for touching the lives of people everywhere was overwhelming. She was the consummate crowd-pleaser and she was surely at her best when addressing other human beings in a large setting. Everywhere we went, throngs and multitudes followed us, touching Joan's robes, and reverentially chanting, "Papa! Papa! Papa!" Joan made several important Papal pronouncements – or, to be more accurate, she delivered several of Benedict's important pronouncements – and she delivered them well. Benedict was content to let Joan bathe in the spotlight, while he ran the Papacy.

During that year, Joan met with emperors and kings, no matter how small the area ruled over by such a King, provided he was a *Christian* king. She visited Gottschalk, who was now in disfavor, and tried unsuccessfully to prevail upon him to moderate his views. She visited John Scotus Erigena, who, while not entirely favored in every See, was a powerful force to be reckoned with, since he was Charles the Bald's personal chaplain as well as the head of his palace schools. In my official hearing, she said nothing to dissuade or countermand his philosophy. In a private meeting, just the three of us, she teasingly remarked, "Speaking as one John to another, are you crazy, my friend? Your newest work, which I read for the last fortnight, is certainly your most brilliant, but, if you will excuse my saying so, it will roundly piss off everyone."

"Spoken like a true Pope," Scotus replied, never once departing from his sharp humor and his realistic belief that Joan was no more elevated a human being than he was, and that, but for the grace of his devilish wit and his unrepentant mouth and quill, he might have stood in the Shoes of the Fisherman.

"Thank God you're under Charles' protection," I said.

"You may thank God. I prefer to thank Charliebald, and I do so continually and profusely."

Joan said, more seriously, "You know I'll do anything I can," – I noticed that when she was with friends, she never resorted to the Papal "We" – "to protect you."

"I appreciate that, but given the way things have gone this century, that'll give me two or three years of protection. Alas, Joannes, Popes don't have a particularly long record of job security. I don't mean to make you feel bad, but wouldn't it be nice if you had some way of retiring early – and living to enjoy your retirement?"

"Not hardly, Scotus," I answered for Joan. "Our brother in Christ has, if you'll excuse my blasphemy, made one hell of a good start."

"Yes, that and a *nummus* will get you a hundredweight of beans. Or had you not noticed you're only as popular as your last great success?"

"Enough of such talk," Joan said. "Where do you think you'll end up, John?"

"You mean when Charlie dies?"

"Yes."

"Hanged from a gibbet, celebrated in story and song, burning in hell, or, if I'm lucky, buried in Ireland."

"You really love that place, don't you?" I asked.

"It's got a lot to commend it. After all, it was my home."

Later in the year, we visited Moravia and met with the reigning Prince and Princess. Rostislav was amazed, humbled, and honored that His Holiness would grace their small kingdom with his august Presence. The princess stammered, "Your Holiness!" kissed the Papal ring, blushed as red as a beet, and whispered, "Joannes, is it really you?"

"The same, my daughter … Your Royal Highness," Joan said, winking. "Is there some place away from the eyes of your adoring subjects, where the three of us can talk?"

There was and we did, and Little Aegina, now the princess of Greater Moravia, and, I might add, a rather impressive, if somewhat matronly beauty, giggled like a young child. "You've no idea how wonderful it is to see you, Joannes, Martin! I thought you'd gone out of my life forever."

"Seems to me, little girl, you recovered nicely enough after the adder bite," Joan said, brotherly squeezing her shoulders. "Martin and I have followed your career, and I'd say you made a name for yourself, even if you haven't grown as tall as your father."

"One doesn't have to be tall to be large in someone's life," she said, a gentle jibe, or a gentle reminder, of a small, fawn-skinned girl we'd known so many years ago.

"Could you and your Prince husband visit us in Rome?" Joan asked.

"I would in a moment, but, for the time being, we cannot, alas, make a commitment. Greater Moravia is beset once again from Sarmatia. Germania would as soon have a piece of our territory as well. Rostislav fears that leaving his domain for any appreciable period would result in him have no domain left to return to."

We spent the entire winter in residence at Rome, to dispel any grumbling that the Pope was never present at the Holy See. During that time Joan made it a point to visit every single shelter and orphanage and hospital and poorhouse in that part of Italia. She dispensed love and charity, she listened to what everyone had to say, from the poorest two-year-old child to the most ancient grandmother. And she received the love and adoration of the populace in return, for she truly came to be known as the "People's Pope."

At the commencement of her second year as Pope, Joan decided to try to accomplish the truly unthinkable. The Churches of East and West had been at odds with one another for more than five hundred years. Although many had tried before, Joan, as Pope of the Western Church, declared she was going to travel to Constantinople, "and speak with Methodius and Michael and anyone else who'll listen, and I'll chew their ears off until they hear what I say."

I reminded Joan of what she'd said about John Scotus Erigena some years ago, "Once he gets an intellectual bone to chew, he will not stop until that bone is gnawed to powder."

"I never said I was any different," she snapped. "Besides, wouldn't you agree that that's the best thing that could happen and that my Papacy would be complete if I could accomplish even that?"

"*Even* that?" I rejoined. "No pope, and for that matter no patriarch, has even been able to convince the other that such an idea would work. It would be a monumental."

"Well," she smiled. "What else have I got to do, especially since, if I were a merchant, I would say 'Benedict's tending the store?'"

~ ∫ ~

We spent September of 855 in Athens, which was brutally hot, before we continued on to the Queen City, where we arrived at the beginning of October. Joan replicated and amplified the electrifying message she'd delivered in Constantinople in the days when Sergius was still a cardinal, only now it was fleshed out, the product of mature and incisive thought: There should be no earthly – or heavenly – reason why each of the Churches could not function as equal partners in Christ. "After all, there is but One Father and One Son, and regardless of what we call the Trinity, and regardless of the temporal or celestial nature of that Trinity, and for that matter, whether there is Predestination of Free Will or some combination of both, is there really a difference that matters?" she asked.

"We struggle together against the heathen hordes of Arabia, and the closer we come to God, the closer our paths merge with one another, so in the end we all achieve and return to the Holy Spirit that created us. Why can we not unite in our efforts to find Christ and redemption – recognizing and honoring and respecting our differences in doctrine, while reaffirming the unity that exists in our hearts?"

She stated this message in a hundred different ways, but the message was always the same, and in the end, regardless of what happened, she came closer to understanding the ways and the minds behind the Eastern Church, and the leaders of the Eastern Church listened to and understood the words of the Western Pope.

"What are you asking?" said the Patriarch one day in late November.

"Only this," Joan said simply. "Let us abandon the false enmity and competition between the Churches. Let us declare, each from our own pulpit, each from our own emperor, that we are one in Christ, united in spirit. Let us create a federation, a partnership of independent, equal ideas."

It took two weeks before the Patriarch delivered his message. It was frank and direct, entirely devoid of the indirection and circumvention we'd come to associate with the east, and it consisted of two words: *Why not?*

~ ∫ ~

Over the next two months, Joan and I, the Patriarch and the emperors, worked out the language of the announcement. Its meaning had to be exactly the same in both Latin and Greek. It had to answer every question that Churchmen and parishioners would ask – and it had to do so before they asked the questions, so it would issue as a final word from both Churches that would tolerate no misunderstanding.

We finished the document the week before Christmas, and we decided the announcement would be made one year hence, December 25, 856 according to the Roman Calendar. It would take place at exactly eleven o'clock in the morning in Rome and at noon in Constantinople, so they would be delivered simultaneously.

Very few high Church leaders in Constantinople or Rome knew about the magnitude of what was transpiring in these private meetings. Benedict knew, of course, as did Nicola, and, while they wished us the best of all possible good fortune, they were not optimistic that Joan could accomplish what no other Western Church leader had ever accomplished. Methodius, the Patriarch of Byzantium knew what we were about, as did Ignatius, the elderly Patriarch Emeritus of the Eastern Church, and, of course, so did Emperor Michael.

~ ∫ ~

"So you really consummated the bargain?" Benedict was happily incredulous.

"We did, *Magister*," Joan replied with the secret, quiet smile I'd known since she was twelve years old. "I can hardly contain myself, but I promised our Eastern partner we would let only the most trustworthy of our cardinals know about the announcement before Christmas Day, 856."

"I suppose saying it was a 'wonderful deed' would be rather pale, since no Pope has ever brought about such a thing. After you announce this pact, with everything else you've done in your short reign, what is there left to do? What mountain have you not climbed, Holiness?"

"Ah, Nicola," Joan said. In private, we still used the names we'd been using among ourselves for more than thirty years. "I am, like most, more sinner than saint. I suppose I shall continue to do the best I can, which is all anyone can ask of anyone else, until it is time for me to go."

"Your Holiness, you are only forty-two years old," Benedict said. "You have already done more good in your brief period on earth than any number of men could have done in an entire lifetime. Truly, our Cardinal Nicholas is correct when he asks what more you could do. You have accomplished everything a human being is destined to achieve."

CHAPTER 47

The two saddest words in any tongue on earth are "*If only.*"

I cannot think of any other words that convey a deeper, more profound sense of sadness.

Had I known then what I know now, would the result have been any different? I have pondered that question ever since ... but I am getting ahead of myself.

Alone in my cell, with all the time in the world to think, to write, and perhaps to seek consolation, I have, I believe, learned one thing. No matter what a human being has, whether he be rich or poor, healthy or sick, young or old, he is never utterly, completely content – or if he is, it is only a momentary thing and lasts no longer than the flapping of a bat's wings. This is an unfortunate thing, for it is the one thing that prevents us from ever achieving or enjoying heaven on earth. Perhaps God intended it to be that way. I have no other explanation except that's simply the way it is.

There is an old tale, told by the Goths of centuries ago, about a fisherman who lived near the Euxine, the Black Sea. He had a wife who wanted something more than the rude shack in which they lived. One day, the man caught a large fish. The fish begged for its life and promised the man it would grant him wishes without number. The man was satisfied, but when he told his goodwife what had occurred, the woman said the man was a fool, for he could have asked the fish for anything. She sent him back to call out to the fish and ask the fish for a cottage.

The man did, and when he returned to his home, he found that, indeed, where there had once been a rude hut, there was a large and very pleasant cottage. He was now more than satisfied, and for a fortnight, so was his wife. But then she demanded her husband return to the shore and call out to the fish again, for a larger home. And so it was that again and again and again the wife kept demanding more and more and more, until, at the end, she demanded to be on equal terms with God.

Coming back from that final wish, the man found only the rude hut he'd started out with, and his wife in rags and tatters.

~ ∫ ~

Toward the middle of May in the Year of Our Lord 856, the most beautiful season of the year in the Eternal City, I came to Joan's chambers where we met every so often for a private walk. We'd been friends for so many years, each of us knew the other's thoughts, almost by heart. We would almost always know exactly what the other was going to say, and many times we engaged in a verbal collision, when we'd say almost the same thing at the same time. This was our private joke, but it never ceased to remind us of how close we truly were.

I knocked softly on the door. "Martin? Come in. I'll only be a moment."

When I entered, Joan was in the bathroom, attending to her ablutions or whatever. She emerged momentarily. I stared at my friend uncertainly.

"I've left my beard off this evening. Sometimes it chafes so much I simply need a night off from wearing it. What are you staring at?"

"It's just that it's been so long since I've seen you without the beard. You look … beautiful, Joan, and very womanly."

She raised her eyebrows. "You'd say that to a Pope? I might find such a remark impertinent, but I'm flattered that my dearest friend still remembers how I started out."

I felt a faint, but definite, rush of desire. I'd not been with a woman since Eva, not that I hadn't thought about it from time to time. I quashed such an unseemly feeling immediately. This was Joannes – the Pope – and I felt guilty about my decidedly *un*-Christian feelings. "Time for our evening walk?"

"Would you mind if I begged off tonight?" she said. "I'm truly tired. What I really need is a holiday. If only I could disappear for even a fortnight to a place where I'd not be recognized. But, of course, that's impossible. Everywhere the Pope goes he is certain to attract attention."

At that moment, a thought came to my mind. As I said, we could almost fathom one another's every thoughts.

"No, Martin. I dressed the part of a smelly old Jew once, and it became irritating after a couple of days."

"I was thinking along those lines. I was also recalling some of the adventures we've had together over the past thirty years. You just said it became irritating after a couple of days. Could you stand it for even one day?"

"What then?"

"You could spirit yourself out of town unseen and make it as far as Neapolis. Remember how badly we both wanted to see Neapolis? As things turned out, we've never had the chance?"

"Aye."

"A few moments ago, when I first came in, I was surprised – unnerved – because wearing a simple bathrobe and with no beard I could hardly recognize you. What if you pulled off the biggest gamble of all? You could be a woman for a fortnight, and no one would know when you returned to Rome."

"But how would I manage to come by womanly clothing?"

"I could attend to that."

"I'd love it if we could share a holiday together – just us and no retinue."

In the end, we could, and we did, arrange things. A week before we were to leave, Joan announced to Benedict, Nicola, and me that she was going to Spalatius for private talks with the Patriarch Methodius. She asked that I leave for Spalatius on the morrow, to ensure that everything would properly be set up.

Of course, I used that week to absent myself from Rome. I traveled in a plain tunic to Neapolis, where I procured some elegant, and some not-so-elegant, women's clothing. Joan had given me her measurements so, with the help of several merchants, I was able to approximate the sizes that would best fit her.

We had arranged to meet at the top of a rise from whence we'd first seen Neapolis so many years ago, when we'd been summoned to Rome for our investiture as bishops. And so it was that on the very day and at the very time we'd planned, an old Jew, wearing a caftan and high skullcap, slowly wended his way up the hill.

~ ∫ ~

I'd arranged for lodgings for us in a rather sumptuous villa overlooking Neapolis, and the sea beyond. We arrived just after noon.

"All right, friend, I can't wait to get out of these scratchy, smelly clothes. I trust you've bought me some decent things?"

"Aye. They're in your bedchambers, your Holiness," I said. "I've even made certain you can take a hot, relaxing Roman bath if that is your wish."

"Very well, my *Scriptus Scriptorum*. I suggest you bathe yourself. Let's meet right here in an hour or so."

When next I saw the Pope, my mouth dropped open and hung agape. Joan had not looked like this since that afternoon in St. Gallen, when she'd met Torvald. She was no longer in the first blush of youth, but she had grown even more womanly lovely in the intervening years. She was possessed of a feminine and enticing figure. She'd applied light makeup, and her short hair framed her face in a most attractive way. My heart leapt inside my chest. Eva was a long-ago beloved memory, but this was Joan and this was now.

"Is there something wrong?" she asked. Her eyes were large and luminous. She could not deny how beautiful she looked, and she didn't try to deny it. "By the way, thank you for the lovely flowers."

"Something is most definitely *not* wrong my friend, but I think we might want to go into Neapolis now, before I have thoughts that I should not have."

"You don't have to tell me what those thoughts are, Martin. I can see what you're thinking." She laughed gaily. "But I agree. Let's go."

~ ∫ ~

As beautiful as it had been to see Neapolis from afar, once we got into the city, it was an altogether different story. The dregs of humanity seemed to erupt into the streets at all hours. Fat priests waddled through the alleys of the city. Every one of them we saw was eating some kind of pastry or greasy grilled chicken or nuts or olives in a show of shameless gluttony. They seemed not to mind that they were passing through areas of poverty, although I'll admit even the poorest of the poor seemed remarkably well-fed, and streets were filled with the odors of frying olive oil and garlic and onions, roasting meats, and stale urine, which puddled in a steady stream down sewers in the middle of the alleys.

I found Neapolis singularly unattractive, and not an easy city to enjoy, but Joan waxed rapturous. "Oh, Martin, you see the poverty and you smell the ordure, and you think, 'How awful!' But you're so busy preserving your sensibilities that you miss the very soul of this place."

"What do you mean?"

"Look, listen, and feel with your heart! Smell the beauty beyond the stink and sweat! Let this place surround you and touch you with its heartbreaking sadness, its earth-shattering gaiety!"

"That great, eh?"

"Dolt!" She stopped at the next corner, bought a small container of roasted nuts, popped a few into her mouth, and spilled the rest of them down the neck of my tunic. "There. Now you're more like a Neapolitan. You're only missing some olive oil running down your beard!"

She was right. It seemed that every human being in the city – at least through middle age – was garbed in the brightest, most varicolored clothing, mostly reds and oranges and blues and yellows, imaginable. The young people – and at that moment I certainly felt young, for I was holding the hand of the most beautiful woman in Neapolis – were preening birds. Although they were strict Roman Christians, and their young women were under the perennial and watchful eyes of staunch older women duennas, the pulse of life was such that members of each sex were out to attract and tease and tantalize the opposite sex.

"Joan, er, Joannes, how dare the Church allow clothing to be so tight and so revealing?" I said, expressing my own wildly mixed feelings.

"They do seem to love life. Can you tell me you don't find it enticing?"

"I certainly find *you* enticing." For the first time in many years, I caught her blushing.

"Oh, Martin, just let your senses enjoy the world as it goes by."

As we approached a large, three-story building at a four-way intersection of streets, I stopped in my tracks and stared at a man far shorter than me, with a shirt opened at the neck revealing a barrel chest, a huge belly, and an almost totally bald head. He started singing as he entered the street. I felt a chill go through my bones. His voice was strong, filled with emotion, and what he sang was as far from Church hymns as London is from Constantinople: folk songs and gay parodies and songs of unrequited, or lost, love that reached deep into my heart. So powerful was his voice, so tender the music, that I felt uncontrollable tears brimming in my eyes. I could have simply stood and listened to him for the entire afternoon and into the night, but a crowd had circled him, and most of his audience was singing with him as well. Any number of their voices were as strong as his. A stunning, dark-haired woman moved from the center of the crowd to stand next to the man, and her voice, a clear, sharp soprano that hit every note perfectly, without a screech and with seemingly no effort, joined him in a brilliant series of duets. The crowd erupted in spontaneous applause. As instantly as they had come together, the man and the woman turned and walked their separate ways, leaving Joan and me alone in the street.

"Do you still doubt that life is larger than life in Neapolis, Martin?"

"Your point is made."

"I saw you holding back tears," she said gently. "Perhaps we might visit the Amalfius Coast as long as we're on holiday." She squeezed my hand.

We had not once since our arrival talked about the Church or Joan's or my position in it. We were simply Joan and Martin, a man and a woman, two of millions in the world, and we were enjoying each other's companionship ... and something more.

When we arrived at our villa later than evening, I felt tense, as though Joan and I had suddenly stepped over an invisible threshold of a new relationship. For the first time since I'd been fired up with jealousy when I first learned about Joan's momentary ... event ... with Anastasius, I found it difficult to speak with she who had been my closest friend for three decades. I could tell Joan felt the same thing, for she was quiet once we'd entered the villa. Yet, her eyes were bright and there was high color in her cheeks. "I guess we must have had too much wine tonight," I said, trying to lighten the tension in the room.

"Perhaps," she said dreamily. "Time for bed." She came over and lightly kissed me on the cheek. Why did it feel so different? I didn't say anything about it, nor did she. We each adjourned to our own bedroom. I slept fitfully that night.

Nor did the sense of tension decrease the next morning when Joan appeared in a summery yellow outfit, cut low about her neck and cut short, just below her knees. She wore a green scarf about her neck. I won't speculate on whether she knew the effect this would have on me, but I do know this was not one of the tunics I'd purchased for her in the last week. I had carefully chosen what I would wear that day, and even more carefully trimmed my own beard. Neither of us said anything about how we looked to one another.

Our first stop that day was at Pompeii. There was almost nothing there worth seeing. "You must remember," our guide said, "this place was covered with tons upon tons of lava and fiery rock, which hardened instantly into a covering at least thirty feet deep. The town died in less than an hour. Twenty-five thousand souls gone in an instant."

"You could imagine the same thing anywhere." I remarked dryly.

"I suppose you could," the man said, "but we know it happened here, and it has been the subject of story and song for at least six hundred years. So it has become a bit of a voyager's destination, even though there's little to commend it."

Sorrentium was truly a lovely place, a small town of three thousand people, bundled onto a small rise above the Tyrrhenian Sea. There were small shops all up and down its single main street, but it seemed the merchants there had selected a grade of merchandise that was dearer and of substantially higher quality than we'd seen in Neapolis. One of the shopkeepers smiled at us and said, "You lovers should really take a launch out to Capri."

Without batting an eye and, surprisingly, without denying the shopkeeper's comment about our relationship, Joan asked why.

"It's once of the most romantic places in the world. There's the portside town of Capri itself, and higher up there is the town of Anacapri, and some rather well-preserved villas of the very wealthy who, at one time, occupied the place. There's also a rather unique surprise, if you're so inclined to see it."

Joan looked at me and said, "Why not?"

Capri was a lovely extension of Sorrentium, not far from the Italian coast. Teams of mules patiently carried visitors up and down the hill from one town to the other. Seafood was plentiful, and prepared in deliciously different ways than I'd ever eaten it before. For our midday meal, we started out with a rich broth in a bowl filled to the brim with all manner of crustaceans and fresh fish. Afterward, we enjoyed calamari stuffed with White Sea rockfish, leeks, and onions, and then grilled over a wood fire. During the meal, Joan quite casually remarked, "Oysters are said to be a great aphrodisiac."

I glanced directly into her eyes and, trying to keep things light – or maybe to keep at bay what I was feeling at that moment – I said, "What separates a Pope from an aphrodisiac?"

"This table," she said. We both broke into gales of laughter simultaneously, and that broke the tension. It was the same remark John Scotus Erigena had made to the long-deceased Gurgis so many years ago.

After the meal we walked around the upper town for a while, then descended on mule back to the port of Capri. Boatmen were calling and cajoling visitors to see what I thought I heard as the "Blue Grotto."

"I wonder if that's the 'surprise' the shopkeeper talked about," Joan said. "You're the man among us. Find out about it."

What I did find out in short order was that it was no use bargaining with any of the skippers. Each boatman charged exactly the same. I engaged a small skiff for us. There were five places in the boat, one hard bench toward the front, another where two of us could sit, and a third at the back of the boat, which could also accommodate two people. Our boatman whistled sharply, and a young lad of fifteen joined him in the boat. The two of them rowed us out two hundred fifty feet from the island, then started circling the island.

If you've never seen a grotto before, I must here write that it is a cave, but a cave where you cannot walk, for it is filled with water from the sea. As the boat entered the grotto, we felt an immediate damp coolness in the air. Our captain told us that rain or shine, winter or summer, the temperature remains constant.

"Aren't you frightened to ply these waters?" Joan asked. "If it's always dark like this, how can you tell where you're going?"

"You'll know in a few moments," our captain said. "I've probably spent as much time in these waters as I've spent on land."

Moments later, I saw what the boatman meant. Joan and I gasped involuntarily at the same moment, for suddenly we were surrounded, bathed in an eerie, extraordinarily bright blue light. Everything around us, water, the ceiling and walls of the cavern, everything was that remarkable shade of blue the Byzantines call turquoise. There were fish swimming around in the water underneath us, and they, too, were a light shade of blue. When I held my hand out and looked at it, it was as bright blue as the rest of the place. It was as though we had gone into a different world. It was too fascinating to be frightening, but too striking not to be jarring. I looked at Joan's blue face and she looked at mine, and we suddenly started giggling uncontrollably. That happens sometimes when you don't know quite how to react.

What I was not prepared for was that Joan snuggled up against me and, when we slid through the darkness on the way out of the grotto, she took my hand and pressed it against her breast. I felt a shock when I realized that her nipples had hardened perceptibly. Returning to Sorrentium later that afternoon, we were still silent, each of us thinking of the remarkable phenomenon we'd just experienced, and by that I don't mean simply the grotto.

~ ∫ ~

As if by prearrangement, we rented a small villa above Anacapri for the night. Late that afternoon, we purchased the fixings of a light supper and a small amphora of wine. I was already feeling a bit dizzy, but not from the wine.

The villa's balcony overlooked the town of Anacapri. The view of the island's two towns basking in the glow of a red sunset, and, farther out to sea, that sunset itself, was the perfect ending to what had been a perfect day.

I don't know when it started or how, but one of us reached over and touched the other and soon we were kissing passionately. As the sun descended into the sea, Joan said, "Come," and led me inside. "I think we'd better sit and talk," she said huskily, "or something might happen that shouldn't."

Talk did not come lightly or easily. No sooner we'd sat on the sofa, we reached hungrily for one another again. She turned to me and I felt warm lips on mine. I gulped and tried to steady myself as her tongue slipped through my lips. My hand went to her breasts, this time of my own accord, and she pressed harder against me. Joan was moaning and harshly muttering all manner of endearments.

"Enough," she said, breaking away at the last moment. "I think I could use a cool bath. This really is getting out of control."

As she went into the bath, my mind was a jumble of thoughts. We'd been friends, closer than brother and sister, since she'd been twelve years old. There'd been Torvald and Eva, and we'd weathered those crises as supportive friends. Could it possibly be that we'd repressed our true feelings for one another for thirty years? My God, she was — the most extraordinary woman I'd ever known.

As if there were unseen wires between our hearts, Joan emerged from the bath totally nude. She came to me proudly, holding her breasts in her hands, holding them out to me as if they were the greatest gift she could bring me. How could I not have been affected? I'd been without a woman for so many years ... for so many years. Pope she may have been, but as I saw her now, she was a goddess.

"Martin?"

"You know what could happen?"

"I know what will happen," she said throatily. "And I'm much more than ready for it. I've loved you since the day we met. I always wanted you, but you were unavailable to me."

"How could you possibly have thought I didn't want you, agonize over you? Couldn't you tell how I felt when we talked about ... Anastasius? And there was Torvald — "

"Yes, but that was only because I couldn't have you."

"You never said anything. I could never have even have suspected — "

In answer, she took my hand and pressed it to her womanhood, then led me to the large, soft bed and pulled me onto her. "Shouldn't we have some protection? What if you were to — ?"

"Darling," she said. "As youthful as we are to each other, we are not what the world would call young people. I've observed signs that my menstruus is coming to an end. I don't think we need worry about anything like that. But we've talked too much. We've waited for so long, I can't wait a moment longer."

By that time, she was lost in the passion of a strong, healthy female animal. She grabbed me, alternately moaned in exquisite agony and shouted guttural grunts and obscenities, and when we climaxed it was so explosive it left us both gasping for a long time after.

That night, we slept peacefully in one another's arms, but not that peacefully that we didn't make love twice more during the night, and a final time the following morning. The shopkeeper had been absolutely correct – Capri was a most romantic place, and we were, after thirty years, lovers at long last. But, as so often has been said, man proposes, God disposes.

CHAPTER 48

It was not until August that we knew for absolute certain. Joan had not experienced her *menstruum* since that night, and she told me she was becoming nauseous every morning. She did not emerge from her chambers until just before noon each day, and by that time her complexion was apple-red and radiant. Under Benedict's direction, the Papacy continued to function smoothly. Joan continued to hold weekly Masses for the masses. They adored her and they had cause to be doubly thankful that she now seemed to be permanently in residence at Rome.

In September, when the morning sickness had passed, we asked Nicola to walk with us after sunset. We'd been walking about half an hour when Joan announced, "Nicola, I am with child."

"What?" Nicola gasped. "But that's impossible! You're … you're the Pope!"

"Also very much a woman," said Joan, smiling.

Nicola was so thunderstruck he was rendered speechless for at least five minutes. "My God!" he finally swore softly. "How could that have happened?"

"Very much in the normal way," Joan said, with a wistful half-smile.

"May I ask — ?"

"No, you may not," Joan said.

"Have you thought about what you are saying? What you are doing? Surely there are ways — "

"*Ne*, Nicola, it is too late for that."

"What a horrid, inopportune time for this to happen."

"Why, Nicola?"

"You've not heard the rumors, then?"

"*Ne.*"

"Anastasius is making outrageous claims that the Pope is really a woman. What's more, he is boasting that he can prove he's lain with the Pope."

I paled, but my voice stayed calm. "How did anyone find this out? He's supposed to be in Sarmatia."

"And he is," Nicola said. "But he's sent messengers to the few powerful friends he has left in the Vatican, and they've started asking uncomfortable questions."

"My God, what can we do?" Joan asked.

"I met with these so-called friends and told them Anastasius' brain must have been addled by his long time in Sarmatia. When I told Benedict about Anastasius' blasphemy, he decreed that the Archbishop of Sarmatia be relieved of his duties while he is undergoing treatment for mental disorder. He is presently confined at an institution in western Sarmatia."

"Thank God," I said.

"Perhaps. Certainly things have calmed down for the time being. But we must plan for this new eventuality."

Nicola had proved himself time and again to be a humane man, filled with understanding for his fellow man's foibles, even if that fellow man – woman – was the Holy Father. Now, he proved his friendship – and his great wisdom – once again.

"I will not question either of you any further," he said. "The options are very few. You have gone so long it is too late for one of them – that is just as well, for the Church views abortion as a mortal sin. That leaves only two alternatives, as far as I can see. The first is to go far away, where no one knows who you are, and give birth to the child. But you will have to separate yourself from the child forever, and it can never be known that you gave birth."

"That is not an option," Joan said. "I could never live with so monstrous a crime."

"Well, then, my friends, that leaves only one alternative, doesn't it?"

"To step down from the Papacy before the child is born," Joan said.

We pondered that for a few moments. The lights of myriad torches and candles reflected in the waters of the Tiber. I wondered how many generations of humankind had experienced this very problem – well, not exactly this very problem, but certainly one similar.

"When is the child due?" Nicola asked.

"At the beginning of February."

Nicola smiled and squeezed Joan's hand. "Enough time, but barely."

"I thought so, myself."

We all knew what that meant. Joan was going to announce the federation of the Eastern and Western Churches on December 25, well more than a month before the baby was due.

"You must still be Pope on that day, for it will be the very pinnacle of your achievement."

"Nicola, you are a very smart man. I feel you may have a future in the Church."

"And on that day," I picked up for Nicola, "Joan will announce to the multitudes that she has done what she set out to do as Pope, and that she will be stepping aside to let another Holy Father stand in St. Peter's Shoes?"

"You are both prescient and correct," Joan said. "Can you think of a better plan?"

"One other matter," Nicola said. "How do we answer Anastasius' scurrilous charge?" I noticed that Nicola did not say, "Anastasius' *false* and scurrilous charge."

"We will immediately deny it, of course," Joan replied, "and we will spread the word everywhere Anastasius has tried to spread his poisonous heresy that on December 25, the Pope will answer Anastasius' insane charges with absolute proof."

We turned and headed back toward the Vatican. "You seem to have thought of everything except what you'll do after you withdraw from the Papacy," Nicola said.

"That's the easiest part," Joan said. "I will remain in Rome for seven days after my retirement, to bid farewell to my friends. Then I will travel to a place where not even the two of you will know where I'm going. After my child is born, you may hear from me again."

"Have you decided where and how you will make the announcement of the federation and ... the ... ah ... other matters?"

"*Aye*," she said. "On that day, I will walk in full regalia, accompanied by a cortege of all the cardinals and bishops in Rome, from St. Peter's to the Church of St. John Lateran. I will make my announcements from there. Now, my friends, I suggest we return to my Papal Chambers, so we might start preparations for the grandest day of my life, save perhaps one."

CHAPTER 49

We awoke early on Christmas morning. Thus far, miraculously, not one person in Christendom, even Benedict, had any idea either that Joan was a woman, or that she was with child. The Papal robes, particularly in winter, are huge and capacious, and a man three times Joan's girth would not have attracted attention.

Once again, Nicola and I tried to get Joan to ride in the Papal sedan chair, which was the normal means of conveyance on high Church occasions. But Joan steadfastly refused. "I am the people's Pope," she said, "and on such a propitious occasions it is my privilege and joy to walk among my people, as one of them."

"But Your Holiness?" Nico began.

"*Ne*, Cardinal Nicholas, I am strong and fine, and the exercise will do me good."

Our breakfast was a light one. The walk from St. Peter's basilica to St. John Lateran normally takes half an hour at most. With the huge retinue – well over eight hundred Church elders and their hangers-on – scheduled to accompany us, and with another ten thousand of the Roman *publica* expected to line the road enroute to the Lateran, we had set aside two hours for the walk and another hour to have everything settled and arranged for Joan's speech.

The cardinals and bishops had been told only that Pope John would give two major pronouncements at the midday service.

We started out at the eighth hour after midnight. The Papal Guard preceded the Pope. Joan followed at the head of the procession. Benedict stood to her left and Nicola to her right. I was immediately behind her. The officers of Christ's Army, in full array, from the Generals down to the Captains, ranged behind us for more than a Roman mile. The cheering throng stood on both sides of the road and the day, although brisk, was not unbearably cold. We reached the Colosseum, the halfway point in the journey, and had just started for St. Clement's Church, less than one-quarter mile away, when I suddenly saw Joan turn pale and clutch at her stomach.

"Your Holiness!" I was at her side in a moment.

"It's nothing, Cardinal Paschal. Most likely the residue of last night's heavy meal, or maybe — " She gasped, in obvious pain.

"The Papal sedan, fetch the Papal sedan immediately!" I ordered one of the guards, who ran off to do my bidding.

"Holiness, perhaps if we rested a moment," I said, directing another guard to bring the Pope a draught of water.

The water seemed to help. After a few moments, Joan said, "Ah, I feel better now. Perhaps it is the unbearable heat of my garments." There was a thin sheen of perspiration on her forehead. I wiped it away with my sleeve.

We resumed the procession and had gotten another hundred feet down the road when the Pope clutched at her midsection once again. I had a dreadful premonition of something unspeakable, but said nothing about it. "Holiness?"

She gasped, "That was much more painful than the last one. Perhaps I should follow your advice and travel the rest of the way on the palanquin."

I glanced about, looking for the sedan, but the guard who'd gone to fetch it was nowhere in sight.

"Is there a place I might perhaps sit for a moment?"

The crowd around us was starting to shuffle uncomfortably. Could the Holy Father be having a seizure or, worse, a heart attack? The Papal guard cleared the immediate area to give the Pope the breathing space she needed – and she needed this space, for her breath was starting to come in rapid, shallow rasps.

"Mother of Jesus, no!" the crowd started to wail.

I removed my own cardinal's robes and lay them on the ground. The guards, ever alert, lay the Pope on my robes and started to untie the binding on her robes.

"*Ne*," Joan said, but very weakly. "I'll only need a moment to calm down. The palanquin will be here in a moment, won't it?"

"Aye," I said, but panic was rising within my throat.

Suddenly a sharp, angry, and very familiar voice barked out from the crowd, "I tried to tell everyone she was a woman! No one believed me! Now you pious hypocrites, you will see that I was right!"

"Shut the hell up, Anastasius, you son of a bitch," I growled through clenched teeth. "I swear if you don't shut up this instant, I will kill you with my bare hands!"

But the crowd either hadn't heard Anastasius or they weren't paying any attention, for the drama unfolding before our eyes riveted every eye to Joan.

Now she was screaming in agony and her body was moving in paroxysms of pain. For the briefest moment, I thought back to Eva's death throes, but this was different. In between her screams, she whispered, "Cut my robe open, Martin, and be quick. My water has burst and I'm — " She panted and moaned, trying hard not to scream again. It took me only a moment to cut away the bottom portion of her robe.

She was bleeding now, and the crowd pressed in on us, their eyes observing the impossible. Joan gave one last gasp and pushed mightily. As Benedict, Nicola, and I struggled to hold the crowd back, the air was suddenly pierced by the strong, high-pitched cry of a baby boy.

The gasp that emerged from the crowd was like nothing I'd ever heard. Over a thousand people in the immediate vicinity, including myself, were absolutely paralyzed. All but one person.

Padraigh – and to this day God only knows where he came from – swiftly cut the cord binding mother and child. Despite Joan's weak protestations, he grabbed the baby and merged into the crowd. Since everyone's eyes were on the Pope who had given birth, no one seemed to notice or care that one Churchman had broken through the ranks, holding a newborn babe in his arms, and had disappeared.

While this was going on, Joan lay in the street serenely, blood flowing from between her legs, semi-conscious. Not one person uttered a sound, nor tried to stop me, as I picked her up and carried her into St. Clement's and into a private cell behind the worship hall.

~ ∫ ~

We made it unseen into the cell. I found water and wiped the blood off Joan as best I could. She looked up at me, fully conscious now.

"We almost made it," she said. "Is the baby alive?"

"Aye, Joan, so far as I know."

I was weeping and I was trembling, but this was a time to be strong, for I knew the time we had was very limited.

"Who — ?"

"Padraigh. Paddy," I said. "I'm sure the baby's safe, but I don't think anyone cares one way or the other about him."

"Him?" She smiled. "It was a boy, then?"

"Aye. Joan, listen, we've almost no time at all. You're in no condition to move right now, but you have to. Can you — ?"

"I don't know. I can try."

I heard the crowd starting to converge on the Church. It was now only a matter of minutes. There was a sharp knock on the very small door at the rear of the Church. "Uncle Isaac, Uncle Isaac, open the door quickly! The Christians are coming and I fear for my life! Help me, Uncle Isaac!"

I could not believe what I was hearing. It couldn't be! It was nearly as impossible as Joan becoming Pope, or, once she'd become the Pope, becoming pregnant. There was absolutely no way, but the shout emerged again, louder than before, "Uncle Isaac, I saw you go in there! Uncle Isaac, open up the door this instant! They are less than two minutes away! Please, Uncle Isaac! For the love of God, don't wait another moment or I'm a dead man!"

I left Joan for the briefest of moments and thrust open the door. God's own gift smiled indulgently at me. "Doctor ben Halevi?"

"Don't look so surprised. I thought I'd come to hear the great speech. I didn't expect such a surprise. *Mazal Tov*! But enough of this. Go and bar the door. Do what you have to do, say what you have to say, and I'll handle matters here."

~ ∫ ~

Anastasius, as might have been expected, incited a near riot when, in the midst of the crowd, he demanded that Joan be summarily tried for every sin imaginable unto God and some that weren't even mentioned. Heresy, witchcraft, apostasy … the list continued on and on. It was a veritable alphabet of charges, and the inflamed crowd demanded the immediate and ultimate punishment to be accorded such a base and reprehensible being – that she have her feet tied together and be dragged on the ground behind a horse while the populace of Rome, always in the mood for entertainment of any kind – would stone her until she died.

I ran to the front and barred the doors of St. Clement's not a moment too soon. The infuriated crowd set fire to the wooden doors of the Church and used heavy sledge hammers to break the doors down. It still took them a quarter of an hour before they could enter the church.

The crowd ranged everywhere, Anastasius at their head. They scoured every room and every tiny corner of every square foot of that Church, but ultimately they found no one except me in that house of worship. I was kneeling and praying as my brother cardinals bore me away, and within hours I was thrust into Hadrian's Mausoleum, where I sit to this day.

~ ʃ ~

Joan was tried in absentia. Of course the verdict was the only verdict that could have been given, since what had happened had been witnessed by hundreds of people. I heard later that one voice, Nicola's, raised the novel defense that this could well have been a miracle – a second coming of Christ. "After all," he argued, "it was a boy child, born on

Christmas day, and no man has ever come forth to claim the child's parentage." Incredibly enough, a substantial number of cardinals and bishops and people actually believed him!

In the end, the sentence was exactly what Anastasius had demanded, but once again that evil man was frustrated, for neither Joan nor her baby could be found anywhere in Rome, or, for that matter, in the Papal States. In an agony of bitterness, Anastasius erected effigies and incited the Roman populace to set fires to these effigies in front of every Church in Rome, including St. Peter's itself. All to no avail.

I am told it was ultimately Nicola whose quiet demeanor finally calmed the crowds, and who preached it was God's Will that we had been delivered of this tragedy, but that God would surely give Mother Church and its followers the strength, the courage, and the spirituality to overcome even this horrendous event. To give him his due, Nicola publicly anathematized she who had been Pope John VIII, and afterward led services throughout the city.

~ ∫ ~

Benedict was immediately cast up, and became Pope in name as well as in deed, but not without a substantial – and characteristically vicious – contest from Anastasius, who claimed that Benedict had known all along who – and what – Joan was, and that Benedict had sanctioned this fraud on the Roman Church. He demanded Benedict's immediate excommunication, and, I'm told, he demanded Benedict's head as well. Nevertheless, in the end, Benedict prevailed. Anastasius refused to give up his fight. He declared himself as the only justifiable Pope, the only one without sin and without blemish, and he claimed he was the true Pope and Benedict the false pope. Such was the character of this man that he, far more than Joan, tried to rip the fabric of the Church apart, consumed as he was by his hatred, bitterness, and frustration, and ever more so by his own ambition. Nicola retained his position. And I, who had been found in St. Clement's Church, from which Joan had disappeared, was cast down into the dungeons, where I languish to this day, while they decide what to do with me – if, in fact, anyone but Nicola even remembers me.

I have been at this task for more than eight months, and here I still languish. I shall put down my quill ...

ANNO DOMINI: II APRILIUS DCCCLVIII.

A.D. 2011

"That's all there is? That's the *end* of it? My God, how can there not be more?"

It was a bright, sunny day in Viona. The sky was cerulean blue and there were only a few small clouds in the sky.

"Well…" Signor Bertelli chuckled. His face, as usual, was ruddy and he shrugged his shoulders. "I wanted to see if you were really serious about the translation."

"So you made me work for over a year for this? Listen!" I said, angrily pounding on the table. "You've got your translation and you know it's a damned good one! If there's nothing more, I demand you tell me now – and if you're lying —"

My own frustration was guiding me to angrier heights, and it was the usually ebullient Signor Bertelli who was trying to calm me down. "Professor — "

"Don't 'Professor' me, Signor Bertelli! I want a straight answer. Is there more to this story or not? I want to know and I want to know now!"

"Ah, you Americans, always so impatient," he said, waving his hands about. "We Italians have lived long enough to know impatience will get you nothing but disease. If you must know, there is more, but not much more. I imagine you'll be able to complete the translation in two weeks, maybe three."

I felt like an utter fool, for even had there not been more to the story, what could I have done about it? Nothing, of course.

I made my apologies to Signor Bertelli, who shrugged, smiled, and turned his hands up.

The last words I heard as I went out the door, clutching several more pages of parchment, were, "So I'll see you in three weeks, Professor?"

A.D. DCCCLVIII

On the seventeenth day of April in the Year of Our Lord 858, my reverie was interrupted by a gentle knock on the door of my cell. Honorius, a boy of twenty years, obviously a simple peasant and equally obviously a devout monk, who had been my jail guard for the past year, entered my cell. "Eminence," he said. Given the low station to which I'd fallen, I found his continued – and utterly faithful – pronouncement of my former position to be mildly amusing. "Pope Benedict is dead."

"I'm sorry," I said. There was really no other answer I could give. If I were guilty of anything, Benedict would have known about it and known exactly what charges to bring. Perhaps – and here I only speculate – that good and wise man had kept me imprisoned in Hadrian's Mausoleum so that I would be safe, and so that he could honestly tell his detractors that I was in Hadrian's Tower awaiting trial on numerous charges. "When will they elect the new Pope?"

"I don't know, Eminence."

"More parchment, Honorius? But I told you to tell whoever sent it to you that I was finished." The young monk shrugged. "I told you I have nothing more to write," I snapped.

"I'm sorry, young Honorius. None of this is your fault. Have you finished your *Aves* and *Paters* this morning?"

"I have, Eminence."

"Good boy," I said, smiling and patting him on the shoulder.

After the boy had gone, I leafed through the several large pages of bare parchment he'd left with me. I'd gotten about halfway through them, and my eyes had started to get heavy from boredom when I saw it. It occupied nothing more than a tiny part of the lower right hand corner of one of the parchments, and an untrained eye would have seen it for what it most likely was, a bit of miniature writing that had been mostly erased, as though an unpracticed hand had written a practice script, then tried to erase it, but not altogether successfully. I looked at it very carefully. Then read it very carefully. Then I smiled, held that corner of parchment to the large candle in my cell, and watched it burn to a blackened crisp.

~ ʃ ~

"Your Eminence!" Honorius said, barely able to contain himself. "He who has been providing you with materials, and the one to whom I have delivered them has been elected Pope on the thirtieth ballot. He has taken the Papal name of Nicholas the First."

"Nicola is Pope?" I sucked my breath in, amazed. That was all I said, for I knew nothing of what this would mean for me. Two nights later, I found out. It was in the evening, two hours after sunset. I was reading *The Consolation of Philosophy* for perhaps the tenth time, or maybe it was the twentieth, when there was a knock at my cell door. This was out of the ordinary, since it was well after my last light meal of the day. I had, of course, faithfully recited most of the orders of service each day, although I had consolidated them into one short service whenever I awoke, one brief service at the midday meal, and one even shorter service at sunset.

"Honorius?" I asked. "Is something wrong, boy?"

"*Ne.*" The voice was deep and familiar. The door was opened and I was face to face with his Holiness, Pope Nicholas I.

"Nicola?"

"*Aye*, Martin."

"The Holy Father wrapped me in his strong arms as he would a child, and held me tight. After awhile, I stopped and looked at him. Nicola was older, but it was a vigorous, strong age. He reminded me of that long-ago Orestes.

"You're looking well, Nicola."

"Which is more than I can say for you. You look sixty, and an emaciated wretch at that."

"How kind of you to say," I remarked acidly. "I wonder how you'd look after a year-and-a-half in this prison."

Nicola smiled at that remark. "I saved your life in case you hadn't noticed," he said. We drifted into that familiar pattern of friendship again, a friendship of thirty-three years, and one that had weathered many storms.

"What of Anastasius?"

"One of my very first acts was to anathematize and excommunicate that low scum. He's been banished from the Holy Roman Empire for the rest of his life, and I've left strict word that if anyone sees him anywhere in the areas controlled by Western Christendom, he is to be brought to Rome where he will be publicly hanged and stoned."

"A fitting end. What ever happened to Joan's magnificent achievement to bring the Churches together?"

"Alas, when the Patriarch heard what had happened the Eastern Church wanted nothing more to do with the Roman Church. So we are back to where we have always been as far as the Byzantine Empire is concerned."

"I'm sorry I can't offer you anything, Nicola, not even a proper seat."

"I wouldn't have expected you to."

"It's night and I daresay no one of consequence in this rathole is even awake, save mayhap little Honorius."

"That's why I'm here," Nicola said. "I have an offer, if you're willing to accept it."

"How can I not accept it, whatever it is, Nicola? You've given me back my life."

"What I propose is something more substantial."

"Which is?"

"Tomorrow night at this same time, you will escape from Hadrian's Mausoleum. Young Honorius will show you the way. You will be provided with appropriate clothing and money. If you accept my offer, you will secretly be accorded the full pay and privileges of a cardinal for the rest of your life, although, of course, you will have no official affiliation with the Church in any manner unless you choose to become a country priest or such."

"That's certainly more than acceptable, Nicola. I would say it's Godly-generous, even though, as you well know, I have more than ample funds to keep me in luxury for the remainder of my days. Surely there is something you want in return?"

"There is. You must promise me you will never return to Rome. You must be forever silent about what happened, for it has now been completely erased from the slate of Christianity. I will keep your scandalous, heretical, and totally false writings with me in Rome for safekeeping. Of course, I expect you will continue to write your blasphemous and scandalous lies. Indeed I order you, under threat of excommunication, to send them to me privately, when – and as – you write them. All of your writings will, of course, disappear soon and forever – officially at any rate." He smiled at me and I smiled back.

"All of these conditions are acceptable Holiness. I intend to honor them with a full heart."

"I've only one more question. We will probably never see one another again, my friend, and now that what's happened has happened, and it's over — "

"That you will never know, Nicola, whether you are His Holiness or a craven tavern maid."

"I thought as much," he said. "Good bye, Martin Paschal. May you live a long, healthy life."

Chapter 50

There is little to write about the trip, which was uneventful. I knew where I'd planned to go, and where I planned to live out as many days as God had to give me – the one place in the world that had not changed, and where people would welcome me as they had so many years ago.

I landed at Dun Laoghaire once again, and once again I set out for the west, and once again I was accompanied by my great and good friend Padraigh, who was now a cardinal and who was still as rowdy and boisterous and hard-drinking and filled with tales as he'd ever been.

"So ye're goin' to the Burren, then, laddy?" he said.

"*Aye*, Paddy."

"Hard life there."

"I've had harder."

"Gonna' be a priest again?"

"Mayhap, mayhap not. Don't need the money."

"Ye'll write?"

"Don't know that either."

It was now the middle of April 859, nearly fourteen years to the day since Hrinc and his brother had saved my life, when

I'd stumbled and lost my footing and rolled uncontrollably toward the edge of the Cliffs of Moher, that Padraigh and I reached the Burren.

"Ha'n't changed much, has it?"

"*Ne*, Paddy," I said, adopting his lilt. "Ha'n't changed a'tall, a'tall."

"A few new houses. A few new parishioners. Like that 'un atop yonder hill."

I looked where Padraigh was pointing and saw a small, neat stone house, surrounded by a field of spring flowers.

"Lovely," I said. "Y'know, Paddy, it's not been easy for me these past couple of years. I fear I'm getting old and I know I'm tired, and now that there's no one left to me, in the words of your hero Coohoolen, 'tis a sweet country. I could rest my weapon there.'"

"Why'd you come here, then?"

"I've decided to quit the world for a spell. Let them batter themselves all they want. All I'd like is to live the rest of my life in peace."

"Them that live up on yonder hill are a bit like Hrinc and his folk. If y'er going to do any priestin' around here, you may as well meet them."

"That's all right by me. I don't know exactly where I'm headed, and it might be wise to ask the neighbors what they think."

"Give me a few moments then, boyo," he said. "They're new in the territory and I'd like to give 'em warnin' that there's a new fella' about."

"That's fine by me, Paddy. I'll simply walk along the cliffs. It's been a long time."

"Aye. Whyn't you come on up after ye've looked? It'll take you half an hour or so to make the trip to there and back."

As I moved closer to the Great Ocean, the clouds became heavier and took on the color of a bruise. The wind whipped up and soon I found myself in a driving rain. Recalling my last adventure there, I kept a ways back from the cliffs themselves.

"I wonder what other changes there've been," I said softly, relishing the wind and the rain and the solitude.

"As far as you're concerned, you won't live long enough to see any changes." I turned abruptly and found myself staring into the murderous eyes of Anastasius. "That's right, it's me, you pigshit excuse for a high-and-mighty churchman. You were the one who claimed you were so moral when you found I'd been with a common slut. You, who impregnated the Pope!" He spat on the ground in front of me. "I should have spit in your face like you did in mine, you emaciated old nothing! How old are you now? Sixty? Seventy?"

"Very funny," I said, moving toward him.

"Stop right there your holy *Cardinalship*," he blazed, drawing a long-handled knife from his cloak. "Now it's just you and me. Your fat little cardinal friend has gone a'wandering, and your great friend, that pretender of a Pope is a thousand miles away. God knows if that whore of a Pope you played with is even alive. That means it's you and me – a fair fight."

"I'd hardly call it a fair fight," I said. "You've got a knife and I've got my bare hands."

"That's as fair a fight as I want it to be," he said.

With that, he lunged toward me. I jumped to the side, barely avoiding the thrusting blade, but Anastasius was faster than me and he immediately followed the blade toward me. His second thrust was more successful, and I felt a sharp pain go through my left shoulder. I fell to the ground, and Anastasius, pursuing his advantage, stood over me. "All right, fallen priest," he said. "Say your prayers, because I'm about to administer the last rites." He raised his knife to bring it down on my head.

I made a last, desperate twist to avoid the descending knife. In so doing, my foot struck Anastasius' leg. Backing away, he tripped over a small rock in the road, and started rolling uncontrollably toward the cliffs. Even had I wanted to save him, it would have been impossible for me to do so. Anastasius grasped for purchase anywhere he could find a rock, a shrub, anything, but it was raining and it was slippery, and there was nothing he could find.

As he rolled over the cliff and I heard a last piercing scream, the safety net raised up and flapped in the wind. "Damn!" I heard a voice say. "I guess we missed one, but at least if the other feller starts to roll, we'll save him." There wasn't the faintest trace of regret or unhappiness in Hrinc's voice. He came over to me. "Friend?" he asked. "Me or the other fellow?"

"Hell, I know you – you're Paddy's friend. The other one."

"Can't say he is. You saw, then?"

"Yup." He grinned at me. "I think Paddy's waitin' up yonder hill. Ye'd best not keep him waitin'."

I climbed the hill and a shaft of sunlight broke through the gray at that moment. From the summit of the hill, I could see out to the Cliffs of Moher and beyond. "Here do be monsters," I said softly, as I stared out at the angry sea, which was always dashing itself against the great stone cliffs. Spring had made western Ireland even greener than I remembered, and the wildflowers laid a rainbow-colored carpet out before me.

Padraigh was waiting at the top of the rise. "Heard ye had a little adventure, laddy. No great loss to the church so far as I can tell. Well, I talked to the people in the new place and they've no objection to meetin' you. Come along, now."

When we got to the stout wooden door, Paddy pounded upon it. "A good day t'ye," he sang out, "'tis Paddy the priest and his friend."

The door opened.

I stared, speechless and unmoving.

"Joan?"

"Martin."

We stood there transfixed. Neither of us could move. Neither of us could say a word. Neither of us wanted to.

The instant passed. I held my hands out, grasping her arms, and looked hard at her, as she was looking hard at me. Time had not been especially kind to her, but there was no question it was my Joan.

"Your hair's grown longer, and there's a bit of gray in it," I finally managed.

"And you've aged some, too," she said.

"Fifty."

"*Aye*, that's an age."

Silly little inanities between us masked the incredible miracle of the moment. Our awkward silence was shattered as a small boy toddled toward us. "Ma ... who 'dat?" he said, curiously.

"John Martin, this here's your *da*."

"Oh. Hi, *da*." He smiled. His question having been answered, he toddled back into another room from which he'd come.

"He looks a lot like you, don't you think?"

"I don't know what to think, Joan. Do you?"

"It'll take time."

"I think the first thing we ought to do is make him legitimate, don't you?"

A smile started to form on her lips. A smile that came from deep within her heart. "Mayhap we should at that."

"D'you think there's time left to give him a brother or a sister?"

"Don't know that," she said. "We'll never know 'til we try, will we now?" I was astounded as to how quickly she'd picked up the local dialect, the charming lilt. But then, Joan had always amazed me.

We still hadn't moved from the position we were in when I'd first touched her arms. We still held each other a little apart, staring at one another, drinking in the other.

"Ahem." Padraigh interrupted the moment. "Listen up lad, lassie. Neither of ye're gonna' do a thing like that until ye'r legal this time."

I felt myself grinning and I couldn't stop. "But Paddy m'dear, there's not a priest to marry us within several days, and there's the banns, and — "

"Listen, young Martin," he said. "There ain't no banns in these parts, and the last time I recall, a cardinal still qualifies to marry folks, and, unless I'm deeply mistaken, one of ye's is still a cardinal and the other of ye's was the Pope himself, er, *her*self. Ye've been married forever in the eyes of the Lord, and I'm prepared to make ye married in the eyes of man as well, so's ye can get started on that brother or sister – and f'r sure ye ain't got a lot of time to do that, ye's bein' old folk and all."

"Now you listen, you old *ferta*," I started to say, but by that time Joan was all over me, hugging, kissing, giggling like a twelve-year-old child.

The ceremony was very short. Only Padraigh and John Martin witnessed it, and John Martin only for a few seconds at a time, because he was in and out, trying unsuccessfully to get both of our attentions. And then it was over and, after we'd each had a generous draught of the warm, honeyed mead Joan had brought out, Paddy said, "Well, 'tis time I'm on my way. Hrinc promised me stronger stuff down the hill, and I'm sure the two of ye've got things to talk about and things to do where ye don't need a priest about. God be with ye then." And off he went.

For a few moments, Joan and I drank in the miracle God had wrought.

Finally, I managed to say what was on both our minds. "Well, here we are, far from the world and everything else. What do we do with the rest of our lives?"

"Ah, Martin, we have weathered so much together. We are old, and we are friends. Let us be … old friends."

And so it was, and so it is.

And here ends my tale.

ANNO DOMINI XVII JUNIUS DCCCLX.

Translator's Final Historical Note

There have been many great popes, but posterity has awarded the title of "the Great" to only four. One of them was St. Nicholas I, the Great, who sat on the Papal throne from A.D. 858 to 867. He was noted for charity and justice. He took loving care of his poor, and he was a mighty protector of the oppressed and wronged. When one adds great strength of soul and a dynamic character, it is easy to see why this man made so strong an impression on his age.

Nicholas dispensed justice and mercy with an equal hand. He devoted his greatest energy to maintaining peace in Europe as the descendants of Charlemagne continued to fight one another and further fragment the Holy Roman Empire. But as the Carolingian Dynasty continued its inexorable descent into collapse, not even Nicholas could do much to stop it. Nicholas the Great died on November 13, 867. His feast is kept on that day.

~ ∫ ~

It is historical fact that from A.D. 860 until early in the Fifteenth Century, as part of the medieval papal consecration ceremony, each newly elected Pope sat on the *sella stercoraria*, a chair pierced in the middle like a toilet, where his genitals were examined to give proof of his manhood. Afterward, the examiner solemnly informed the gathered people, "*Mas nobis nominus est*" – "Our nominee is a man." Only then was the Pope handed the keys of St. Peter.

~ ∫ ~

A word about that child of the West Saxon King Ethelwulf, whom Leo had baptized Alfred. The young lad was, like Torvald, epileptic and suffered a seizure at his wedding feast. But he was a vigorous hunter, handsome, graceful, and wise, and he ultimately drove the Danes from England. He died at fifty-two, after reigning for twenty-eight years.

Alfred the Great, as he came to be known by posterity, offered the English nation a model that it gratefully received and soon forgot. Still, many centuries later, no less a giant than the often cynical Voltaire wrote of him, "I do not think that there was ever in the world a man more worthy of the regard of posterity than Alfred the Great."

~ ∫ ~

Finally, I raise the two words "If only" once again. If only Joan could have brought off her grand scheme to reunite the Eastern and Roman churches, would there have been a need for Protestantism? Might we all be speaking Greek or Latin instead of the polyglot languages that blanket the world today? Would there have been two World Wars, massive genocides on an unparalleled scale, and human misery beyond anything either Church could have conceived in the Ninth Century?

I am reminded of a story I once read. The protagonist had the opportunity to travel back in time to the beginning of life on earth, but he was warned not to stray from the path on which he landed, and not to touch a leaf or a blade of grass or any living thing. When he saw a beautiful butterfly, he reached out to grasp it, if for no other reason than to bring it back with him and look at the beauty God had wrought, even at the dawn of time. When he returned to his own time, he found a world changed so radically that he could not even speak the language, or familiarize himself with anything he saw, and he died within moments trying to breathe the air that was poisonous to his lungs.

And so it was, and so it is, and so it will be.

And here ends my tale.

THE END

www.ingramcontent.com/pod-product-compliance
Lightning Source LLC
Chambersburg PA
CBHW030742030726
47497CB00001B/102